"A cross betwe
and a poli

"Nothing is true. Everything is permissible."
—Hassan i Sabbah, founder (1090 A.D.)

Have YOU ever wondered:

WHO IS the MAN in ZURICH that
some SWEAR is LEE HARVEY OSWALD?

IF there's an ESOTERIC ALLEGORY concealed
in the APPARENTLY INNOCENT legend of
Snow White and the Seven Dwarfs?

WHY scholarly anthropologists TURN PALE
with terror at the very MENTION of the
FORBIDDEN name YOG-SOTHOTH?

Find out in the original and genuine
trilogy of CONSPIRACIES
battling for world control—

ILLUMINATUS!

Volume I   THE EYE IN THE PYRAMID
Volume II   THE GOLDEN APPLE
Volume III   LEVIATHAN

— by Robert Shea and Robert Anton Wilson —

PUBLISHED
BY SPHERE BOOKS

ILLUMINATUS! Part II

The Golden Apple

ROBERT SHEA and ROBERT ANTON WILSON

SPHERE BOOKS LIMITED

First published in Great Britain
by Sphere Books Ltd 1977
27 Wrights Lane, London W8 5TZ
Copyright © 1975 by
Robert J. Shea and Robert Anton Wilson
Reprinted 1978, 1979, 1980, 1982, 1986

Published by arrangement with
Dell Publishing Co. Inc.,
New York, N.Y., U.S.A.

To Arlen and Yvonne

Set in Intertype Times

Printed and bound in Great Britain by
Cox & Wyman Ltd, Reading

There is no god but man.

Man has the right to live by his own law – to live in the way that he wills to do: to work as he will: to play as he will: to rest as he will: to die when and how he will.

Man has the right to eat what he will: to drink what he will: to dwell where he will: to move as he will on the face of the earth.

Man has the right to think what he will: to speak what he will: to write what he will: to draw, paint, carve, etch, mold, build as he will: to dress as he will.

Man has the right to love as he will.

Man has the right to kill those who thwart these rights.

—*The Equinox: A Journal of Scientific Illuminism*, 1922 (edited by Aleister Crowley)

PROLOGUE

(You already know *some* of this if you read
ILLUMINATUS!, *Vol. I*,
The Eye in the Pyramid)

Hagbard Celine, a mad genius fully qualified to practice several varieties of engineering and law, chooses instead to be a pirate and attempts to design the world's first Self-Destruct Mynah Bird.

'Here, kitty-kitty-kitty! Here, kitty-kitty-kitty!' Hagbard can be heard saying as we dolly in for a close-up on his swarthy Sicilian face. (Actually, he's half Norwegian and has a raft of Irish relatives named McGee and Marlowe in Ohio somewhere.) As the camera pulls back, we see Hagbard standing between two rows of Mynah Birds, each perched on a separate miniature lemon tree. 'Here, kitty-kitty-kitty! Here, kitty-kitty-kitty!' the birds robotically repeat, thereby being programmed for self-destruct when he unleashes them in New York City.

'Honest to God,' Epicene Wildeblood (New York's bitchiest literary critic) is later heard telling a crowd of skeptics in the office of *Confrontation* magazine. 'The damned bird committed suicide. I was sitting in Washington Square and I heard him cackling. "Here, kitty-kitty-kitty!" Just like that. "Here, kitty-kitty-kitty!" It was a big Siamese that got him, but every cat in the neighborhood was on the prowl by then. I tell you, this city has reached the end of its rope if even the birds are turning depressive-psychotic.'

'Tell that to the *Occult Digest*,' Joe Malik said skeptically. Actually, Joe – who had edited *Confrontation* all through the eras of Joe McCarthy and Jim Garrison and flying saucers and Watergate and Linda Lovelace – was almost a transcendental agnostic by now, ready to embrace any insane rumor as possibly true. 'If the real is so often bizarre, then the bizarre may often be real' had become his motto; 'but,' he always added, 'you've got to draw the line *somewhere*. As Mason said to Dixon.' Drawing the line had admittedly become increasingly difficult for him, especially since the Democratic Convention in Chicago, 1968, when he met Simon Moon of the Nameless Anarchist Horde and learned of the mysterious and diabolical Bavarian Illuminati.

Cut. Tight close-up on Simon Moon as he tells us about himself. 'Well uh Dad and Mom were both anarchists, dig? He was the Bakuninist, I.W.W., One Big Union and keep a steel helmet handy, boys, the Revolution is coming any day now. She was the Tolstoyan, nonviolence, the Jesus Trip, the next step in evolution is Universal Love. So naturally I rebelled against both of them and became a disciple of Donatien Alphonse François de Sade. For a while. But then Padre Pederastia introduced me to the JAMs.'

The JAMs – Justified Ancients of Mummu – are an ancient Babylonian secret society, worshippers of Mummu, god of chaos. ('The Chinese Taoist laughs at civilization and goes elsewhere,' Simon explains helpfully, 'but the Babylonian Chaoist sets termites at the Foundations.') When Simon and Padre Pederastia recruited Joe Malik – a process begun at the last-ever SDS convention, 1969, and continued into the 1970s, Joe being then still a confirmed skeptic – the JAMs were engaged in the 59th century of their war against the Illuminati, not counting a few centuries of alliance.

Joe Malik, whose narrow, intelligent face contained all the ambiguities of an Arabian-American intellectual who was raised Roman Catholic, joined the Trotskyists during the Hitler-Stalin Pact, and edits a magazine radical enough to attract tons of crackpot mail every week, smiles tiredly. 'Before meeting Simon and the Padre, the only people I ever heard talk about the Illuminati Conspiracy were right-wing cranks. I was sure Simon was putting me on at first. But then I met the leader of the JAMs . . .' (Thunder on the soundtrack; eerie shadows cross Joe's face.)

We are standing outside a bungalow in the suburbs of Los Angeles. Simon knocks, Joe looks nervous. The door opens and a feisty little man says, 'So you're the new recruit. Come in and tell me how a goddam intellectual can help us beat the shit out of the cocksucking Illuminati motherfuckers.' This little old fellow has a peculiarly mocking and stony glitter in his eyes. He is John Dillinger, now living under the name Frank Sullivan, and president of Laughing Phallus Productions, king of the rock music industry.

Dillinger's first robbery, in 1923, was a travesty. The victim, a grocer named B. F. Morgan, gave the Masonic Signal of Distress and John was quickly apprehended. He made a deal with the D.A. but landed in prison anyway. Sure that the Masons were behind this betrayal, John joined the JAMs and subsequently used their motto – 'Lie down on the floor and keep calm' – during each of his bank heists. This was his way of taunting J. Edgar Hoover, a thirty-third-degree Mason and high Illuminatus Primus. Hoover, in turn, recognizing the 'leaping bandit' (the tabloids' gaudy title for John) as a JAM agent, gave orders which resulted in the shooting of the three innocent businessmen at Little Bohemia Lodge, Lake Geneva, Wisconsin, when they were mistaken for the Dillinger gang. Smarting from criticism after this blunder, the FBI subsequently kept quiet when the man they shot at the Biograph Theatre, July 22, 1934, also turned out to be an innocent bystander. Dillinger meanwhile was promoted to a higher rank in the JAMs and gave up such crude tactics as knocking over banks.

Now an old man in the mid-1970s, Dillinger has decided to amalgamate the JAMs with a new anti-Illuminati group, the Legion of Dynamic Discord, headed by the madcap Hagbard Celine, pirate extraordinary and breeder of Self-Destruct Mynah Birds.

Simon Moon : 'Hagbard's a right-wing crank!'

Joe Malik : 'I dunno. Hagbard's a genius, that's for sure. Unfortunately, his IQ is devoted mostly to keeping the world confused about what his real motives and aims are. I just don't know . . .'

Hagbard, in fact, is the discoverer of the Snafu Principle, which holds that *communication is possible only between equals*. Every hierarchy, therefore, in order to repress equality, must also repress communication. This, he claims,

is the Achilles' heel of armies, corporations, governments
and other front groups used by the Illuminati in their conspiracy to govern mankind.

Where the JAMs worship the Babylonian god of chaos,
Mummu, Hagbard's Legion of Dynamic Discord worships
Eris, Greek goddess of confusion, who is also known in
Latin as Discordia. (Conversations among the Discordians
usually begin: 'Hail Eris!' 'All hail Discordia!' *'Kallisti!'*)
Unknown to the JAMs, Hagbard also has an alliance with
the Erisian Liberation Front (ELF), a super-Zen supersecret insurrection following a program known as Operation Mindfuck (OM) and directed by the Dealy Lama, who
lives in the sewers below Dealy Plaza, Dallas, Texas.

Close-up of a computer face almost as bland as HAL-
9000. This is FUCKUP (First Universal Cybernetic Kinetic
Uni-Programmer), Hagbard's greatest invention. FUCKUP
'throws' *I Ching* hexagrams internally, reading random
open circuits as *yin* lines and closed circuits as *yang*; these
are then correlated with three thousand years of *I Ching*
scholarship, current astronomical and astrological data,
CBS news, and reports from Hagbard's agents in world
capitals, thereby combining in FUCKUP's memory integration
circuits a Worldgame Report unique in its comprehensive
objectivity. 'World War III is imminent,' FUCKUP reports
blandly, 'Prognosis: many megadeaths. No blame.'

'My *ass*, no blame!' Hagbard rages; he now realizes the
true importance of the Fernando Poo incident.

Fernando Poo is a tiny island in the bay of Biafra, off the
coast of Africa, where Captain Ernesto Tequila y Mota
has arranged his own promotion to generalissimo by stag-
ing a blitz coup d'etat. Crack CIA agents quickly report to
Washington that the new regime is under the control of
Russia and China; but Russian agents report to Moscow
that it is under the control of China; and Chinese agents
report to Peking that it is under the control of Moscow.
Hagbard, recognizing the fine hand of the Illuminati, re-
programs FUCKUP to locate the source of major danger and
is told that Las Vegas needs watching.

Sherri Brandi (née Sharon O'Farrell) gives us her version: 'The only way to make some scratch is to sell your
snatch. At least, that's the story in this hard-ass town. So I

work for Carmel, who isn't bad as pimps go, if you don't mind getting beat all black and blue every so often. But now Carmel thinks we can get rich . . .'

Carmel, indeed, is convinced that Sherri's latest john, Charlie Mocenigo, has discovered the ultimate secret weapon. Obviously, if he and Sherri can steal it and sell it to the Goddam Commies, they'll both be millionaires. Alas, the secret weapon is Anthrax Leprosy Pi (ALP), a virus with certain unpredictable properties. Mocenigo and Sherri are both killed by an accidental infection, and Carmel unknowingly becomes a kind of Typhoid Mary. Since nobody else is aware of this significant fact either, the world is dancing on the edge of an abyss, watching Fernando Poo with trepidation, while only FUCKUP and Hagbard Celine know the real threat is coming from Las Vegas.

(Fission Chips, English Secret Agent 00005, has already discovered that all the American, Russian and Chinese reports from Fernando Poo are inaccurate. He, alas, has jumped to his own Wrong Conclusion and believes that BUGGER – Bad Unreformed Goons, Gangsters and Espionage Renegades, headed by Eric 'the Red' Blowhard – is behind the coup there. Chips has never heard of the Illuminati . . .)

Acting on orders from Hagbard, Joe Malik sends *Confrontation*'s star reporter, George Dorn, to Mad Dog, Texas, to investigate the right-wing groups there, one of which is widely rumored to be behind the assassinations of John and Robert Kennedy, Martin Luther King, George Lincoln Rockwell and Spiro Agnew. (Joe smiles knowingly. 'That's what I told George,' he winks.)

In Mad Dog, George is busted for possession of marijuana and hustled off to jail by Sheriff Jim Cartwright. George's cell-mate, a snaky-looking individual named Harry Coin, first brags about killing various famous people, then attempts to rape George. The jail is then invaded by a mysterious group led by Mavis, a young lady in a trench coat carrying a Tommy gun, and they remove George after blowing holes in the walls. On the way out, George sees a hidden chapel with a pyramid-shaped altar and an open eye on top, with the slogan *'Ewige Blumenkraft!'* Mavis tells him that Mad Dog Jail is a secret headquarters of the Bavarian Illuminati.

George is driven to the Gulf of Mexico, where he and Mavis just have time to argue politics and engage in a little friendly oral sex before the *Leif Erikson* appears. This is a gigantic golden-yellow submarine owned by Hagbard Celine, who explains to George that he is neither left-wing nor right-wing but a political non-Euclidean. The Illuminati, Hagbard goes on, is the cause of all unhappiness in the world: a vast secret society founded by the Mason and former Jesuit Adam Weishaupt in Ingolstadt, Bavaria, May 1, 1776.

Back in New York, however, Saul Goodman, Inspector of the Homicide Squad, is investigating the bombing of *Confrontation* and the mysterious disappearance of editor Joe Malik. The strange aspect of the case is that Malik's dogs – he had an apartment full of them, according to neighbors – also disappeared. Stranger yet is the fact that magazine staffers insist Joe was allergic to dogs. Strangest of all is a series of memos found in Joe's apartment. Quoting various authorities, academic and otherwise, these memos give a strange variety of theories about the Illuminati, to wit:

1. According to French sociologist Jacques Ellul, the Illuminati was founded in the 11th century by disciples of Joachim of Floris and tried to redistribute wealth by robbing the rich; they were vanquished by Law and Order in 1507 and ceased to exist. But the *National Review* claims Joachim's followers still survive and are seeking to imminentize the Eschaton.

2. According to Daraul's *History of Secret Societies*, the Illuminati was begun by Hassan i Sabbah in 1092, entered Spain in 1623, spread throughout Europe and infiltrated Masonry via Adam Weishaupt in 1776.

3. According to *Encyclopaedia Britannica*, the Illuminati was founded by Weishaupt in 1776 and suppressed by the Bavarian government in 1785.

4. According to a letter in *Playboy*, the Illuminati is still in existence and masterminded the assassinations of recent years.

5. According to *Teenset* magazine, the Illuminati controls the rock music business.

6. According to *American Opinion* magazine, the Council on Foreign Relations is the latest manifestation of the One World conspiracy originally founded by Weishaupt's Illuminati.

7. According to *The Spark*, a Chicago newspaper, Mayor Richard Daley used the Illuminati slogan '*Ewige Blumenkraft*' during his diatribe against Abe Ribicoff at the 1968 Convention. Furthermore, Weishaupt and George Washington were the same man.

8. According to CBS radio, paintings of Washington are so different that they look like more than one man.

9. According to *East Village Other*, New York, the current leaders of the Illuminati (1969) are Malaclypse the Younger, Mao Tse-tung, Mordecai the Foul, Richard Nixon, Aga Khan, Saint Yossarian, Nelson Rockefeller, Saint McMurphy, Lord Omar and Mark Lane. ('This one *must* be a hoax,' Saul Goodman concludes thoughtfully . . .)

10. According to Virginia Brasington's *Flying Saucers in the Bible*, the eye-in-pyramid Illuminati symbol was given to Jefferson by a mysterious man in a black cloak. Neither Jefferson nor any of the other Founding Fathers knew what it meant, but they put it on the Great Seal anyway.

11. According to *Planet*, San Francisco, the eye-in-pyramid design is the symbol of Timothy Leary, Ph.D.

12. According to *Proofs of a Conspiracy* by 18th-century Mason John Robison, the Illuminati was not destroyed by the 1785 crackdown by the Bavarian government and was still trying to infiltrate Masonic groups everywhere. They supervised the French Revolution, Robison says, and are plotting more revolutions.

13. According to *World Revolution* by Nesta Webster, the Illuminati controls all socialist, communist and anarchist groups; the celebration of May 1 as International Labor Day by these groups actually honors the founding of the Illuminati on May 1, 1776.

14. According to *History of Magic* by French cabalist Eliphas Levi, the Illuminati was founded by Zoroaster and

introduced to Europe by the Knights Templar in the 12th century.

15. According to *High IQ Bulletin*, the Illuminati are invaders from the planet Venus.

16. According to *Libertarian American*, the Illuminati is the political front of the Vril Society, where Adolf Hitler received his occult education; their aim is Christian Socialism, as distinguished from 'godless Russian socialism.'

17. According to *Los Angeles Free Press*, the Theosophical Society has been accused by John Birch Society members of being the chief front for Illuminati activities; and the founder of the Illuminati, they say, was Cain, son of Eve and the Serpent.

18. According to Levi's *History of Magic* again, the Holy Vehm (a kind of medieval Catholic version of the Ku Klux Klan) was the morals-enforcement wing of the Illuminati in the Middle Ages.

19. According to Daraul's *History of Secret Societies*, the Nazis revived the Holy Vehm and it may still be active today.

After comparing and reviewing these memos, Saul Goodman deduces by rigorous logic that the Illuminati have inspired much of this literature to conceal their real identity and actual motives. Meanwhile, Barney Muldoon of the Bomb Squad finds evidence, annoying to himself, that the Illuminati are controlled by the Jesuits. Comparing notes, Saul and Barney conclude that the Illuminati are actually Satanists who have infiltrated every organization from Catholicism to Masonry to sow conflict and achieve their own ends. Unfortunately, soon after arriving at this deduction, Saul is kidnapped, held prisoner in a fake mental hospital and put through a psychedelic brainwashing process intended to convince him he is Barney Muldoon, a patrolman on the Newark Police Force, suffering from the hallucination that he is Saul Goodman, an Inspector on the New York Police Force.

Hagbard Celine, meanwhile, races toward sunken Atlantis in the *Leif Erikson*, hoping to seize some golden statues which the Illuminati are planning to melt down to finance their current projects. George Dorn is hurriedly initiated into the Legion of Dynamic Discord (with the lusty assistance of a lovely black lady named Stella Maris) – but let George tell it himself:

'Well, wow, like, man, uh I'm no hero, you know. I'd rather be initiated again – especially by Stella – or maybe Mavis – I *mean* a Discordian initiation is something special – ('*I'll say,*' Stella interjects lewdly) – but the next thing I know Hagbard has me up on the bridge and we're talking to a dolphin named Howard and about to be attacked by five Illuminati spider ships. Maybe I'd been smoking too much of that great Kallisti Gold grass that Hagbard grows, but it was all a big freakout. What's it like to drown at the bottom of the Atlantic? The water pressure must crush you atom by atom, I imagine. And the Illuminati are ready to blast us with everything they have. I just go away from there in my head, you know, and I'm back in the Morituri Underground, in my younger days, when Carlo wanted me to kill a pig to show my dedication to the revolution. So there I am trailing this cop down Broadway in the '70s, trying to get the courage to pull the gun out of my pocket, and Howard the dolphin is yelling through the intercom "Here come the spider ships!" and I'm still remembering Stella's luscious-lovely-yummy pussy, and I don't know if I'm in a porny novel, a science-fiction movie, or the real world, and I got this ESP flash that this cop had a retarded four-year-old child and suddenly that made him human so I knew I couldn't kill him. Wow, man, you see? It was heavy.' George later – or earlier: it depends on which of his time tracks we're in – tried to shoot himself in the head, despising his cowardice, but the gun provided by Morituri Underground didn't fire.

'Well, yeah, sure' – Simon Moon is horning in on the narrative again – 'Morituri is no kindergarten, we all know that. But every time I hear "Joe Hill" I think of my father:

> The copper bosses killed you, Joe.
> "I never died," says he.

And both lines are true, and mourning never ends, and the revolution never ends, whatever way you're fighting it. Read De Sade. Or ask John Dillinger. You don't come *alive*, as a Person, until you break the laws. Inside the legal cage, you're nothing but a robot.' He bursts into song: 'Tho' cowards cringe and traitors sneer/ We'll keep the Red Flag flying here . . .' (Down, boy. Go on, George.)

'Well, yeah, Hagbard finally blasted all five of those Illuminati spider ships and we salvaged the golden Atlantean statues. They were gorgeous, if you like antediluvian porno, I mean, but then Hagbard told me my first mission as a Discordian was to take them to the headquarters of the leader of the Mafia. I shit.'

Actually, George did fairly well on his visit to the Blue Point, Long Island, home of Robert Putney Drake, famous banker and philanthropist, unacknowledged governor of the Mafia, and Illuminatus Primus. It was arranged that, in return for the statues, Drake would break with the Illuminati, sign a treaty with the Discordians and arrange the assassinations of twenty-three top Illuminati officials in the United States as a gesture of good faith. Afterwards, George was entertained in his bedroom by Tarantella Serpentine, the lady who taught Linda Lovelace *everything*. George was very entertained indeed.

(But the Fernando Poo incident was escalating: the President of the United States gave Russia and China twenty-four hours to get their troops out of Fernando Poo *or else*. The *or else* was taken by terrorized earth-people everywhere to mean all-out thermonuclear war; the Kremlin and Peking were leaked the information that it also meant Anthrax Leprosy Pi – which, in fact, was already loose on the person of the little Las Vegas pimp Carmel, unknown to anyone . . . And, in Fernando Poo, the brave but dumb English agent Fission Chips, after a glorious fuck with a lady named Concepcion Galore, learned about a mysterious Church of Saint Toad and decided to investigate it . . . Whilst the rulers of Russia and China, having no troops in Fernando Poo, politely informed the world that the President of the U.S. was a mental case. The Chairman of the Chinese Communist Party thereupon, finding Marx no source of inspiration in such parlous times, threw the *I Ching* sticks and puzzled over Hexagram 23: 'Breaking Apart' . . .)

And (things are moving faster now) Saul Goodman discovers that the phony psychiatrist 'treating' him in the fake

mental hospital is actually the missing editor Joe Malik.
They are both aboard Hagbard's submarine, *Leif Erikson*,
bound for Ingostadt, Bavaria, where the Illuminati hope to
use the energies of Woodstock Europa – a gigantic rock
festival – to imminentize the Eschaton. 'What does imminentize the Eschaton mean?' Saul demands; but just then
the submarine is attacked by the Illuminati spider ships
and we are back in Simon Moon's interminable mono-
logue again:

'A glorious fuck? What the hell does a government
agent like Fisson Chips know about glorious fucking? Let
me call a witness for the antigovernment forces. She'll tell
you about glorious fucking. Mary Lou?'

Documentary-style close-up on Mary Lou Servix, a
black cop sent to infiltrate the Nameless Anarchist Horde,
who ended up learning Tantra from Simon Moon also.

'At first I thought Mr. Simon Motherfucking Moon was
a stone kink, an Ignatz, you know? I mean, trying to ball
sitting up – it's from Bizarresville. And I got a backache
the first half-hour. But he kept telling me, "Just hang in
there, just hold on, baby." And then it started to happen –
that *kundalini* he calls it. Earthquake City! Wilder than
the time I hadda take acid with the Weather people, trying
to infiltrate them. The Ancient Babylonian Secret of Serpent Power he calls it . . .'

Simon coughs modestly. 'Our secret weapon against the
Illuminati. Neuroprogramming the sixth circuit. See Dr.
Leary for details.'

'To reveal everything is an ineptness,' Hagbard Celine
remonstrates. 'Truth must come to bloom slowly, like a
secret flower in the heart. We don't communicate much
better than the dogs most of the time – as per my famous
Snafu Principle. True communication, in the egalitarianism
of neurology, is more complex than galactic law.' He stares
into the distance, remembering Uncle John Feather . . .

Uncle John, a Mohawk Indian, gives us the Moral of
This Fable, fairly straightforwardly for once: 'You are a
good lawyer, Hagbard; I know that. But can you tell the
truth in a government court? I doubt it. They make their
own rules and everything relevant is declared irrelevant . . .'
But that was over twenty years ago, and after the Mohawk

land was taken from them, Hagbard abandoned law for piracy . . . 'Seeking a more honest way of making a living,' he says with that hawklike look in his eye.

But, back in present time again, Danny Pricefixer of Homicide Squad, New York, is investigating the disappearances of Joe Malik, Saul Goodman and Barney Muldoon. Some of the references in the Illuminati memos draw him, like most of our characters, into past time, where he was once a detective on the Arkham, Massachusetts, Police Force and investigated the disappearance of Professor Joshua Marsh of Miskatonic University. Professor Marsh had written a book on the lost continent of Atlantis, claiming that the Atlanteans worshiped gods, called the Iloigor, who actually existed – extrasolar visitors to earth from higher civilizations in remote galaxies. Alas, every clue in the Marsh case led to a dead end, and Danny never did find out what happened to the eccentric professor.

'The one lead that bothered me most,' Danny tells our interviewer, 'was the fnords. What in hell are fnords? But just the day before his disappearance, Professor Marsh was overheard by several witnesses talking to himself in the Miskatonic Library. "I've seen the fnords," he kept saying. Now, I ask you, what can a poor cop do with a clue like that? It's depressing.'

A visit to the New York Public Library and some browsing among occult books gives Danny the information that many traditions trace the Illuminati back to Atlantis, or to some interstellar source.

Waking in the big bed, George Dorn finds Tarantella has left him. But how did Mavis get here? Looking down at his elderly hands, he sobs, 'You've won. I'm no longer sure *who* I am or which way Time runs . . .'

'No,' Mavis says, 'you've won, Saul. You're waking up at last.'

'You mean I *am* Saul Goodman but I'm all the others, too . . .'

'Who asks that question?' Mavis responds like a Zen Master . . .

But returning to his hotel suite, Fission Chips finds Concepcion Galore lying in his bed with her throat cut from ear to ear, and beside her the emblematic Flame Dagger of

Hassan i Sabbah. 'Damn, blast and thunder! Every time I find a good piece of ass, those fuckers from BUGGER come along and shaft her!'

And the White House order is given; the SAC bombers head toward Fernando Poo and the Third World War . . .

(Rising organ music.)

Can World War III be averted? Will Carmel infect the whole world with Anthrax Leprosy Pi? What is Hagbard's real angle anyway? Who are the Illuminati and what's *their* angle? Continue reading for the next psychotic episode . . .

BOOK THREE

UNORDNUNG

Believe not one word that is written in *The Honest Book of Truth* by Lord Omar nor any that be in *Principia Discordia* by Malaclypse the Younger; for all that is there contained are the most pernicious and deceptive truths.

> —'Epistle to the Episkopi,' *The Dishonest Book of Lies*, by Mordecai Malignatus, K.N.S.

THE SIXTH TRIP, OR TIPARETH
(THE MAN WHO MURDERED GOD)

> To choose order over disorder, or disorder over order, is
> to accept a trip composed of both the creative and the
> destructive. But to choose the creative over the destructive
> is an all-creative trip composed of both order and disorder.
> —'The Curse of Grayface and the Introduction
> of Negativism,' *Principia Discordia,* by
> Malaclypse the Younger, K.S.C.

April 25 began, for John Dillinger, with a quick skimming
of the *New York Times*; he noticed more fnords than
usual. 'The fit's about to hit the shan,' he thought grimly,
turning on the eight o'clock news – only to catch the story
about the Drake Mansion, another bad sign. In Las Vegas,
in rooms where the light never changed, none of the gamblers
noticed that it was now morning; but Carmel, returning
from the desert, where he had buried Sherri Brandi, drove
out of his way to look over Dr. Charles Mocenigo's home,
hoping to see or hear something helpful; he heard only a
revolver shot, and quickly sped away. Looking back, he
saw flames leaping toward the sky. And, over the mid-
Atlantic, R. Buckminster Fuller glanced at his three
watches, noting that it was two in the morning on the plane,
midnight at his destination (Nairobi) and 6 A.M. back home
in Carbondale, Illinois. (In Nairobi itself, Nkrumah Fubar,
maker of voodoo dolls that caused headaches to the President of the United States, prepared for bed, looking forward to Mr. Fuller's lecture at the university next morning.
Mr. Fubar, in his sophisticated-primitive way, like Simon

Moon in his primitive-sophisticated way, saw no conflict between magic and mathematics.)

In Washington, D.C., the clocks were striking five when Ben Volpe's stolen Volkswagen pulled up in front of the home of Senator Edward Coke Bacon, the nation's most distinguished liberal and leading hope of all those young people who hadn't yet joined Morituri groups. 'In quick and out quick,' Ben Volpe said tersely to his companions, 'a *cowboy*.' Senator Bacon turned in his bed (Albert 'the Teacher' Stern fires directly at the Dutchman) and mumbled, 'Newark.' Beside him, his wife half woke and heard a noise in the garden (*Mama mama mama*, the Dutchman mumbles): 'Mama,' she hears her son's voice saying, as she sinks back toward a dream. The rain of bullets jolts her awake into a sea of blood and in one flash she sees her husband dying beside her, her son twenty years ago weeping for a dead turtle, the face of Mendy Weiss, and Ben Volpe and two others backing out of the room.

But, in 1936, when Robert Putney Drake returned from Europe to accept a vice presidency in his father's bank in Boston, the police already knew that Albert the Teacher really hadn't shot the Dutchman. There were even a few, such as Elliot Ness, who knew the orders had come from Mr. Lucky Luciano and Mr. Alphonse 'Scarface' Capone (residing in Atlanta Penitentiary) and had been transmitted through Federico Maldonado. Nobody, outside the Syndicate itself, however, could name Jimmy the Shrew, Charley the Bug and Mendy Weiss as the actual killers – nobody except Robert Putney Drake.

On April 1, 1936, Federico Maldonado's phone rang and, when he answered it, a cultivated Boston voice said conversationally, 'Mother is the best bet. Don't let Satan draw you too fast.' This was followed by an immediate click as the caller hung up.

Maldonado thought about it all day and finally mentioned it to a very close friend that evening. 'Some nut calls me up today and gives me part of what the Dutchman told the cops before he died. Funny thing about it – he gives one of the parts that would really sink us all, if anybody in the police or the Feds could understand it.'

'That's the way some nuts are,' pronounced the other

Mafioso don, an elegant elderly gentleman resembling one
of Frederick II's falcons. 'They're tuned in like gypsies.
Telepathy, you know? But they get it all scrambled because they're nuts.'

'Yeah, I guess that's it,' Maldonado agreed. He had a
crazy uncle who would sometimes blurt out a Brotherhood
secret that he couldn't possibly know, in the middle of
ramblings about priests making it with altar boys and
Mussolini hiding on the fire escape and nonsense like that.
'They tune in – like the Eye, eh?' And he laughed.

But the next morning, the phone rang again, and the
same voice said with elaborate New England intonation,
'Those dirty rats have tuned in. French Canadian bean
soup.' Maldonado broke into a cold sweat; it was that moment, in fact, when he decided his son, the priest, would
say a mass for the Dutchman every Sunday.

He thought about it all day. Boston – the accent was
Boston. They had witches up there once. French Canadian
bean soup. Christ, Harvard is just outside Boston and
Hoover is recruiting Feds from the Harvard Law School.
Were there lawyers who were witches, too? Cowboy the
son of a bitch, I told them, and they found him in the
men's crapper. That damned Dutchman. A bullet in his
gut and he lives long enough to blab everything about the
Segreto. The goddam *tedeschi* . . .

Robert Putney Drake dined on lobster Newburg that
evening with a young lady from one of the lesser-known
branches of the House of Morgan. Afterward, he took her
to see *Tobacco Road* and, in the cab back to his hotel,
they talked seriously about the sufferings of the poor and
the power of Henry Hull's performance as Jeeter. Then he
took her up to his room and fucked her from hell to breakfast. At ten in the morning, after she had left, he came out
of the shower, stark naked, thirty-three years old, rich,
handsome, feeling like a healthy and happy predatory
mammal. He looked down at his penis, thought of snakes
in mescaline visions back in Zurich and donned a bath-
robe which cost enough to feed one of the starving families
in the nearby slums for about six months. He lit a fat
Cuban cigar and sat down by the phone, a male mammal,
predatory, happy. He began to dial, listening to the clicks,

the dot and the dot and the dot-dot, remembering the perfume his mother had worn leaning over his crib one night thirty-two years ago, the smell of her breasts, and the time he experimentally tried homosexuality in Boston Common with the pale faggot kneeling before him in the toilet stall and the smell of urine and Lysol disinfectant, the scrawl on the door saying ELEANOR ROOSEVELT SUCKS and his instant fantasy that it wasn't a faggot genuflecting in church before his hot hard prick but the President's wife . . . 'Yes?' said the taut, angry voice of Banana Nose Maldonado.

'When I reached the can, the boy came at me,' Drake drawled, his mild erection becoming warm and rubbery. 'What happened to the other sixteen?' He hung up quickly. ('The analysis is brilliant,' Professor Tochus at Harvard had said of his paper on the last words of Dutch Schultz. 'I particularly like the way you've combined both Freud and Adler in finding sexuality and power drives expressed in the same image at certain places. That is quite original.' Drake laughed and said: 'The Marquis de Sade anticipated me by a century and a half, I fear. Power – and possession – *are* sexual, to some males.')

Drake's brilliance had also been noted by Jung's circle in Zurich. Once – when Drake was off taking mescaline with Paul Klee and friends on what they called their Journey to the East – Drake had been a topic of long and puzzled conversation in Jung's study. 'We haven't seen his like since Joyce was here,' one woman psychiatrist commented. 'He is brilliant, yes,' Jung said sadly, 'but evil. So evil that I despair of comprehending him. I even wonder what old Freud would think. This man doesn't want to murder his father and possess his mother; he wants to murder God and possess the cosmos.'

Maldonado got two phone calls the third morning. The first was from Louis Lepke, and was crudely vehement: 'What's up, Banana Nose?' The insult of using the forbidden nickname in personal conversation was deliberate and almost unforgivable, but Maldonado forgave it.

'You spotted my boys following you, eh?' he asked genially.

'I spotted your *soldiers*,' Lepke emphasized the word,

'and that means you wanted me to spot them. What's up? You know if I get hit, you get hit.'

'You won't get hit, *caro mio*,' Don Federico replied, still cordial. 'I had a crazy idea about something I thought might be coming from inside and you're the only one who would know enough to do it, I thought. I was wrong. I can tell by your voice. And if I was right, you wouldn't have called me. A million apologies. Nobody will be following you anymore. Except maybe Tom Dewey's investigators, eh?' he laughed.

'Okay,' Lepke said slowly, 'Call them off, and I'll forget it. But don't try to scare me again. I do crazy things when I'm scared.'

'Never again,' Maldonado promised.

He sat frowning at the phone, after Lepke hung up. *Now I owe him*, he thought. *I'll have to arrange to bump off somebody who's annoying him, to show the proper and most courteous apology.*

But, Virgin Mother, if it isn't the Butcher, who is it? A real witch?

The phone rang again. Crossing himself and calling on the Virgin silently, Maldonado lifted the receiver.

'Let him harness himself to you and then bother you,' Robert Putney Drake quoted pleasantly, 'fun is fun.' He did not hang up.

'Listen,' Don Federico said, 'who is this?'

'Dutch died three times,' Drake said in a sepulchral tone. 'When Mendy Weiss shot him, when Vince Coll's ghost shot him and when that dumb junkie, the Teacher, shot him. But Dillinger never even died once.'

'Mister, you got a deal,' Maldonado said. 'I'm sold. *I'll meet you anywhere. In broad daylight.* In Central Park. *Any place* you'll feel safe.'

'No, you will not meet me just now,' Drake said coolly. 'You are going to discuss this with Mr. Lepke and Mr. Capone, first. You will also discuss it with –' he read, off a card in his hand, fifteen names. 'Then, after you have all had time to consider it, you will be hearing from me.' Drake farted, as he always did in the nervous moments when an important deal was being arranged, and hung up quickly.

Now, he said to himself, *insurance*.

A photostat of his second analysis of the last words of Dutch Schultz – the private one, not the public version which he had turned in to the Department of Psychology at Harvard – was on the hotel desk before him. He folded it smartly and pinned on top of it a note saying, 'There are five copies in the vaults of five different banks.' He then inserted it in an envelope, addressed it to Luciano and strolled out to drop it down the hotel mail chute.

Returning to his room he dialed Louis Lepke, born Louis Buchalter, of the organization later to be named Murder Inc. by the sensational press. When Lepke answered, Drake recited solemnly, still quoting the Dutchman, 'I get a month. They did it. Come on, Illuminati.'

'Who the hell is this?' Lepke's voice cried as Drake gently cradled the phone. A few moments later, he completed checking out of the hotel and flew home on the noon flight, to spend five grueling twenty-hour days reorganizing and streamlining his father's bank. On the fifth night he relaxed and took a young lady of the Lodge family to dance to Ted Weems's orchestra and listen to their new young vocalist, Perry Como. Afterwards, he fucked her thirteen to the dozen and seven ways to a Sunday. The next morning, he took out a small book, in which he had systematically listed all the richest families in America, and placed her first name and a check after *Lodge*, as he had done with *Morgan* the week before. A Rockefeller would be next.

He was on the noon flight to New York and spent the day negotiating with Morgan Trust officials. That night he saw a breadline on Fortieth Street and became profoundly agitated. Back in his hotel, he made one of his rare, almost furtive diary entries:

Revolution could occur at any time. If Huey Long hadn't been shot last year, we might have it already. If Capone had let the Dutchman hit Dewey, the Justice Department would be strong enough now, due to the reaction, to ensure that the State would be secure. If Roosevelt can't maneuver us into the war when it starts, all will be lost. And the war may be three or

four years away yet. If we could bring Dillinger back,
the reaction might strengthen Hoover and Justice, but
John seems to be with the other side. My plan may be
the last chance, and the Illuminati haven't contacted
me yet, although they must have tuned in. Oh, Weishaupt, what a spawn of muddleheads are trying to
carry on your work.

He tore the page out nervously, farted and crumbled it
in the ashtray, where he burned it slowly. Then, still agitated, he dialed Mr. Charles Luciano on the phone and
said softly, 'I am a pretty good pretzler, Winifred. Department of Justice. I even got it from the department.'
　'Don't hang up,' Luciano said softly. 'We've been waiting to hear from you. Are you still there?'
　'Yes,' Drake said carefully, with tight lips and a tighter
sphincter.
　'Okay,' Mr. Lucky said. 'You know about the Illuminati. You know what the Dutchman was trying to say to
the police. You even seem to know about the *Liberteri*
and Johnnie Dillinger. How much do you want?'
　'Everything,' Drake replied. 'And you are all going to
offer it to me. But not yet. Not tonight.' And he hung up.
　(The wheel of time, as the Mayans knew, spins three
ways; and just as the earth revolves on its own axis, simultaneously orbits about the sun and at the 'same' time trails
after the sun as that star traverses the galaxy's edge, the
wheel of time, which is a wheel of *ifs*, is come round again,
as Drake's phone clicks off, to Gruad the Grayface calcu-
lating the path of a comet and telling his followers: 'See?
Even the heavenly bodies are subject to law, and even the
Iloigor, so must not men and women also be subject to
law?' And in a smaller cycle, Semper Cuni Linctus, centurion stationed in a godforsaken outpost of the Empire,
listens in boredom as a subaltern tells him excitedly: 'That
guy we crucified last Friday – people all over town are
swearing they've seen him walking around. One guy even
claims to have put a hand through his side!' Semper Cuni
Linctus smiles cynically. 'Tell that to the gladiators,' he
says. And Albert Stern turns on the gas, takes one last
fix, and full of morphine and euphoria, dies slowly, con-

fident that he will always be remembered as the man who shot Dutch Schultz, not knowing that Abe Reles will reveal the truth five years later.)

Camp-town racetrack five miles long . . .

During Joe's second trip on the *Leif Erikson*, they went all the way to Africa, and Hagbard had an important conference with five gorillas. At least, he said afterwards that it was important; Joe couldn't judge, since the conversation was in Swahili. 'They speak some English,' Hagbard explained back on the sub, 'but I prefer Swahili, since they're more eloquent in it and can express more nuances.'

'Are you the first man to teach an ape to speak,' Joe asked, 'in addition to your other accomplishments?'

'Oh, not at all,' Hagbard said modestly. 'It's an old Discordian secret. The first person to communicate with a gorilla was an Erisian missionary named Malaclypse the Elder, who was born in Athens and got exiled for opposing the imposition of male supremacy when the Athenians created patriarchy and locked up their women. He then wandered all over the ancient world, learning all sorts of secrets and leaving behind a priceless collection of mind-blowing legends – he's the Phoenix Madman mentioned in the Confucian scriptures, and he passed himself off as Krishna to recite that gorgeous Bible of revolutionary ethics, the Bhagavad Gita, to Arjuna in India, among other feats. I believe you met him in Chicago while he was pretending to be the Christian Devil.'

'But how have you Discordians concealed the fact that gorillas talk?'

'We're rather close-mouthed, you might say, and when we do speak it's usually to put somebody on or blow their minds—'

'I've noticed that,' Joe said.

'And the gorillas themselves are too shrewd to talk to anybody but another anarchist. They're all anarchists themselves, you know, and they have a very healthy wariness about people in general and government people in particular. As one of them told me once, "If it got out that we can talk, the conservatives would exterminate most of us and make the rest pay *rent* to live on our own land; and the liberals would try to train us to be engine-lathe oper-

ators. Who the fuck wants to operate an engine lathe?"
They prefer their own pastoral and Eristic ways, and I, for
one, would never interfere with them. We do communicate,
though, just as we communicate with the dolphins. Both
species are intelligent enough to realize that it's in their
interest, as part of earth's biosphere, to help the handful of
human anarchists to try to stop, or at least slow down, the
bloodletting and slaughter of our Aneristic rulers and
Aneristic mobs.'

'Sometimes I still get confused about your theological
terms – or are they psychological? The Aneristic forces,
especially the Illuminati, are structure freaks : they want
to impose their concept of order on everybody else. But I
still get confused about the differences between the Erisian,
the Eristic and the Discordian. Not to mention the JAMs.'

'The Eristic is the opposite of the Aneristic,' Hagbard
explained patiently, 'and, therefore, identical with it. Remember the Hodge-Podge. Writers like De Sade, Max
Stirner and Nietzsche are Eristic; so are the gorillas. They
represent total supremacy of the individual, total negation
of the group. It isn't necessarily the war-of-all-against-all,
as Aneristic philosophers imagine, but it can, under stress,
degenerate into that. More often, it's quite pacifistic, like
our hairy friends in the trees back there. The Erisian position is modified; it recognizes that Aneristic forces are part
of the world drama, too, and can never be totally abolished.
We merely stress the Eristic as a balance, because human
society has been tilted grotesquely toward the Aneristic
side all through the Piscean age. We Discordians are the
activists in the Erisian movement; we do things. The pure
Erisians work in more mysterious ways, in accordance
with the Taoist principle of *wu-wei* – doing nothing effec-
tively. The JAMs are left-wingers, who might have become
Aneristic except for special circumstances that led them in
a libertarian direction. But they've fucked it all up with
typical left-wing hatred trips. They haven't mastered the
Gita : the art of fighting with a loving heart.'

'Strange,' Joe said. 'Dr. Iggy, in the San Francisco JAM
cabal, explained it to me differently.'

'What would you expect?' Hagbard replied. 'No two
who *know*, know the same in their knowing. By the way,

why haven't you told me that you're sure those gorillas back there were just men I dressed up in gorilla suits?'

'I'm becoming more gullible.' Joe said.

'Too bad,' Hagbard told him sadly. 'They really *were* men in gorilla suits. I was testing how easily you could be bamboozled, and you flunked.'

'Now, wait a minute. They smelled like gorillas. That was no fake. You're putting me on *now*.'

'That's right,' Hagbard agreed. 'I wanted to see if you'd trust your own senses or the word of a Natural-Born Leader and Guru like me. You trusted your own senses, and you pass. My put-ons are not just jokes, friend. The hardest thing for a man with dominance genes and piratical heredity like me is to avoid becoming a goddam authority figure. I need all the feedback and information I can get – from men, women, children, gorillas, dolphins, computers, any conscious entity – but nobody contradicts an Authority, you know. *Communication is possible only between equals:* that's the first theorem of social cybernetics – and the whole basis of anarchism – and I have to keep knocking down people's dependence on me or I'll become a fucking Big Daddy and won't get accurate communication anymore. If the pig-headed Illuminati and their Aneristic imitators in all the governments, corporations, universities and armies of the world understood that simple principle, they'd occasionally find out what's actually going on and stop screwing up every project they start. I am Freeman Hagbard Celine and I am not anybody's bloody leader. As soon as you fully understand that I'm your equal, and that my shit stinks just like yours, and that I need a lay every few days or I get grouchy and make dumb decisions, and that there is One more trustworthy than all the Buddhas and sages but you have to find him for yourself, then you'll begin to understand what the Legion of Dynamic Discord is all about.'

'One more trustworthy than all the Buddhas and sages . . .?' Joe repeated, finding himself most confused when he had been closest to total comprehension a second earlier.

'To receive light you must be receptive,' Hagbard said curtly. 'Work that one out for yourself. Meanwhile, take this back to New York and chew on it a bit.' And he presented Joe with a book entitled *Never Whistle While You're Pissing: A Guide to Self-Liberation*, by Hagbard Celine, H.M., S.H.

Joe read the book carefully in the following weeks – while Pat Walsh, in *Confrontation*'s research department, checked out every assertion about the Illuminati that Joe had picked up from Hagbard, Simon, Dillinger and Dr. Ignotius – but, although some of the book was brilliant, much was obscure, and he found no clue to the One more trustworthy than all Buddhas. Then, one night high on Alamout Black hashish, he started working on it with expanded and intensified consciousness. Malaclypse the Elder? No, he was wise, and somewhat benevolent in a fey sort of style, but certainly not trustworthy. Simon? For all his youth and nuttiness, he had moments of incredible perception, but he was almost certainly less enlightened than Hagbard. Dillinger? Dr. Ignotius? The mysterious Malaclypse the Younger, who had disappeared, leaving behind only the inscrutable *Principia Discordia*?

Christ, Joe thought, what a male chauvinist I am! Why didn't I think of Stella? The old joke came back to him . . . 'Did you see God?' 'Yes, and she's black.' *Of course.* Hadn't Stella presided over his initiation, in Dr. Iggy's chapel? Hadn't Hagbard said she would preside over George Dorn's initiation, when George was ready? *Of course.*

Joe always remembered that moment of ecstasy and certainty: it taught him a lot about the use and misuse of drugs and why the Illuminati went wrong. For the unconscious, which always tries to turn every good lay into a mother figure, had contaminated the insight which his supraconscious had almost given him. It was many months later, just before the Fernando Poo crisis, that he finally discovered beyond all doubt the One who was more trustworthy than all Buddhas and all sages.

Do-da, do-da, do-da-do-da-DAY . . .

(And Semper Cuni Linctus, the very night that he reamed his subaltern for taking native superstitions seriously, passed an olive garden and saw the Seventeen . . . and with them was the Eighteenth, the one they had crucified the Friday before. *Magna Mater*, he swore, creeping

closer, *am I losing my mind?* The Eighteenth, whatshis-
name, the preacher, had set up a wheel and was distributing
cards to them. Now, he turned the wheel and called out
the number at which it stopped. The centurion watched,
in growing amazement, as the process was repeated several
times, and the cards were marked each time the wheel
stopped. Finally, the big one, Simon, shouted 'Bingo!' The
scion of the noble Linctus family turned and fled . . . Behind him, the luminous figure said, 'Do this in commemoration of me.'

'I thought we were supposed to do the bread and wine
bit in commemoration of you?' Simon objected.

'Do both,' the ghostly one said. 'The bread and wine is
too symbolic and arcane for some folks. This one is what
will bring in the mob. You see, fellows, if you want to bring
the Movement to the people, you have to start from where
the people are at. You, Luke, don't write that down. This
is part of the *secret* teachings.')

Slurp, slurp . . . *Camp-town ladies sing this song* . . .

(But how do you account for a man like Drake? one of
Carl Jung's guests asked at the Sunday afternoon *Kaf-
feeklatsch* where the strange young American had inspired
so much speculation. Jung sucked on his pipe thoughtfully
– wondering, actually, how he could ever cure his associates
of treating him like a guru – and answered finally, 'A fine
mind strikes on an idea like the arrow hitting bull's-eye.
The Americans have not yet produced such a mind, because they are too assertive, too outgoing. They land on an
idea, even an important idea, like one of their fullbacks
making a tackle. Hence, they always crumple or cripple it.
Drake has such a mind. He has learned everything about
power – more than Adler knows, for all his obsession on
the subject – but he has not learned the important thing.
That is, of course, how to *avoid* power. What he needs, and
will probably never achieve, is religious humility. Impossible in his country, where even the introverts are extro-
verted most of the time.')

It was a famous novelist, who was later to win the Nobel
Prize, who actually gave Drake his first lead on what the
Mafia always called *il Segreto*. They had been talking
about Joyce and his unfortunate daughter, and the novelist

mentioned Joyce's attempts to convince himself that she wasn't really schizophrenic. 'He told Jung, "After all, I do the same sorts of things with language myself." Do you know what Jung, that old Chinese sage disguised as a psychiatrist, answered? "You are diving, but she is sinking." Incisive, of course; and yet, all of us who write anything that goes below the surface of naturalism can understand Joyce's skepticism. We never know for sure whether we're diving or just sinking.'

That reminded Drake of his thesis, and he went and got the last words of Mr. Arthur Flegenheimer, a.k.a. Dutch Schultz, from his bureau. He handed the sheets to the novelist and asked, 'Would you say the author of this was diving or sinking?'

The novelist read slowly, with increasing absorption, and finally looked up to regard Drake with extremely curious eyes. 'Is it a translation from the French?' he asked.

'No,' Drake said. 'The author was an American.'

'So it's not poor Artaud. I thought it might be. He's been around the bend, as the English say, since he went to Mexico. I understand he's currently working on some quite remarkable astrological charts involving Chancellor Hitler.' The novelist lapsed into silence, and then asked, 'What do you regard as the most interesting line in this?'

' "A boy has never wept nor dashed a thousand kim," ' Drake quoted, since that was the line that bothered him most.

'Oh, that boy imagery is all personal, just repressed homosexuality, quite ordinary,' the novelist said impatiently. ' "I was in the can and the boy came at me." I think the author hurt the boy in some way. All the references are tinged with more than normal homosexual guilt.'

My God, Drake thought, *Vince Coll. He was young enough to seem like a boy to Schultz. The Dutchman thought Coll's ghost was shooting at him in that john in Newark.*

'I would imagine the author killed himself, or is in a mental hospital by now,' the novelist went on thoughtfully.

'He's dead,' Drake said grudgingly. 'But I won't give you any more clues. It's fascinating to see how well you're doing on your own.'

'This is the interesting line,' the novelist said. 'Or three lines rather. "I would hear it, the Circuit Court would hear it, and the Supreme Court might hear it. If that ain't the payoff. Please crack down on the Chinaman's friends and Hitler's commander." You swear this author was American?'

'Well, he came of German ancestry,' Drake said, thinking of Jung's theory of genetic memory. 'But Chancellor Hitler would hate to admit it. His people were not Aryan.'

'He was Jewish?' the novelist exclaimed.

'What's so surprising about that?'

'Only that scarcely two or three people in the whole world, outside the inner circle of the Nazi Party, would understand what was meant by the Chinaman and Hitler's commander. This author must have delved very deeply into occult literature – things like Eliphas Levi, or Ludvig Prinn, or some of the most closely guarded Rosicrucian secrets, and then made a perfectly amazing guess in the right direction.'

'What in the world are you talking about?'

The novelist looked at Drake for a long time, then said, 'I hate to even discuss it. Some things are too vile. Some books, as your Mr. Poe said, should not allow themselves to be read. Even I have coded things in my most famous work, which is admired for all the wrong reasons. In my search for the mystical, I have learned things I would rather forget, and the real goal of Herr Hitler is one of those things. But you must tell me: who was this remarkable author?'

('He just called me,' Luciano told Maldonado, 'and I got this much at least: he's not a shakedown artist. He's aiming big, and he's big already himself. I'm getting my lawyer out of bed, to run down all the best Boston families, and find one with a son who shows signs of having the old larceny in his heart. I bet it's a banking family. I can hear money in a voice, and he has it.')

Drake was persistent, and finally the novelist said, 'As you know, I refuse to live in Germany because of what is happening there. Nevertheless, it is my home, and I do hear things. If I try to explain, you must get your mind out of the arena of ordinary politics. When I say Hitler does have a Master, that doesn't mean he is a front man in the pedestrian political sense.' The novelist paused. 'How can I present the picture so you will understand it? You are not German . . . How can you understand a people of whom it has been said, truthfully, that they have one foot in their own land and one foot in Thule? Have you ever heard of Thule? That's the German name for the fabulous kingdom the Greeks called Atlantis. Whether this kingdom ever existed is immaterial; the belief in it has existed since the dawn of history and beliefs motivate actions. In fact, you cannot understand a man's actions unless you understand his beliefs.'

The novelist paused again, and then began talking about the Golden Dawn Society in England in the 1890s. 'Strange things were written by the members. Algernon Blackwood, for instance, wrote of intelligent beings who preexisted mankind on earth. Can you take such a concept seriously? Can you think about Blackwood's warnings, of his guarded phrases, such as, "Of such great powers or beings there may conceivably be a survival, of which poetry and legend alone caught a flying memory and called them gods, monsters, mythical beings of all sorts and kinds"? Or, Arthur Machen, who wrote of the "miracles of Mons" during the Great War, describing the angels, as they were called, and published this two days before the soldiers at the scene sent back reports of the incident. Machen was in the Golden Dawn, and he left it to rejoin the Catholic Church, warning, "There are sacraments of Evil as well as of Good." William Butler Yeats was a member, too, and you must certainly know his remarkable lines, "What rough beast/ Its hour come round at last/ Slouches toward Bethlehem to be born?" And the Golden Dawn was just the outer portal of the Mysteries. The things that Crowley learned after leaving the Golden Dawn and joining the Ordo Templi Orientis . . . Hitler suppressed both the Dawn and the Ordo Templi Orientis, you know. He belonged to the Vril Society himself, where the really extraterrestrial secrets are kept . . .'

'You seem to be having a hard time getting to the point,' Drake said.

'Some things need to be approached in hints, even in

allegories. You have taken mescaline with Klee and his friends, and spent the night seeing the Great Visions. Do I need to remind you that reality is not a one-level affair?'

'Very well,' Drake said. 'Behind the Golden Dawn and the OTO and the Vril Society is a hidden group of real Initiates. There was a German branch of the Golden Dawn, and Hitler was a member. You want me to understand that to treat these sacraments of Evil and these beings from Atlantis as no more than fictions would be to oversimplify; is that right?'

'The Golden Dawn was founded by a German woman, carrying on a tradition that was already a hundred years old in Bavaria. As for these powers or beings from Thule, they do not exist in the sense that bricks and beefsteak exist, either. The physicist, by manipulating these fantastic electrons – which, I remind you, have to be imagined as moving from one place to another without passing through any intervening space like a fairy or a ghost – produces real phenomena, visible to the senses. Say, then, that by manipulating these beings or powers from Thule, certain men are able to produce effects that can also be seen and experienced.'

'What was the Golden Dawn?' Drake asked, absorbed. 'How did it begin?'

'It's very old, more than medieval. The modern organization began in 1776, with a man who quit the Jesuits because he thought he was an atheist, until his researches into Eastern history had surprising results . . .'

(It's him! Hitler screamed, *He has come for me!* And then, as Herman Rauschning recorded, 'he lapsed into gibberish.' *The boss himself,* Dutch Schultz moaned, *Oh, mama, I can't go through with it. Please. Come on, open the soap duckets. The chimney sweeps. Take to the sword. Shut up. You got a big mouth.)*

We've got two real possibilities, Lepke's lawyer reported. *But one of them is Boston Irish and what you described was the old original Boston accent. The second one is probably your man, then. His name is Robert Putney Drake.*

Standing before the house on Benefit Street, Drake could see, across the town, the peak of Sentinel Hill and the old deserted church that had harbored the Starry Wisdom Sect in the 1870s. He turned back to the door and raised the old Georgian knocker *(remembering: Lillibridge the reporter and Blake the painter had both died investigating that sect)*, then rapped smartly three times.

Howard Phillips Lovecraft, pale, gaunt, cadaverous, opened the door. 'Mr. Drake?' he asked genially.

'It was good of you to see me,' Drake said.

'Nonsense,' Lovecraft replied, ushering him into the Colonial hallway. 'Any admirer of my poor tales is always welcome here. They are so few that I could have them all here on a single day without straining my aunt's dinner budget.'

He may be one of the most important men alive, Drake thought, *and he doesn't really suspect.*

('He left Boston by train this morning,' the soldier reported to Maldonado and Lepke. 'He was going to Providence, Rhode Island.')

'Of course, I have no hesitation in discussing it,' Lovecraft said after he and Drake were settled in the old booklined study and Mrs. Gamhill had served them tea. 'Whatever your friend in Zurich may feel, I am and always have been a strict materialist.'

'But you have been in touch with *these* people?'

'Oh, certainly, and an absurd lot they are, all of them. It began after I published a story called "Dagon" in, let me see, 1919. I had been reading the Bible and the description of the Philistine sea god, Dagon, reminded me of sea serpent legends and of the reconstructions of dinosaurs by paleontologists. And the notion came to me: suppose Dagon were real, not a god, but simply a long-lived being vaguely related to the great saurians. Simply a story, to entertain those who enjoy the weird and Gothic in literature. You can't imagine my astonishment when various occult groups began contacting me, asking which group I belonged to and which side I was on. They were all terribly put out when I made perfectly clear that I didn't believe any such rubbish.'

'But,' Drake asked perplexed, 'why did you pick up more and more of these hidden occult teachings and incorporate them in your later stories?'

'I am an artist,' Lovecraft said, 'a mediocre artist, I fear – and don't contradict me. I value honesty above all the other virtues. I would like to believe in the supernatural, in a world of social justice and in my own possession of genius. But reason commands that I accept the facts: the world is made of blind matter, the wicked and brutal always have and always will trample on the weak and innocent, and I have a very microscopic capacity to create a small range of esthetic effects, all macabre and limited in their appeal to a very special audience. Nevertheless, I would that things were otherwise. Hence, although a conservative, I support certain social legislation that might improve the conditions of the poor, and, although a poor writer, I try to elevate the status of my own wretched prose. Vampires and ghosts and werewolves are worn out; they provoke chuckles rather than terror. Thus, when I began to learn of the old lore, after "Dagon" was published, I began to use it in my stories. You can't imagine the hours I have spent with those old volumes at Miskatonic, wading through tons of trash – Alhazred and Levi and Von Juntzt were all mental cases, you know – to sift out the notions that were unfamiliar enough to cause a genuine shock, and a real shudder, in my readers.'

'And you've never received threats from any of these occult groups for mentioning Iok Sotot or Cthulhu outright in your stories?'

'Only when I mentioned Hali,' Lovecraft said with a wry smile. 'Some thoughtful soul reminded me of what happened to Bierce after *he* wrote a bit frankly on that subject. But that was a friendly warning, not a threat. Mr. Drake, you are a banker and a businessman. Certainly, you don't take any of this seriously?'

'Let me reply with a question of my own,' Drake said carefully. 'Why, in all the exoteric lore which you have chosen to make exoteric through your stories, have you never mentioned the Law of Fives?'

'In fact,' Lovecraft said, 'I did hint at it, rather broadly, in "At the Mountains of Madness." Have you not read that? It's my longest, and, I think, my best effort to date.' But he seemed abruptly paler.

'In "The Case of Charles Dexter Ward,"' Drake pursued, 'you quote a formula from Eliphas Levi's *History of Magic*. But you don't quote it in full. Why was that?'

Lovecraft sipped his tea, obviously framing his answer carefully. Finally he said, 'One doesn't have to believe in Santa Claus to recognize that people will exchange presents at Christmas time. One doesn't have to believe in Yog Sothoth, the Eater of Souls, to realize how people will act who do hold that belief. It is not my intent, in any of my writings, to provide information that will lead even one unbalanced reader to try experiments that will result in the loss of human life.'

Drake arose. 'I came here to learn,' he said, 'but it appears that my only possible function is to teach. Let me remind you of the words of Lao-tse: "Those who speak do not know; those who know do not speak." Most occult groups are in the first class, and their speculations are as absurd as you think. But those in the second class are not to be so lightly dismissed. They have left you alone because your stories appear only in magazines that appeal to a small minority. These magazines, however, have lately been printing stories about rockets and nuclear chain reactions and other matters that are on the edge of technological achievement. When these fantasies start coming true, which will probably occur within a decade, there will be much wider interest in such magazines, and your stories will be included in that renaissance. Then you will receive some very unwelcome attention.'

Lovecraft remained seated. 'I think I know of whom you are speaking; I can also read newspapers and make deductions. Even if they are mad enough to attempt it, they do not have the means. They would have to take over not one government but many. That project would keep them busy enough, I should think, to distract them from worrying about a few lines here and there in stories that are published as fiction. I can conceive of the next war leading to breakthroughs in rocketry and nuclear energy, but I doubt that even that will lead many people to take my stories seriously, or to see the connections between certain rituals, which I have never described explicitly, and acts which will be construed as the normal excesses of despotism.'

'Good day, sir,' Drake said formally. 'I must be off to New York, and your welfare is really not a major concern in my life.'

'Good day,' Lovecraft said, rising with Colonial courtesy. 'Since you have been so good as to give me a warning, I will return the favor. I do not think your interest in these people is based on a wish to oppose them, but to serve them. I beg you to remember their attitude toward servants.'

Back out on the street, Drake experienced a momentary dejection. *For nearly twenty years he's been writing about them and they haven't contacted him. I've been rocking the boat on two continents, and they haven't contacted me. What does it take to make them show their hand? And if I don't have an understanding with them, anything I work out with Maldonado and Capone is written on the wind. I just can't afford to deal with the Mafia before I deal with them. What should I do – put an ad in the* New York Times: *'Will the All-Seeing Eye please look in my direction? R. P. Drake, Boston?'*

And a Pontiac (stolen an hour before in Kingsport) pulled away from the curb, several houses back, and started following Drake as he left Benefit Street and walked back toward the downtown area. He wasn't looking back, so he didn't see what happened to it, but he noticed an old man coming toward him stop in his tracks and turn white.

'Jesus on a pogo stick,' the old man said weakly.

Drake looked over his shoulder and saw nothing but an empty street. 'What is it?' he asked.

'Never mind,' the old man replied. 'You'd *never* believe me, mister.' And he cut across the sidewalk toward a saloon.

('What do you mean, you lost four soldiers?' Maldonado screamed into the phone.

'Just what I'm saying,' Eddie Vitelli, of the Providence gambling, heroin and prostitution Vitellis, said. 'We found your Drake at a hotel. Four of the best soldiers we've got followed him. They called in once to say he was at a house on Benefit Street. I told them to pick him up as soon as he comes out. And that's it, period, it's all she wrote.

They're all gone, like something picked them off the face of the earth. I've got everybody looking for the car they were in, and that's gone, too.')

Drake canceled his trip to New York and went back to Boston, plunging into bank business and mulling over his next move. Two days later, the janitor came to his desk, hat in hand, and asked, 'Could I speak to you, Mr. Drake?'

'Yes, Getty, what is it?' Drake replied testily. His tone was deliberate; the man was probably about to ask for a raise, and it was best to put him on the defensive immediately.

'It's this, sir,' the janitor said, laying a card on Drake's desk. Drake looked down impatiently and saw a rainbow of colors – the card was printed on some unknown plastic and created a prismatic effect recalling his mescaline trips in Zurich. Through the rainbow, shimmering and radiant, he saw the outlines of a thirteen-step pyramid, with a red eye at the top. He stared up at the janitor and saw a face without subservience or uncertainty.

'The Grand Master of the Eastern United States is ready to talk to you,' the janitor said softly.

'Holy Cleopatra!' Drake cried, and tellers turned to stare at him.

'Kleopatra?' Simon Moon asked, twenty-three years later. 'Tell him about Kleopatra.'

It was a sunny afternoon in October and the drapes in the living room of the apartment on the seventeenth floor of 2323 Lake Shore Drive were pulled back to reveal a corner window view of Chicago's Loop skyscrapers and the whitecap-dotted blue surface of Lake Michigan. Joe sprawled in a chair facing the lake. Simon and Padre Pederastia were on a couch under an enormous painting titled 'Kleopatra.' She looked a good deal like Stella Maris and was holding an asp to her bosom. The eye-and-pyramid symbol appeared several times in the hieroglyphs on the tomb wall behind her. Sitting in an armchair opposite the painting was a slender man with sharp, dark features, shoulder-length chestnut hair, a forked brown beard and green eyes.

'Kleopatra,' said the man, 'was an instant study. Would

have made her Polymother of the great globe itself, if she'd
lived. She damned near brought down the Roman Empire,
and she did shorten its life by centuries. She forced
Octavius to bring so much Aneristic power to bear that
the Empire went prematurely into the state of bureaucracy.'

'What do I call you?' said Joe. 'Lucifer? Satan?'

'Call me Malaclypse the Elder,' said the fork-bearded
man with a smile that seemed to beam through endless
shifting veils of warm self-regard.

'I don't get it,' said Joe. 'The first time I saw you, we
were all terrified out of our minds. Though when you
finally showed up looking like Billy Graham, I didn't know
whether to laugh or go catto. But I know I was scared.'

Padre Pederastia laughed. 'You were so terrified, my
son, that you were trying to climb right inside our little
redhead's big red bird's nest. You were so frightened that
that hefty cock of yours' – he licked his lips – 'was squirting juice all over the carpet. Oh, you were terrified, all
right. Oh, my, yes.'

'Well, I wasn't so scared just at that moment you mention,' said Joe with a smile. 'But a little later, when our
friend here was about to appear. You were terrified yourself, Padre Pederastia. You kept hollering, "Come not in
that form! Come not in that form!" Now we're all sittting
around the living room behaving like old chums – and
this – this *being* here is reminiscing about the good old
days with Kleopatra.'

'They were terrible days,' said Malaclypse. 'Very cruel
days, very sad days. Constant wars, tortures, mass murders,
crucifixions. Bad times.'

'I believe you. And what's worse, I can understand what
it means if I believe you, and I can live knowing that you
exist. And even sit down in this living room and smoke a
cigarette with you.'

Two lit cigarettes appeared between Malaclypse's fingers.
He passed one to Joe. Joe drew on it; it tasted sweet, with
just a hint of marijuana.

'That's a corny trick,' said Joe.

'Just so you don't lose your old associations to me too
quickly,' said Malaclypse. 'Too quick to understand, too
soon to misunderstand.'

Padre Pederastia said, 'The night of that Black Mass, I simply had worked myself up to the point where I totally believed. That's what magic is, after all. The people who were here that night relate to left-hand magic, to the Satan myth, to the Faust legend. It's a quick way to get them involved. It worked with you at the time, but we've brought you along fast, because we want more help from you. So now you don't need the trappings.'

'You don't have to be a Satanist to love Malaclypse,' said Malaclypse.

'In fact, its better if you're not,' said Simon. 'Satanists are creeps. They skin dogs alive and shit like that.'

'Because most Satanists are Christians,' said Joe. 'Which is a very masochistic religion.'

'Now, just a minute—' said Padre Pederastia with some asperity.

'He's right, Pederastia,' said Malaclypse. 'Nobody knows that better than you – or me, for that matter.'

'Did you ever meet Jesus?' Joe asked, awed in spite of his skepticism.

Malaclypse smiled. 'I *was* Jesus.'

Padre Pederastia flapped his hands and bounced up and down in his chair. 'You're telling too much!'

'For me, trust is total or nonexistent,' said Malaclypse. 'I perceive that I can trust Joe. I wasn't the original Jesus, Joe, the one they crucified. But – this happened a few centuries after I experienced transcendental illumination at Melos – I was passing through Judea in the persona of a Greek merchant when they crucified Jesus. I met some of his followers the day he died, and I talked with them. If you think Christianity is a bloody religion as it is, this is nothing to what it would have been if Jesus hadn't seemed to come back. If the seventeen original apostles – five of them have been purged from the records – had been left on their own, they would have passed from horror and terror at Jesus's death to vindictive fury. It would have been as if Islam had come seven centuries earlier. Instead of slowly taking over the Roman Empire and preserving much of the Greco-Roman world intact, it would have swept and mobilized the East, destroyed most of Western civilization and replaced it with a theocracy more oppressive than Pharaonic Egypt. I stopped that with a few magic tricks. Appearing in the persona of the ressurrected Jesus, I taught there was no need for hatred and vengeance after my death. I even tried to get them to realize that life is a game by teaching them Bingo. To this day, nobody understands and critics call it part of the *commercialism* of the Church. The sacred Tarot wheel, the moving Mandala! So despite my influence, Christianity focused obsessively on the crucifixion of Jesus – which is really irrelevant to what he taught while he was alive – and remained a kind of death worship. When Paul went to Athens and made the link-up with the Illuminati, who were using Plato's Academy as a front, the ideology of Plato combined with the mythology of Christ to deliver the knockout blow to pagan humanism and lay the foundations for the modern world of superstates. After that, I changed my appearance again and took the name of Simon Magus and had some success spreading ideas contradictory to Christianity.'

'You can change your appearance at will, then,' said Joe.

'Oh, sure thing. I'm just as quick with a thought projection as anybody.' He pushed his pinkie thoughtfully into his left nostril and worked it around. Joe stiffened; he didn't care to watch people picking their noses in public. He looked resolutely over Malaclypse's left shoulder. 'Now that you know as much as you do about us, Joe, it's time you started working with us. Chicago, as you know, is the Illuminati nerve center in this hemisphere, so we'll use this town to test AUM, a new drug with astonishing properties, if ELFs technicians are correct. It's supposed to turn neophobes into neophiles.'

Simon slapped his forehead and shouted 'Wow, man!' and started laughing. Pederastia gasped and whistled.

'You look blank, Joe,' said Malaclypse. 'Has no one explained to you that the human race is divided into two distinct genotypes – neophobes, who reject new ideas and accept only what they have known all their lives, and neophiles, who love new things, change, invention, innovation? For the first four million years of man's history, all humans were neophobes, which is why civilization did not develop. Animals are all neophobes. Only mutation can change

them. Instinct is simply the natural behavior of a neo-
phobe. The neophile mutation appeared about a hundred
thousand years ago, and speeded up thirty thousand years
ago. However, there has never been more than a handful of
neophiles anywhere on the planet. The Illuminati themselves sprang from one of the oldest neophile-neophobe
conflicts on record.'

'I take it the Illuminati were trying to hold back progress,' said Joe. 'Is that their general aim?'

'You're still thinking like a liberal,' said Simon. 'Nobody gives a fuck for progress.'

'Right,' said Malaclypse. 'They were the innovators in
that instance. All the Illuminati were – and are – neophiles.
Even today, they see their work as directed toward progress. They want to become like gods. It's possible for
humans, given the right methods, to translate themselves
into sentient latticeworks of pure energy that will be more
or less permanent. The process is called transcendental
illumination, to distinguish it from the acquisition of insight into the true nature of man and the universe, which
is ordinary illumination. I've gone through transcendental
illumination and am a being composed altogether of
energy, as you may have guessed. However, prior to becoming energy fields men often fall victim to hubris. Their
actions cause pain to others and make them insensitive,
uncreative and irrational. Mass human sacrifice is the most
reliable method of achieving transcendental illumination.
Human sacrifice can, of course, be masked as other things,
such as war, famine and plague. The vision of the Four
Horsemen vouchsafed to Saint John is actually a vision of
mass transcendental illumination.'

'How did you achieve it?' Joe asked.

'I was present at the massacre of the male inhabitants
of the city of Melos by the Athenians in 416 B.C. Have you
read Thucydides?'

'A long time ago.'

'Well, Thucydides had it wrong. He presented it as an
out-and-out atrocity, but there were extenuating circumstances. The Melians had been stabbing Athenian soldiers
in the back, poisoning them, filling them full of arrows
from ambush. Some of them were working for the Spartans

and some were on the side of Athens, but the Athenians didn't know which ones they could trust. They didn't want to do any unnecessary killing, but they did want to get back to Athens alive. So they rounded up all the Melian men one day and hacked them to pieces in the town square. The women and children were sold into slavery.'

'What did you do?' said Joe. 'Were you there with the Athenians?'

'Yes, but I didn't do any killing, I was a chaplain. Of the Erisian denomination, of course. But I was prepared to perform services to Hermes, Dionysus, Heracles, Aphrodite, Athena, Hera and some of the other Olympians. I almost went mad with horror – I didn't understand that Pangenitor is Panphage. I was praying to Eris to deliver me or deliver the Melians or do something, and she answered me.'

'Hail, she what done it all,' said Simon.

'I almost believe you,' said Joe. 'But every once in a while the suspicion creeps in that you're simply doing a two-thousand-year-old-man routine and the butt of the joke is me.'

Malaclypse stood up with a little smile. 'Come here, Joe.'

'What for?'

'Just come here.' Malaclypse held his hands away from his sides, palms turned toward Joe appealingly. Joe walked over and stood before him.

'Put your hand into my side,' said Malaclypse.

'Oh, come on,' said Joe. Pederastia snickered. Malaclypse just looked at him with a gentle, encouraging smile, so he reached out to touch Malaclypse's shirt. His hands still felt nothing. He closed his eyes to verify that. There was no sensation whatever. Thin air. Eyes still shut, he moved his hand forward. He opened his eyes, and when he saw his arm sunk into Malaclypse's body up to the elbow, he almost barfed his cookies.

He drew back. 'It can't be a movie. I'd be almost willing to say a moving holograph, but the illusion is too perfect. You're looking right at me. To my eyes you are unquestionably there.'

'Try a few karate chops,' said Malaclypse. Joe obliged, swinging his hand like a scythe through Malaclypse's waist, chest and head. For a finale, Joe brought his hand straight down through the top of the being's head.

'I suspend judgment,' said Joe. 'Maybe you are what you say you are. But it's pretty hard to take. Can you feel anything?'

'I can create temporary sensory organs for myself whenever I want to. I can enjoy just about anything a human enjoys or experiences. But my primary mode of perception is a very advanced form of what you would call intuition. Intuition is a kind of sensitivity in the mind to events and processes; what I have is a highly developed intuitional receptor which is completely controllable.'

Joe went back and sat down, shaking his head. 'You certainly are in an enviable position.'

'Like I said, it's the real reason for human sacrifice,' said Malaclypse. He, too, sat down, and Joe now noticed that the soft upholstery of his chair didn't sink beneath his weight. He seemed to rest on the surface of the cushions. 'Any sudden or violent death releases a burst of consciousness energy, which can be controlled and channeled as any explosive energy can be. The Illuminati would all like to become as gods. That has been their ambition for longer than I care to say.'

'Which means they have to perpetrate mass murder,' said Joe, thinking of nuclear weapons, gas chambers, chemical-biological warfare.

Malaclypse nodded. 'Now, I don't disapprove of that on moral grounds, since morals are purely illusory. I do have a personal distaste for that sort of thing. Although, when you've lived as long as I have, you have lost so many friends and lovers that it is impossible not to take the deaths of humans as a matter of course. So it goes. And, since I achieved my own immortality and nonmateriality as the result of a mass murder, it would be hypocritical of me to condemn the Illuminati. For that matter, I don't condemn hypocrisy, though it is also personally distasteful to me. But I do say that the method of the Illuminati is stupid and wasteful, since everybody is already everything. So, why fuck around with things? It is absurd to try to be something else when there is nothing else.'

'That kind of statement is simply beyond my comprehension,' said Joe. 'I don't know, maybe it's my engineering training. But even after my own partial illumination in San Francisco with Dr. Iggy, this kind of talk doesn't make any more sense than Christian Science to me.'

'Soon you'll understand more,' said Malaclypse. 'About the history of man, about some of the esoteric knowledge that has been lying around for tens of thousands of years. Eventually you'll know all that's worth knowing about absolutely everything.'

(Tobias Knight, the FBI agent monitoring the bugging equipment in Dr. Mocenigo's home, heard the pistol shot the same time Carmel did. 'What the hell?' he said out loud, sitting up straight. He had heard the door open and footsteps walking about and had been waiting for a conversation . . . and then, without warning, he had heard the shot. Now a voice spoke, 'Sorry Dr. Mocenigo. You were a great patriot, and this is a dog's death. But I will share it with you.' Then there were more footsteps and *something else* . . . Knight recognized the sound: it was liquid being poured. The steps and the pouring liquid continued, and Knight abruptly tore himself out of his state of shock and pressed the intercom. 'Knight?' asked a voice which he recognized as Esperando Despond, the Special Agent in Charge for Las Vegas. 'Mocenigo's house,' Knight said crisply. 'Get a whole crew out there double-quick. Something is happening, one killing at least.' He released the intercom and listened, paralyzed, to the footsteps and the liquid sounds, which were now mixed with subdued humming. A man doing an unpleasant job, but trying to keep his cool. Knight recognized the tune, finally: 'Camp-town Races.' The humming and walking and slurping continued. 'Do-da-Do-da . . .' Then the voice spoke again: 'This is General Lawrence Stewart Talbot, speaking to the CIA, the FBI and whoever else has this house bugged. I discovered at two this morning that several people in our Anthrax Leprosy Pi project have accidentally been subjected to live cultures. All of them are living at the installation, and can easily be isolated while the antidote works. I have already given orders to that effect. Dr. Mocenigo himself unknowingly received the worst dose, and was in advanced morbidity, a few minutes from death, when I arrived. His

whole house, obviously, will have to be burned down, and
I am also, due to my proximity while examining him, too
far gone to be saved. I will therefore shoot myself after
setting fire to the house. There is one remaining problem.
I found evidence that a woman had been in Dr. Mocenigo's
bed earlier – that's what comes of allowing important
people to live off base – and she must be found and given
the antidote and each of her contacts must be traced. Needless to say, this must be done quietly, or there will be a
nationwide panic. Tell the President to see that my wife
gets the medal for this. Tell my wife that with my last
breath I still insist she was wrong about that girl in Red
Lion, Pennsylvania. In closing, I firmly believe that this is
the greatest country in the history of the world, and can
still be saved if Congress will lock up those damned college
kids for once and for all. God bless America!' There was
a scratching sound – my God! Knight thought, the match
– and the sound of flames, in the midst of which General
Talbot tried to add a postscript but couldn't get the words
out because he was screaming. Finally, the second shot
came, and the screaming stopped. Knight raised his head,
jaw clenched, repressed tears in his steely eyes. 'That was
a great American,' he said aloud.)

    Over cigars and brandy, after George had been sent off
to bed to be distracted by Tarantella, Richard Jung asked
pointedly, 'Just how sure are you that this Discordian
bunch is a match for the Illuminati? It's kind of late in the
game to change sides.'

    Drake started to speak, then turned to Maldonado. 'Tell
him about Italy in the 19th century,' he said.

    'The Illuminati are just men and women,' Maldonado
replied obligingly. 'More women than men, in fact. It was
Eve Weishaupt who started the whole show; Adam just
acted as her front because people are used to taking orders
from men. This Atlantis stuff is mostly bullshit. Everybody
who knows about Atlantis at all traces his family, or his
clan, or his club, back there. Some of the old dons in the
Maf even try to trace *la Cosa Nostra* back there. All bullshit. Just like all the WASPs tracing themselves back to
the *Mayflower*. For everyone who can prove it, like Mr.
Drake, there's a hundred who are just bluffing.

'You see,' Maldonado went on more intensely, chewing his cigar ferociously, 'originally the Illuminati was just a – how do you call it – a kind of 18th-century women's liberation front. Behind Weishaupt was Eve; behind Godwin, who started all this socialism and anarchism with his *Political Justice* book, was his mistress Mary Wollstonecraft, who started the woman revolution with a book called, uh . . .'

'*Vindication of the Rights of Women,*' Drake contributed.

'And they got Tom Paine to write on women's lib, too, and to defend their French Revolution and try to import it here. But that all fell through and they didn't get a real controlling interest in the U.S. until they hoodwinked Woody Wilson into creating the Federal Reserve in 1914. And that's the way it usually goes. In Italy they had a front called the Haute Vente, that was so damn secret Mazzini was a member all his life and never knew the control came from Bavaria. My grandpa told me all about those days. We had a three-way dogfight. The Monarchists on one side, the Haute Vente and the Liberteri, the anarchists, on the other, and the Maf in the middle trying to roll with the punches and figure out which way the bread was buttered, you know? Then the Liberteri got wise to the Haute Vente and split from it, and it was a four-way fight. You look it up in the history books, they tell it like it was except they don't mention who ran the Haute Vente. And then the good old Law of Fives came into it, and we had the Fascisti and it was a five-way dogfight. Who won? Not the Illuminati. It wasn't until 1937, manipulating the English government to discourage Mussolini's peace plans and using Hitler to get Benito into the Berlin-Tokyo axis, that the Illuminati had some kind of control in Italy. And even then it was indirect. When we made our deal with the CIA – it was called the OSS back in those days – Luciano got out of the joint and we turned over Italy and delivered Mussolini dead.'

'And the point of all this?' Jung asked coldly.

'The point is,' Maldonado said, 'the Maf has been against the Illuminati more of the time than we've been with them, and we're still doing business and we're stron-

ger than ever. Believe me, their bark is much worse than
their bite. Because they know some magic, they scare everybody. We've had magicians and belladonnas – witches, to
you – in Sicily since before Paris got hot pants for Helen,
and believe me a bullet kills them as dead as it kills anybody else.'

'The Illuminati *do* have a bit,' Drake interjected, 'but it
is my judgment that they are going out with the Age of
Pisces. The Discordians, I think, represent an Aquarian
swing.'

'Oh, I don't go for that mystic stuff,' Jung said. 'Next
thing you'll be quoting *I Ching* at me, like my old man.'

'You're an anal type, like most accountants,' Drake replied coolly. 'And a Capricorn as well. Down-to-earth and
conservative. I won't attempt to persuade you about this
aspect of the matter. Just take my word, I didn't get where
I am by ignoring significant facts just because they won't fit
on a profit-and-loss statement. On the profit-and-loss level,
however, I have had reasons to believe that the Discordians
can currently outbid the Illuminati. These reasons date
back many months before the appearance of those mar-
velous statues today.'

Later, in bed, Drake turned the matter around in his
head and looked at it from several sides. Lovecraft's words
came back to him: 'I beg you to remember their attitude
toward their servants.' That was it, basically. He was an
old man, and he was tired of being their servant, or satrap,
or satellite. When he was thirty-three, he was ready to take
them over, as Cecil Rhodes had once done. Somehow, he
had been maneuvered into taking over just one section of
their empire. If he could think, truthfully, that he owned
the United States more thoroughly than any President in
four decades, the fact remained that he did not own himself. Not until he signed his Declaration of Independence
tonight by joining the Discordians. The other Jung, the
alter Zauber in Zurich, had tried to tell him something
about power once, but he had dismissed it as sentimental
slop. Now he tried to remember it . . . and, suddenly, all
the old days came back, Klee and his numinous paintings,
the Journey to the East, old Crowley saying, 'Of course,
mixing the left-hand and right-hand paths is dangerous. If

you fear such risks, go back to Hesse and Jung and those old ladies. Their way is safe and mine isn't. All that can be said for me is that I have real power and they have dreams.' But the Illuminati had crushed Crowley, just as they smashed Willie Seabrook, when those men revealed too much. *'I beg you to remember their attitude toward their servants.'* Damn it, what was it Jung had said about power?

And he turned the card over, and on the back was an address on Beacon Hill with the words '8:30 tonight.' He looked up at the janitor, who backed away deferentially, saying, 'Thank you, Mr. Drake, sir,' without a touch of irony in his face or voice. And it hadn't surprised him at all that, for deliberate contrast, the Grand Master he met that night, one of the five Illuminati Primi for the U.S., was an official of the Justice Department. (And what had Jung said about power?) 'A few of them will have to fall. Lepke, I would recommend. Perhaps Luciano also.' No mystical trappings: just a businesslike meeting. 'Our interest is the same as yours: increasing the power of the Justice Department. An equal increment in the power of the other branches of government will proceed nicely when we get the war into gear.' Drake remembered his excitement: it was all as he had foreseen. The end of the Republic, the dawn of the Empire.

'After Germany, Russia?' Drake asked once.

'Very good; you are indeed farseeing,' the Grand Master replied. 'Mr. Hitler, of course, is only a medium. Virtually no ego at all, on his own. You have no idea how dull and prosaic such types are, except when under proper Inspiration. Naturally, his supplied ego will collapse, he will become psychotic, and we will have no control over him at all, then. We are prepared to help him fall. Our real interest now is here. Let me show you something. We do not work in general outlines; our plans are always specific, to the last detail.' He handed Drake a sheaf of papers. 'The war will probably end in '44 or '45. We will have Russia built up as the next threat within two years. Read this carefully.'

Drake read what was to become the National Security

Act of 1947. 'This abolishes the Constitution,' he said almost in ecstasy.

'Quite. And believe me, Mr. Drake, by '46 or '47, we will have Congress and the public ready to accept it. The American Empire is closer than you imagine.'

'But the isolationists and pacifists – Senator Taft and that crowd—'

'They will wither away. When communism replaces fascism as the number one enemy, your small-town conservative will be ready for global adventures on a scale that would make the heads of poor Mr. Roosevelt's liberals spin. Trust me. We have every detail pinpointed. Let me show you where the new government will be located.'

Drake stared at the plan and shook his head. 'Some people will recognize what a pentagon means,' he said dubiously.

'They will be dismissed as superstitious cranks. Believe me, this building will be constructed within a few years. It will become the policeman of the world. Nobody will dare question its actions or judgments without being denounced as a traitor. Within thirty years, Mr. Drake, *within thirty years,* anyone who attempts to restore power to the Congress will be cursed and vilified, not by liberals but by conservatives.'

'Holy God,' Drake said.

The Grand Master rose and walked to an old-fashioned globe nearly as large as King Kong's head. 'Pick a spot, Mr. Drake. Any spot. I guarantee you we will have American troops there within thirty years. The Empire that you dreamed of while reading Tacitus.'

Robert Putney Drake felt humbled for an instant, even though he recognized the gimmick: using one single example of telepathy, plucking Tacitus out of his head, to climax the presentation of the incredible dream. At last he understood firsthand the awe that the Illuminati created in both its servitors and its enemies.

'There will be opposition,' the Grand Master went on. 'In the 1960s and early 1970s especially. That's where your notion for a unified crime syndicate fits into our plan. To crush the opposition, we will need a Justice Department equivalent in many ways to Hitler's Gestapo. If your scheme works – if the Mafia can be drawn into a syndicate that is not entirely under Sicilian control, and the various other groups can be brought under the same umbrella – we will have a nationwide outlaw cartel. The public itself will then call for the kind of Justice Department that we need. By the mid-1960s, wiretapping of all sorts must be so common that the concept of privacy will be archaic.' And, tossing sleeplessly, Drake thought how smoothly it had all worked out; why then was he rebelling against it? Why did it give him no pleasure? And what *was* it Jung had said about power?

Richard Jung, wearing Carl Jung's old sweater and smoking his pipe, said, 'And next the solar system.' The room was crowded with white rabbits, Playboy bunnies, Bugs Bunny, the Wolf Man, Ku Kluxers, Mafiosos, Lepke with accusing eyes, a dormouse, a mad hatter, the King of Hearts, the Prince of Wands, and Jung was shouting over the din. 'Billions to reach the moon. Trillions to get to Mars. All pouring into our corporations. Better than the gladiatorial games.' Linda Lovelace elbowed him aside. 'Call me Ishmaelian,' she said suggestively; but Jung handed Drake the skeleton of a Biafran baby. 'For Petruchio's feast,' he explained, producing a piece of ticker tape. 'We now own,' he began to read, 'seventy-two percent of earth's resources, and fifty-one percent of all the armed troops in the world are under our direction. Here,' he said, passing the body of an infant that had died in Appalachia, 'see that this one gets an apple in its mouth.' A bunny passed Drake a 1923 Thompson machine gun, the model that had been called an automatic rifle because the Army had no funds to buy submachine guns that year. 'What's this for?' Drake asked, confused. 'We have to defend ourselves,' the bunny said. 'The mob is at the gates. The hungry mob. An astronaut named Spartacus is leading them.' Drake handed the gun to Maldonado and crept upstairs to his private heliport. He passed through the lavatory to the laboratory (where Dr. Frankenstein was attaching electrodes to Linda Lovelace's jaws) and entered the golf course again, where the door opened to the airplane cabin.

He was escaping in his 747 jet, and below he could see Black Panthers, college kids, starving coal miners, Indians,

Viet Cong, Brazilians, an enormous army pillaging his
estate. 'They must have seen the fnords,' he said to the
pilot. But the pilot was his mother and the sight of her
threw him into a rage. 'Leaving me alone!' he screamed.
'Always leaving me alone to go to your damned parties
with father. I never had a mother, just one nigger maid
after another acting as mothers. Were the parties that fucking important?'

'Oh,' she said reddening, 'how can you use that word
in front of your own mother?'

'To hell with that. All I remember is your perfume hanging in the air, and some strange black face coming when I
called for you.'

'You're such a baby,' she said sadly. 'All your life,
you've always been a big baby.' It was true: he was wearing diapers. A vice president of Morgan Guarantee Trust
stared at him incredulously. 'I say, Drake, do you really
think that is appropriate garb for an important business
meeting?' Beside him Linda Lovelace bent in ecstasy to
kiss the secret ardor of Ishmael. 'A whale of a good time,'
the vice president said, suddenly giggling inanely.

'Oh, fuck you all,' Drake screamed. 'I've got more money
than any of you.'

'The money is gone,' Carl Jung said, wearing Freud's
beard. 'What totem will you use now to ward off insecurity
and the things that go bump in the night?' He sneered.
'What childish codes! M.A.F.I.A. – *Morte Alla Francia
Italia Anela.* French Canadian bean soup – the Five Con-
secrated Bavarian Seers. *Annuit Coeptis Novus Ordo Sec-
lorum* – Anti-Christ Now Our Savior. A boy has never
wept nor dashed a thousand kim – Asmodeus Belial Hastur
Nyarlathotep Wotan Niggurath Dholes Azathoth Tindalos
Kadith. Child's play! *Glasspielen!*'

'Well, if you're so damned smart, who are the inner Five
right now?' Drake asked testily.

'Groucho, Chico, Harpo, Zeppo and Gummo,' Jung
said, riding off on a tricycle. 'The Illuminati is your
mother's breast, sucker,' added Albert Hoffman, peddling
after Jung on a bicycle.

Drake awoke as the Eye closed. It was all clear in an
instant, without the labor he had spent working over the

Dutchman's words. Maldonado stood by the bedside, his face Karloff's, and said, 'We deserve to be dead.' Yes: that was what it was like when you discovered you were a robot, not a man, like Karloff in the last scene of *Bride of Frankenstein.*

Drake awoke again and this time he was really awake. It was clear, crystal clear, and he had no regrets. Far away over Long Island Sound came the first distant rumble of thunder, and he knew this was no storm that any scientist less heretical than Jung or Wilhelm Reich would ever understand. 'Our job,' Huxley wrote before death, 'is waking up.'

Drake put on his robe quickly and stepped out into the dark Elizabethan hallway. Five hundred thousand dollars this house and grounds had cost, including the cottages, and it was only one of his eight estates. Money. What did it mean when Nyarlathotep appeared and 'the wild beasts followed him and licked his hands' as that damned stupid-smart Lovecraft wrote? What did it matter when 'the blind idiot God Chaos blew earth's dust away?'

Drake pushed open the dark paneled doorway of George's room. Good: Tarantella was gone. The thunder rumbled again, and Drake's own shadow looming over the bed reminded him once more of a Karloff movie.

He bent over the bed and shook George's shoulder gently. 'Mavis,' the boy said. Drake wondered who the hell Mavis was; somebody terrific, obviously, if George could be dreaming about her after a session with the Illuminati-trained Tarantella. Or was Mavis another ex-Illuminatus? There were a lot of them with the Discordians lately, Drake had surmised. He shook George's shoulder again, more vigorously.

'Oh, no, I can't come again,' George said. Drake gave another shake, and two weary and frightened eyes opened to look at him.

'What?'

'Up,' Drake grunted, grabbing George under the arms and pulling him to a sitting position. 'Out of bed,' he added, panting, rolling the boy to the edge.

Drake was looking through waves upward at George.

Damn it, the thing has already found my mind. 'You've got to get out,' he repeated. 'You're in danger here.'

October 23, 1935: Charley Workman, Mendy Weiss and Jimmy the Shrew charge through the door of the Palace Chop House and, according to orders, cowboy the joint . . . Lead pellets like rain; and rain like lead pellets hitting George's window, 'Christ, what is it?' he asked. Drake stood him up stark naked and handed him his drawers, repeating 'Hurry!' *Charley the Bug looked over the three bodies: Abadaba Berman, Lulu Rosenkrantz and somebody he didn't recognize. None of them was the Dutchman. 'My God, we fucked up,' he said, 'Dutch ain't here.'* But a commotion has started in the alleys of the dream: Albert Stern, taking his last fix of the night, suddenly recalls his fantasy of killing somebody as important as John Dillinger. *'The can,' Mendy Weiss says excitedly; he had a hard-on, like he always did on this kind of job.* 'Man is a giant,' Drake says, 'forced to live in a pigmy's hut.' 'What does that mean?' George asks. 'It means we're all fools,' Drake says excitedly, smelling the old whore Death, 'especially those of us who try to act like giants by bullying the others in the hut instead of knocking the goddam walls down. Carl Jung told me that, only in more elegant language.' George's dangling penis kept catching his eye: homosexuality (an occasional thing with Drake), heterosexuality (his normal state) and the new lust for the old whore Death were all tugging at him. *The Dutchman dropped his penis, urine squirting his shoes, and went for his gun as he heard the shots in the barroom. He turned quickly, unable to stop pissing, and Albert Stern came through the door, shooting before Dutch could take aim. Falling forward, he saw that it was really Vince Coll, a ghost. 'Oh, mama mama mama,' he said, lying in his urine.*

'Which way do we go?' George asked, buttoning his shirt.

'You go,' Drake said. 'Down the stairs and out the back, to the garage. Here's the key to my Silver Wraith Rolls Royce. It won't be any use to me anymore.'

'Why aren't you coming?' George protested.

'We deserve to be dead,' Drake said, 'all of us in this house.'

'Hey, that's crazy. I don't care what you've done, a guilt trip is always crazy.'

'I've been on a crazier trip, as you'd call it, all my life,' Drake said calmly. 'The power trip. Now, *move!*'

'George, don't make no bull moves,' the Dutchman said. *'He's talking,'* Sergeant Luke Conlon whispered at the foot of the hospital bed; the police stenographer, F. J. Lang, began taking notes. *'What have you done with him?'* the Dutchman went on. *'Oh, mama, mama, mama. Oh, stop it. Oh, oh, oh, sure. Sure, mama.'* Drake sat down in the window seat and, too nervous for a cigar, lit one of his infrequent cigarettes. One hundred and fifty-seven, he thought, remembering the last entry in his little notebook. One hundred and fifty-seven rich women, one wife, and seventeen boys. And never once did I really make contact, never once did I smash the walls . . . The wind and the rain were now deafening outside . . . Fourteen billion dollars, thirteen billion illegal and tax-free; more than Getty or Hunt, even if I could never publicize the fact. And that Arab boy in Tangier who picked my pocket after he blew me, my mother's perfume, hours and hours in Zurich puzzling over the Dutchman's words.

Outside Flegenheimer's livery stable in the Bronx, Phil Silverberg is teasing young Arthur Flegenheimer in 1913, holding the burglar's tools out of reach, asking mockingly, 'Do you really think you're big enough to knock over a house on your own?' In the Newark hospital, the Dutchman cries angrily, 'Now listen, Phil, fun is fun.' The seventeen Illuminati representatives vanished in the dark; the one with the goat's head suddenly returned. 'What happened to the other sixteen?' Dutch asked the hospital walls. The blood from his arm signed the parchment. 'Oh, he done it. Please,' he asked vaguely. Sergeant Conlon looks bemusedly at the stenographer, Lang. *The lightning seemed dark, and the darkness seemed light. It's taking hold of my mind completely, Drake thought, sitting by the window.*

I will hold onto my sanity, Drake swore silently. What was that rock song about Jesus I was remembering?

'Only five inches between me and happiness,' was it? No, that's from *Deep Throat*. The whiteness of the whale. The waves covered his vision again: wrong song, obviously. I have to reach him, to unify the forces. No, dam-mit, that's not *my* thought. That's his thought. He's coming up, up out of the waves, I must rise. I must rise. To unify the forces.

Dillinger said, 'You're right, Dutch. Fuck the Illuminati. Fuck that Maf. The Justified Ancients of Mummu would be glad to have you.' The Dutchman looked right into Sergeant Conlon's eyes and asked, 'John, please, oh, did you buy the whole tale? You promised a million, sure. Get out, I wished I knew. Please make it quick. Fast and furi-ous. Please. Fast and furious. Please help me get out.'

I should have gotten out in '42, when I first learned about the camps, Drake thought. I never realized until then that they really meant to do it. And next Hiroshima. Why did I stay after Hiroshima? It was so obvious, it was just the way Lovecraft wrote, the idiot God Chaos blew earth's dust away, and back in '35 I knew the secret: if a cheap hoodlum like Dutch Schultz had a great poet buried in him, what might be released if any man looked the old whore Death in the eye? Say that I betrayed my country and my planet, but worse, add that I betrayed Robert Putney Drake, the giant of psychology I murdered when I used the secret for power and not for healing.

I see the plumbers, the cesspool cleaners, the colorless all-color of atheism. I am the Fate's lieutenant: I act under ardors. White, White void. Ahab's eye. Five inches from happiness, the Law of Fives, always. Ahab schlurped down, down.

'This Bavarian stuff is all bullshit,' Dillinger said. 'They're mostly Englishmen, since Rhodes took command in 1888. And they've already infiltrated Justice, State and Labor, as well as the Treasury. That's who you're playing ball with. And let me tell you what they plan to do with your people, the Jews, in this war they're cooking up.'

'Listen,' the Dutchman interrupted. 'Capone would have a bullet in me if he knew I was even talking to you, John.'

'Are you afraid of Capone? He arranged to have the Feds put a bullet in me at the Biograph and I'm still sassy and lively as ever.'

'I'm not afraid of Capone or Lepke or Maldonado or . . .' The Dutchman's eyes brought back the hospital room.

'I'm a pretty good pretzler,' he told Sergeant Conlon anxiously. 'Winifred, Department of Justice. I even got it from the department.' The pain shot through him, sharp as ecstasy. 'Sir, please stop it!' He had to explain about DeMolay and Weishaupt. 'Listen,' he urged, 'the last Knight. I don't want to holler.' It was so hard, with the pulsings of the pain. 'I don't know, sir. Honestly, I don't. I went to the toilet. I was in the can and the boy came at me. If we wanted to break the Ring. No, please. I get a month. Come on, Illuminati, cut me off.' It was so hard to explain. 'I had nothing with him and he was a cowboy in one of the seven days. *Ewige!* Fight . . . No business, no hangouts, no friends. Nothing. Just what you pick up and what you need.' The pain wasn't just the bullet; they were working on his mind, trying to stop him from saying too much. He saw the goat head. 'Let him harness himself to you and then bother you,' he cried. 'They are Englishmen and they are a type and I don't know who is best, they or us.' So much to say, and so little time. He thought of Francie, his wife. 'Oh, sir, get the doll a rofting.' The Illuminati formula to summon the lloigor: he could at least reveal that. 'A boy has never wept nor dashed a thousand kim. Did you hear me?' They had to understand how high it went, all over the world. 'I would hear it, the Circuit Court would hear it, and the Supreme Court would hear it. If that ain't the pay-off. Please crack down on the Chinaman's friends and Hitler's Commander.' Eris, the Great Mother, was the only alternative to the Illuminati's power; he had to tell them that much. 'Mother is the best bet and don't let Satan draw you too fast.'

'He's blabbing too much,' the one who wore the goat head, Winifred, from Washington, said. 'Increase the pain.'

'The dirty rats have tuned in,' Dutch shouted.

'Control yourself,' Sergeant Conlon said soothingly.

'But I am dying,' Dutch explained. Couldn't they understand anything?

Drake met Winifred at a cocktail party in Washington, in '47, just after the National Security Act was passed by the Senate. 'Well?' Winifred asked, 'do you have any further doubts?'

'None at all,' Drake said. 'All my open money is now invested in defense industries.'

'Keep it there,' Winifred smiled, 'and you'll get richer than you ever dreamed. Our present projection is that we can get Congress to approve *one trillion dollars* in war preparations before 1967.'

Drake thought fast and asked softly, 'You're going to add another villain beside Russia?'

'Watch China,' Winifred said calmly.

For once, curiosity surpassed cupidity in Drake; he asked, 'Are you really keeping *him* in the Pentagon?'

'Would you like to meet him, face to face?' Winifred asked with a faint hint of a sneer in his voice.

'No thank you,' Drake said coolly. 'I've been reading Herman Rauschning. I remember Hitler's words about the Superman: "He is alive, among us. I have met him. He is intrepid and terrible. I was afraid of him." That's enough for my curiosity.'

'Hitler,' Winifred replied, not hiding the sneer now. 'Saw him in his more human form. He's . . . progressed . . . since then.'

Tonight, Drake thought, as the thunder rose to a maddening crescendo, I will see him, or one of them. Surely, I could have picked a more agreeable form of suicide? The question was pointless; Jung had been right all along, with his Law of Opposites. Even Freud knew it: every sadist becomes a masochist at last.

On an impulse, Drake arose and fetched a pad and pen from the bedside Tudor table. He began to scribble by the light of the increasing electrical storm outside:

> What am I afraid of? Haven't I been building up to this rendezvous ever since I threw the bottle at mother when I was $1\frac{1}{2}$ years old?
>
> And it is kin to me. We both live on blood, do we not, even if I have prettied it over by taking the blood money instead of the blood itself?
>
> Dimensions keep shifting, whenever it gets a fix on me. Prinn was right in his *De Vermis Mysteriis*, they don't really participate in the same space-time as us. That's what Alhazred meant when he wrote, 'Their

hand is at your throat but you see them not. They
walk serene and unsuspected, not in the spaces we
know, but between them.'

'Pull me out,' the Dutchman moaned. 'I am half crazy.
They won't let me get up. They dyed my shoes. Give me
something. I am so sick.'

I can see Kadath and the two magnetic poles. I must
unify the forces by eating the entity.

Which me is the real me? Is it so easy to flow into
my soul because there is so little soul left? Is that what
Jung was trying to tell me about power?

I see Newark Hospital and the Dutchman. I see the
white light and then the black that does not pulsate or
move. I see George trying to drive the Rolls in this
damnable rain. I see the whiteness of whiteness is
black.

'Anybody,' the Dutchman pleaded, 'kindly take my
shoes off. No, there's a handcuff on them. The Baron says
these things.'

I see Weishaupt and the Iron Boot. No wonder only
five ever withstand the ordeal to become the top of
the pyramid. Baron Rothschild won't let Rhodes get
away with that. What is time or space, anyway? What
is soul, that we claim to judge it? Which is real – the
boy Arthur Flegenheimer, seeking for his mother, the
gangster Dutch Schultz, dealing in murder and corrup-
tion with the cool of a Medici or a Morgan, or the
mad poet being born in the Newark hospital bed as
the others die?

And Elizabeth was a bitch. They sang 'The Golden
Vanity' about Raleigh, but none could speak a word
against me. Yet he received the preference. The Globe
Theatre, new drama by Will Shakespeare, down the
street they torture Sackerson the bear for sport.

Christ, they opened the San Andreas Fault to hide
the most important records about Norton. Sidewalks
opening like mouths, John Barrymore falling out of

bed, Will Shakespeare in his mind, my mind, Sir
Francis's mind. Roderick Usher. Starry Wisdom, they
called it.

'The sidewalk was in trouble,' the Dutchman tried to
explain, 'and the bears were in trouble and I broke it up.
Please put me in that room. Please keep him in control.'

I can hear it! The very sounds recorded by Poe and
Lovecraft: Tekeli-li, tekeli-li! It must be close.
I didn't mean to throw the bottle, mother. I just
wanted your attention. I just wanted attention.

'Okay,' the Dutchman sighed. 'Okay, I am all through.
Can't do another thing. Look out, mama, look out for her.
You can't beat Him. Police. Mama. Helen. Mother. Please
take me out.'

I can see it and it can see me. In the dark. There
are things worse than death, vivisections of the spirit.
I should run. Why do I sit here? The bicycle and the
tricycle. 23 skiddoo. Inside the pentagon, the cold of
interstellar space. They came from the stars and
brought their images with them. Mother. I'm sorry.

'Come on, open the soap duckets,' the Dutchman said
hopelessly. 'The chimney sweeps. Take to the sword.'

It is like a chimney without end. Up and up forever,
in deeper and deeper darkness. And the red all-seeing
eye.

'Please help me up. French Canadian bean soup. I want
to pay. Let them leave me alone.'

I want to join it. I want to become it. I have no
more will of my own. I take thee, old whore Death,
as my lawful wedded wife. I am mad. I am half mad.
Mother. The bottle. Linda, schlurped, sucked down.
Unity.

A nine-year-old girl named Patty Cohen lived three

miles down the coast from the Drake estate, and she went mad in those early morning hours of April 25. At first, her parents thought she had gotten hold of some of the LSD which was known to be infiltrating the local grammar school and, being fairly hip, they fed her niacin and horse doctor's doses of vitamin C as she ran about the house alternately laughing and making faces at them, howling about 'he's laying in his own piss' and 'he's still alive inside it' and 'Roderick Usher.' By morning they knew it was more than acid, and months of sadness began as they took her to clinics and private psychiatrists and more clinics and more private psychiatrists. Finally, just before Chanukah in December, they took her to an elegant shrink on Park Avenue, and she had a virtual epileptic fit in the waiting room, staring at a statue on the end table and screaming, 'Don't let him eat me! Don't let him eat me!' Her recovery began from that day, and the sight of that miniature representation of the giant Tlaloc in Mexico City.

But three hours after Drake's death, George Dorn lay on his bed in the Hotel Tudor, holding a phone to his ear, listening to it ring. A young woman's voice on the other end suddenly said hello.

'I'd like to speak to Inspector Goodman,' said George.

There was a momentary pause, then the voice said, 'Who's calling, please?'

'My name is George Dorn, but it probably wouldn't mean anything to the Inspector. But would you ask him to come to the phone please and tell him I have a message for him about the case of Joseph Malik.'

There was a constricted silence, as if the woman on the other end of the phone wanted to scream and had stopped breathing. Finally she said, 'My husband is working just now, but I'll be glad to give him any message you have.'

'That's funny,' said George. 'I've been told Inspector Goodman's duty hours are noon to 9 P.M.'

'I don't think it's any of your business where he is,' the woman suddenly blurted. George felt a little shock. Rebecca Goodman was frightened and she didn't know where her husband was: something in the tone of her last three words revealed her mental state to George. I must be getting more sensitive to people, he thought.

'Do you ever hear from him?' he said gently. He was feeling sorry for Mrs. Inspector Saul Goodman, who was, come to think of it, the wife of a pig. If, just a few years ago, George had read in the paper that this woman's husband had been shot down at random by some unknown revolutionary-type assailants, he would probably have whispered, 'Right on.' One of George's own friends of that period might have killed Inspector Goodman. There was even a moment when George himself might have done it. Once, one of the kids in George's group had called up the young widow of a policeman killed one December by young blacks and called her a bitch and the wife of a pig and told her that her husband was guilty of crimes against the people and that those who had shot him would go down in history as heroes. George had approved of this verbal action as a means of hardening oneself against bourgeois sentimentality. The papers had been full of stories about how this policeman's three little kids would have no Christmas this year; such tripe made George urgently want to throw up.

But now this woman's anguish was coursing through the wire and he was feeling it, just because her husband was not known to be dead, just missing. And probably not dead at all; otherwise why would Hagbard have said that George should get in touch with him?

'I – I don't know what you mean,' she said. She was starting to break, George thought. In another minute she'd be blurting out all her fears to him. Well, for Christ's sake, *he* didn't know where Goodman was.

'Look,' he said sharply, pushing back again the flow of emotion coming through to him, 'if you hear from Inspector Goodman, tell him if he wants to know more about the Bavarian Illuminati he should call George Dorn at the Hotel Tudor. That's D-O-R-N, Hotel *Tudor*. Have you got that?'

'The Illuminati! Look, uh, Mr. Dorn, whatever you want to tell, you can tell me. I'll pass it on to him.'

'I can't do that, Mrs. Goodman. Thank you, now. Goodbye.'

'Wait! Don't hang up.'

'I can't help you, Mrs. Goodman. I don't know where he is, either.' George dropped the phone into its cradle with a sigh. His hands were cold and moist. Well, he'd have to tell Hagbard he couldn't reach Inspector Goodman. But he had learned something – that Saul Goodman, who was supposed to be investigating Joe Malik's disappearance, had himself disappeared, and the words 'Bavarian Illuminati' meant something to his wife. George crossed the small room and turned on the TV. The noon news would be on. He went back to his bed, lay down and lit a cigarette. He was still exhausted, from his sexual bout of the night before with Tarantella Serpentine.

The announcer said, 'The Attorney General has announced that he will speak at six this evening on the early morning epidemic of gangland-style assassinations at widely separated locations all over the country. The death toll from killings of this type has reached twenty-seven, though local officials refuse to say whether all – or any – of these deaths are connected. Among those shot are Senator Edward Coke Bacon; two high-ranking Los Angeles police officers; the mayor of a town called Mad Dog, Texas; a New York fight promoter; a Boston pharmacist; a Detroit ceramicist; a Chicago Communist; three New Mexico hippie leaders; a New Orleans restaurateur; a barber in Yorba Linda, California; and a sausage manufacturer in Sheboygan, Wisconsin. There were bomb explosions at fifteen locations, killing thirteen more people. Six persons around the country have disappeared, and four of these were seen being forced into cars at different times last night and this morning. The Attorney General today called this "a reign of terror perpetrated by organized crime," pointing out that though the motives for the widely scattered slayings is obscure they bear the ear-marks of gangster killings. However, new FBI director George Wallace, who has ordered FBI agents around the country into action, issued a written statement declaring – quote – "Once again the Attorney General has treed the wrong coon, proving that law enforcement should be left to the experienced professionals. We have reason to think that these murders are the work of Negro Communists directed from Peking." – end of quote. Meanwhile, the office of the Vice President has issued an apology to the Italian-American Anti-Defamation League for his reference to "Mafioso rubouts" and the League has withdrawn its picket line from the White House. Remember, the Attorney General will address the nation at 6 P.M. tonight.' The announcer suddenly changed his facial expression from neutral newscaster to pugnacious patriot. 'Certain dissident elements keep complaining that people don't get a chance to participate in decisions made by their government. Yet, at a time like this, when the whole nation has an opportunity to hear the Attorney General, the ratings are not always as good as they should be. So let's do everything we can to build up those ratings tonight, and let the whole world know that this is still a democracy.'

'Fuck!' George shouted at the screen. He didn't recall TV newscasters being that obnoxious. Must be a fairly recent development, something that had happened after he left for Mad Dog – maybe a late outgrowth of the Fernando Poo crisis. It was in this very hotel, George remembered, just after the bloody Fernando Poo demonstrations at the UN that Joe Malik had first broached the subject of Mad Dog. Now Joe had disappeared, not unlike those people who, as George knew, the Syndicate had snuffed in earnest of their good intentions, having accepted Hagbard's gift of objets d'art. Not unlike Inspector Saul Goodman who perhaps had gone down the same rabbit hole as Joe.

There was a knock at the door. George went to it, turning off the TV set in passing. It was Stella Maris.

'Well, glad to see you, baby. Strip off that dress and come over to the bed, so we can reaffirm my initiation rites.'

Stella put her hands on his shoulders. 'Never mind that now, George. We've got things to worry about. Robert Putney Drake and Banana Nose Maldonado are dead. Come on. We've got to get back to Hagbard right away.'

Traveling first by helicopter, then by executive jet and finally by motorboat to Hagbard's Chesapeake Bay submarine base, George was exhausted and dazed in terror's aftermath. He rallied when he saw Hagbard again.

'You motherfucker! You sent me to get goddam killed!'

'And that has given you the courage to tell me off,' said Hagbard with an indulgent smile. 'Fear is a funny thing, isn't it, George? If we weren't afraid of dying of diseases, we'd never develop the science of microbiology. That science in turn creates the possibility of germ warfare. And each superpower is so afraid that the others may wage germ warfare against it, each develops its own plagues to wipe out the human race.'

'Your mind is wandering, you stupid old fart,' said Stella. 'George isn't kidding about nearly being killed.'

'The fear of death is the beginning of slavery,' Hagbard said simply.

Even though it was early, George found himself on the verge of collapse, ready to sleep for twenty-four hours or more. The submarine's engines vibrated under his feet as he trudged to his cabin, but he wasn't even curious about where they were going. He lay down on his bed, and picked a book off the headpost bookshelf, part of his getting-ready-for-sleep ritual. *Sexuality, Magic and Perversion* said the binder. Well, that sounded juicy and promising. Author named Francis King, whoever that is. Citadel Press, 1972. Only a few years ago.

Well, then. George opened at random:

> Within a few years Frater Paragranus had become Chief of the Swiss section of the OTO, had entered into friendly relationships with the disciples of Aleister Crowley – notably Karl Germer – and had established a magazine. Subsequently Frater Paragranus inherited the chieftainship of Krumm-Heller's Ancient Rosi-crucian Fraternity and the Patriarchate of the Gnostic Catholic Church – this latter dignity he derived from Chevillon, murdered by the Gestapo in 1944, who was himself the successor of Johnny Bricaud. Frater Para-granus is also the head of one of the several groups who claim to be the true heirs and successors of the Illuminati of Weishaupt as revived (circa 1895) by Leopold Engel.

George blinked. *Several* Illuminati? He had to ask Hagbard about this. But he was already beginning to visualize into hypnogogic revery and sleep was coming.

In less than a half-hour, Joe had distributed ninety-two paper cups of tomato juice containing AUM, the drug that

promised to turn neophobes into neophiles. He stood in
Pioneer Court, just north of the Michigan Avenue Bridge,
at a table from which hung a poster reading FREE TOMATO
JUICE. Each person who took a cupful was invited to fill
out a short questionnaire and leave it in a box on Joe's
table. However, Joe explained, the questionnaire was op-
tional, and anyone who wanted to drink the tomato juice
and run was welcome to do so.

AUM would work just as well either way, but the questionnaire would give ELF an opportunity to trace its effect
on some of the subjects.

A tall black policeman was suddenly standing in front
of the table. 'You got a permit for this?'

'You bet,' said Joe with a quick smile. 'I'm with the
General Services Corporation, and we're running a test on
a new brand of tomato juice. Care to try some, officer?'

'No thanks,' said the cop unsmilingly. 'We had a bunch
of yippies threatening to put LSD in the city's water supply
two years ago. Let's just see your credentials.' There was
something cold, hard and homicidal in this cop's eyes, Joe
thought. Something beyond the ordinary. This would be a
unique guy, and the stuff would affect him uniquely. Joe
looked down at the nameplate on the policeman's jacket,
which read WATERHOUSE. The line behind Patrolman
Waterhouse was getting longer.

Joe found the paper Malaclypse had given him. He
handed it to Waterhouse, who glanced at it and said,
'This isn't enough. You apparently didn't tell them you
were going to set up your stand in Pioneer Court. You're
blocking pedestrian traffic here. This is a busy area. You'll
have to move.'

Joe looked out at the street where crowds walked back
and forth, at the bridge across the green, greasy Chicago
river and at the buildings surrounding Pioneer Court. The
brick-paved area was an ample public square, and there
was clearly room for everyone. Joe smiled at Waterhouse.
He was in Chicago and knew what to do. He took a ten-
dollar bill out of his pocket, folded it twice lengthwise and
wrapped it around a cup of the tomato juice, which he
deftly filled from the plastic jug on his table. Waterhouse
drained the tomato juice without comment, and when he

tossed the cup into the wastebasket the ten-dollar bill was gone.

A bunch of baldheaded, cackling small-town business-man types was lined up in front of the table. Each one wore an acetate-covered badge bearing a red Crusaders' cross, the letters KCUF and the words, 'Dominus Vobis-cum! My name is ———— .' Joe smilingly handed them cups of tomato juice, noting that the lapels of several bore an additional decoration, a square white plastic cross with the letters CL printed across it. Any of these men, Joe knew, would love to put him in jail for the rest of his life because he was the publisher of a radical magazine that occasionally got very explicit about sex and several times had published what Joe considered very beautiful erotica. The Knights of Christianity United for the Faith were rumored to be behind the firebombing of two theaters in the Midwest and the lynching of a news dealer in Alabama. And, of course, they had close ties with Atlanta Hope's God's Lightning Party.

AUM would be strong medicine for this bunch, Joe thought. He wondered if it would get them off their censor-ship kick or just make them more formidable. In either case, they would be bound to bust loose from Illuminati control for a time. If only there were a way he and Simon could get into their convention and administer AUM to more of them . . .

Behind the KCUF contingent there was a small man who looked like a rooster with a gray comb. When Joe read the questionnaire later, he found out that he had ad-ministered AUM to Judge Caligula Bushman, a shining ornament of the Chicago judiciary.

These followed a succession of faces Joe did not find memorable. They all had that complex, stupid, shrewd, angry, defeated, cynical, gullible look characteristic of Chicago, New York and other big cities. Then he found himself confronting a tall redhead whose features seemed to combine the best of Elizabeth Taylor and Marilyn Monroe. 'Any vodka in that?' she asked him.

'No, ma'am, just straight tomato juice,' said Joe.

'Too bad,' she said as she tossed it down.' 'I could use one.'

Caligula Bushman, known as the toughest judge on the Chicago bench, was trying six people who were charged with attacking a draft board, destroying all its furniture, ruining its files and dumping a wheelbarrow full of cow manure on the floor. Suddenly Bushman interrupted the trial about halfway through the prosecution's presentation of its case with the announcement that he was going to hold a sanity hearing. To the bewilderment of all, he then asked State's Attorney Milo A. Flanagan a series of rather odd questions:

'What would you think of a man who not only kept an arsenal in his home, but was collecting at enormous financial sacrifice a second arsenal to protect the first one? What would you say if this man so frightened his neighbors that they in turn were collecting weapons to protect themselves from him? What if this man spent ten times as much money on his expensive weapons as he did on the education of his children? What if one of his children criticized his hobby and he called that child a traitor and a bum and disowned it? And he took another child who had obeyed him faithfully and armed that child and sent it out into the world to attack neighbors? What would you say about a man who introduces poisons into the water he drinks and the air he breathes? What if this man not only is feuding with the people on his block but involves himself in the quarrels of others in distant parts of the city and even in the suburbs? Such a man would clearly be a paranoid schizophrenic, Mr. Flanagan, with homicidal tendencies. This is the man who should be on trial, though under our modern, enlightened system of jurisprudence we would attempt to cure and rehabilitate him rather than merely punish.

'Speaking as a judge,' he continued, 'I dismiss this case on several grounds. The State is clinically insane as a corporate entity and is absolutely unfit to arrest, try and incarcerate those who disagree with its policies. But I doubt that this judgment, though obvious to any man of common sense, quite fits into the rules of our American jurisprudential game. I also rule, therefore, that the right to destroy government property is protected by the First Amendment to the U.S. Constitution and therefore the crime with which these people are charged is not a crime under the Constitution. Government property belongs to all of the people, and the right of any of the people to express displeasure with their government by destroying government property is precious and shall not be infringed.' This doctrine had come to Judge Bushman suddenly while he was speaking without his robe. It startled him, but he had noticed that his mind was working better and faster this afternoon.

He went on, 'The State does not exist as a person or thing exists, but is a legal fiction. A fiction is a form of communication. Anything said to be owned by a form of communication must also thereby be itself a form of communication. Government is a map and government paper is a map of the map. The medium, in this case, is definitely the message, as any semanticist would agree. Furthermore, any physical act directed against a communication is itself a communication, a map of the map of the map. Thus, destruction of government property is protected by the First Amendment. I will issue a more ample written opinion on this point, but I feel now that the defendants need suffer in durance no longer. Case dismissed.'

Many spectators trooped out of the courtroom sullenly, while those who loved the defendants surrounded them with tears, laughter and hugs. Judge Bushman, who stepped down from the bench but remained in the courtroom, was the benign center of a cluster of reporters. (He was thinking that his opinion would be a map of the map of the map of the map, or a fourth-order map. How many potential further orders of symbolism were there? He barely heard the praises showered on him. Of course, he knew his decision would be overturned; but the judge business already bored him. It would be interesting to get into mathematics, really *deep*.)

Harold Canvera had not bothered to fill out a questionnaire and therefore was not under observation and was not protected. He returned to his home, and his job as an accountant, and his avocation, which was recording telephone spiels against the Illuminati, the Communists, the Socialists, the Liberals, the Middle-of-the-Roaders and all insufficiently conservative Republicans. (Mr. Canvera also mailed out similar pamphlets whenever anybody was in-

trigued enough by his phone messages to send him twenty-
five cents for additional information. He performed these
worthy educational services for a group calling itself White
Heroes Opposing Red Extremism, which was a splinter off
Taxpayers Warring Against Tyranny, which was a splinter
off God's Lightning.) In the following weeks, however,
strange new ideas began to appear in Canvera's taped
phone messages.

'*Lower* taxes aren't enough,' he said, for instance. 'When
you hear some so-called conservative Bircher or some
follower of Willam Buckley Jr. call for lower taxes, *be-
ware*. There's a man who's *squishy soft* on Illuminism. All
taxes are robbery. Instead of attacking Joan Baez, a real
American should support her for refusing to pay any more
money into the Illuminati treasury in Washington.'

The next week was even more interesting: 'White
Heroes Opposing Red Extremism has often told you that
there's no real difference between the Democrats and Republicans. Both are pawns of the Illuminati scheme to
destroy private property and make everybody a slave of
the State, so the International Bankers *of a certain minority
group* can run everything. Now it's time for all thinking
patriots to take an even more skeptical look than before at
the so-called anti-Illuminati John Birch Society. Why are
they always putting up those stickers saying, "Support
Your Local Police"? Ever wonder about that? What's the
most important thing to a police state? Isn't it police? And
if we got rid of the police, how could we ever have a
police state? Think about it, fellow Americans, and Remember the Alamo!'

A few of these new strange ideas had come from various
right-wing anarchist periodicals (all secretly subsidized by
Hagbard Celine) that Canvera had mysteriously received
three months earlier and hadn't glanced at until swallowing
the AUM. The periodicals had been mailed by Simon
Moon, as a joke, in an envelope with the return address
Illuminati International, 34 East 68th Street, New York
City – the headquarters of the Council on Foreign Relations,
long regarded by the Birchers as an Illuminati hotbed.
'Remember the Alamo,' Canvera had picked up from
Bowie Knife, a publication of the Davy Crockett Society,

a paramilitary right-wing fascist group which had splintered off God's Lightning when their leader, a Texas oil millionaire of gigantic paranoias, became convinced that many apparent Mexicans were actually Red Chinese agents in slight disguise. Later, the dogma became retroactive and he claimed that the Chinese had always been Communists, *all* Mexicans had always been Chinese, and the attack on the Alamo was the first Communist assault against American capitalism.

The third week was quite remarkable. Evidently, AUM, like LSD, changed some personality traits but left others fairly intact; in any event, in Canvera's irregular evolution from right-wing authoritarianism to right-wing libertarianism, he had somehow managed to arrive at a thesis never before enunciated except by Donatien Alphonse François de Sade. What this rare man did was to give a three-minute spiel in favor of the right of any person, of either sex, to use any other person, of either sex, *with or without* their consent, for sexual gratification of any sort needed or at least *desired*. The only option he granted the recipients of these intimate invasions was the reciprocal right to use the initiator for their own needs or desires. Now, most of the people who regularly called Canvera's phone service were not offended by any of this; they were Lincoln Avenue hippies and dialed him only when stoned, for what they called 'a really weird and far-out head trip,' and they were bored that he was no longer as funky as in his old Negro-baiting, Jew-hating and Illuminati-castigating days. However, there were a few members of White Heroes Opposing Red Extremism who called occasionally to check that their contributions were still financing the dissemination of true Americanism, and these people were severely puzzled and finally disturbed. Some of them even wrote to WHORE headquarters in Mad Dog, Texas, to complain that there was something a little bit peculiar in the Americanism lately. However, the president of WHORE, Dr. Horace Naismith, who also ran the John Dillinger Died for You Society, Veterans of the Sexual Revolution, and the Colossus of Yorba Linda Foundation, was in it only for the money, sad to say, and had no time for such petty complaints. He was too busy implementing his newest fund-raising scheme, the Male Chauvinist Organization (MACHO), which he hoped would milk *mucho* denaros from Russ Meyers, illegal abortionists, pimps, industrialists who regularly paid female workers thirty percent of the salaries of men doing the same jobs, and all others threatened by the Women's Liberation Movement.

The fourth week was, to be frank about it, definitely bizarre. Canvera discoursed at length on the lost civilization that once existed in the Gobi Desert and denounced those, such as Brion Gysin, who believed it had destroyed itself in atomic war. Rather, he asserted, it had been obliterated when the Illuminati arrived from the planet Vulcan in flying saucers. 'Remember the Alamo' was now replaced by 'Remember Carcosa,' Canvera having discerned that both Ambrose Bierce and H. P. Lovecraft were describing this tragic Gobian society in their fiction. The hippies were again delighted – this was the funky kind of trip that had originally made Canvera a mock folk hero among them – and they especially appreciated his call for the U.S. to abandon the next moon shot and launch a punitive expedition to Vulcan both to wipe out Illuminism at its source and to avenge poor Carcosa. The WHORE regulars, however, were again upset; all that concern with Carcosa struck them as creeping one-worldism.

The fifth week, Canvera took a new turn, denouncing the masses for their stupidity and proclaiming that the boobs probably deserved being governed by the Illuminati since most of them were too dumb to find their own behinds in a dark room even using both hands. He had been browsing through a volume of H. L. Mencken (sent to him over a year earlier by El Haj Stackerlee Mohammed, né Pearson, after one of his put-prayers-back-in-the-public-schools tirades); but he had also been pondering an invitation to *join* the Illuminati. This document, which came in an envelope with no return address, informed him that he was too smart to stay with the losers all his life and ought to climb on the winning side before it was too late. It added that membership dues were $3125, which should be put in a cigar box and buried in his back yard, after which it promised 'one of our underground agents will contact you.' At first, Canvera had considered this a hoax – he received many put-ons in the mail, together with pornography, Rosicrucian pamphlets, illustrated with the eye-and-pyramid design, and pretended fan letters signed by such names as *Eldridge Cleaver, Fidel Castro, Anton Szandor Levay* or *Judge Crater*, all of course cooked up by his Lincoln Avenue audience. Later, however, it struck him that 3125 was *five to the fifth power* and that convinced him a True Illuminatus was indeed communicating with him. He took the $3125 out of his savings account, buried it as instructed, made a pro-Illuminati recording as a gesture of good faith and waited. The next day he was shot, several times, in the head and shoulders, dying of natural causes as a result.

(In present time again, Rebecca Goodman enters the Hotel Tudor lobby in answer to the second mysterious phone call of the day, while Hagbard decides George Dorn needs to be illuminized further before Ingolstadt, and Esperando Despond clears his throat and says, 'I want to explain the mathematics of plague to you men . . .')

Actually, poor old Canvera's death had nothing to do with the Illuminati or with his former compatriots in WHORE. The man had been practicing the libertine philosophy of his post-AUM phone editorials and had tampered with Cassandra Acconci, the beloved daughter of Ronald Acconci, Chicago Regional Commander of God's Lightning and a long-time contributor to KCUF. Acconci arranged, via State's Attorney Milo A. Flanagan, for the local Maf to do a hit on Canvera. But there are no endings, any more than there are any beginnings; it next developed that Canvera's seed lived on in wedlock with Cassandra's ovum and was in danger of becoming a human being within her previously trim abdomen.

Saul Goodman had no idea that the room he was in had last been rented to George Dorn; he was conscious only of his impatience, not knowing that Rebecca was at that moment on an elevator approaching his floor . . . And a mile north, Peter Jackson, still trying to put together the July issue of *Confrontation* virtually singlehanded, dives into the slush pile (which is the magazine industry's elegant name for unsolicited manuscripts) and comes up with more fallout from the Moon-Malik AUM project of 1970. 'Orthodox Science: The New Religion,' he reads. *Well, let's sample it, what the hell.* Opening at random he finds:

> Einstein's concept of spherical space, furthermore, suffers from the same defect as the concept of a smoothly or perfectly spherical earth: it rests upon the use of the irrational number, π. This number has no operational definition; there is no place on any engineer's scale to which one can point and say 'This is exactly π,' although these scales are misleadingly marked with such a spot. π, in fact, can never be found in the real world, and there are historical and archeological reasons to believe it was created by a Greek mathematician under the influence of the mind-warping hallucinogenic mushroom *Amanita muscaria.* It is pure surrealism. You cannot write π as a real number; you can only approximate it, as 3.1417 . . . etc. Chemistry knows no such units: three atoms of an element may combine with four atoms of another element, but you will never find π atoms combining with anything. Quantum physics reveals that an electron may jump three units or four units, but it will not jump π units. Nor is π necessary to geometry, as is sometimes claimed; R. Buckminster Fuller has created an entire geometric system, at least as reliable as that of the ancient Greek dope fiends, in which π does not appear at all. Space, then, may be slanted or kiltered in various ways, but it cannot be smoothly spherical . . .

'What the ring-tailed rambling hell?' Peter Jackson said aloud. He flipped to the end:

> In conclusion, I want to thank a strange and uncommon man, James Mallison, who provided the spark which set me thinking about these matters. In fact, it was due to my meeting with Mr. Mallison that I sold my hardware business, returned to college and majored in cartography and topology. Although he was a religious fanatic (as I was at the time of our meeting) and would, therefore, not appreciate many

of my discoveries, it is due to this man's perverse, peculiar and yet brilliant prodding that I embarked on the search which has lead to this new theory of a Pentahedroidal Universe.

W. Clement Cotex, Ph.D

'Far fucking *out*,' Peter muttered. James Mallison was a pen name Joe Malik sometimes used, and here was another James Mallison inspiring this guy to become a Ph.D. and invent a new cosmological theory. What was the word Joe used for such coincidences? Synch-something . . .

('1472,' Esperando Despond concludes his gloomy mathematical calculations. 'That's the number of plague cases we might have right now, at noon, if the girl had only two contacts after leaving Dr. Mocenigo. Now, if she had three contacts . . .' The assembled FBI· agents are gradually turning a pale greenish color from the neck up. Carmel, the only actual contact, is busy two blocks away stuffing money into a briefcase.)

'That's him!' Mrs. Edward Coke Bacon cried excitedly, addressing Basil Banghart, another FBI agent, in an office in Washington. She is pointing at a photo of Albert 'the Teacher' Stern. 'Ma'am,' Banghart says kindly, 'that can't be him. I don't even know why his picture's still in the file. That's a no-account junkie who once got on our most-wanted list because he confessed to a murder he didn't even commit.' In Cincinnati, an FBI artist is completing a portrait under the direction of the widow of a slain TV repairman: the face of the killer, gradually emerging, combines various features of Vincent 'Mad Dog' Coll, George Dorn and the lead vocalist of the American Medical Association, which group was at that moment boarding a plane at Kennedy International Airport for the Ingolstadt gig. Rebecca Goodman, rising in the Hotel Tudor elevator, has a flash memory of a nightmare of the night before: Saul being shot by the same vocalist, dressed as a monk, in red-and-white robes, while a Playboy bunny danced in front of some kind of giant pyramid. In Princeton, New Jersey, a nuclear physicist named Nils Nosferatu – one of the few survivors of the early morning shootings – babbles to the detective and police stenographer at his bed-

side, 'Tlaloc sucks. You can't trust them. The midget is
the one to watch. We'll be moved, all right, when the tear
gas hits. Fun is fun. Omega. George's brother met the
dolphins first, and that was the psychic hook that brought
George in. She's at the door. She's buried in the desert.
Any deviation will result in termination. Unify the forces.
You hold the hose. I'll get Mark.'

'I've got to start telling you the truth, George,' Hagbard
began hesitantly, *as the Midget, Carmel and Dr. Horace
Naismith collided in front of the door of the Sands Hotel
('Watch the fuck where you're going,' Carmel growled)*,
and she was at the door, her heart was pounding, an intuition was forming in her mind, and she knocked *(and Peter
Jackson began dialing Epicene Wildblood)*, and she was
sure of it, and she was afraid of being sure because she
might be wrong, *and the Midget said to Dr. Naismith
'Rude bastard, wasn't he?'* and the door opened, *and the
door of Milo O. Flanagan's office opened to admit Cassandra Acconci*, and her heart stopped, *and Dr. Nosferatu
screamed, 'The door. She's in the door. The door in the
desert. He eats Carmels,'* and it was him and she was in
his arms and she was weeping and laughing and asking,
'Where have you *been*, baby?' And Saul closed the door
behind her and drew her further into the room. 'I'm not a
cop anymore,' he said, 'I'm on the other side.'

'*What?*' Rebecca noticed there was a new thing in his
eyes, a thing for which she had no word.

'You can stop worrying that you'll get back on horse,' he
went on gaily. 'And if you've ever been afraid of your sexual
fantasies, don't be. We've all got them. Saint Bernards!'

But even that wasn't as weird as the new thing in his
eyes.

'Baby,' she said, '*baby*. What the hell is this?'

'I wanted sex with my father, when I was two years old.
When did you have that thing about the Saint Bernard?'

'When I was eleven or twelve, I think. Just before my
first period. My God, you must have been a lot further
away than I ever imagined.' She was beginning to recognize
the new thing. It wasn't intelligence; he had always had
that. With awe, she realized it was what the ancients called
wisdom.

'I've always had a thing about black women, just like your thing about black men,' he went on. 'I think everybody in this country has a touch of it. The blacks have it about *us*, too. I was in one head, a brilliant black guy, musician, scientist, poet, a million talents, and white women were like the Holy Grail to him. And your fantasy about Spiro Agnew – I had one just like that about Ilse Koch, a Nazi bitch from before your time. It was the same thing in both cases, revenge. Not real sex, hate-sex. Oh, we're all so crazy-in-the-head.'

Rebecca backed up and sat down on the bed. 'It's too much, too fast, I'm scared. I can see you don't have any contempt for me, but, Lord, can I *live* knowing that somebody else knows every single repressed desire I have?'

'Yes,' Saul said calmly. 'And you're mistaken about Time. I can't know every secret, darling. I've only had a smattering of them. A handful. There are a dozen people right now who've been through my head the same way, and I can look any one of them in the eye. The things I know about *them*!' He laughed.

'It's still too fast,' Rebecca said. 'You disappear, and then you come back knowing things about me that I only half know myself, and you're not a cop anymore . . . What do you mean, you've joined "the other side"? The Mafia? The Morituri groups?'

'No,' Saul answered happily. 'Much further out than that. Darling, I've been driven mad by the world's best brainwashers and put back together again by a computer that does psychotherapy, predicts the future and steers a submarine all at once. On the way, I learned things about humanity and the universe that it would take a year to tell you. And I don't have much time right now, because I've got to fly to Las Vegas. In two or three days, if everything works out, I'll be able to show you, not just tell you—'

'Are you reading my mind right now?' Rebecca asked, still awed and nervous.

Saul laughed again. 'It isn't that simple. It takes years of training, and even then it's like an old radio full of static. If I "tune in" right now, I'll get a flash of whatever's in your head, but it will be so jumbled with other things that relate to my resonance in one way or another that I won't know for sure which part is you.'

'Do it,' Rebecca said. 'I'll be more comfortable with you if I see a sample of whatever-it-is that you've become.'

Saul sat down on the bed beside her and took her hand. 'Okay,' he said thoughtfully, 'I'll do it aloud, and don't be afraid. I'm the same man, darling, there's just more of me now.' He inhaled deeply. 'Here goes . . . Five million bucks. Never find her where I buried her. 1472. George, don't make no bull moves. Unify the forces. One helping hand deserves another. New York Jew doctors. Remember Carcosa! In quick and out quick, a cowboy. They're all coming back. Lie down on the floor and keep calm. It's a League of Nations, a young people's League of Nations. One was for fighting, the other for fun . . . *Good Lord*,' he broke off and closed his eyes. 'I've got a whole street and I can see them. They're still singing. "We rose up in arms and none failed to come, we're the Vets of the Sex Revolooooootion!" *What the hell?*' He turned to her and explained, 'It's like a split-screen movie, but split a thousand ways, and with a thousand soundtracks. I only pick up a few random bits. When one jumps out like that last one, it's important; I'll bet that street is in Las Vegas and I'll be walking on it myself in a few hours. Anyway,' he added, 'none of that seemed to come from you. Did it?'

'No,' she said, 'and I'm glad. This takes some reorientation. When you said you're going to show me in a few days, did you mean show me how to do it?'

'You *are* doing it. Everybody is. All the time.'

'But?'

'But most of the time it's just background noise. I can teach you to become more aware of it. Learning to focus – to pick out one person and one time – that takes years, decades.'

Rebecca finally smiled. 'You sure did go a long way in a day and a half.'

'If it were a year and a half,' Saul said simply, 'or a century and a half – I'd still be trying to to find my way back to you all through it.'

She kissed him. 'Yes, it's still you,' she said, 'just *more* of you. Tell me: if we both studied it for years and years could we get to the point where we were reading each other's minds constantly, tuned in on each other completely?'

'Yes,' Saul said, 'there are couples like that.'

'Mm. That's even more intimate than sex.'

'No. It *is* sex.'

An intimation came to Rebecca, like a voice whispering far down at the end of a dark hall, and she knew that some part of her already knew, and had always known, what Saul was about to explain. 'Your new friends who taught all this,' she said quietly. 'They're way ahead of Freud, aren't they?'

'Way ahead. For instance, what am I thinking now?'

'You're feeling horny,' Rebecca grinned. 'But that's not my background noise, or telepathy, that picked that up. It's your breathing and the kind of light in your eyes and all sorts of other small cues that a woman learns to recognize. The way you moved a little closer after I kissed you. Things like that.'

Saul took her hand again. '*How* horny am I?' he asked.

'*Very* horny. In fact, you've already decided that you've got time enough and *that's* more important than talking . . .'

Saul touched her cheek gently. 'Did you read that from kinesic cues, or was it the background noise or telepathy?'

'I guess the background noise helped me to read the cues . . .'

Saul glanced at his watch. 'I have to meet Barney Muldoon in the lobby in exactly fifty minutes. How would you like to hear a scientific lecture while you're being laid? That's a perversion we've never tried before.' His hand moved down from her cheek to her neck and then began unbuttoning her blouse.

('There's a Morituri bomb factory in your building,' Cassandra Acconci said flatly. 'On the seventeenth floor. The name on the buzzer is the same as yours.'

'My brother!' Milo O. Flanagan bellowed. 'Right under my nose! That freaking faggot!')

'Oh, Saul. Oh, Saul, Saul,' Rebecca closed her eyes as the mouth tightened on her nipple . . . *and Dr. Horace Naismith crossed the lobby of the Sands, affixing the VSR*

badge to his lapel, and passed the Midget again . . . 'Well,'
the Attorney General told the President, 'one solution, of
course, is to *nuke* Las Vegas. But that wouldn't solve the
problem of the possible carriers who could have hopped a
plane already and might be anywhere in the country now,
or anywhere in the world.' While the President washes
down three Librium, a Tofranil and an Elavil, the Vice
President asks thoughtfully, 'Suppose we just distribute the
antidote to party workers and ride this thing out?' He is
feeling more than usually misanthropic, having had an
appalling evening in New York due to his impulsiveness
in answering a personal ad which had touched his
heart . . .

('Thank you Cassandra,' Milo A. Flanagan said fer-
vently. 'I'm eternally grateful to you.'

'One helping hand deserves another,' Cassandra replied;
she remembered how Milo and Smiling Jim Trepomena
had helped her get the abortion the time she was knocked
up by that Canvera character. Her father had wanted to
send her to New York for a legal D & C, but Milo had
pointed out that it would look kind of funny to some people
for the daughter of a high KCUF spokesman to have an
official abortion. 'Besides,' Smiling Jim had added, 'you
don't want to fool around with them New York Jew
doctors. They might do dirty things to you. Just trust me,
child; we've got the country's best-qualified criminal abortionists in Cincinnati.' Actually, though, the real reason
Cassandra was blowing the whistle on Padre Pederastia's
bomb emporium was to annoy Simon Moon, whom she
had been trying to get into her bed ever since she met him
at the Friendly Stranger Coffee House six months before.
Simon hadn't been interested, due to his obsession with
black women, who represented the Holy Grail to him.)

'Wildeblood here,' the cultured drawl came over the
wire.

'Have you finished your review yet?' Peter Jackson
asked, crushing another cigarette butt in his ashtray and
worrying about lung cancer.

'Yes, and you'll love it. I really tear these two smart-
asses apart.' Wildeblood was enthusiastic. 'Listen to this:
"a pair of nursery Nietzsches dreaming of a psychedelic

Superman." And this: "a plot that is only a put-on, characters who are cardboard, and a pretense of scholarship that amounts to sheer bluff." But *this* is the crusher; listen: "a constant use of obscene language for shock effect until the reader begins to feel as depressed as an unwilling spectator at a quarrel between a fishwife and a lobster-pot pirate." Don't you think that will get quoted at all the best cocktail parties this season?'

'I suppose so. The book's a real stinker, eh?'

'Heavens, I wouldn't know for sure. I told you yesterday, it's absurdly *long*. Three volumes, in fact. Boring as hell. I only had time to skim it. But listen to this, dear boy: "If *The Lord of the Rings* is a fairy tale for adults, sophisticated readers will quickly recognize this monumental miscarriage as a fairy tale for paranoids." That refers to the ridiculous conspiracy theory that the plot, if there is one, seems to revolve around. Nicely worded, wouldn't you say?'

'Yeah, sure,' Peter said, crossing off *book review* on his pad. 'Send it over. I'll pay the messenger.'

Epicene Wildeblood, hanging up, crossed off *Confrontation* on his own pad, found *Time* next on the list, and picked up another book to be immortalized by his devastating witticisms. He was feeling more than unusually misanthropic, having had a disastrous evening the night before. Somebody had answered his personal ad about his 'interest in Greek Culture' and he had thrilled at the thought of a new asshole to conquer; the asshole, unfortunately, had turned out to be the Vice President of the United States, who was interested only in declaiming about the glorious achievements of the military junta that had ruled in Athens. When Eppy, despairing of sex, had tried to steer the conversation to Plato at least, the VP asked, 'Are you sure he was a Greek? That sounds like a wop name to me.'

(Tobias Knight and two other FBI agents elbow past the Midget searching for whores who might have been with Dr. Mocenigo the night before, while outside the VSR's first contingent, the Hugh M. Hefner Brigade, led by Dr. Horace Naismith himself, marches by singing: 'We're Vet'rans of the *Sexule* Revolution/ Our rifles were issued, we had our own guns/ One was for fighting, the other for fun/ We rose

up in arms and none failed to come/ We're Vets of the Sex
Revoloooooooooooootion!')

You see, darling, it all revolves around sex, but not in
the sense that Freud thought. Freud never understood sex.
Hardly anybody understands sex, in fact, except a few poets
here and there. Any scientist who starts to get an inkling
keeps his mouth shut because he knows he'd be drummed
out of the profession if he said what he knew. Here, I'll
help you unhook that. What we're feeling now is supposed
to be tension, and what we'll feel after orgasm is supposed
to be relaxation. Oh, they're so pretty. Yes, I know I always say that. But they are pretty. Pretty, pretty, pretty.
Mmmm. Mmmm. Oh, yes, yes. Just hold it like that a moment. Yes. Tension? Lord, yes that's what I mean. How
can this be tension? What's it got in common with worry
or anxiety or anything else that we call tension? It's a
strain, but not a tension. It's a drive to break out, and a
tension is a drive to hold in. Those are the two polarities.
Oh, stop for a minute. Let me do this. You like that? Oh,
darling, yes, darling, I like it, too. It makes me happy to
make you happy. You see, we're trying to break through
our skins into each other. We're trying to break the walls,
walls, walls. Yes, Yes. Break the walls. Tension is trying
to hold up the walls, to keep the outside from getting in.
It's the opposite. Oh, Rebecca. Let me kiss them again.
They're so pretty. Pretty pretty titties. Mmm. Mmm.
Pretty. And so big and round. Oh, you've got two hard-
ons and I've only got one. And this, this, ah, you like it,
don't you, that's three hard-ons. You want me to take my
finger away and kiss it? Oh, darling, pretty belly, pretty.
Mmm. Mmm. Darling, Mmm. MMMMM. Mmm. Lord,
Lord. You never came so fast before, oh, I love you. Are
you happy? I'm so happy. That's right, just for a minute.
Oh, God, I love watching you do that. I love to see it go
into your mouth. Lord, God, Rebecca, I love it. Yes, now
I'll put him in. Little Saul, there, coming up inside you,
there. Does little Rebecca like him? I know, I know. They
love each other, don't they? The way we love each other.
She's so warm, she welcomes him so nicely. You're inside
me, too. That's what I'm trying to say. My field. You're
inside my field, just like I'm inside yours. It's the fields, not

the physical act. That's what people are afraid of. That's why they're tense during sex. They're afraid of letting the fields merge. It's a unifying of the forces. God, I can't keep talking. Well, if we slow way down, yes, this is nicer, isn't it? That's why it's so fast for most people. They rush, complete the physical act, before the fields are charged. They never experience the fields. They think it's poetry, fiction, when somebody who's had it describes it. One scientist knew. He died in prison. I'll tell you about him later. It's the big taboo, the one all the others grow out of. It isn't sex itself they're trying to stop. That's too strong, they can't stop it. It's this. Darling, yes. This. The unifying. It happens at death, but they try to steal it even then. They've taken it out of sex. That's why the fantasies. And the promiscuity. The search. Blacks, homosexuality, our parents, people we know we hate, Saint Bernards. Everything. It's not neuroses or perversion. It's a search. A desperate search. Everybody wants sex with an enemy. Hate mobilizes the field, too, you see. And hate. Is safer. Safer than love. Love too dangerous. Lord, Lord, I love you. I love you. Let me more. Get the weight on my elbows, hold your ass with my hands. Yes. Poetry isn't poetry. I mean it doesn't lie. It's true when I say I worship you. Can't say it outside bed. Can only say love then, usually. Worship too scary. Some people can't even say love in bed. Searching, partner to partner. Never able to say love. Never able to feel it. Under control. They can't let us learn, or the game is up. Their name? They got a million names. Monopolize it. Keep it to themselves. They had to stamp it out in the rest of us, to control. To control us. Drove it underground, into background noise. Mustn't break through. That's how. How it happened. Darling. First they repressed telepathy, then sex. That's why schizos. Darling. Why schizos break into crazy sex things first. Why homosexuals dig the occult. Break one taboo, come close to the next. Finally break the wall entirely. Get through. Like we get through, together. They can't have that. Got to keep us apart. Schisms. Always splitting and schisms. White against black, men against women, all the way down the line. Keep us apart. Don't let us merge. Make sex a dirty joke. A few more minutes. A few more. My tongue in your ear. Oh, God.

Soon, So fast. A miracle. Whole society set up to prevent this. To destroy love. Oh, I do love you. Worship you. Adore you. Rebecca. Beautiful, beautiful. Rebecca. They don't want us to. Unify. The. Forces. Rebecca. Rebecca. Rebecca.

THE SEVENTH TRIP, OR NETZACH
(THE SNAFU PRINCIPLE)

The most thoroughly and relentlessly Damned, banned, excluded, condemned, forbidden, ostracized, ignored, suppressed, repressed, robbed, brutalized and defamed of all Damned Things is the individual human being. The social engineers, statisticians, psychologists, sociologists, market researchers, landlords, bureaucrats, captains of industry, bankers, governors, commissars, kings and presidents are perpetually forcing this Damned Thing into carefully prepared blueprints and perpetually irritated that the Damned Thing will not fit into the slot assigned to it. The theologians call it a sinner and try to reform it. The governor calls it a criminal and tries to punish it. The psychotherapist calls it a neurotic and tries to cure it. Still, the Damned Thing will not fit into their slots.
—*Never Whistle While You're Pissing*,
by Hagbard Celine, H.M., S.H.

The Midget, whose name was Markoff Chaney, was no relative of the famous Chaneys of Hollywood, but people *did* keep making jokes about that. It was bad enough to be, by the standards of the gigantic and stupid majority, a freak; how much worse to be so named as to remind these big oversized clods of the cinema's two most famous portrayers of monstro-freaks; by the time the Midget was fifteen, he had built up a detestation for ordinary mankind that dwarfed (he hated that word) the relative misanthropies of Paul of Tarsus, Clement of Alexandria, Swift of Dublin and even Robert Putney Drake. Revenge, for sure, he would have. He would have revenge.

It was in college (Antioch, Yellow Springs, 1962) that

Markoff Chaney discovered another hidden joke in his
name, and the circumstances were – considering that he
was to become the worst headache the Illuminati ever encountered – appropriately synchronistic. It was in a math
class, and, since this was Antioch, the two students directly
behind the Midget were ignoring the professor and discussing their own intellectual interests; since this was Antioch,
they were a good six years ahead of intellectual fads elsewhere. They were discussing ethology.

'So we keep the same instincts as our primate ancestors,'
one student (he was from Chicago, his name was Moon,
and he was crazy even for Antioch) was saying. 'But we
superimpose culture and law on top of this. So we get split
in two, dig? You might say,' Moon's voice betrayed pride
in the aphorism he was about to unleash, 'mankind is a
statutory ape.'

'. . . and,' the professor, old Fred 'Fidgets' Digits, said
at just that moment, 'when such a related series appears
in a random process, we have what is known as a Markoff Chain. I hope Mr. Chaney won't be tormented by jokes
about this for the rest of the term, even if the related series
of his appearances in class do seem part of a notably random process.' The class roared; another ton of bile was
entered in the Midget's shit ledger, the list of people who
were going to eat turd before he died.

In fact, his cuts were numerous, both in math and in
other classes. There were times when he could not bear to
be with the giants, but hid in his room, *Playboy* gatefold
open, masturbating and dreaming of millions and millions
o: nubile young women built like Playmates. Today, however, *Playboy* would avail him not; he needed something
raunchier. Ignoring his next class, Physical Anthropology
(always good for a few humiliating moments), he hurried
across David Street, passing Atlanta Hope without noticing
her, and slammed into his room, chain-bolting the door behind him.

Damn old Fidgets Digits, and damn the science of mathematics itself, the line, the square, the average, the whole
measurable world that pronounced him a bizarre random
factor. Once and for all, beyond fantasy, in the depth of
his soul he declared war on the statutory ape, on law and

order, on predictability, on negative entropy. He would be
a random factor in every equation; from this day forward,
unto death, it would be civil war: the Midget versus the
Digits.

He took out the pornographic Tarot deck, which he used
when he wanted a really far-out fantasy for his orgasm,
and shuffled it thoroughly. Let's have a Markoff Chain
masturbation to start with, he thought with an evil grin.

And, thus, without ever contacting the Legion of Dynamic Discord, the Erisian Liberation Front or even the
Justified Ancients of Mummu, Markoff Chaney began his
own crusade against the Illuminati, not even knowing that
they existed.

His first overt act – his Fort Sumter, as it were – began
in Dayton the following Saturday. He was in Norton's
Emporium, a glorified 5 & 10¢ store, when he saw the sign:

NO SALESPERSON MAY LEAVE THE FLOOR WITHOUT
THE AUTHORIZATION OF A SUPERIOR.
THE MGT.

What!, he thought, are the poor girls supposed to pee
in their panties if they can't find a superior? Years of
school came back to him ('Please, may I leave the room,
sir?') and rituals which had appeared nonsensical suddenly
made sense in a sinister way. Mathematics, of course. They
were trying to reduce us all to predictable units, robots.
Hah! not for nothing had he spent a semester in Professor
'Sheets' Kelly's intensive course on textual analysis of
modern poetry. The following Wednesday, the Midget was
back at Norton's and hiding in a coffee urn when the staff
left and locked up. A few moments later, the sign was
down and a subtly different one was in its place:

NO SALESPERSON MAY LEAVE THE FLOOR OR GO TO THE
DOOR WITHOUT THE AUTHORIZATION OF A SUPERIOR.
THE MGT.

He came back several times in the next few weeks, and
the sign remained. It was as he suspected: in a rigid hierarchy, nobody questions orders that seem to come from

above, and those at the very top are so isolated from the
actual work situation that they never see what is going on
below. It was the chains of communication, not the means
of production, that determined a social process; Marx had
been wrong, lacking cybernetics to enlighten him. Marx
was like the engineers of his time, who thought of electricity in terms of work done, before Marconi thought of it
in terms of information transmitted. Nothing signed 'THE
MGT.' would ever be challenged; the Midget could always
pass himself off as the Management.

At the same time, he noticed that the workers were more
irritable; the shoppers picked this up and became grouchier
themselves; sales, he guessed correctly, were falling off.
Poetry was the answer: poetry in reverse. His interpolated
phrase, with its awkward internal rhyme and its pointlessness, bothered everybody, but in a subliminal, preconscious
fashion. Let the market researchers and statisticians try to
figure this one out with their computers and averages.

His father had been a stockholder in Blue Sky Inc.,
generally regarded as the worst turkey on the Big Board
(it produced devices to be used in making landings on low-
gravity planets); profits had soared when John Fitzgerald
Kennedy had announced that the U.S. would put a man
on the moon before 1970; the Midget now had a guaran-
teed annuity amounting to thirty-six hundred dollars per
year, three hundred dollars per month. It was enough for
his purposes. Revenge, in good measure, he would have.
He would have revenge.

Living in Spartan fashion, dining often on a tin of sar-
dines and a pint of milk from a machine, traveling always
by Greyhound bus, the Midget criss-crossed the country
constantly, placing his improved surrealist signs whenever
the opportunity presented itself. A slowly mounting wave
of anarchy followed in his wake. The Illuminati never got
a fix on him: he had little ego to discover, burning all his
energies into Drive, like a dictator or a great painter – but,
unlike a dictator or a great painter, he had no desire for
recognition. For years, the Illuminati attributed his efforts
to the Discordians, the JAMs or the esoteric ELF. Watts
went up, and Detroit; Birmingham, Buffalo, Newark, a
flaming picnic blanket spread across urban America as the

Midget's signs burned in the stores that had flaunted them; one hundred thousand marched to the Pentagon and some of them tried to expel the Demon (the Illuminati foiled that at the last minute, forbidding them to form a circle); a Democratic convention was held behind barbed wire; in 1970 a Senate committee announced that there had been three thousand bombings in the year, or an average of ten per day; by 1973 Morituri groups were forming in every college, every suburb; the SLA came and came back again; Atlanta Hope was soon unable to control God's Lightning, which was going in for its own variety of terrorism years before Illuminati planning had intended.

'There's a random factor somewhere,' technicians said at Illuminati International; 'There's a random factor somewhere,' Hagbard Celine said, reading the data that came out of FUCKUP; 'There's a random factor somewhere,' the Dealy Lama, leader of ELF, said dreamily in his underground hideout beneath Dealy Plaza.

Drivers on treacherous mountain roads swore in confusion at signs that said:

> SLIPPERY WHEN WET
> MAINTAIN 50 M.P.H.
> FALLING ROCK ZONE
> DO NOT LITTER

Men paid high initiation fees to revel in the elegance of all-WASP clubs whose waiters were carefully trained to be almost as snobbish as the members, then felt vaguely let down by signs warning them:

> WATCH YOUR HAT AND COAT
> NOT RESPONSIBLE FOR LOST PROPERTY.
> THE MGT.

The Midget became an electronic wizard in his spare time. All over the country, pedestrians stood undecided on curbs as electric signs said WALK while the light was red and then switched to DON'T WALK when the light went green. He branched out and expanded his activities; office workers received memos early in the morning (after he had spent a night with a Xerox machine) and puzzled over:

1. All vacation requests must be submitted in triplicate to the Personnel Department at least three weeks before the planned vacation dates.

2. All employees who change their vacation plans must notify Personnel Department by completing Form 1472, Vacation Plan change, and submitting it three weeks before the change in plans.

3. All vacation plans must be approved by the Department Supervisor and may be changed if they conflict with the vacation plans of employees of higher rank and/or longer tenure.

4. Department Supervisors may announce such cancellations at any time, provided the employee is given 48 hours notice, or two working days, whichever is longer, as the case may be. (Employees crossing the International Date Line, see Form 2317.)

5. Employees may not discuss vacation plans with other employees or trade preferred dates.

6. These few simple rules should prevent a great deal of needless friction and frustration if all employees cooperate, and we will all have a happy summer.

THE MGT.

On April 26 of the year when the Illuminati tried to imminentize the Eschaton, the Midget experienced aches, pains, nausea, spots before his eyes, numbness in his legs and dizziness. He went to the hotel doctor, and a short while after describing his symptoms he was rushed in a closed car to a building that had a Hopi Indian Kachina Doll Shop in front and the Las Vegas CIA office in the back. He was fairly delirious by then, but he heard somebody say, 'Ha, we're ahead of the FBI *and* the Cesspool Cleaners on this one.' Then he got an injection and began to feel better, until a friendly silver-haired man sat down by his cot and asked who 'the girl' was.

'What girl?' the Midget asked irritably.

'Look, son, we know you've been with a girl. She gave you this.'

'Was it the clap?' the Midget asked, dumbfounded. Except for his pornographic Tarot cards, he was still a virgin (the giant women were all so damned patronizing, but his own female equivalents bored him; the giantesses were the Holy Grail to him, but he had never had the courage to approach one). 'I never knew the clap could be this bad,' he added, blushing. His greatest fear was that somebody would discover his virginity.

'No, it wasn't the clap,' said the kindly man (who didn't deceive the Midget one bit; if this guy couldn't pump him, he knew, they would send in the mean, tough one; the nice cop and the nasty cop; oldest con in the business). 'This girl had a certain, uh, rare disease, and we're with the U.S. Public Health Service.' The gentle man produced forged credentials to 'prove' this last allegation. Horseshit, the Midget thought. 'Now,' the sweet old codger went on, 'we've got to track her down, and see that she gets the antidote, or a lot of people will get this disease. You understand?'

The Midget understood. This guy was Army Intelligence or CIA and they wanted to crack this before the FBI and get the credit. The disease was started by the government, obviously. Some fuckup in one of their biological war laboratories, and they had to cover it up before the whole country got wise. He hesitated; none of his projects had ever been consciously intended to lead to death, just to make things a little unpredictable and spooky for the giants.

'The U.S. Public Health Service will be eternally grateful to you,' the grandfatherly man said, eyes crinkling with sly affection. 'It isn't often that a *little* man gets a chance to do such a *big* job for his country.'

That did it. 'Well,' the Midget said, 'she was blonde, in her mid-twenties I guess, and she told me her name was Sarah. She had a scar on her neck – I suppose somebody tried to cut her throat once. She was, let's see, about five-five and maybe 110-115 pounds. And she was superb at giving head,' he concluded, thinking that was a very plausible Las Vegas whore he had just created. His mind was racing rapidly; they wouldn't want people running around loose knowing about this. The antidote had been to keep him alive while they pumped him. He needed insurance. 'Oh, and here's a real lead for you,' he said 'I just remembered. First, I want to explain something about, uh, people

who are below average in stature. We're very sexy. You
see, our sex gland or whatever it's called works extra, because our growth gland doesn't work. So we never get
enough.' He was making this up off the top of his head and
enjoying it. He hoped it would spread; he had a beautiful
vision of bored rich women seeking midgets as they now
seek blacks. 'So you see,' he went on, 'I keep her a long
time, having encores and encores and encores. Finally, she
told me she'd have to raise her price, because she had another customer waiting. I couldn't afford it so I let her go.'
Now the clincher. 'But she mentioned his name. She said,
"Joe Blotz will be pissed if I disappoint him," only the
name wasn't Joe Blotz.'

'Well, what was it?'

'That's the problem,' the Midget said sadly. 'I can't remember. But if you leave me alone awhile,' he added
brightly, 'maybe it'll come back to me.' He was already
planning his escape.

*And, twenty-five hours earlier, George Dorn, quoting
Pilate, asked, 'What is Truth?'* (Barney Muldoon just then,
was lounging in the lobby of the Hotel Tudor, waiting for
Saul to finish what he had called 'a very important, very
private conversation' with Rebecca; Nkrumah Fubar was
experimentally placing a voodoo doll of the president of
American Express inside a tetrahedron – their computer
was still annoying him about a bill he'd paid over two
months ago, on the very daynight that Soapy Mocenigo
dreamed of Anthrax Leprosy Pi; R. Buckminster Fuller,
unaware of this new development in his geodesic revolution, was lecturing the Royal Institute of Architects in
London and explaining why there were no nouns in the
real world; August Personage was breathing into a telephone in New York; Pearson Mohammed Kent was ex-
uberantly balling a female who was not only *white* but *from
Texas*; the Midget himself was saying 'Rude bastard isn't
he?' to Dr. Naismith; and our other characters were variously pursuing their own hobbies, predilections, obsessions
and holy missions). *But Hagbard, with uncharacteristic
gravity, said,* 'Truth is the opposite of lies. The opposite of
most of what you've heard all your life. The opposite of
most of what you've heard from me.'

They were in Hagbard's funky stateroom and George, after his experience at the demolished Drake mansion, found the octopi and other sea monsters on the wall murals distinctly unappetizing. Hagbard, as usual, was wearing a turtleneck and casual slacks; this time the turtleneck was lavender – an odd, faggoty item for him. George remembered, suddenly, that Hagbard had once told him, anent homosexuality, 'I've tried it, of course,' but added something about liking women better. (Goodness, was that only two mornings ago?) George wondered what it would be like to 'try it' and if he would ever have the nerve. 'What particular lies,' he asked cautiously, 'are you about to confess?'

Hagbard lit a pipe and passed it over. 'Alamout Black hash,' he said croakingly, holding the smoke down. 'Hassan i Sabbah's own private formula. Does wonders when heavy metaphysics is coming at you.'

George inhaled and felt an immediate *hit* like cocaine or some other forebrain stimulant. 'Christ, what's this shit cut with?' he gasped, as somebody somewhere seemed to turn colored lights on in the gold-and-nautical-green room and on that outasight lavender sweater.

'Oh,' Hagbard said casually, 'a hint of belladonna and stramonium. That was old Hassan's secret, you know. All that crap in most books about how he had turned his followers on with hash, and they'd never had it before so they thought it was magic, is unhistorical. Hashish was known in the Mideast since the neolithic age; archeologists have dug it up in tombs. Seems our ancestors buried their priests with a load of hash to help them negotiate with their gods when they got to Big Rock Candy Mountain or wherever they thought they were going. Hassan's originality was blending hashish with just the right chemical cousins to produce a new synergetic effect.'

'What's *synergetic*?' George asked slowly, feeling seasick for the first time aboard the *Leif Erikson*.

'Nonadditive. When you put two and two together and get five instead of four. Buckminster Fuller uses synergetic gimmicks all the time in his geodesic domes. That's why they're stronger than they look.' Hagbard took another toke and passed the pipe again.

What the hell? George thought. Sometimes increasing the dose got you past the nausea. He toked, deeply. Hadn't they started out to discuss Truth, though?

George giggled. 'Just as I suspected. Instead of using your goddam *prajna* or whatever it is to spy on the Illuminati, you're just another dirty old man. You use it to play Peeping Tom in other people's heads.'

'*Heads?*' Hagbard protested, laughing. 'I never scan the *heads.* Who the hell wants to watch people eliminating their wastes?'

'I thought you were going to be Socrates,' George howled between lunatic peals of tin giggles, 'and I was prepared to be Plato, or at least Glaucon or one of the minor characters. But you're as stoned as I am. You can't tell me anything important. All you can do is make bad puns.'

'The pun,' Hagbard replied with dignity (ruined somewhat by an unexpected chortle), 'is mightier than the sword. As James Joyce once said.'

'Don't get pedantic.'

'Can I get semantic?'

'Yes. You can get semantic. Or antic. But not pedantic.'

'Where were we?'

'Truth.'

'Yes. Well, Truth is like marijuana, my boy. A drug on the market.'

'I'm getting a hard-on.'

'You too? That's the way the balling bounces. At least, with Alamout Black. Nausea, then microamnesia, then the laughing jag, then sex. Be patient. The clear light comes next. Then we can discuss Truth. As if we haven't been discussing it all along.'

'You're a hell of a guru, Hagbard. Sometimes you sound even dumber than me.'

'If the Elder Malaclypse were here, he'd tell you a few about some other gurus. And geniuses. Do you think Jesus never whacked off? Shakespeare never got on a crying jag at the Mermaid Tavern? Buddha never picked his nose? Gandhi never had the crabs?'

'I've still got a hard-on. Can't we postpone the philosophy while I go look for Stella – I mean, Mavis?'

'That's Truth.'

'What is Truth?'

'Up in the cortex it makes a difference to you whether it's Stella or Mavis. Down in the glands, no difference. My grandmother would do as well.'

'That's not Truth. That's just cheap half-assed Freudian cynicism.'

'Oh, yes. You saw the mandala with Mavis.'

'And you were inside my head somehow. Dirty voyeur.'

'Know thyself.'

'This will never take its place beside the Platonic Dialogues, not in a million years. We're both stoned out of our gourds.'

'I love you, George.'

'I guess I love you, too. You're so damned overwhelming. Everybody loves you. Are we gonna fuck?'

(Mavis had said, 'Wipe the come off your trousers.' Fantasizing Sophia Loren while he masturbated. Or fantasizing that he masturbated while actually . . .)

'No. You don't need it. You're starting to remember what really happened in Mad Dog jail.'

'Oh, no.' Coin's enormous, snaky cock . . . the pain . . . the pleasure . . .

'I'm afraid so.'

'Damn it, now I'll never know. Did you put that in my head, or did it really happen? Did I fantasize the interruption then or did I fantasize the rape just now?'

'Know thyself.'

'Did you say that twice or did I just hear it twice?'

'What do you think?'

'I don't know. I don't know, right now. I just don't know. Is this some devious homosexual seduction?'

'Maybe. Maybe it's a murder plot. Maybe I'm leading up to cutting your throat.'

'I wouldn't mind. I've always had a big self-destructive urge. Like all cowards. Cowardice is a defense against suicide.'

Hagbard laughed. 'I never knew a young man who had so much pussy and risked death so often. And there you sit, still worrying about being whatever it was they called you when you first started letting your hair grow long in your early teens.'

'Sissy. That was the word in good old Nutley, New Jersey. It meant both faggot and coward. So I've never cut my hair since then, to prove *they* couldn't intimidate *me*.'

'Yeah. I'm tracking a black guy now, a musician, who's balling a white lady, a fair flower from Texas. Partly, because she really turns him on. But partly because she could have a brother who might come after him with a gun. He's proving *they* can't intimidate *him*.'

'That's the Truth? We spend all our time proving we can't be intimidated? But all the time we are intimidated on another level?' The colors were coming back strong again; it was that kind of trip. Every time you thought you were the pilot, it would go off in an unexpected direction to remind you that you were just a passenger.

'That's part of the Truth, George. Another part is that every time you think you're intimidated you're really rebelling on another level. Oh, what idiots the Illuminati really are, George. I once collected statistics on industrial accidents in a sample city – Birmingham, England, actually. Fed all the relevant facts into FUCKUP and got just what I expected. Sabotage. Unconscious sabotage. Every case was a blind insurrection. Every man and woman is in rebellion, but only a few have the guts to admit it. The others jam the system by accident, har har har, or by stupidity, har har har again. Let me tell you about the Indians, George.'

'What Indians?'

'Did you ever wonder why nothing works right? Why the whole world seems completely fucked up all the time?'

'Yeah. Doesn't everybody?'

'I suppose so. Pardon me, I've got to get more stoned. In a little while, I go into FUCKUP and we put our heads together – literally, I attach electrodes to my temples – and I'll try to track down the problem in Las Vegas. I don't spend *all* my time on random voyeurism,' Hagbard pronounced with dignity. He refilled the pipe, asking pettishly, 'Where was I?'

'The Indians in Birmingham. How did they get there?'

'There weren't any fucking Indians in Birmingham. You're getting me confused.' Hagbard toked deeply.

'You're getting yourself confused. You're bombed out of your skull.'

'Look who's talking.' Hagbard toked again. 'The Indians. The Indians weren't in Birmingham. Birmingham was where I did the study that convinced me most industrial accidents are unconscious sabotage. So are most misfiled documents among white-collar workers, I'd wager. The Indians are another story. I was a lawyer once, when I first came to your country and before I went in for piracy. I usually don't admit that, George. I usually tell people I played the piano in a whorehouse or something else not quite so disreputable as the truth. If you want to know why nothing makes sense in government forms, remember there are two hundred thousand lawyers working for the bureaucracy these days.

'The Indians were a band of Shoshones. I was defending them against the Great Land Thief, or as it pretentiously titles itself, the Government, in Washington. We were having a conference. You know what an Indian conference is like? Nobody talks for hours sometimes. A good yoga. When somebody does finally speak, you can be sure it comes from the heart. That old movie stereotype, "White man speak with forked tongue," has a lot of truth in it. The more you talk, the more your imagination colors things. I'm one of the most long-winded people alive and one of the worst liars.' Hagbard toked again and finally held the pipe out inquiringly; George shook his head. 'But the story I wanted to tell was about an archeologist. He was hunting for relics of the Devonian culture, the Indians who lived in North America just before the ecological catastrophe of 10,000 B.C. He found what he thought was a burial mound and asked to dig into it. Grok this, George. The Indians looked at him. They looked at me. Then looked at each other. Then the oldest man spoke and, very gravely, gave permission. The archeologist hefted his pick and shovel and went at it like John Henry trying to beat that steam drill. In two minutes he disappeared. Right into a cesspool. Then the Indians laughed.

'*Grok*, George. I knew them as well as any white man ever knows Indians. They had learned to trust me, and I, them. And yet I sat there, while they played their little joke, and I didn't get a hint of what was about to happen. Even though I had begun to discover my telepathic talents

and even focus them a little. Think about it, George. Think
about all the pokerfaced blacks you've seen. Think about
every time a black has done something so fantastically,
outrageously stupid that you had a flash of racism – which,
being radical, you were ashamed of, right? – and wondered if maybe they *are* inferior. And think of ninety-nine
percent of the women in the Caucasian world, outside
Norway, who do the Dumb Dora or Marilyn Monroe act
all the time. Think a minute, George. Think.'

There was a silence that seemed to stretch into some long
hall of near-Buddhist emptiness – George recognized a
glimpse, *at last!*, into the Void all his acidhead friends had
tried to describe – and then he remembered this was not
the trip Hagbard was pushing him toward. But the silence
lingered as a quietness of spirit, a calm in the tornado of
those last few days, and George found himself ruminating
with total dispassion, without hope or dread of smugness
or guilt; if not totally without ego, or in full *darshana*, at
least without the inflamed and voracious ego that usually
either leaped forward or shrunk back from naked fact. He
contemplated his memories and was unmoved, objective,
at peace. He thought of blacks and women and of their
subtle revenges against their Masters, acts of sabotage that
could not be recognized clearly as such because they took
the form of acts of obedience; he thought of the Shoshone
Indians and their crude joke, so similar to the jokes of
oppressed peoples everywhere; he saw, suddenly, the meaning of Mardi Gras and the Feast of Fools and the Satur-
nalia and the Christmas Office Party and all the other
limited, permissible, structured occasions on which Freud's
Return of the Repressed was allowed; he remembered all
the times he had gotten his own back against a professor,
a high school principal, a bureaucrat, or, further back, his
own parents, by waiting for the occasion when, by doing
exactly what he was told, he could produce some form of
minor catastrophe. He saw a world of robots, marching
rigidly in the paths laid down for them from above, and
each robot partly alive, partly human, waiting its chance
to drop its own monkey wrench into the machinery. He
saw, finally, why everything in the world seemed to work
wrong and the Situation Normal was All Fucked Up. 'Hag-

bard,' he said slowly. 'I think I get it. Genesis is exactly backwards. Our troubles started from obedience, not disobedience. And humanity is not yet created.'

Hagbard, more hawk-faced than ever, said carefully, 'You are approaching Truth. Walk cautiously now, George. Truth is not, as Shakespeare would have it, a dog that can be whipped out to kennel. Truth is a tiger. Walk cautiously, George.' He turned in his chair, slid open a drawer in his Danish Modern quasi-Martian desk and took out a revolver. George watched, as cool and alone as a man atop Everest, as Hagbard opened the chamber and showed six bullets inside. Then, with a snap, the gun was closed and placed on the desk blotter. Hagbard did not glance at it again. He watched George; George watched the pistol. It was the scene with Carlo all over again, but Hagbard's challenge was unspoken, gnomic; his level glance did not even admit that a contest had begun. The gun glittered maliciously; it whispered of all the violence and stealth in the world, treacheries undreamed of by Medici or Machiavelli, traps set for victims who were innocent and blameless; it seemed to fill the room with an aura of its presence, and yes, it even had the more subtle menace of a knife, weapon of the sneak, or of a whip in the hands of a man whose smile is too sensual, too intimate, too knowing; into the middle of George's tranquility it had come, inescapable and unexpected as a rattlesnake in the path on the afternoon of the sweetest spring day in the world's most manicured and artificial garden. George heard the adrenalin begin to course into his bloodstream; saw the 'activation syndrome' moisten his palms, accelerate his heart, loosen his sphincter a micrometer; and still, high and cool on his mountain, felt nothing.

'The robot,' he said, glancing finally at Hagbard, 'is easily upset.'

'Don't put your hand in that fire,' Hagbard warned, unimpressed. 'You'll get burned.' He watched; he waited; George could not tear his glance from those eyes and in them, then, he saw the merriment of Howard, the dolphin, the contempt of his grade school principal ('A high IQ, Dorn, does not justify arrogance and insubordination'), the despairing love of his mother, who could never understand him, the emptiness of Nemo, his tomcat of childhood days, the threat of Billy Holtz, the school bully, and the total otherness of an insect or a serpent. More: he saw the child Hagbard, proud like himself of intellectual superiority and frightened like himself of the malice of stupider but brawnier boys, and the very old Hagbard, years hence, wrinkled as a reptile but still showing an endless searching intelligence. The ice melted; the mountain, with a roar of protest and defiance, crumbled; and George was borne down, down in the river racing toward the rapids where the gorilla howled and the mouse trotted quickly, where the saurian head raised above the Triassic foliage, where the sea slept and the spirals of DNA curled backward toward the flash that was this radiance now, this raging eternally against the quite impossible dying of the light, this storm and this centering.

'Hagbard . . .' he said at last.

'I know. I can see it. Just don't fall back into that other thing. It's the Error of the Illuminati.'

George smiled weakly, still not quite back into the world of words. ' "Eat and ye shall be as gods"?' he said.

'I call it the no-ego ego trip. It's the biggest ego trip of all, of course. Anybody can learn it. A child of two months, a dog, a cat. But when an adult rediscovers it, after the habit of obedience and submission has crushed it out of him for years or decades, what happens can be a total disaster. That's why the Zen Roshis say, "One who achieves supreme illumination is like an arrow flying straight to hell." Keep in mind what I said about caution, George. You can release at any moment. It's great up there, and you need a mantra to keep you away from it until you learn how to use it. Here's your mantra, and if you knew the peril you are in you'd brutally burn it into your backside with a branding iron to make sure you'd never forget it: I Am The Robot. Repeat it.'

'I Am The Robot.'

Hagbard made a face like a baboon and George laughed again, at last. 'When you get time,' Hagbard said, 'look into my little book, *Never Whistle While You're Pissing* — there are copies all over the ship. That's *my* ego tip. And keep it in mind: you are the robot and you'll never be anything else. Of course, you're also the programmer, and even the meta-programmer; but that's another lesson, for another day. For now, just remember the mammal, the robot.'

'I know,' George said. 'I've read T. S. Eliot, and now I understand him. "Humility is endless".'

'And humanity *is* created. The . . . other . . . is not human.'

George said then, 'So I've arrived. And it's just another starting place. The beginning of another trip. A harder trip.'

'That's another meaning in Heracleitus. "The end is the beginning".' Hagbard rose and shook himself like a dog. 'Wow,' he said. 'I better get to work with FUCKUP. You can stay here or go to your own room, but I suggest that you don't rush off and talk about your experience to somebody else. You can talk it to death that way.'

George remained in Hagbard's room and reflected on what had happened. He had no urge to scribble in his diary, the usual defense against silence and aloneness since his early teens. Instead, he savored the stillness of the room and of his inner core. He remembered Saint Francis of Assisi called his body 'Brother Ass,' and Timothy Leary used to say when exhausted, 'The robot needs sleep.' Those had been their mantras, their defenses against the experience of the mountaintop and the terrible arrogance it triggered. He remembered, too, the old classic underground press ad: 'Keep me high and I'll ball you forever.' He felt sorry for the woman who had written that: pitiful modern version of the maddened Saint Simon on his pillar in the desert. And Hagbard was right: any dog or cat could do it, could make the jump to the mountaintop and wait without passion until the robot, Brother Ass, survived the ordeal or perished in it. That was what primitive rites of initiation were all about – driving the youth through sheer terror to the point of letting go, the mountaintop point, and then bringing him back down again. George suddenly understood how his generation, in rediscovering the sacred drugs, had failed to rediscover their proper use . . . had failed, or had been prevented. The Illuminati, it was clear, didn't want any competition in the godmanship business.

You could talk it to death in your own head as well as in conversation, he realized, but he went back over it again trying to dissect it without mutilating it. The homosexuality bit had been a false front (with its own reality, of course, like all false fronts). Behind that was the conditioned terror against the Robot: the fear, symbolized in Frankenstein and dozens of other archetypes, that if it were let loose, unrestrained, the Robot would run amok, murder, rape, go mad . . . And then Hagbard had waited until the Alamout Black brought him to freedom, showed him the peak, the place where the cortex at last could idle, as a car motor or a dog or cat idles, the last refuge where the catatonic hides. When George was safely in that harbor, Hagbard produced the gun – in a more primitive, or more sophisticated, society, it would have been the emblem of a powerful demon – and George saw that he could, indeed, idle there and not blindly follow the panic signals from the Robot's adrenalin factory. And, because he was a human and not a dog, the experience had been ecstasy to him, and temptation, so Hagbard, with a few words and a glance from those eyes, pushed him off the peak into . . . what?

Reconciliation was the word. Reconciliation with the robot, with the Robot, with himself. The peak was not a victory; it was the war, the eternal war against the Robot, carried to a higher and more dangerous level. The end of the war was his surrender, the only possible end to that war, since the Robot was three billion years old and couldn't be killed.

There were two great errors in the world, he perceived: the error of the submissive hordes, who fought all their lives to control the Robot and please their masters (and who always sabotaged every effort without knowing it, and were in turn sabotaged by the Robot's Revenge: neuroses, psychoses and all the tiresome list of psychosomatic ailments); and the error of those who recaptured the animal art of letting the Robot run itself, and who then tried to maintain this split from their own flesh indefinitely, until they were lost forever in that eternally widening chasm. One sought to batter the Robot to submission, the other to slowly starve it; both were wrong.

And yet, on another plane of his still-zonked mind,

George knew that even this was a half truth; that he was, indeed, just beginning his journey, not arrving at his destination. He rose and walked to the bookshelves and, as he expected, found a stack of Hagbard's little pamphlets on the bottom: *Never Whistle While You're Pissing,* by Hagbard Celine, H.M., S.H. He wondered what the H.M. and S.H. stood for, then flipped open to the first page, where he found only the large question:

WHO
IS THE ONE
MORE TRUSTWORTHY
THAN
ALL THE BUDDHAS
AND SAGES
? ?

George laughed out loud. The Robot, of course. Me. George Dorn. All three billion years' worth of evolution in every gene and chromosome of me. And that, of course, was what the Illuminati (and all the petty would-be Illuminati who made up power structures everywhere) never wanted a man or woman to realize.

George turned to the second page and began reading:

> If you whistle while you're pissing, you have two minds where one is quite sufficient. If you have two minds, you are at war with yourself. If you are at war with yourself, it is easy for an external force to defeat you. This is why Mong-tse wrote, 'A man must destroy himself before others can destroy him.'

That was all, except for an abstract drawing on page three that seemed to suggest an enemy figure moving out toward the viewer. About to turn to page four, George got a shock: from another angle, the drawing was two figures engaged in attacking each other. I and It. The Mind and the Robot. His memory leaped back twenty-two years and he saw his mother lean over the crib and remove his hand from his penis. Christ, no wonder I grab it when I'm frightened: the Robot's Revenge, the Return of the Repressed.

George started to turn the page again, and saw another trick in Hagbard's abstraction: from a third angle, it might be a couple making love. In a flash, he saw his mother's face above his crib again, in better focus, and recognized the concern in her eyes. The cruel hand of repression was moved by love: she was trying to save him from Sin.

And Carlo, dead three years now, together with the rest of that Morituri group – what had inspired Carlo when he and the four others (all of them less than eighteen, George remembered) blasted their way into a God's Lightning rally and killed three cops and four Secret Service agents in their attempts to gun down the Secretary of State? Love, nothing but mad love . . .

The door opened and George tore his eyes from the text. Mavis, back again in her sweater and slacks outfit, walked in. For a proclaimed right-wing anarchist, she sure dresses a lot like a New Leftist, George thought; but then Hagbard wrote like a cross between Reichian Leftist and an egomaniacal Zen Master – there was obviously more to the Discordian philosophy than he could grasp yet, even though he was now convinced it was the system he himself had been groping toward for many years.

'Mmm,' she said, 'I like that smell. Alamout Black?'

'Yeah,' George said, having trouble meeting her eyes. 'Hagbard's been illuminating me.'

'I can tell. Is that why you suddenly feel uncomfortable with me?'

George met her eyes, then looked away again; there was tenderness there but it was, as he had expected, sisterly at best. He muttered, 'It's just that I realize our sex' (why couldn't he say fucking or, at least, balling?) 'was less important to you than to me.'

Mavis took Hagbard's chair and smiled at him affectionately. 'You're lying, George. You mean it was *more* important to me than to you.' She began to refill the pipe; *Christ God,* George thought, *did Hagbard send her in to take me to the next stage, whatever it is?*

'Well, I guess I mean both,' he said cautiously. 'You were more emotionally involved than I was *then,* but *now*

I'm more emotionally involved. And I know that what I want, I can't have. Ever.'

'Ever is a long time. Let's just say you can't have it now.'

' "Humility is endless",' George repeated.

'Don't start feeling sorry for yourself. You've discovered that love is more than a word in poetry, and you want it right away. You just had two other things that used to be just words to you – *sunyata* and *satori*. Isn't that enough for one day?'

'I'm not complaining. I know that "humility is endless" also means surprise is endless. Hagbard promised me a happy truth and that's it.'

Mavis finally got the pipe lit and, after toking deeply, passed it over. 'You can have Hagbard,' she said.

George, sipping very lightly since he was still fairly high, mumbled 'Hm?'

'Hagbard will love you as well as ball you. Of course, it's not the same. He loves everybody. I'm not at that stage yet. I can only love my equals.' She grinned wickedly. 'Of course, I can still get horny about you. But now that you know there's more than that, you want the whole package deal, right? So try Hagbard.'

George laughed, feeling suddenly lighthearted. 'Okay! I will.'

'Bullshit,' Mavis said bluntly. 'You're putting us both on. You've liberated some of the energies and right away, like everybody else at this stage, you want to prove that there are no blocks anywhere anymore. That laugh was not convincing, George. If you have a block, face it. Don't pretend it isn't there.'

Humility is endless, George thought. 'You're right,' he said, unabashed.

'That's better. At least you didn't fall into feeling guilty about the block. That's an infinite regress. The next stage is to feel guilty about feeling guilty . . . and pretty soon you're back in the trap again, trying to be the governor of the nation of Dorn.'

'The Robot,' George said.

Mavis toked and said, 'Mm?'

'I call it the Robot.'

'You picked that up from Leary back in the mid-'60s. I keep forgetting you were a child prodigy. I can just see you, with your eyeglasses and your shoulders all hunched, poring over one of Tim's books when you were eight or nine. You must have been quite a child. They've sure mauled you over since then, haven't they?'

'It happens to most prodigies. And nonprodigies, too, for that matter.'

'Yeah. Eight years' grade school, four high school, four college, then postgraduate studies. Nothing left but the Robot at the end. The ever-rebellious nation of Me with poor old I sitting on the throne trying to govern it.'

'There's no governor anywhere,' George quoted.

'You *are* coming along nicely.'

'That's Chuang Chou, the Taoist philosopher. But I never understood him before.'

'So that's where Hagbard stole it! He has little cards that say, "There is no enemy anywhere." And ones that say, "There is no friend anywhere." He said once he could tell in two minutes which card was right for a particular person. To jolt them awake.'

'But words alone can't do it. I've known most of the words for years . . .'

'Words can help. In the right situation. If they're the wrong words. I mean, the right words. No, I *do* mean the wrong words.'

They laughed, and George said, 'Are we just goofing, or are you taking up the liberation of the nation of Dorn where Hagbard left off?'

'Just goofing. Hagbard did tell me that you had passed one of the gateless gates and that I might drop in, *after* you had a while alone.'

'A gateless gate. That's another one I've known for years, without understanding it. The gateless gate and the governorless nation. The chief cause of socialism is capitalism. What the hell does that bloody apple have to do with all this?'

'The apple is the world. Who did Goddess say owns it?'

' "The prettiest one." '

'Who is the prettiest one?'

'You are.'

'Don't make a pass right now. Think.'

George giggled. 'I've been through too much already. I think I'm getting sleepy. I have two answers, one communist and one fascist. Both are wrong, of course. The correct answer has to fit in with your anarcho-capitalism.'

'Not necessarily. Anarcho-capitalism is just *our* trip. We don't mean to impose it on everybody. We have an alliance with an anarcho-communist group called the JAMs. John Dillinger's their leader.'

'Come off it. Dillinger died in 1935 or something.'

'John Dillinger is alive and well today, in California, Fernando Poo and Texas,' Mavis smiled. 'As a matter of fact, he shot John F. Kennedy.'

'Give me another toke. If I have to listen to this, I might as well be in a state where I won't try to understand it.'

Mavis passed the pipe. 'The prettiest one has quite a few levels to it, like all good jokes. I'll give you the Freudian one, as beginners. You know the prettiest one, George. You gave it to the apple just yesterday.'

'Every man's penis is the prettiest thing in the world to him. From the day he's born until the day he dies. It never loses its endless fascination. And, I kid you not, baby, the same is true of every woman and her pussy. It's the closest thing to a real, blind, helpless love and religious adoration that most people ever achieve. But they'd rather die than admit it. Homosexuality, the urge to kill, petty spites and treacheries, fantasies of sadism, masochism, transvestism, any weird thing you can name, they'll confess all that in a group therapy session. But that deep submerged constant narcissism, that perpetual mental masturbation, is the earliest and most powerful block. They'll never admit it.'

'From what I've read of psychiatric literature, I thought most people had rather squeamish and negative feelings about their genitals.'

'That, to quote Freud himself, is a reaction formation. The primordial emotional tone, from the day the infant discovers the incredible pleasure centers there, is perpetual astonishment, awe and delight. No matter how much society tries to crush it and repress it. For instance, everybody has some pet name for their genitals. What's yours?'

'Polyphemus,' he confessed.

'What?'

'Because it has one eye, you know? Also, Polyphemus rhymes with penis, I guess. I mean, I can't remember exactly what my mental process was when I invented that in my early teens.'

'Polyphemus was a giant, too. Almost a god. You see what I mean about the primary emotional tone? It's the origin of all religion. Adoration of your own genitals and of your lover's genitals. *There's* Pan Pangenitor and the Great Mother.'

'So,' George said owlishly, still not sure whether this was profundity or nonsense, 'the earth belongs to our genitalia?'

'To their offspring, and their offspring's offspring, and so on, forever. The world is a verb, not a noun.'

'The prettiest one is three billion years old.'

'You've got it, baby. We're all tenants here, including the ones who think they're owners. Property is impossible.'

'Okay, okay, I think I've got most of it. Property is theft because the Illuminati land titles are arbitrary and unjust. And so are their banking charters and railroad franchises and all the other monopoly games of capitalism—'

'Of state capitalism. Not of true laissez-faire.'

'Wait. Property is impossible because the world is a verb, a burning house as Buddha said. All things are fire. My old pal Heracleitus. So property is theft and property is impossible. How do we get to property is liberty?'

'Without private property there can be no private decisions.'

'So we're back where we started from?'

'No, we're one flight higher up on the spiral staircase. Look at it that way. Dialectically, as your Marxist friends say.'

'But we *are* back at private property. After proving it's an impossible fiction.'

'The Statist form of private property is an impossible fiction. Just like the Statist form of communal property is an impossible fiction. Think outside the State framework, George. Think of property in freedom.'

George shook his head. 'It beats the hell out of my ass. All I can see is people ripping each other off. The war of all against all, as what's-his-name said.'

'Hobbes.'

'Hobbes, snobs, jobs. Whoever. Or whatever. Isn't he right?'

'Stop the motor on this submarine.'

'What?'

'Force me to love you.'

'Wait, I don't . . .'

'Turn the sky green or red, instead of blue.'

'I still don't get it.'

Mavis took a pen off the desk and held it between two fingers. 'What happens when I let go of this?'

'It falls.'

'Where do you sit if there are no chairs?'

'On the floor?' *If I wasn't so stoned, I would have had it by then. Sometimes drugs are more a hindrance than a help.* 'On the ground?' I added.

'On your ass, that's for sure.' Mavis said. 'The point is, if the chairs all go away, you still sit. Or you build new chairs.' She was stoned, too; otherwise she'd be explaining it better, I realized. 'But you can't stop the motor without learning something about marine engineering first. You don't know what switch to pull. Or switches. And you can't change the sky. And the pen will fall without a gravity-governing demon rushing into the room to make it fall.'

'Shit and pink petunias,' I said disgustedly. 'Is this some form of Thomism? Are you trying to sell me the Natural Law argument? I can't buy that at all.'

'Okay, George. Here's the next jolt. Keep your ass-hole tight.' She spoke to the wall, to a hidden microphone, I guessed. 'Send *him* in now.'

The Robot is easily upset; my sphincter was already tightening as soon as she warned me there was a jolt coming and she didn't really need to add that bit about my asshole. Carlo and his gun. Hagbard and his gun. Drake's mansion. I took a deep breath and waited to see what the Robot would do.

A panel in the wall opened and Harry Coin was pushed into the room. I had time to think that I should have guessed, in this game where both sides were playing with illusion constantly, Coin's death could have been faked, artificial intestines dangling and all, and of course Mavis

and her raiders could have taken him out of Mad Dog jail
even before they took me out of course, and I remembered
the pain when he slapped my face and when his cock
entered me, and the Robot was already moving, and I
hardly had time to aim of course, and then his head was
banging against the wall, blood spurting from his nose, and
I had time to clip him again on the jaw as he went down
of course, and then I came all the way back and stopped
myself as I was about to kick him in the face as he lay
there unconscious. Zen in the art of face-punching. I had
knocked a man out with two blows; I who hated Heming-
way and Machismo so much that I'd never taken a boxing
lesson in my life. I was breathing hard, but it was good and
clean, the feeling of after-an-orgasm; the adrenalin was
flowing, but a fight reflex instead of a flight reflex had been
triggered, and now it was over, and I was calm. A glint in
the air: Hagbard's pistol was in Mavis's hand, then flying
toward me. As I caught it, she said, 'Finish the bastard.'

But the rage had ended when I held back the kick on
seeing him already unconscious.

'No,' I said. 'It *is* finished.'

'Not until you kill him. You're no good to us until you're
ready to kill, George.'

I ignored her and rapped on the wall. 'Haul the bastard
out,' I said clearly. The panel opened, and two Slavic-
looking seamen, grinning, grabbed Coin's arms and
dragged him out. The panel closed again, quietly.

'I don't kill on command,' I said, turning back to Mavis.
'I'm not a German shepherd or a draftee. *My* case with
him is settled, and if you want him dead, do the dirty work
yourself.'

But Mavis was smiling placidly. 'Is that a Natural Law?'
she asked.

*And twenty-three hours later Tobias knight listened to
the voice in his earphones:* 'That's the problem. I can't
remember. But if you leave me alone for a while maybe
it'll come back to me.' Smoothing his mustache nervously,
Knight set the button for automatic record, removed the
earphones and buzzed Esperando Despond's office.

'Despond,' the intercom said.

'The CIA has one. A man who was with the girl after

Mocenigo. Send somebody down for the tape – it's got a pretty good description of the girl.'

'Wilco,' Despond said tersely. 'Anything else?'

'He thinks he might remember the name of her next customer. She mentioned it to him. We might get that, too.'

'Let's hope so,' Despond said and clicked off. He sat back in his chair and addressed the three agents in his office. 'The guy we've got – what's his name? Naismith – is probably the next customer. We'll check the two descriptions of the girl against each other and get a much more accurate picture than the CIA has, since they're working from only one description.'

But fifteen minutes later, he was staring in puzzlement at the chart which had been chalked on the blackboard:

DESCRIPTION OF SUSPECT

	First Witness	Second Witness
Height	5'2"	5'5"
Weight	90–100 lbs	110–115 lbs
Hair	Black	Blond
Race	Negro	Caucasian
Name or alias	Bonnie	Sarah
Scars, etc.	None	Scar on throat
Age	Late teens	Mid-twenties
Sex	Female	Female

A tall, bearish agent named Roy Ubu said thoughtfully, 'I've never seen two eyewitness descriptions match exactly, but *this* . . .'

A small, waspish agent named Buzz Vespa snapped, 'One of them is lying for some reason. But which one?'

'Neither of them has any reason to lie,' Despond said. 'Gentlemen, we've got to face the facts. Dr. Mocenigo was unworthy of the trust that the U.S. government placed in him. He was a degenerate sex maniac. He had *two* women last night, one of them a Nigra.'

'What do you mean that little sawed-off bastard is gone?' Peter Kurten of the CIA was shouting at that very moment. 'The only way out of his room was right through that door, there, and we've all had it under constant surveillance. The door was only opened once when DeSalvo took out

the coffee urn to have it refilled at the sandwich shop next
door. Oh . . . my . . . *God* . . . the . . . *coffee* . . . *urn* . . .'
As he slumped back in his chair, mouth hanging open, an
agent with a device that looked like a mine sweeper stepped
forward.

'Daily sweep for FBI bugs, sir,' he said uncomfortably.
'I'm afraid the machine is registering one under your desk.
If you'll let me just reach in and . . . uh . . . that gets it . . .'

And Tobias Knight, listening, heard no more. It would
be a few hours, at least, until their man in the CIA was
able to plant a new bug.

And Saul Goodman stepped hard on the brakes of his
rented Ford Brontosaurus as a tiny and determined figure,
dashing out of the Papa Mescalito Sandwich Shop, ran
right in front of the fender. Saul heard a sickening thud and
Barney Muldoon's voice beside him saying, 'Oh Christ,
no . . .'

*I was at the end of my ropes. The Syndicate I could see,
but why the Feds?* I was flabbygastered. I said to that dumb
cunt Bonnie Quint, 'Are you a thousand percent sure?'

'Carmel,' she says. 'I know the Syndicate. They're not
that smooth. These guys were just what they claimed.
Feds.'

Oh, Christ Jesus. Christ Jesus with egg in his beard. I
couldn't help myself, I just hauled off and bopped her in
the kisser, the dumb cunt. 'What'd you tell them?' I
screamed. 'What'd you tell them?'

She started to snivel. 'I didn't tell them nothing,' she
says.

So I had to bop her again. Christ, I hate hitting women,
they always blubber so much. 'I'll use the belt,' I howled.
'So help me, God, I'll use the belt. Don't tell me you didn't
tell them nothing. Everybody tells them something. Even a
clam would sing like Sinatra when they're finished with
him. So what'd you tell them?' I bopped her again, Christ,
this was terrible.

'I just told them I wasn't with this Mocenigo. Which I
wasn't.'

'So who did you tell them you were with?'

'I made up a prescription. A midget. A guy I saw on

the street. I wouldn't give the name of a real john, I know
that could come back against you. And me.'

I didn't know what to do, so I bopped her again. 'Go
away,' I says. 'Be missing. Let me think.'

She goes out, still blubbering, and I go over to the window and look at the desert to calm my head. My rose
fever was starting to act up; it was that time of year. Why
did people have to bring roses to the desert? I tried to
contemplate hard on the problem and forget my health.
There was only one explanation: that damned Mocenigo
figured out that Sherri was pumping him and told the Feds.
The Syndicate wasn't in it yet. They were all still running
around the East like chickens with their legs cut off, trying to figure who rubbed Maldonado, and why it happened
at the house of a straight like this banker Drake. So they
hadn't got the time yet to find out that five million of
Banana Nose's money had disappeared into my own safe
as soon as I heard he was dead. The Feds weren't in on
that at all, and the connection was circumsubstantial.

And then it hit me so hard that I almost fell over. Besides my own girls, who wouldn't talk, there were a dozen
or two cab drivers and bartenders and whatnots who knew
that Sherri worked for me. The Feds would get it out of
somebody sooner or later, and probably sooner. It was like
a light bulb going on over my head in a comic strip:
TREASON. AIDING AND ABEDDING THE ENEMY. I remembered
from when I was a kid those two Jewish scientists who the
Feds got for that. The hot squat. They fried them, Christ
Jesus, I thought I'd vomit. Why does the fucking government have to be that way about somebody just trying to
make a buck? Even the Syndicate would only shoot you or
give you a lead enema, but the cocksucking government
has to go and put you in an electrical chair. Christ Jesus, I
was hot as a chimney.

I took a candy out of my pocket and started chewing it,
trying to think what to do. If I ran, the Syndicate would
guess I was the one who emptied the till when Maldonado
was rubbed, and they'd get me. If I *didn't* run, the Feds
would be at the door with a high treason warrant. It was a
double whammy. I might try to highjack a plane to Panama, but I didn't know nearly enough about Mocenigo's

bugs to make a deal with the Commie government down there. They'd just send me right back. It was hopeless, like trying to fill a three-card inside straight. The only thing to do was find a hole and bury myself.

And then it was just like a light bulb in my head again, and I thought: Lehman Cave.

'*What does the computer say now?*' the President asked the Attorney General.

'What does the computer say now?' the Attorney General barked into the open phone before him.

'If the girl had two contacts before she died, at this moment the possible carriers number,' the phone paused, '428,000. If the girl had three contacts, 7,656,000.'

'Get the Special Agent in Charge,' the President snapped. He was the calmest man at the table – ever since Fernando Poo, he had been supplementing his Librium, Tofranil and Elovil with Demerol, the amazing little pills that had kept Hermann Goering so chipper and cheerful during the Nuremberg Trials while all the other Nazis crumbled into catatonic, paranoid or other dysfunctional conditions.

'Despond,' a second open phone said.

'This is your President,' the President said. 'Give it to us straight. Have you treed the coon?'

'Uh, sir, no, sir. We have to find the procurer, sir. The girl can't possibly be alive, but we haven't found her. It is now mathematically certain that somebody hid her body. The obvious theory, sir, is that her procurer, being in an illegal business, hid the body rather than report it. We have two descriptions of the girl, sir, and, uh, although they don't tally *completely* they should lead us to her procurer. Of course, he should die soon, sir, and then we'll find him. That's the Rubicon of the case, sir. Meanwhile, I'm happy to report, sir, that we're lucking out amazingly. Only two definite cases off the base so far and both of them injected with the antidote. It is possible, just possible, that the procurer went into hiding after disposing of the body. In that case, he hasn't contacted another human being and is not spreading it. Sir.'

'Despond,' the President said, 'I want *results*. Keep us informed. Your country depends on you.'

'Yes, sir.'

'*Tree that coon*, Despond.'

'We will, sir.'

Esperando Despond turned from the phone as an agent from the computer section entered the room. 'Got something?' he snapped nervously.

'The first girl, the Nigra, sir. She was one of the pros we questioned yesterday. Her name is Bonnie Quint.'

'You look worried. Is there a hitch?' Despond asked shrewdly.

'Just another of the puzzles. She didn't admit being with Mocenigo the night before, but that kind of lying we expected. Here's what's weird: her description of the guy she says she *was* with.' The computer man shook his head dubiously. 'It doesn't fit Naismith, the guy who said he was with *her*. It fits the little mug, the dwarf, that the CIA grabbed. Only *he* said she was the second girl.'

Despond mopped his brow. 'What the heck has been going on in this town?' he asked the ceiling. 'Some kind of *sex* orgy?'

In fact, several kinds of sex orgies had been going on in Las Vegas ever since the Veterans of the Sexual Revolution had arrived two days earlier. The Hugh M. Hefner Brigade had taken two stories of the Sands, hired a herd of professional women, and hadn't yet come out to join the Alfred Kinsey Brigade, the Norman Mailer Guerrillas and the others in marching up and down the Strip, squirting young girls in the crotch with water pistols, passing bottles of hooch back and forth and generally blocking traffic and annoying pedestrians. Dr. Naismith himself, after a few token appearances, had avoided most of the merriment and retired to a private suite to work on his latest fund-raising letter for the Colossus of Yorba Linda Foundation. Actually, the VSR, like White Heroes Opposing Red Extremism, was one of Naismith's lesser projects and brought in only peanuts. Most of the real veterans of the sexual revolution had succumbed to syphilis, marriage, children, alimony or some such ailment, and few white heroes were prepared to oppose red extremism in the bizarre manner suggested by Naismith's pamphlets; in both of those cases, he had recognized two nut markets that nobody else was exploiting and had quickly moved in.

Even the John Dillinger Died For You Society, of which
he was inordinately proud since it was probably the most
implausible religion in the long history of humanity's in-
fatuation with metaphysics, didn't earn much less per
annum than these fancies. The real bread was in the
Colossus of Yorba Linda Foundation, which had been
successfully raising money for several years to erect a
heroic monument, in solid gold and *ten feet taller than the
statue of Liberty,* honoring the martyred former president
Richard Milhous Nixon. This monument, paid for entirely
by the twenty million Americans who still loved and re-
vered Nixon despite the damnable lies of the Congress, the
Justice Department, the press, the TV, the law courts, *et
al.,* would stand outside Yorba Linda, Tricky Dicky's boy-
hood home, and scowl menacingly toward Asia, warning
those gooks not to try to get the jump on Uncle Sammie.
Beside the gigantic idol's right foot, Checkers looked ador-
ingly upward; beneath the left foot was a crushed alle-
gorical figure representing Cesar Chavez. The Great Man
held a bunch of lettuce in his right hand and a tape recording in the left. It was all most tasteful, and so appealed
to Fundamentalist Americans that hundreds of thousands
of dollars had already been collected by the Colossus fund,
and Naismith planned to hop to Nepal with the loot at the
first sign that contributors or postal inspectors were beginning to wonder when the statue would actually start rising
on the plot he had purchased, amid much publicity, after
the first few thousand arrived.

Naismith was a small, slight man and, like many Texans,
affected a cowboy hat (although he had never herded
cattle) and a bandito mustache (although his thefts were
all based on fraud rather than force). He was also, for his
nation at this time in history, an uncommonly honest man,
and, unlike most corporations of the epoch, none of his
enterprises had poisoned or mutilated the customers whose
money he took. His one vice was cynicism based on lack
of imagination: he reckoned most of his countrymen as
total mental basket cases and fondly believed that he was
exploiting their folly when he told them that a vast Illuminati conspiracy controlled the money supply and interest
rates or that a bandit of the 1930s was, in a sense, a re-

deemer of the atrophying human spirit. That there was an element of truth in these bizarre notions never crossed his mind. In short, even though born in Texas, Naismith was as alienated from the pulse, the poetry and the profundity of American emotion as a New York intellectual.

But his cynicism served him well when, after reporting certain strange symptoms to the hotel doctor, he found himself rushed to a supposed U.S. Public Health Service station which was manned by individuals he quickly recognized as *laws*. This is an old Texas word, probably an abbreviation of *lawmen* (Texans don't know much about abbreviating) and is as charged with suspicion and wariness, although not quite so much rage, as the New Left's word *pig*. Bonnie Parker had used it, eloquently, in her last ballad:

> Someday they'll go down together
> They'll bury them side by side
> For some it means grief
> For the laws a relief
> But it's death for Bonnie and Clyde.

That about summed it up: the *laws* were not necessarily fascist Gestapo racist pigs (words largely unknown in Texas), but they were people who would find it a relief if bothersome and rebellious individualism disappeared, however bloody the disappearance might be. If you were ornery enough, the laws would bushwhack you – shoot you dead from ambush, without a chance to surrender, as they did to Miss Parker and Mr. Barrow – but even if you were merely a mildly larcenous hoaxter like Dr. Naismith, they would be much cheered to put you someplace where you couldn't throw any more entropy into the functioning of the Machine they served. And so, recognizing laws, Dr. Naismith narrowed his eyes, thought deeply, and when they began their questioning, lied as only an unregenerate old-school Texas confidence man can lie.

'You got it from somebody who had body contact with you. So either you were in a very crowded elevator or you got it from a prostitute. Which was it?'

Naismith thought of the collision on the sidewalk with

the Midget and the weasel-faced character with the big
suitcase, but he also thought that the questioner leaned
heavily on the second possibility. They were looking for a
woman; and, if you tell the laws what they want to hear,
they don't keep coming back and asking more personal
questions. 'I was with a prostitute,' he said, trying to sound
embarrassed.

'Can you describe her?'

He thought back over the pros he had seen with other
VSR delegates, and one stood out. Being a kindly man, he
didn't want to implicate an innocent whore in this messy
business (whatever it was), so he combined her with another woman, the first that he ever successfully penetrated
in his long-ago youth in the 1950s.

Unfortunately for Dr. Naismith's kindly intentions, the
laws never expect an eyewitness description to match the
person described in *all* respects, so when his information
was coded into an IBM machine, three cards came out.
Each one had more similarities to his fiction than differences from it, and they came from a card file of several
hundred prostitutes whose description had been gathered
and coded in the past twenty-four hours. Running the three
cards through a different sorting in the machine, limited to
outstanding bodily characteristics most commonly remembered correctly, the technicians emerged, after all, with
Bonnie Quint. Forty-five minutes later she was in Esperando Despond's office, nervously twirling her mink stole,
picking at the hem of her mini-skirt, evading questions
nimbly and remembering intensely Carmel's voice saying,
'I'll use the belt. So help me, God. I'll use the belt.' She
was also smarting from the injection.

'You *don't* work free-lance,' Despond told her, nastily,
for the fifth time. 'In this town, the Maf would put a knife
up your ass and break off the handle if you tried that.
You've got a pimp. Now, do we throw the book at you or
do we get his name?'

'Don't be too hard on her,' Tobias Knight said. 'She's
only a poor, confused kid. Not twenty yet, are you?' he
asked her kindly. 'Give her a chance to think. She'll do
the right thing. Why should she protect a lousy pimp who
exploits her all the time?' He gave her a reassuring glance.

'Poor confused kid, my ass!' Despond exploded. 'This is a matter of life and death and no Nigra whore is going to sit here lying her head off and get away with it.' He did a good imitation of a man literally trembling with repressed fury. 'I'd like to kick her head in,' he screamed.

Knight, still playing the friendly cop, looked shocked. 'That's not very professional,' he said sadly. 'You're over-tired, and you're frightening the child.'

Three hours later – after Despond had nearly done a complete psycho schtick and virtually threatened to behead poor Bonnie with his letter opener, and Knight had become so fatherly and protective that both he and she were beginnning to feel that she was actually his very own six-year-old daughter being set upon by Goths and Vandals – a sobbing but accurate description of Carmel emerged, including his address.

Twelve minutes later, Roy Ubu, calling via car radio, reported that Carmel was not in his house and had been seen driving toward the Southwest in a jeep with a large suitcase beside him.

In the next eighteen hours, eleven men in jeeps were stopped on various roads southwest of Las Vegas, but none of them was Carmel, although most of them were around the height and weight and general physical description given by Bonnie Quint, and two of them even had large suitcases. In the twenty-four hours after that, nearly a thousand men of all sizes and shapes were stopped on roads, north, south, east and west, in cars not remotely like jeeps and some driving toward, not away from, Las Vegas. None of them was Carmel either.

Among all the men wandering around the Desert Door base and the city of Las Vagas with credentials from the U.S. Public Health Service, one who really was employed by USPHS, had a long lean body, a mournful countenance, a general resemblance to the late great Boris Karloff, and the name Fred Filiarisus. By special authority of the White House, Dr. Filiarisus was able to gain access to everything known by the scientists at Desert Door, including the course of the disease in those originally infected, among whom two had died before the antidote took effect and three had shown a total lack of symptoms even though exposed along with the others. He also had access to both FBI and CIA information as it came in, without having to bug either office. It was he, therefore, who finally put together the correct picture, on April 30, and reported directly to the White House at eleven that morning.

'Some people are naturally immune to Anthrax Leprosy Pi, Mr. President,' Filiarisus said. 'Unfortunately, they serve as carriers. We found three like that at the base, and it is mathematically, scientifically certain that a fourth is still at large.

'Everybody was lying to the FBI and CIA, sir. They were all afraid of punishment for various activities forbidden by our laws. No variation or permutation on their stories will hang together reasonably. Each witness lied about something, and usually about several things. The truth is other than it appeared. In short, the government, being an agency of punishment, acted as a distorting factor from the beginning, and I had to use information-theory equations to determine the degree of distortion present. I would say that what I finally discovered may have universal application: no governing body can ever obtain an accurate account of reality from those over whom it holds power. From the perspective of communication analysis, government is not an instrument of law and order, but of law and disorder. I'm sorry to have to say this so bluntly, but it needs to be kept in mind when similar situations arise in the future.'

'He sounds like an *eff*ing anarchist,' the Vice President muttered.

'The true picture, with a ninety-seven percent probability, is this,' Filiarisus continued. 'Dr. Mocenigo had only one contact, and she died. The FBI hypothesis is correct: her body was then hidden, probably in the desert, by an associate wishing to avoid involvement with law enforcement agencies. If prostitution were legal, we might never have had this nightmare.'

'I told you he was an *eff*ing anarchist,' the Vice President growled. 'And a sex maniac, too!'

'The associate who hid the body,' Filiarisus went on, 'is our fourth carrier, personally immune but lethal to others. It was this person who infected Mr. Chaney and Dr.

Naismith. This person was probably not a prostitute. These men lied, among other reasons, because they knew what the government agents wanted them to say. When power is wielded over people, they *say* as well as *do* what they think is expected of them – another reason government always finds it difficult to learn the truth about anything.

'The only hypothesis that mathematical logic will accept, when all the known data was fed into a computer, is that the fourth carrier is the procurer who disappeared, Mr. Carmel. Experiencing no symptoms himself, he is unaware that he carries the world's most dangerous disease. For reasons of his own, which we cannot guess, he has been hiding since he disposed of the woman's body. Probably, he feared that the corpse might be found and a case of manslaughter or homicide could be made against him. Or he might have a motive completely unrelated to her death. Only twice has he contacted other human beings. I would suggest that his contact with Miss Quint was typical of their professional relationship; he either hit her or had sex relations with her. His contact with Dr. Naismith and Mr. Chaney was some sort of accident – perhaps the crowded elevator that has been suggested by Mr. Despond. Otherwise, he had been, as it were, underground.

'This is why we only found three cases instead of the thousands or millions we feared.

'However, the problem still remains. Carmel is immune, will never know he has the disease unless he is told it, and will eventually surface somewhere. When he does, we will learn of it through the outbreak of Anthrax Leprosy Pi cases in the vicinity. At that point, the whole nightmare begins again, sir.

'Our best hope, and the computer backs me on this, is public disclosure. The panic we tried to avoid will have to be faced. Every medium of communication in the nation must be given the full facts, and Carmel's description must be circulated everywhere. This is our last chance. The man is a walking biological Doomsday Machine and he must be found.

'Psychologists and social psychologists have fed all the relevant facts about this case, and about previous panics and plagues, into the computer also. The conclusion, with ninety-three percent certainty, is that the panic will be nationwide and martial law will have to be declared everywhere. Liberals in Congress should be placed under house arrest as the first step, and the Supreme Court must be stripped of its powers totally. The Army and the National Guard will have to be sent into every city with authority to override any policies of local officials. Democracy, in short, must cease until the emergency is ended.'

'He's not an anarchist,' the Secretary of the Interior said. 'He's a goddam fascist.'

'He's a realist,' said the President, clear-minded, crisp, quick on the uptake and stoned clear round the corner of schizophrenia by his usual three tranquilizers, a stronger dose of amphetamines than usual, and loads of those happy little Demerol tablets. 'We start implementing his suggestions right now.'

And so those few tattered remnants of the Bill of Rights which had survived into the fourth decade of the Cold War were laid to rest – temporarily, it was thought by those present. Dr. Filiarisus, whose name in the Ancient Illuminated Seers of Bavaria was Gracchus Gruad, had completed on the day known as May Eve or *Walpurgisnacht* the project begun when the first dream of Anthrax Leprosy Pi was planted in Dr. Mocenigo's mind on the day known as Candelmas. These dates were known by much older names in the Illuminati, of course, and the burial of the Bill of Rights was expected, by them, to be permanent.

(Two hours before Dr. Filiarisus spoke to the President, four of the world's five Illuminati Primi met in an old graveyard in Ingolstadt; the fifth could not be present. They agreed that all was going as scheduled, but one danger remained: nobody in the order, however developed his or her ESP, had been able to trace Carmel. Leaning on a tombstone – where Adam Weishaupt had once performed rites so unique that the psychic vibration had bounced off every sensitive mind in Europe, leading to such decidedly peculiar literary productions as Lewis's *The Monk*, Maturin's *Melmoth*, Walpole's *Castle of Otranto*, Mrs. Shelley's *Frankenstein*, and DeSade's *One Hundred*

Twenty Days of Sodom – the eldest of the four said, 'It can still fail, if one of the mehums finds the pimp before he infects a city or two.' Mehums was an abbreviation for all descendants of those not part of the original Unbroken Circle; it meant *mere humans*.

'Why can none of our ultra-sensitives find him?' a second asked. 'Does he have no ego or soul at all?'

'He has a vibration but it's not distinctly human. Whenever we seem to have a fix on it, we're usually picking up a bank vault or the safe of some paranoid millionaire,' the eldest replied.

'We have that problem with an increasing number of Americans,' the third commented morosely. 'In that nation, we have done our work too well. The conditioning to those pieces of paper is so strong that no other psychic impulse remains to be read.'

The fourth spoke. 'Now is no time for trepidation, my brothers. The plan is virtually realized, and this man's lack of ordinary mehum qualities will prove an advantage when we do fix on him. No ego, no resistance. We will be able to move him at our whim. The stars are right, He Who Is Not To Be Named is impatient, and now we must be intrepid!' She spoke with fervor.

The others nodded. '*Heute die Welt, Morgens das Sonnensystem!*' the eldest cried out fiercely.

'*Heute die Welt,*' all repeated, '*Morgens das Sonnensystem!*')

But two days earlier, as the *Leif Erikson* left the Atlantic and entered the underground Ocean of Valusia beneath Europe, George Dorn was listening to a different kind of chorus. It was, Mavis had explained to him in advance, the weekly Agape Ludens, or Love Feast Game, of the Discordians, and the dining hall was newly bedecked with pornographic and psychedelic posters, Christian and Buddhist and Amerindian mystic designs, balloons and lollypops dangling from the ceiling on Day-Glo-dabbed strings, numinous paintings of Discordian saints (including Norton I, Sigismundo Malatesta, Guillaume of Aquitaine, Chuang Chou, Judge Roy Bean, various historical figures even more obscure, and numerous gorillas and dolphins), bouquets of roses and forsythia and gladiolas and orchids,

clusters of acorns and gourds, and the inevitable prolifer-
ation of golden apples, pentagons and octopi.

The main course was the best Alaskan king crab Newburg that George had ever tasted, only lightly dusted with
a mild hint of Panamanian Red grass. Dozens of trays of
dried fruits and cheeses were passed back and forth among
the tables, together with canapes of an exquisite caviar
George had never encountered before ('Only Hagbard
knows where those sturgeon spawn,' Mavis explained) and
the beverage was a blend of the Japanese seventeen-herb
Mu tea with Menomenee Indian peyote tea. While everyone
gorged, laughed and got gently but definitely zonked, Hagbard – who was evidently satisfied that he and FUCKUP
had located 'the problem in Las Vegas' – merrily con-
ducted the religious portion of the Agape Ludens.

'Rub-a-dub-dub,' he chanted, 'O hail Eris!'

'Rub-a-dub-dub,' the crew merrily chorused, 'O Hail
Eris!'

'*Sya-dasti*,' Hagbard chanted. 'All that I tell you is true.'

'*Sya-dasti*,' the crew repeated, 'O hail Eris!' George
looked around; there were three, or five, races present (depending upon which school of physical anthropology you
credited) and maybe half a hundred nationalities, but the
feeling of brotherhood and sisterhood transcended any
sense of contrast, creating instead a blend, as in musical
progression.

'*Sya-davak-tavya*,' Hagbard chanted now. 'All that I
tell you is false.'

'*Sya-davak-tavya*,' George joined in, 'O hail Eris!'

'*Sya-dasti-sya-nasti*,' Hagbard intoned. 'All that I tell
you is meaningless.'

'*Sya-dasti-sya-nasti*,' all agreed, some jeeringly, 'O hail
Eris!'

If they had services like this in the Baptist church back
in Nutley, George thought, I never would have told my
mother religion is all a con and had that terrible quarrel
when I was nine.

'*Sya-dasti-sya-nasti-sya-davak-tav-yaska*,' Hagbard sang
out. 'All that I tell you is true and false and meaningless.'

'*Sya-dasti-sya-nasti-sya-davak-tav-yaska*,' the massed
voices replied, 'O hail Eris!'

'Rub-a-dub-dub,' Hagbard repeated quietly. 'Does anyone have a new incantation?'

'All hail crab Newburg,' a Russian-accented voice
shouted.

That was an immediate hit. 'All hail crab Newburg,'
everyone howled.

'All hail these bloody fucking beautiful roses,' an Ox-
fordian voice contributed.

'All hail these bloody fucking beautiful roses,' all agreed.

Miss Mao arose. 'The Pope is the chief cause of Pro-
testantism,' she recited softly.

That was another roaring success; everybody chorused,
and one Harlem voice added, 'Right *on*!'

'Capitalism is the chief cause of socialism,' Miss Mao
chanted, more confident. That went over well, too, and
she then tried, 'The State is the chief cause of anarchism,'
which was another smashing success.

'Prisons are built with the stones of law, brothels with
the bricks of religion,' Miss Mao went on.

'PRISONS ARE BUILT WITH THE STONES OF
LAW, BROTHELS WITH THE BRICKS OF RE-
LIGION,' the hall boomed.

'I stole that last one from William Blake,' Miss Mao
said quietly and sat down.

'Any others?' Hagbard asked. There was none, so he
went on after a moment, 'Very well, then, I will preach
my weekly sermon.'

'Balls!' cried a Texan voice.

'Bullshit!' added a Brazilian female.

Hagbard frowned. 'That wasn't much of a demonstration,' he commented sadly. 'Are the rest of you so
passive that you're just going to sit here on your dead asses
and let me bore the piss out of you?'

The Texan, the Brazilian lady and a few others got up.
'We are going to have an orgy,' the Brazilian said briefly,
and they left.

'Well, sink me, I'm glad there's some life left on this
old tub,' Hagbard grinned. 'As for the rest of you – who
can tell me, without uttering a word, the fallacy of the
Illuminati?'

A young girl – she was no more than fifteen, George

guessed, and the youngest member of the crew; he had heard she was a runaway from a fabulously rich Italian family in Rome – slowly raised her hand and clenched her fist.

Hagbard turned on her furiously. 'How many times must I tell you people: no faking! You got that out of some cheap book on Zen that neither the author nor you understood a damned word of. I hate to be dictatorial, but phony mysticism is the one thing Discordianism can't survive. You're on shitwork, in the kitchen, for a week, you wise-ass brat.'

The girl remained immobile, in the same position, fist raised, and only slowly did George read the slight smile that curled her mouth. Then he started to smile himself.

Hagbard lowered his eyes for a second and gave a Sicilian shrug. '*O oi che siete in piccioletta barca,*' he said softly, and bowed. 'I'm still in charge of nautical and technical matters,' he announced, 'but Miss Portinari now succeeds me as *episkopos* of the *Leif Erikson* cabal. Anyone with lingering spiritual or psychological problems, take them to her.' He lunged across the room, hugged the girl, laughed with her happily for a moment and placed his golden apple ring on her finger. 'Now I don't have to meditate every day,' he shouted joyously, 'and I'll have more time for some thinking.'

In the next two days, as the *Leif Erikson* slowly crossed the Sea of Valusia and approached the Danube, George discovered that Hagbard had, indeed, put all his mystical trappings behind him. He spoke only of technical matters concerning the submarine, or other mundane subjects, and was sublimely unconcerned with the role-playing, role-changing and other mind-blowing tactics that had previously made up his persona. What emerged – the new Hagbard, or the old Hagbard of days before his adoption of guru-hood – was a tough, pragmatic, middle-aged engineer, with wide intelligence and interests, an overwhelming kindness and generosity, and many small symptoms of nervousness, anxiety and overwork. But mostly he seemed happy, and George realized that the euphoria derived from his having dropped an enormous burden.

Miss Portinari, meanwhile, had lost the self-effacing

quality that made her so eminently forgettable before, and, from the moment Hagbard passed her the ring, she was as remote and gnomic as an Etruscan sybil. George, in fact, found that he was a little afraid of her – an annoying sensation, since he thought he had transcended fear when he found that the Robot was, left to itself, neither cowardly nor homicidal.

George tried to discuss his feelings with Hagbard once, when they happened to be seated together at dinner on April 28. 'I don't know where my head is at anymore,' he said tentatively.

'Well, in the immortal words of Marx, putta your hat on your neck, then,' Hagbard grinned.

'No, seriously,' George murmured as Hagbard hacked at a steak. 'I don't feel really awakened or enlightened or whatever. I feel like K. in *The Castle:* I've seen it once, but I don't know how to get back there.'

'Why do you *want* to get back?' Hagbard asked. 'I'm damned glad to be out of it all. It's harder work than coal mining.' He munched placidly, obviously bored by the direction of the conversation.

'That's not true,' George protested. 'Part of you is still there, and always will be. You've just given up being a guide for others.'

'I'm *trying* to give up,' Hagbard said pointedly. 'Some people seem to be trying to reenlist me. Sorry. I'm not a German shepherd or a draftee. *Non serviam,* George.'

George fiddled with his own steak for a minute, then tried another approach. 'What was that Italian phrase you used, just before you gave your ring to Miss Portinari?'

'I couldn't think of anything else to say,' Hagbard explained, embarrassed. 'So, as usual with me, I got arty and pretentious. Dante addresses his readers, in the First Canto of the *Paradiso,* "*O voi che siete in piccioletta barca*" – roughly, Oh, you who are sailing in a very small boat astern of me. He meant that the readers, not having had the Vision, couldn't really understand his words. I turned it around, "*O oi che siete in piccioletta barca,*" admitting I was behind her in understanding. I should get the Ezra Pound Award for hiding emotion in tangled erudition.

That's why I'm glad to give up the guru gig. I never was much better than second-rate at it.'

'Well, I'm still way astern of *you* . . .' George began.

'Look,' Hagbard growled. 'I'm a tired engineer at the end of a long day. Can't we talk about something less taxing to my depleted brain? What do you think of the economic system I outline in the second part of *Never Whistle While You're Pissing?* I've decided to start calling it techno-anarchism; do you think that's more clear at first sight than anarcho-capitalism?'

And George found himself, frustrated, engaged in a long discussion of non-interest-bearing currencies, land steward-ship replacing land ownership, the inability of monopoly capitalism to adjust to abundance, and other matters which would have interested him a week ago but now were very unimportant compared to the question which Zen masters phrased as 'getting the goose out of the bottle without breaking the glass' – or specifically, getting George Dorn out of 'George Dorn' without destroying GEORGE DORN.

That night, Mavis came again to his bed, and George said again, 'No. Not until you love me the way I love you.'

'You're turning into a stiff-necked prig,' Mavis said. 'Don't try to walk before you can crawl.'

'Listen,' George cried. 'Suppose our society crippled every infant's legs systematically, instead of our minds? The ones who tried to get up and walk would be called neurotics, right? And the awkwardness of their first efforts would be published in all the psychiatric journals as proof of the regressive and schizzy nature of their unsocial and unnatural impulse toward walking, right? And those of you who know the secret would be superior and aloof and tell us to wait, be patient, you'll let us in on it in your own good time, right? Crap. I'm going to do it on my own.'

'I'm not holding anything back,' Mavis said gently. 'There's no field until *both* poles are charged.'

'And I'm the dead pole? Go to hell and bake bagels.'

After Mavis left, Stella arrived, wearing cute Chinese pajamas. 'Horny?' she asked bluntly.

'Christ Almighty, yes!'

In ninety seconds they were naked and he was nibbling at her ear while his hand rubbed her pubic mat; but a saboteur was at work at his brain. 'I love you,' he thought, and it was not untrue because he loved all women now, knowing partially what sex was really all about, but he couldn't bring himself to say it because it was not totally true, either, since he loved Mavis more, much more. 'I'm awfully fond of you,' he almost said, but the absurdity of it stopped him. Her hand cupped his cock and found it limp; her eyes opened and looked into his enquiringly. He kissed her lips quickly and moved his hand lower, inserting a finger until he found the clitoris. But even when her breathing got deeper, he did not respond as usual, and her hand began massaging his cock more desperately. He slid down, kissing nipples and bellybutton on the way, and began licking her clitoris. As soon as she came, he cupped her buttocks, lifted her pelvis, got his tongue into her vagina and forced another quick orgasm, immediately lowering her slightly again and beginning a very gentle and slow return in spiral fashion back to the clitoris. But still he was flaccid.

'Stop,' Stella breathed. 'Let me do you, baby.'

George moved upward on the bed and hugged her. 'I love you,' he said, and suddenly it did not sound like a lie.

Stella giggled and kissed his mouth briefly. 'It takes a lot to get those words out of you, doesn't it?' she said bemusedly.

'Honesty is the worst policy,' George said grimly. 'I was a child prodigy, you know? A freak. It was rugged. I had to have some defense, and somehow I picked honesty. I was always with older boys so I never won a fight. The only way I could feel superior, or escape total inferiority, was to be the most honest bastard on the planet earth.'

'So you can't say "I love you" unless you mean it?' Stella laughed. 'You're probably the only man in America with *that* problem. If you could only be a woman for a while, baby! You can't imagine what liars most men are.'

'Oh, I've said it at times. When it was at least half true. But it always sounded like play-acting to me, and I felt it sounded that way to the woman, too. This time it just came out, perfectly natural, no effort.'

'That *is* something,' Stella grinned. 'And I can't let it go unrewarded.' Her black body slid downward and he enjoyed the esthetic effect as his eyes followed her – black on white, like the *yin-yang* or the Sacred Chao – what was the psychoses of the white race that made this beauty seem ugly to most of them? Then her lips closed over his penis and he found that the words had loosened the knot: he was erect in a second. He closed his eyes to savor the sensation, then opened them to look down at her Afro hairdo, her serious dark face, his cock slipping back and forth between her lips. 'I love you,' he repeated, with even more conviction. 'Oh, Christ, Oh, Eris, oh baby baby, I love you!' He closed his eyes again, and let the Robot move his pelvis in response to her. 'Oh, stop,' he said, 'stop,' drawing her upward and turning her over, 'together,' he said, mounting her, 'together,' as her eyes closed when he entered her and then opened again for a moment meeting his in total tenderness, 'I love you, Stella, I love,' and he knew it was so far along that the weight wouldn't bother her, collapsing, using his arms to hug her, not supporting himself, belly to belly and breast to breast, her arms hugging him also and her voice saying, 'I love you, too, oh, I love you,' and moving with it, saying 'angel' and 'darling' and then saying nothing, the explosion and the light again permeating his whole body not just his penis, a passing through the mandala to the other side and a long sleep.

The next morning, he and Stella fucked some more, wildly and joyously; they said 'I love you' so many times that it became a new mantra to him, and they were still whispering at breakfast. The problem of Mavis and the problem of reaching total enlightenment had both vanished from his mind. Enjoying bacon and eggs that seemed tastier than he had ever eaten before, exchanging pointless and very private jokes with Stella, George Dorn was at peace.

(But nine hours earlier, at that 'same' time, the Kachinas gathered in the center of the oldest city in North America, Orabi, and began a dance which an excited visiting anthropologist had never seen before. As he questioned various old men and old women among the People of Peace – which is what *ho-pi* means – he found that the dance was dedicated to She-Woman-Forever-Not-Change. He knew enough not to try to convert that title into his own grammar, since it represented an important aspect of the Hopi philosophy of Time, which is much like the Simon Moon and Adam Weishaupt philosophies of Time and nothing like what physics students learn, at least until they reach graduate level studies. Only four times, he was told, had this dance ever been necessary: four times when the many worlds were all in danger, and this was the time of the fifth and greatest danger. The anthropologist, who happened to be a Hindu named Indole Ringh, quickly jotted in his notebook: 'Cf. four yugas in *Upanishads*, Wagadu legend in Sudan, and Marsh's queer notions about Atlantis. This could be big.' The dance went on, the drums pounded monotonously, and Carmel, far away, broke into a sudden perspiration . . .)

And, in Los Angeles, John Dillinger calmly loaded his revolver, dropped it in his briefcase and set a Panama hat on his neatly combed silver-gray hair. He was humming a song from his youth: 'Those wedding bells are breaking up that old gang of mine . . .' I hope that pimp is where Hagbard says, he thought; I've only got eighteen hours before they declare martial law . . . 'Good-bye forever,' he hummed on, 'old fellows and pals . . .'

I saw the fnords the same day I first heard about the plastic martini. Let me be very clear and precise about this, since many of the people on this trip are deliberately and perversely obscure: I would not, *could not*, have seen the fnords if Hagbard Celine hadn't hypnotized me the night before, on the flying saucer.

I had been reading Pat Walsh's memos, at home, and listening to a new record from the Museum of Natural History. I was adding a few new samples to my collection of Washington-Weishaupt pictures on the wall, when the saucer appeared hovering outside my window. Needless to say, it didn't particularly surprise me; I had saved a little of the AUM, after Chicago, contrary to the instructions from ELF, and had dosed myself. After meeting the Dealy Lama, not to mention Malaclypse the Elder, and seeing that nut Celine actually talk to gorillas, I assumed my mind was a point of receptivity where the AUM would trigger something truly original. The UFO, in fact, was a bit of a letdown; so many people had seen them already, and I was ready for something nobody had ever seen or imagined.

It was even more a disappointment when they psyched me, or slurped me aboard, and I found, instead of Martians or Insect Trust delegates from the Crab Galaxy, just Hagbard, Stella Maris and a few other people from the *Leif Erikson.*

'Hail Eris,' said Hagbard.

'All hail Discordia,' I replied, giving the three-after-two pattern, and completing the pentad. 'Is this something important, or did you just want to show me your latest invention?'

The inside of the saucer was, to be trite, eerie. Everything was non-Euclidean and semitransparent; I kept feeling that I might fall through the floor and hurtle to the ground to smash myself on the sidewalk. Then we started moving and it got worse.

'Don't let the architecture disturb you,' Hagbard said. 'My own adaptation of some of Bucky Fuller's synergetic geometry. It's smaller, and more solid, than it looks. You won't fall out, believe me.'

'Is this contraption behind all the flying saucer reports since 1947?' I asked curiously.

'Not quite,' Hagbard laughed. 'That's basically a hoax. The plan was created in the United States government, one of the few ideas they've had without direct Illuminati inspiration since about the middle of Roosevelt's first term. A reserve measure, in case something happens to Russia and China.'

'Hi, baby,' I said softly to Stella, remembering San Francisco. 'Would you tell me, minus the Celine rhetoric and paradox, what the hell he's talking about?'

'The State is based on threat,' Stella said simply. 'If people aren't afraid of something, they'll realize they don't need that big government hand picking their pockets all the time. So, in case Russia and China collapse from internal dissension, or get into a private war and blow each other to hell, or suffer some unexpected natural calamity like a series of earthquakes, the saucer myth has been planted. If there are no earthly enemies to frighten the American people with, the saucer myth will immediately change. There will be "evidence" that they come from Mars and are planning to invade and enslave us. Dig?'

'So,' Hagbard added, 'I built this little gizmo, and I can travel anywhere I want without interference. Any sighting of this craft, whether by a radar operator with twenty years' experience or a little old lady in Perth Amboy, is regarded by the government as a case of autosuggestion – since they know they didn't plant it themselves. I can hover over cities, like New York, or military installations that are Top Secret, or any place I damned well please. Nice?'

'Very nice,' I said. 'But why did you bring me up here?'

'It's time for you to see the fnords,' he replied. Then I woke up in bed and it was the next morning. I made breakfast in a pretty nasty mood, wondering if I'd seen the fnords, whatever the hell they were, in the hours he had blacked out, or if I would see them as soon as I went out in the street. I had some pretty gruesome ideas about them, I must admit. Creatures with three eyes and tentacles, survivors from Atlantis, who walked among us, invisible due to some form of mind shield, and did hideous work for the Illuminati. It was unnerving to contemplate, and I finally gave in to my fears and peeked out the window, thinking it might be better to see them from a distance first.

Nothing. Just ordinary sleepy people, heading for their buses and subways.

That calmed me a little, so I set out the toast and coffee and fetched in the *New York Times* from the hallway. I turned the radio to WBAI and caught some good Vivaldi, sat down, grabbed a piece of toast and started skimming the first page.

Then I saw the fnords.

The feature story involved another of the endless squabbles between Russia and the U.S. in the UN General Assembly, and after each direct quote from the Russian delegate I read a quite distinct 'Fnord!' The second lead was about a debate in Congress on getting the troops out of Costa Rica; every argument presented by Senator Bacon was followed by another 'Fnord!' At the bottom of the page was a *Times* depth-type study of the growing pollution problem and the increasing use of gas masks among New Yorkers; the most distressing chemical facts were interpolated with more 'Fnords.'

Suddenly I saw Hagbard's eyes burning into me and heard his voice: 'Your heart will remain calm. Your adrenalin gland will remain calm. Calm, all-over calm. You will not panic. You will look at the fnord and see it. You will not evade it or black it out. You will stay calm and face it.' And further back, way back: my first-grade teacher writing FNORD on the blackboard, while a wheel with a spiral design turned and turned on his desk, turned and turned, and his voice droned on, IF YOU DON'T SEE THE FNORD IT CAN'T EAT YOU, DON'T SEE THE FNORD, DON'T SEE THE FNORD . . .

I looked back at the paper and still saw the fnords.

This was one step beyond Pavlov, I realized. The first conditioned reflex was to experience the panic reaction (the activation syndrome, it's technically called) whenever encountering the word 'fnord.' The second conditioned reflex was to black out what happened, including the word itself, and just to feel a general low-grade emergency without knowing why. And the third step, of course, was to attribute this anxiety to the news stories, which were bad enough in themselves anyway.

Of course, the essence of control is fear. The fnords produced a whole population walking around in chronic low-grade emergency, tormented by ulcers, dizzy spells, nightmares, heart palpitations and all the other symptoms of too much adrenalin. All my left-wing arrogance and contempt for my countrymen melted, and I felt genuine pity. No wonder the poor bastards believe anything they're told, walk through pollution and overcrowding without complaining, watch their sons hauled off to endless wars and butchered, never protest, never fight back, never show much happiness or eroticism or curiosity or normal human emotion, live with perpetual tunnel vision, walk past a slum without seeing either the human misery it contains or the potential threat it poses to their security . . . Then I got a hunch, and turned quickly to the advertisements. It was as I expected: no fnords. That was part of the gimmick, too: only in consumption, endless consumption, could they escape the amorphous threat of the invisible fnords.

I kept thinking about it on my way to the office. If I

pointed out a fnord to somebody who hadn't been de-conditioned, as Hagbard deconditioned me, what would he or she say? They'd probably read the word before or after it. 'No *this* word,' I'd say. And they would again read an adjacent word. But would their panic level rise as the threat came closer to consciousness? I preferred not to try the experiment; it might have ended with a psychotic fugue in the subject. The conditioning, after all, went back to grade school. No wonder we all hate those teachers so much: we have a dim, masked memory of what they've done to us in converting us into good and faithful servants for the Illuminati.

When I arrived at my desk, Peter Jackson handed me a press release. 'What do you make of this?' he asked with a puzzled frown, and I looked at the mimeographed first page. The old eye-and-pyramid design leaped out at me. 'DeMolay Frères invites you to the premiere debut of the world's first plastic nude martini . . . ,' the press release declared. On second glance the eye in the triangle turned into the elliptical rim of a martini glass, while the pupil in the eye was actually the olive floating in the cocktail.

'What the hell is a plastic nude martini?' said Peter Jackson. 'And why would they invite us to a press party for one?'

'You can bet that it's nonbiodegradable,' said Joe.

'Which will make it very unfashionable with honky ecology freaks,' said Peter sarcastically.

Joe squinted at the design again. It could be a coincidence. But coincidence was just another word for synchronicity. 'I think I'll go,' he said. 'And what's that?' he added as his eye fell upon a half-unfolded poster on his desk.

'Oh, that came with the latest American Medical Association album,' said Peter. 'I don't want it, and I thought you might. It's time you took those pictures of the Rolling Stones off your wall. This is the age of constantly accelerating change, and a man who displays old pictures of the Stones is liable to be labeled a reactionary.'

Four owl-eyed faces stared at him. They were dressed in one-piece white suits, and three of them were joining extended hands to form a triangle, while the fourth, Wolfgang Saure, generally acknowledged to be the leader of the group, stood with his arms folded in the center. The picture was taken from above so that the most prominent elements were the four heads, while the outstretched arms clearly made the sides of the triangle, and the bodies seemed unimportant, dwindling away to nothing. The background was jet black. The three young men and the woman, with their smooth-shaven bony faces, their blond crew-cuts and their icy blue eyes seemed extremely sinister to Joe. If the Nazis had won the war and Heinrich Himmler had followed Hitler as ruler of the German Empire, kids like this would be running the world. And they almost were, in a different sense, because they had succeeded the Beatles and Stones as kings of music, which made them emperors among youth. Although long hair remained the general fashion, the kids had accepted the American Medical Association's antiseptic-clean appearance as a needed reaction against a style that had become too commonplace.

As Wolfgang himself had said, 'If you need an outward sign to know your own, you don't really belong.'

'They give me the creeps,' said Joe.

'What did you think when the Beatles first came out?' said Peter.

Joe shrugged. 'They gave me the creeps. They looked ugly and sexless and like teenage werewolves with all that hair. And they seemed to be able to mesmerize twelve-year-old girls.'

Peter nodded. 'The bulk of the AMA's fans are even younger. So you might as well start conditioning yourself to them now. They're going to be around for a long time.'

'Peter, let's you and me have lunch,' Joe said. 'Then I'm going to get some work done, and then I'm going to leave here at four to go to this plastic martini party. First of all, though, hold the chair for me while I take down the Stones and put up the American Medical Association.'

The DeMolay Frères group wasn't kidding, he found. There were martinis, olives and all (or cocktail onions for those who preferred them) in transparent plastic bags that were shaped like nude women. Pretty terrible taste the manufacturer had, thought Joe. Briefly, Joe wondered if it would be a good idea to infiltrate this company so as to get dosages of AUM in all the plastic nude martinis. But then he remembered the emblem and thought maybe this company was already infiltrated. But by which side?

There was a beautiful Oriental girl in the room. She had black hair that reached all the way down to the small of her back, and when she raised her arms to adjust a head ornament, Joe was surprised to see thick black hair in her armpits. Orientals did not normally have much body hair, he thought. Could she be some relation to the hairy Ainu of northern Japan? It intrigued him, turned him on as he'd never thought armpit hair would, and he went over to her to talk. The first thing he noticed was that the headband she wore had a golden apple with the letter K printed on it right in the center of her forehead. She is one of Us, he thought. His hunch about coming to this party was right.

'These martini bags sure have a silly shape,' said Joe.

'Why? Don't you care for nude women?'

'Well, this has about as much to do with nude women as any other piece of plastic,' said Joe. 'No, my point is that it's in such execrable taste. But, then, all of American industry is nothing but a giant obscene circus to me. What's your name?'

The black eyes fixed his intently. 'Mao Tsu-hsi.'

'Any relation?'

'No. My name means "cat" in Chinese. His doesn't. His name is *Mao* but mine is *Mao*.' Joe was enchanted by her enunciation of the two different tones.

'Well, Miss Cat, You are the most attractive woman I've met in ages.'

She responded with a silent flirtation of her own and they were soon in a wonderfully interesting conversation – which he could never remember afterwards. Nor did he notice the pinch of powder she dropped into his drink. He began feeling strangely groggy Tsu-hsi took his arm and led him to the checkroom. They got their coats, left the building and hailed a cab. In the back seat they kissed for a long time. She opened her coat and he pulled the zipper that went all the way down the front of her dress. He felt her breasts and stroked her belly, then dropped his head into her bush. She was wearing no underwear. She draped her legs over his, using her coat to screen what was going on from the cab driver, and helped him expose his erect

penis. With a few quick, agile movements she had swept
her skirt out of the way, raised her little seat into the air
and slid her well-lubricated cunt down over his cock and
was fucking him sidesaddle. It could have been difficult and
awkward, but she was so light and well coordinated that
she managed to bring herself to orgasm easily and voluptu-
ously. She drew in her breath sharply through her teeth
and a shudder ran through her body. She rested her head
momentarily on his shoulder, then raised herself slightly
and helped Joe to a pleasant climax with a rotary motion
of her ass.

The experience, Joe realized, would have been more
exquisite a few months, or a few years, earlier. Now, with
his growing sensitivity, he was conscious of what had been
missing: the actual energetic contact. The effect of the
JAMs and the Discordians on him, he reflected, had been
paradoxical by ordinary standards. He was no more puri-
tanical than before they started tinkering with his nervous
system (he was less), but at the same time casual sex was
less appealing to him. He remembered Atlanta Hope's
diatribes against 'sexism' in her book *Telemachus Sneezed*
– the Bible of the God's Lightning Movement – and he
suddenly saw some weird kind of sense in her rantings.
'The Sexual Revolution in America was as much of a
fraud as the Political Revolutions in China and Russia,'
Atlanta had written with her usual exuberant capitalization;
she was, in a way, quite right. People today were still
wrapped in a cellophane of false ego, and even if they
fucked and had orgasms together the cellophane was still
there and no real contact had been made.

And yet if Mao was what he suspected she would know
this even better than he did. Was this quick, cool spasm
some kind of test or some lesson or demonstration? If so,
how was he supposed to respond?

And then he remembered that she had not given an
address to the driver. The cab had been waiting only for
them to take them to a predetermined place, for reasons
unknown.

I've seen the fnords, he thought; *now I'm going to see
more.*

The cab stopped on a narrow, heavily shadowed street

that seemed to be all empty stores, factory buildings, loading docks and warehouses.

With Miss Mao leading, they entered an old dilapidated-looking loft building with the aid of a key she had in her handbag, climbed some clanging cast-iron stairs, walked hand in hand down a long dark corridor and came at last through a series of anterooms, each better appointed than the last, to a splendid boardroom. Joe shook his head, amazed at what he saw, but there was something – he suspected a drug – that was keeping him docile and passive.

Around a table sat men and women costumed from various eras of human history. Joe recognized Indian, Chinese, Japanese, Mongol and Polynesian dress, also classical Greek and Roman, medieval and Renaissance. There were other outfits more difficult to recognize at first glance. A flying Dutch board meeting, Joe thought to himself. They were talking about the Illuminati, the Discordians, the JAMs and the Erisians.

A man wearing a steel breastplate and helmet with gold inlay and a neatly trimmed mustache and goatee said, 'It is now possible to predict with ninety-eight percent probability of accuracy that the Illuminati are setting up Fernando Poo for an international crisis. The question is, do we raid the island and get the records now, making sure they're not endangered, or do we wait and take advantage of the trouble as a cover for our raid?'

A man in a dragon-embroidered red silk robe said, 'There will be no way to take advantage of the trouble, in my opinion. It will seem like chaos on the surface, but underneath the Illuminati will have everything very much under control. Now is the time to move.'

A woman in a translucent silk blouse whose little vest did not hide her dark, rounded breasts, said, 'You realize this could be a lovely scoop for your magazine, Mr. Malik. You could send a reporter there to look into conditions on Fernando Poo. Equatorial Guinea has all the usual problems of a developing African nation. Will tribal rivalries flare up between the Bubi and the Fang, preventing the further development of national cooperation? Will the poverty of the mainland province lead to attempts to expropriate the wealth of Fernando Poo? And what of the army? What, for example, of a certain Captain Jesus Tequila y Mota? An interview with the captain might prove to be a journalistic coup three years from now.'

'Yes,' said a big woman in colourfully dyed furs who played incessantly with the carved leg bone of some large animal. 'We don't expect C. L. Sulzberger to grasp the importance of Fernando Poo until the crisis is upon the world. So· if advance warning is desirable – as we think it is – why not through *Confrontation*?'

'Is that why you asked me here?' said Joe. 'To tell me something is going to happen in Fernando Poo? Where the hell is Fernando Poo, anyway?'

'Look it up in an atlas when you get back to work. It's one of several volcanic islands off the coast of Africa,' said a dark-skinned, slit-eyed man wearing a buffalo hide decorated with feathers. 'Of course, you understand that you could only hint at the real forces at work there,' he added. 'For instance, we wouldn't want you to mention that Fernando Poo is one of the last outcroppings of the continent of Atlantis, you know.'

Mao Tsu-hsi was standing beside Joe with a glass containing a pinkish liquid. 'Here, drink this,' she said. 'It will sharpen your perceptions.'

A man in gold-braid-encrusted field marshal's uniform said, 'Mr. Malik is the next business in order on our agenda. We are to educate him, to some extent. Let's do it, to that extent.'

The lights in the room went out. There was a rustling at one end, and suddenly Joe was looking at a brightly lit movie screen.

WHEN ATLANTIS RULED THE EARTH

The title appears in letters that look like blocks of stone piled on top of one another to form a kind of step pyramid. It is followed by shots of the earth as it looked thirty thousand years ago, during the great ice ages, showing woolly mammoths, saber-toothed tigers and Cro-Magnon hunters, while a narrator explains that at the same time the greatest civilization ever known by man is flourishing on the continent of Atlantis. The Atlanteans do not know anything about good or evil, the narrator explains. However, they all live to be five hundred years old and have no fear of death. The bodies of all Atlanteans are covered with fur, as with apes.

After seeing various domestic scenes in Zukong Gimorlad-Siragosa, the largest and most central city on the continent (but not the capital, because the Atlanteans do not have a government), we move to a laboratory where the young (one hundred years old) scientist GRUAD is displaying a biological experiment to an associate, GAO TWONE. The experiment is a giant water-dwelling serpent-man. Gao Twone is impressed, but Gruad declares that he is bored; he wishes to change himself in some unexpected way. Gruad is already strange – unlike other Atlanteans, he is not covered with fur, but has only short blond hair on top of his head and a close-cropped beard. In comparison to other Atlanteans he seems hideously naked. He wears a high-collared pale green robe and gauntlets. He tells Gao Twone that he is tired of accumulating knowledge for the sake of knowledge. 'It's just another guise for the pursuit of pleasure, to which too many of our fellow Atlanteans devote their lives. Of course, there's nothing wrong with pleasure – it moves the energies – but I feel that there is something higher and more heroic. I have no name for it yet, but I know it exists.'

Gao Twone is somewhat shocked. 'You, as a scientist, can talk of *knowing* something exists when you have no evidence?'

Gruad is dejected by this and admits, 'My lens needs polishing.' But after a moment he bounces back. 'And yet, even though I have my moments of doubt, I think my lens really is clear. Of course, I must find the evidence. But even now, before I start, I feel that I know what I will find. We could be greater and finer than we are. I look at what I am and sometimes I despise myself. I'm just a clever animal. An ape who has learned to play with tools. I want to be much more. I say we can be what the lloigor are, and even more. We can conquer time and seize eternity, even as they have. I mean to achieve that or destroy myself in the attempt.'

The scene shifts to a banquet hall where INGEL RILD, a venerable Atlantean scientist, has called together prominent Atlanteans to celebrate a space research achievement, the production of a solar flare. Ingel Rild and his associates have developed a missile which, when it strikes the sun, can cause an explosion. He tells the marijuana-smoking gathering, 'We can control to the second the timing of the flare and to the millimeter the distance it will spring out from the sun. A flare of sufficient magnitude could burn our planet to a crisp. A smaller flare could bombard the earth with radiations such that the area closest to the sun would be destroyed, while the rest of our world would suffer drastic changes. Most serious of all, perhaps, would be the biological changes these excessive radiations would bring about. Life forms would be damaged and perhaps become extinct. New life forms would arise. All of nature would undergo a tremendous upheaval. This has happened naturally once or twice. It happened seventy million years ago when the dinosaurs were suddenly wiped out and replaced by mammals. We still have much to learn about the mechanism that produces spontaneous solar flares. However, to be able to cause them artificially is a step toward predicting and possibly controlling them. When that stage is reached, our planet and our race will be protected from the kind of catastrophe that destroyed the dinosaurs.'

After the applause, a woman named KAJECI asks whether it might not be disrespectful to tamper with 'our father, the sun.' Ingel Rild replies that man is a part of nature and what he does is natural and can't be construed as tampering. Now Gruad interrupts angrily, pointing out that he, an unattractive mutation, is the product of tampering with nature. He tells Ingel Rild that the Atlanteans do not truly understand nature and the order that controls it. He declares that man is subject to laws. All things in nature are, but man is different because he can disobey the natural laws that govern him. Gruad goes on, 'With humanity we can speak, as we speak of our own machines, in terms of performance expected and performance delivered. If a machine does not do what it is designed for, we try to correct it. We want it to do what it *ought* to do, what it *should* do. I think we have the right and the duty to demand the same of people – that they perform as they *ought* to and *should* perform.' An aged and merry-eyed scientist named LHUV KERAPHT interrupts, 'But people are not machines, Gruad.'

'Exactly,' Gruad answers. 'I have already considered that. Therefore, I have created new words, words even stronger than *should* and *ought*. When a person performs as he or she should and ought, I call that *Good;* and anything less than this I call *Evil*.' This outlandish notion is greeted with general laughter. Gruad tries to speak persuasively, conscious of his lonely position as a pioneer, trying desperately to communicate with the closed minds all around him. After further argument, though, he becomes threatening, declaring, 'The people of Atlantis do not live according to the law. In their pride, they strike the sun itself, and boast of it, as you have, Ingel Rild, this day. I say that if Atlanteans do not live according to the law, a disaster will befall them. A disaster that will shake the entire earth. You have been warned! Heed my words!' Gruad strides majestically out of the banquet hall, seizing his cloak at the door and sweeping it about him as he leaves. Kajeci follows him and tells him that she thinks she partly understands what he has been trying to say. The laws he speaks of are like the wishes of parents, and, 'The great bodies of the universe are our parents. Isn't that so?' Gruad's naked hand strokes Kajeci's furred cheek, and they go off into the darkness together.

Within six months Gruad has formed an organization called the Party of Science. Their banner is an eye inside a triangle which in turn is surrounded by a serpent with its tail in its mouth. The Party of Science demands that Atlantis publish the natural laws Gruad has discovered and make them binding on all with systems of reward and punishment to enforce them. The word 'punishment' is another addition to the Atlantean vocabulary coined by Gruad. One of Gruad's opponents explains to friends of his that it means torture, and everyone's fur bristles. Ingel Rild announces to a gathering of his supporters that Gruad has proven to his own satisfaction – and the demonstration runs to seventy-two scrolls of logical symbols – that sex is part of what he calls Evil. Only sex for the good of the community is to be permitted under Gruad's system, to keep the race alive.

A scientist called TON LIT exclaims, 'You mean we must be thinking about conception during the act? That's impossible. Men's penises would droop, and women's vaginas wouldn't get moist. It's like – well, it's like making the shrill mouth-music while you are urinating. It would take great training, if it can be done at all.' Ingel Rild proposes the formation of a Party of Freedom to oppose Gruad. Discussing Gruad's personality, Ingel Rild says he checked the genealogical records and found that several of the most agitated-energy people in all Atlantean history were among his ancestors. Gruad is a mutation, and so are many of his followers. The energy of normal Atlanteans flows slowly. Gruad's people are impatient and frustrated, and this is what makes them want to inflict suffering on their fellow humans.

Joe sat up with a jolt. If he understood that part of the movie, Gruad – evidently the first Illuminatus – was also the first *homo neophilus*. And the Party of Freedom, which seemed to be the origin of the Discordian and JAM movements, was pure *homo neophobus*. How the hell could that be squared with the generally reactionary attitude of current Illuminati policies, and the innovativeness of the Discordians and JAMs? But the film was moving on—

In a disreputable-looking tavernlike place where men and women smoke dope in pipes that they pass from one to another, while people grope in couples and groups in dark corners, SYLVAN MARTISET proposes a Party of Nothingness that rejects the positions of both the Party of Science and the Party of Freedom.

After this we see street fighting, atrocities, the infliction of punishment on harmless people by men wearing Gruad's eye-and-triangle badge. The Party of Freedom proclaims its own symbol, a golden apple. The fighting spreads, the numbers of the dead mount and Ingel Rild weeps. He and his associates decide on a desperate expedient – unleashing the lloigor Yog Sothoth. They will offer this unnatural soul-eating energy being from another universe its freedom in return for its help in destroying Gruad's movement. Yog Sothoth is imprisoned in the great Pentagon of Atlantis on a desolate moor in the southern part of the continent. The Atlantean electric plan bearing Ingel Rild, Ton Lit and another scientist drifts, trailing feathery sparks, to a landing in a flat field overgrown with gray weeds. Within the Pentagon, an enormous black stone structure, the ground is scorched and the air shimmers like a heat mirage. Flickers of static electricity run through the shimmering from time to time, and an unpleasant noise, like flies around a corpse, pervades the whole moor. The faces of the three Atlantean sages register disgust, sickness and terror. They climb the nearest tower and talk to the guard. Suddenly Yog Sothoth takes control of Ton Lit, speaking in an oily, rich, deep and reverberating voice, and asks them what they seek of him. Ton Lit lets out a terrible shriek and claps his hands over his ears. Froth slips from the side of his mouth, his fur bristles and his penis stands erect. His eyes are delirious and suffering, like those of a dying gorilla. The guard uses an electronic instrument that looks like a magician's wand topped with a five-pointed star to subdue Yog Sothoth. Ton Lit bays like a hound and leaps for Ingel Rild's throat. The electronic ray drives him back and he stands panting, tongue hanging loose, as the Pentagon first and then the ground begin to soften into asymptotic curves. Yog Sothoth chants, 'Ia-nggh-ha-nggh-ha-nggh-fthagn! Ia-nggh-ha-nggh-ha-nggh-hgual! The blood is the life . . . The blood is the life . . .' All faces, bodies and perspectives are skewed and there is a greenish tinge on everything. Suddenly the guard strikes the nearest wall of the Pentagon directly with his electronic wand and Ton Lit shrieks, human intelligence coming back into his eyes together with great shame and revulsion. The three sages flee the Pentagon under a sky slowly turning back to its normal shape and color. The laughter of Yog Sothoth follows them. They decide that they cannot release the lloigor.

Meanwhile Gruad has called his closest followers, known as the Unbroken Circle of Gruad, to announce that Kajeci has conceived. Then he shows them a group of manlike creatures with green, scaly skin, wearing long black cloaks

and black skullcaps with scarlet plumes. These he calls his
Ophidians. Since Atlanteans have a kind of instinctive
check on themselves that prevents them from killing except
in blind fury, Gruad has developed these synthetic hu-
manoids from the serpent, which he has found to be the
most intelligent of all reptiles. They will have no hesitation about destroying men and will act only on Gruad's
command. Some of his followers protest, and Gruad explains that this is not really killing. He says, 'Atlanteans
who will not accept the teachings of the Party of Science
are swinish beings. They are a sort of robot who has no
inner spiritual substance to control it. Our bodies, however,
are deceived into feeling as if they are our own kind, and
we cannot raise our hands against them. Now, however,
the light of science has given us hands to raise.' At this
meeting Gruad also addresses his men for the first time as
the 'illuminated ones.'

At the next meeting of the Party of Freedom the Ophidians attack, using iron bars to club people to death and
slashing throats with their fangs. Then the Party of Freedom holds a funeral for a dozen of its dead at which Ingel
Rild gives an oration describing the ways in which the
struggle between Gruad's followers and the other Atlanteans is changing the character of all human beings:

'Hitherto, Atlanteans have enjoyed knowledge but not
worried over the fact that there is much that we do not
know. We are conservative and indifferent to new ideas,
we have no inner conflicts and we feel like doing the things
that seem wise to us. We think that the things we feel like
doing will usually work out for the best. We consider pain
and pleasure a single phenomenon, which we call sensation, and we respond to unavoidable pain by relaxing or
becoming ecstatic. We do not fear death. We can read each
other's minds because we are in touch with all the energies
of our bodies. The followers of Gruad have lost that ability,
and they are thankful that they have. The Scientists dote
on new things and new ideas. This love of the new thing is
a matter of genetic manipulation. Gruad is even encouraging people in their twenties to have children, though it
is our custom never to have children before we reach a
hundred. The generations of Gruad's followers come thick

and fast, and they are not like us. They agonize over their ignorance. They are full of uncertainty and inner conflict between what they should do and what they feel like doing. The children, who are brought up on Gruad's teachings, are even more disturbed and conflict-filled than their parents. One doctor tells me that the attitudes and the way of life Gruad is encouraging in his people is enough to shorten their life spans considerably. And they are afraid of pain. They are afraid of death. And even as their lives grow shorter, they desperately seek for some means of achieving immortality.'

Gruad tells a meeting of his Unbroken Circle that the time has come to intensify the struggle. If they can't rule the Atlanteans, they will destroy Atlantis. 'Atlantis will be destroyed by light,' says Gruad. 'By the light of the sun.' Gruad introduces the worship of the sun to his followers. He reveals the existence of gods and goddesses. 'They are all energy, conscious energy,' says Gruad. 'This conscious and powerfully directed and focused pure energy I call spirit. All motion is spirit. All light is spirit. All spirit is light.'

Under Gruad's direction, the Party of Science builds a great pyramid, thousands of feet high. It is in two halves; the upper half, made of an indestructible ceramic substance and inscribed with a terrible staring eye, floats five hundred feet above the base, held in place by antigravity generators.

A band of men and women led by LILITH VELKOR, chief spokeswoman for the Party of Nothingness, gathers at the base of the great pyramid and laughs at it. They carry Nothingarian signs:

DON'T CLEAN OUR LENSES, GRUAD—
GET THE CRACK OUT OF YOUR OWN

EVERY TIME I HEAR THE WORD 'PROGRESS' MY
FUR BRISTLES

THE SUN SUCKS

FREEDOM DEFINED IS FREEDOM DENIED

THE MESSAGE ON THIS
SIGN IS A FLAT LIE

Lilith Velkor addresses the Nothingarians, satirizing all Gruad's beliefs, claiming that the most powerful god is a crazy woman and she is the goddess of chaos. To the accompaniment of laughter she declares, 'Gruad says the sun is the eye of the sun god. That's more of his notion that males are superior and reason and order are superior. Actually, the sun is a giant golden apple which is the plaything of the goddess of chaos. And it's the property of anyone she thinks is fair enough to deserve it.' Suddenly a band of Ophidians attacks followers of Lilith Velkor and kills several of them. Lilith Velkor leads her people in an unprecedented attack on the Ophidians. They storm up the side of the great pyramid and throw the Ophidians down to the street, killing them. Amazingly, they succeed in wiping out all the Ophidians. Gruad declares that Lilith Velkor must die. When the opportunity presents itself, his men seize her and take her to a dungeon. There an enormous wheel has been constructed with four spokes in the shape

Lilith Velkor is crucified with ropes, upside down, on this device. Several members of the Party of Science lounge about, watching her die. Gruad enters, goes to the wheel and looks at the dying woman, who says, 'This is as good a day to die as any.' Gruad remonstrates with her, saying that death is a great evil and she should fear it. She laughs and says, 'All my life I have despised tradition and now I despise innovation also. Surely, I must be a most wicked example for the world!' She dies laughing. Gruad's rage is unbearable. He vows that he will wait no longer; Atlantis is too wicked to save and he will destroy it.

On a windswept plain in the northern region of Atlantis a huge teardrop-shaped rocket with graceful fins is poised on the launching pad. Gruad is in the control room making last-minute adjustments while Kajeci and Wo Topod argue with him. Gruad says, 'The human race will survive. It will survive the better purged of these Atlanteans, who are nothing but swine, nothing but robots, nothing but creatures

who do not understand good and evil. Let them perish.'
His finger strikes a red button and the rocket hurtles on its
way to the sun. It will take several days to reach there, and
meanwhile Gruad has gathered the Unbroken Circle on an
airship which takes them away from Atlantis and into the
huge mountains to the east in a region that will one day be
called Tibet. Gruad calculates that by the time the missile
strikes the sun, they will have been landed and underground
for two hours. The sun rides blinding yellow over the plains
of Atlantis. It is a beautiful day in Zukong Gimorlad-
Siragosa, the sun shining down on its slender, graceful
towers with spiderweb bridges spiraling among them, its
parks, its temples, its museums, its fine public buildings
and magnificent private palaces. Its handsome, richly furred
people gracefully stride amidst the beauties of the first and
finest civilization man has ever produced. Families, lovers,
friends and enemies, all unsuspecting what is about to happen, enjoy their private moments. A quintet plays the
melodius zinthron, balatet, mordan, swaz and fendrar. Over
all, however, the great eye on the side of Gruad's pyramid
glares horrid and red.

Suddenly the sun's body rages. Coiled flames, balls of
gas, roll out. The sun looks like a giant fiery arachnid or
octopus. One great flame comes rolling toward the earth,
burning red gas which turns yellow, then green, then blue,
then white.

There is nothing left of Zukong Gimorlad-Siragosa, except the pyramid with its upper segment now resting on
the base, the antigravity generators having been destroyed.
The baleful eye looks out over an absolutely flat, burnt-
black plain. The ground shakes, great cracks open. The
blackened area is a great circle, hundreds of miles in dia-
meter, beyond which is a dark brown and still desolate
wasteland. Thousands of cracks appear in the brittle surface of the continent, the strength of whose rocks has been
destroyed by the incredible heat of the solar flare. A tide
of mud starts crawling over the empty plain. It leaves only
the top of the pyramid, with the great eye, showing. Water
sweeps over the mud, at first sinking in and standing in
pools, then rising higher so that only the tip of the pyramid
sticks out of a great lake. Under the water enormous paral-

lel fissures open in the ground on either side of the blackened
central circle. The midsection of the continent, including
the pyramid, begins to sink. The pyramid falls into the
depths of the ocean with cliffs rising on either side of it to
the parts of Atlantis that still remain above the ocean.
They will remain for many thousands of years more, and
they will be the Atlantis remembered in the legends of men.
But the true Atlantis – high Atlantis – is gone.

Gruad stares into his crimson-glowing viewplate, watching the destruction of Atlantis. The light changes color,
from red to gray, and the face of Gruad turns gray. It is a
terrible face. It has aged a hundred years in the last few
minutes. Gruad may claim to be in the right, but deep
down he knows that what he has done isn't nice. And yet
deep down there is satisfaction, too, for Gruad, long tor-
tured by unreasonable guilt, now has something he can
really feel guilty about. He turns to the Unbroken Circle
and proposes, since it appears that the earth will survive
the cataclysm (he was not really sure that it would), that
they plan for the future. Most of them, however, are still
in shock. Wo Topod, inconsolable, stabs himself to death,
the first recorded time that a member of the human race
has deliberately killed himself. Gruad calls upon his followers to destroy all remains of the Atlantean civilization
and then, later, to build a perfect civilization when even
the ruins of Atlantis have been forgotten.

The great beasts that inhabited Europe, Asia and North
America die off as a result of mutations and diseases caused
by the solar flare. All relics of the Atlantean civilization
are destroyed. The people who were Gruad's erstwhile
countrymen are either killed or driven forth to wander the
earth. Besides Gruad's Himalayan colony there is one other
remnant of the High Atlantean era: the Pyramid of the
Eye, whose ceramic substance resisted solar flare, earthquake, tidal wave and submersion in the depths of the
ocean. Gruad explains that it is right that the eye should
remain. It is the eye of God, the One, the scientific-technical
eye of ordered knowledge that looks down on the universe
and by perceiving it causes it to be. If an event is not
witnessed, it does not happen; therefore, for the universe
to happen there must be a Witness.

Among the primitive hunters and gatherers a mutation has appeared that seems to be spreading rapidly. More and more people are being born without fur and with hair in the same pattern as Gruad's. The Hour of God's Eye has caused mutations in every species.

From the Himalayas the rocket ships of the Unbroken Circle, painted red and white, swoop out in squadrons. They sweep across Europe and land on the brown islands where Atlantis used to be. There they land and raid a city of refugees from the Atlantean disaster. They kill many of the leaders and intellectuals and herd the rest aboard the ships, fly to the Americas and deposit the helpless people on a vast plain. Far below their route of passage lies the Pyramid of the Eye at the bottom of the Atlantic. The base of the pyramid is covered with silt and the break where the upper part of the pyramid had floated on antigravity projectors is also covered. Still the pyramid itself towers over the mud around it, taller by three times than the Great Pyramid of Egypt, the building of which lies twenty-seven thousand years in the future. A vast shadow descends upon the pyramid. There is a suggestion in the darkness of the ocean bottom of giant tentacles, of sucker disks wide as the rims of volcanos, of an eye as big as the sun looking at the eye on the pyramid. Something touches the pyramid, and enormous as it is, it moves slightly. Then the presence is gone.

The pentagonal trap in which the people of Atlantis had heroically and brilliantly caught the dread ancient being Yog Sothoth has been, amazingly, undamaged by the catastrophe. Being on the southern plain, which was relatively uninhabited, the Pentagon of Yog Sothoth becomes the center of a migration of people who survived the disaster. Emergency cities are set up, those dying of radiation sickness are treated. A second Atlantis begins to take root. And then, from the Himalayas, the ships of the Unbroken Circle come swooping down on one of their raids. Lines of Atlantean men and women are marched to the walls of the Pentagon and there mowed down by laser fire. Then explosive charges are placed amid the heaps of bodies and the masked, uniformed men of the Unbroken Circle withdraw. There is a series of explosions; horrid yellow smoke goes coiling up. The gray stone walls crumble. There is a moment of stillness, balance, tension. Then the piled-up boulders of one side of the wall fly apart as if thrust by the hand of a giant. An enormous claw print appears in the soft soil around the ruins of the Pentagon. The masked men of the Unbroken Circle race frantically for their ships and take off. The ships dart into the sky, stop suddenly, waver and plummet like stones to explosive crashes on the earth. The surviving refugees scream and scatter. Like a scythe going through wheat, death sweeps among them in great arcs as they run in massed mobs. Mouths open in soundless screams, they fall. Only a handful escapes. Over the scene a colossal reddish figure of indeterminate shape and number of limbs stands triumphant.

In the Himalayas, Gruad and the Unbroken Circle watch the destruction of the Pentagon and the massacre of the Atlanteans. The Unbroken Circle cheers, but Gruad strangely weeps. 'You think I hate walls?' he says. 'I love walls. I love any kind of wall. Anything that separates. Walls protect good people. Walls lock away the evil. There must always be walls and the love of walls, and in the destruction of the great Pentagon that held Yog Sothoth I read the destruction of all that I stand for. Therefore I am stricken with regret.'

At this the face of EVOE, a young priest, takes on a reddish glow and a demoniac look. There is more than a hint of possession. 'It is good to hear you say that,' he says to Gruad. 'No man yet has befriended me, though many have tried to use me. I have prepared a special place for your soul, oh first of the men of the future.' Gruad attempts to speak to Yog Sothoth, but the possession has apparently passed, and the other members of the Unbroken Circle praise a new beverage that Evoe has prepared, made of the fermented juice of grapes. At dinner, later that day, Gruad tries the new beverage and praises it, saying, 'This juice of grapes relaxes me and does not cause the disturbing visions and sounds that makes the herb the Atlanteans used to smoke so unpleasant for a man of conscience.' Evoe gives him more to drink from a fresh jar, and Gruad takes it. Before drinking he says, 'Any culture that arises in the next twenty thousand years or so is going to have the rot of Atlantis in it. Therefore I decree a noncultural time of eight hundred generations. After that we may allow man free reign on his propensity for building civilizations. The culture he builds will be under our guidance, with our ideas implicit in its every aspect, with our control at every stage. Eight hundred generations from now the new human culture will be planted. It will follow the natural law. It will have the knowledge of good and evil, the light that comes from the sun, the sun that blasphemers say is only an apple. It is no apple, I tell you, though it is a fruit, even as this beverage of Evoe's that I now quaff is from a fruit. From the grape comes this drink and from the sun comes the knowledge of good and evil, the separation of light and darkness over the whole earth. Not an apple, but the fruit of knowledge!' Gruad drinks. He puts down his glass, clutches his throat and staggers back. His other hand goes to his heart. He topples over and lies on his back, his eyes staring upward.

Naturally, everyone accuses Evoe of poisoning Gruad. But Evoe calmly answers that it was Lilith Velkor who did it. He was doing research on the energies of the dead and had learned how to take them into him. But sometimes the energies of the dead could take control of him, so that he would be just a medium through which they act. He cries, 'When you write this tragedy into the archives, you must say, not that Evoe the man did it, but Evoe-Lilith, possessed by the evil spirit of a woman. The woman did tempt me, I tell you! I was helpless.' The Unbroken Circle is persuaded, and agree that since Lilith Velkor and the crazy goddess she worshipped were responsible for Gruad's death, henceforward women must be subordinate to men so such evils will not be repeated. They decide to build a tomb for Gruad and to inscribe upon it, 'The First Illuminated One: Never Trust A Woman.' They decide that since the lloigor is loose they will offer sacrifices to it, and the sacrifices will be pure young women who have never lain with a man. Evoe seems to be taking control of the group and Gao Twone protests this. To prove his dedication to the true and the good, Evoe declares, he has had his penis amputated as a sacrific to the All-Seeing Eye. He pulls open his robe. All look at his truncated crotch and im-

mediately retch. Evoe goes on, 'Furthermore, it is decreed
by the Eye and Natural Law that all male children who
would be close to goodness and truth must imitate my
sacrifice, at least to the extent of losing the foreskin or
being cut enough to bleed.' Kajeci comes in at this point,
and they plan a great funeral, agreeing that they will not
burn Gruad as was the Atlantean custom, signifying that
one is dead forever, but will preserve his body, symbolizing
the hope that he is not really dead but will rise again.

There follow several thousand years of warfare between
the remnants of the Atlanteans and the inhabitants of
Agharti, the stronghold of the Scientists, who now call
themselves variously the Knowledgeable or the Enlightened
Ones. The last remnants of the Atlantean culture are destroyed. Great cities were built, then destroyed by nuclear
explosions. All the inhabitants of the city of Peos are killed
in one night by the eater of souls. Chunks of the continent
break off and sink into the sea. There are earthquakes and
tidal waves. Finally, only outcroppings like the cone-shaped
island of Fernando Poo rise alone from the sea where
Atlantis had been.

About 13,000 B.C. a new culture is planted on a hillside
near the headwaters of the Euphrates and it starts to
spread. A tribe of Cro-Magnons, magnificently tall, strong,
large-headed people, is marched at gunpoint down from
the snows of Europe to the fertile lands of the Middle East.
They are taken to the site chosen for the first agricultural
settlement and show how to plant crops. For several years
they do so while the Unbroken Circle's men guard them
with flame throwers. Their generations pass rapidly, and
once the new way of life has taken hold the Illuminated
Ones leave them alone. The tribe divides into kings, priests,
scribes, warriors, and farmers. A city surrounded by farms
rises up. The kings and priests are soft, weak and fat. The
peasants are stunted and dulled by malnutrition. The warriors are big and strong, but brutal and unintelligent. The
scribes are intelligent, but thin and bloodless. Now the city
makes war on neighboring tribes of barbarians. Being well
organized and technologically superior, the people of the
city win. They enslave the barbarians and plant other cities
nearby. Then a great tribe of barbarians comes down from

the north and conquers the civilized people and burns their
city. This is not the end of the new civilization, though. It
only revitalizes it. Soon the conquerors have learned to
play the roles of kings, priests and warriors, and now there
is a kind of nation consisting of several cities with a large
body of armed men who must be kept occupied. Marching
robotlike in great square formations, they set out over the
plain to find new peoples to conquer. The sun shines down
on the civilization created by the Illuminati. And below the
sea the eye on the pyramid glares balefully upward.

THE END

Lights flashed on suddenly. The screen rolled up into its
receptacle with a snap. Blinded, Joe rubbed his eyes. He
had a ferocious headache. He also had a ferocious need to
urinate at once, before his bladder exploded. He'd had an
awful lot of drinks at the plastic martini party, then made
love to that Chinese girl in the cab, then sat down to watch
this movie without once taking time out to go to the bathroom. The pain in his groin was excruciating. He imagined
it felt something like what Evoe, that fellow in the movie,
had experienced after he castrated himself.

'Where the hell is the john?' said Joe loudly. There was
no one in the room. While he was absorbed in the movie,
they, doubtless having seen it before, had crept away softly,
leaving him alone to watch the death of Atlantis.

'Christ's sake,' he muttered. 'Gotta take a leak. If I don't
find the bathroom right away I'll pee in my pants.' Then
he noticed a wastepaper can under the table. It was walnut
with a metal lining. He bent over and picked it up, sending
new tremors of anguish through a body on the verge of
bursting. He decided to use it as a receptacle, set it down
again, unzipped his fly, took out his dick and let go into
the can. What if they all came trooping back into the room
now, he thought. Well, he would be embarrassed, but what
the hell. It was their fault for springing this movie on him
without giving him a chance to make himself comfortable.
Joe looked somberly down into the foam.

'Piss on Atlantis,' he muttered. Who the hell were those
people he'd seen tonight? Simon and Padre and Big John

had never told him about a group like this. Nor had they ever said anything about Atlantis. But there was the clear implication, if this movie was to be believed, that the Ancient Illuminated Seers of Bavaria might better be called the Ancient Illuminated Seers of Atlantis. And that the word 'Ancient' meant a lot older than 1776.

It was clearly time to leave this place. He could try searching the offices, but he doubted whether he'd find anything, and, anyway, he was much too tired and hung over – not only from the alcohol he'd drunk, but also from the strange drug the Oriental girl had given him before the movie. Still, it had been a very nice drug. It had been Joe's habit since 1969, when he wasn't too busy and didn't have to get up early in the morning, to get stoned and watch late movies on television. He found this so enjoyable a pastime that he'd lost two girlfriends to it; they'd both wanted to go to bed when he was just settling down in front of the tube, laughing himself silly at the incredibly clever witticisms, marveling at the profundity of the philosophical aphorisms tossed off by the characters (such as Johnny's line in *Bitter Rice*: 'I work all week and then on Sundays I watch other people ride the merry-go-round' – what a world of pathos had been expressed in that simple summation of a man's life) or appreciating, as one wordsmith does another, the complex subtlety of the commercials and the secret links between them and the movies into which they were inserted (like the slogan: 'You can take the Salem out of the country but you can't take the country out of Salem,' in the middle of *The Wolf Man*). All of this capacity for appreciating movies had been raised to a new high with the drug Mao Tsu-hsi had given him, and added to this it was a full-color movie on a large screen uninterrupted by commercials or, come to think of it, by fnords – and commercials no matter how trickily interwoven with the plot of the movie did tend to *seem* like interruptions, even to one who was stoned enough to know better. It had been a great movie. The best movie of his life. He would never forget it.

Joe tried the knob of the boardroom door and it opened at once. He stopped, considering whether he should take out his pocket knife and carve 'Malik was here' or some

obscenity into the beautiful wood of the table. That would,
he felt in an obscure way, let them know that he knew
where they were at. But it would be a shame to spoil the
wood, and besides, he was dreadfully tired. He walked
through darkened outer corridors, staggered down the
stairs and let himself out into the street. Looking toward
the East River, he thought he could see light in the sky
over Queens. Was the sun coming up? Had he been there
that long?

A cab cruised by with its light on. Joe hailed it. Sinking
into the back seat as he gave the driver his home address,
he noticed that the man's name on his hack license was
Albert Feather.

> Well, here's that ladder now,
> Come on, let's climb.
> The first rung is yours,
> The rest are mine.

Funny, thought Lieutenant Otto Waterhouse of the
State's Attorney's Police. Every time things get hairy, that
damn song starts going through my head. I must be an
obsessive-compulsive neurotic. He'd first heard the song,
'To Be a Man' by Len Chandler, at the home of a chick he
was balling back in '65. It expressed pretty well for him his
condition as a member of the tribe. The tribe, that was
how he thought of black people; he'd heard a Jew refer to
the Jews that way, and he liked it better than that soul
brother shit. Deep down, he hated other blacks and he
hated being black. You had to climb, that was the thing.
You had to climb, each man alone.

When Otto Waterhouse was eight years old, a gang of
black kids on the South Side had beaten him, knifed him
and thrown him into Lake Michigan to drown. Otto didn't
know how to swim, but somehow he'd pulled himself along
the concrete pilings, clinging to rusty steel where there was
nothing to cling to, his blood seeping out into the water,
and he'd stayed there, hidden, till the gang went away.
Then he pulled himself along to a ladder, climbed up and
dragged himself onto the concrete pier. He lay there, al-

most dead, wondering if the gang would come back and
finish him.

Someone did come along. A cop. The cop nudged Otto's
body with his toe, rolled it over and looked down. Otto
looked up at the Irish face, round, pig-nosed and blue-
eyed.

'Oh, shit,' said the cop, and walked on.

Somehow Otto lived till morning, when a woman came
along and found him and called an ambulance. Years later,
it seemed logical enough to him to join the police force.
He knew the members of the gang that nearly killed him.
He didn't bother with them until after he got on the force.
Then he found cause to kill each of the gang members –
several of whom had by then become respectable citizens –
one by one. Most of them didn't know who he was or why
he was killing them. The number he killed made his reputation in the Chicago Police Department. He was a nigger
cop who could be trusted to deal with niggers.

Otto never did know who the cop was who'd left him
to die – he remembered the face, more or less, but they all
looked alike to him.

He had another oddly vivid memory, of a fall day in
1970 when he'd been walking through Pioneer Court and
had hassled a dude who was giving out free samples of –
of all things – tomato juice. Otto took a ten from the dude
and drank some tomato juice. The guy had a crew hair-
cut and wore horn-rimmed glasses. He didn't seem to mind
having to pay a bribe, and he looked at Otto with an odd
gleam in his eye as the tomato juice went down. For a moment, Otto thought the tomato juice might be poisoned.
There were cop haters everywhere; many people seemed to
have sworn to kill the 'pigs' as they called them. But dozens
of people had already drunk the juice and gone away
happy. Otto shrugged and walked off.

Thinking back over the strange changes that had come
over him, Otto always traced them back to that moment.
There had been something in the juice.

It wasn't till Stella Maris told him about AUM that he
realized how he'd been had. And by then it was too late.
He was a three-way loser, working for the Syndicate, the
Illuminati and Discordian Movement. The only way out

was down – down into the chaos with Stella pointing the way.

'Just tell me one thing, baby,' he said to her one afternoon as they lay naked together in his apartment in Hyde Park. 'Why did they pick you to contact me?'

'Because you hate niggers,' said Stella calmly, running her finger down his dick. 'You hate niggers worse than any white man does. That's why the way to freedom for you lies through me.'

'And what about you?' he said angrily, pulling away from her and sitting up in bed. 'I suppose you can't tell the difference between black and white. Black meat and white meat, it's all the same to you, ain't it, you goddamned *whore!*'

'You'd like to think so,' said Stella. 'You'd like to think only a nigger whore would lay you, a whore who'd lay anybody regardless of race. But you know you are wrong. You know that Otto Waterhouse, the black man who is better than all black men because he hates all black men, is a lie. It's you who can't tell the difference between black and white and thinks the black man should be where the white man is and hates the black man because he isn't white. No, I see color. But I see everything else about a person, too, baby. And I know that nobody is where they should be and everybody should be where they are.'

'Oh, fuck your goddam philosophy,' said Waterhouse. 'Come here.'

But he learned. He thought he'd learned everything Stella and Hagbard and the rest of them had to teach him. And that was a lot, piled on top of all that Illuminati garbage. But now they'd thrown him a total curve.

He was to kill.

The message came, as all the messages did, from Stella.

'Hagbard said to do this?'

'Yes.'

'And I suppose, if I go along with this, I'll be told why later on, or I'll figure it out for myself? Goddam, Stella, this is asking a lot, you know.'

'I know. Hagbard told me you have to do this for two reasons. First, for the honor of the Discordians, so that they will have respect.'

'He *sounds* like a wop for once. But he's right. I understand that.'

'Second. He said because Otto Waterhouse must kill a white man.'

'*What?*' Otto started to tremble in the phone booth. He picked nervously, without reading it, at a sticker that said, THIS PHONE BOOTH RESERVED FOR CLARK KENT.

'Otto Waterhouse must kill a white man. He said you'd know what that meant.'

Otto's hand was still shaking when he hung up. 'Oh, *damn*,' he said. He was almost crying.

So now on April 28 he stood at a green metal door marked '1723.' It was the service entrance to a condominium apartment at 2323 Lake Shore Drive. Behind him stood a dozen State's Attorney's police. All of them, like himself, were wearing body armor and baby-blue helmets with transparent plastic visors. Two were carrying submachine guns.

'All right,' said Waterhouse, glancing at his watch. It had amused Flanagan to set the time for the raid at 5:23 A.M. It was 5:22:30. 'Remember – shoot everything that moves.' He kept his back to the men so they would not see the damned tears that insisted on welling up in his eyes.

'Right on, lieutenant,' said Sergeant O'Banion satirically. Sergeant O'Banion hated blacks, but worse than that he hated filthy, lice-ridden, long-haired, homosexual, Communist-inspired Morituri bomb manufacturers. He believed that there was a whole disgusting nest of them, sleeping together, dirty naked bodies entwined, like a can full of worms, just on the other side of that green metal door. He could see them. He licked his lips. He was going to clean them out. He hefted the machine gun.

'Okay,' said Waterhouse. It was 5:23. Shielding himself with one gloved hand, he pointed his .45 at the lock on the door. The instructions given orally by Flanagan at the briefing were that they would not show a warrant or even knock before entering. The apartment was said to be full of enough dynamite to wipe out the entire block of luxury high-rise apartment houses. Presumably the kids, if they knew they were caught, would set them off. That way they could take a bunch of pigs with them, preserve their reputation for suicidal bravery, protect themselves from giving away any information, use the explosives and avoid having to live with the shaming knowledge that they'd been dumb enough to get caught.

O'Banion was imagining finding a white girl in the arms of a black boy and finishing them off with one burst from his machine gun. His cock swelled in his pants.

Waterhouse fired.

In the next instant he threw his weight against the door and smashed it open. He was in a hallway next to the kitchen. He walked into the apartment. His shoes rang on a bare tile floor. Tears ran down his cheeks.

'My God, my God, why have you forsaken me?' he sobbed.

'Who's that?' a voice called. Waterhouse, whose eyes had adjusted to the darkness, looked across the empty living room into the foyer, where Milo A. Flanagan stood silhouetted in the light from the exterior hall.

Waterhouse raised the heavy automatic in his hand to arm's length, sighted carefully, took a deep breath and held it and squeezed the trigger. The pistol blasted and kicked his hand and the black figure went toppling backwards into the startled arms of the men behind him.

A bat which had been sitting on a windowsill flew out the open window toward the lake. Only Waterhouse saw it.

O'Banion came clumping into the room. He took a bent-kneed stance and fired a burst of six rounds in the direction of the front door.

'Hold it!' Waterhouse snapped. 'Hold your fire. Something's wrong.' Something would really be wrong if the guys at the front door came through again, shooting. 'Turn on the lights, O'Banion,' Waterhouse said.

'There's somebody in here shooting.'

'We're standing here talking, O'Banion. No one is shooting at us. Find a light switch.'

'They're gonna set off the bombs!' O'Banion's voice was shrill with fear.

'With the lights on, O'Banion, we'll see them doing it. Maybe we'll even be able to stop them.'

O'Banion ran to the wall and began slapping it with the

palm of one hand while he kept his machine gun cradled in the free arm. One of the other men who had followed O'Banion through the service entrance found the light switch.

The apartment was bare. There was no furniture. There were no rugs on the floor, no curtains on the windows. Whoever had been living here had vanished.

The front door opened a crack. Before they could start shooting Waterhouse yelled, 'It's all right. It's Waterhouse in here. There's nobody here.' He wasn't crying anymore. It was done. He had killed his first white man.

The door swung all the way open. 'Nobody *there*?' said the helmeted policeman. 'Who the hell shot Flanagan?'

'Flanagan?' said Waterhouse.

'Flanagan's dead. They got him.'

'There isn't anybody here,' said O'Banion, who had been looking through side rooms. 'What the hell went wrong? Flanagan set this up personally.'

Now that the light was on, Waterhouse could see that someone had drawn a pentagram in chalk on the floor. In the center of the pentagram was a gray envelope. Otto picked it up. There was a circular green seal on the back with the word ERIS embossed on it. Otto opened it and read:

> Good going, Otto. Now proceed at once to Ingolstadt, Bavaria. The bastards are trying to imminentize the Eschaton.
>
> S-M

Folding the note and shoving it into his pocket as he holstered his pistol with his other hand, Otto Waterhouse strode across the living room. He barely glanced down at the body of Milo A. Flanagan, the bullet hole in the center of his forehead like a third eye. Hagbard had been right. Despite all the advance terror and sorrow, once he'd done it, he didn't feel a thing. I have met the enemy and he is mine, he thought.

Otto pushed past the men crowded around Flanagan's body. Everyone assumed he was going somewhere to make some sort of report. No one had figured out who shot Flanagan.

By the time O'Banion had puzzled it out. Otto was already in his car. Six hours later, when they had set up blockades at the airports and railway terminals, Otto was in Minneapolis International Airport buying a ticket to Montreal. He had to fly back to Chicago, but he sat out the brief stopover at O'Hare International Airport aboard the plane, while his brother officers searched the terminals for him. Twelve hours later, carrying a passport supplied by Montreal Discordians, Otto Waterhouse was on his way to Ingolstadt.

'Ingolstadt,' said FUCKUP. Hagbard had programmed the machine to converse in reasonably good English this week. 'The largest rock festival in the history of mankind, the largest temporary gathering of human beings ever assembled, will take place near Ingolstadt on the shore of Lake Totenkopf. Two million young people from all over the world are expected. The American Medical Association will play.'

'Did you know or suspect before this that the American Medical Association, Wolfgang, Werner, Wilhelm and Winifred Saure, are four of the Illuminati Primi?' asked Hagbard.

'They were on a list, but fourteenth in order of probability,' said FUCKUP. 'Perhaps some of the other groups I suspected are Illuminati Veri.'

'Can you now state the nature of the crisis that we will face this week?'

There was a pause. 'There were three crises for this month. Plus several subcrises designed to bring the three major crises to a peak. The first was Fernando Poo. The world nearly went to war over the Fernando Poo coup, but the Illuminati had a countercoup in reserve and that resolved the problem satisfactorily. Heads of state are human and this feint has helped to make them jumpier and more irrational. They are in no shape to react wisely to the next two jolts. Unless you wish me to continue discussing the character structures of the present heads of state – which are important elements in the crises through which the world is passing – I will proceed to the next crisis. This is Las Vegas. I still do not know exactly what is going on there, but the sickness vibrations are still com-

ing through strongly. There is, I have deduced from re-
cently acquired information, a bacteriological warfare research center located in the desert somewhere near Las
Vegas. One of my more mystical probes came up with the
sentence, "The ace in the hole is poisoned candy." But
that's one of those things that we probably won't understand until we find out what's going on in Las Vegas by
more conventional means.'

'I've already dispatched Muldoon and Goodman there,'
said Hagbard. 'All right, FUCKUP, obviously the third crisis
is Ingolstadt. What's going to happen at that rock festival?'

'They intend to use the Illuminati science of strategic
biomysticism. Lake Totenkopf is one of Europe's famed
"bottomless lakes," which means it has an outlet into the
underground Sea of Valusia. At the end of World War II
Hitler had an entire S.S. division in reserve in Bavaria. He
was planning to withdraw to Obersalzburg and, with this
fanatically loyal division, make a glorious last stand in the
Bavarian Alps. Instead the Illuminati convinced him that
he still had a chance to win the war, if he followed their
instructions. Hitler, Himmler and Bormann fed cyanide to
all the troops, killing several thousand of them. Then their
bodies, dressed in full field equipment, were placed by
divers on a huge underground plateau near where the Sea
of Valusia surfaces as Lake Totenkopf. Their boots were
weighted at the bottom so that they would stand at attention. The airplanes, tanks and artillery assigned to the
division were also weighted and sunk along with the troops.
Many of them, by the way, knew that there was cyanide
in their last supper, but they ate it anyway. If the Fuehrer
thought it best to kill them, that was good enough for
them.'

'I can't imagine there would be much left of them after
over thirty years,' said Hagbard.

'You are wrong as usual, Hagbard,' said FUCKUP. 'The
S.S. men were placed under a biomystical protective field.
The entire division is as good as it was the day it was
placed there. Of course, the Illuminati had tricked Hitler
and Himmler. The real purpose of the mass sacrifice was to
provide enough explosively released consciousness energy
to make it possible to translate Bormann to the immortal

energy plane. Bormann, one of the Illuminati Primi of his day, was to be rewarded for his part in organizing World War II. The fifty million violent deaths of that war helped many Illuminati to achieve transcendental illumination and were most pleasing to their elder brothers and allies, the lloigor.'

'And what will happen at Ingolstadt during the festival?'

'The American Medical Association's fifth number at Woodstock Europa will send out biomystical waves that will activate the Nazi legions in the lake, and send them marching up the shore. They will be, in their resurrection, endowed with supernormal strength and energy, making them almost impossible to kill. And they will achieve even greater powers as a result of the burst of consciousness energy that will be released when they massacre the millions of young people on the shore. Then, led by the Saures, they will turn against Eastern Europe. The Russians, already made extremely nervous by the Fernando Poo incident, will think an army is attacking them from the West. Their old fear that Germany will once again, with the help of the capitalist powers, rise up and attack Russia and slaughter Russians for the third time in this century will become a reality. They will find that conventional weapons will not stop the resurrected Nazis. They will believe they are up against some new kind of American superweapon, that the Americans have decided to launch a sneak attack. The Russians will then start bringing superweapons of their own into play. Then the Illuminati will play their ace in the hole in Las Vegas, whatever that is.'

The voice of the computer, coming from Hagbard's Polynesian teakwood desk, was suddenly silent.

'What happens after that?' said Hagbard, leaning forward tensely. George saw perspiration on his forehead.

'It doesn't matter what happens after that,' said FUCKUP. 'If the situation develops as I project, the Eschaton will have been imminentized. For the Illuminati, that will mean the fulfillment of the project that has been their goal since the days of Gruad. A total victory. They will all simultaneously achieve transcendental illumination. For the human race, on the other hand, that will be extinction. The end.'

BOOK FOUR

BEAMTENHERRSCHAFT

Well, Hoover performed. He would have fought.
That was the point. He would have defied a few
people. He would have scared them to death. He
has a file on everybody.

—Richard Milhous Nixon

THE EIGHTH TRIP, OR HOD
(TELEMACHUS SNEEZED)

There came unto the High Chapperal one who had studied in the schools of the Purple Sage and of the Hung Mung Tong and of the Illuminati and of the many other schools; and this one had found no peace yet.

Yea: of the Discordians and the teachers of Mummu and of the Nazarene and of the Buddha he had studied; and he had found no peace yet.

And he spake to the High Chapperal and said: Give me a sign, that I may believe.

And the High Chapperal said unto him: Leave my presence, and seek ye the horizon and the sign shall come unto you, and ye shall seek no more.

And the man turned and sought of the horizon; but the High Chapperal crept up behind him and raised his foot and did deliver a most puissant kick in the man's arse, which smarted much and humiliated the seeker grievously.

He who has eyes, let him read and understand.

—'The Book of Grandmotherly Kindness,'
The Dishonest Book of Lies, by Mordecai
Malignatus, K.N.S.

The Starry Wisdom Church was not 00005's idea of a proper ecclesiastical shop by any means. The architecture was a shade too Gothic, the designs on the stained-glass windows a bit unpleasantly suggestive for a holy atmosphere ('My God, they must be bloody wogs,' he thought), and when he opened the door, the altar was lacking a proper crucifix. In fact, where the crucifix should have been he found instead a design that was more than suggestive. It was, in his opinion, downright tasteless.

Not High Church at all, Chips decided.

He advanced cautiously, although the building appeared deserted. The pews seemed designed for bloody reptiles, he observed – a church, of course, should be uncomfortable, that was good for the soul, but this was, well, gross. They probably advertise in the kink newspapers, he reflected with distaste. The first stained-glass window was worse from inside than outside; he didn't know who Saint Toad was, but if that mosaic with his name on it gave any idea of Saint Toad's appearance and predelictions, then, by God, no self-respecting Christian congregation would ever think of sanctifying him. The next feller, a shoggoth, was even less appetizing; at least they had the common decency not to canonize *him*.

A rat scurried out from between two pews and ran across the center aisle, right before Chip's feet.

Fair got on one's nerves, this place did.

Chips approached the pulpit and glanced up at the Bible. That was, at least, one civilized touch. Curious as to what text might have been preached last in this den of wogs, he scrambled up into the pulpit and scanned the open pages. To his consternation, it wasn't the Bible at all. A lot of bragging and bombast about some Yog Sothoth, probably a wog god, who was both the Gate and the Guardian of the Gate. Absolute rubbish. Chips hefted the enormous volume and turned it so he could read the spine. *Necronomicon*, eh? If his University Latin could be trusted, that was something like 'the book of the names of the dead.' Morbid, like the whole building.

He approached the altar, refusing to look at the abominable design above it. Rust – now what could one say of brutes who let their altar get rusty? He scraped with his thumbnail. The altar was marble, *and marble doesn't rust*. A decidedly unpleasant suspicion crossed his mind, and he tasted what his nail had lifted. Blood. Fairly fresh blood.

Not High Church at all.

Chips approached the vestry, and walked into a web. 'Damn,' he muttered, hacking at it with his flashlight – and something fell on his shoulder. He brushed if off quickly and turned the light to the floor. It started to run up his trouser leg and he brushed if off again, beginning to

breathe heavily, and stepped on it hard. There was a satis-
factory snapping sound and he stomped again to be sure.
When he removed his shoe and turned the light down
again, it was dead.

A damned huge ugly brute of a spider. Black gods,
Saint Toads, rats, mysterious and heathenish capitalized
Gates, that nasty-looking shoggoth character, and now
spiders. A buggering tarantula it looked like, in fact. Next,
Count Dracula, he thought grimly, testing the vestry door.
It slid open smoothly and he stepped back out of visible
range, waiting a moment.

They were either not home or cool enough to allow him
the next move.

He stepped through the door and flashed his light
around.

'Oh, God, no,' he said. 'No. God, *no*.'

'Good-bye, Mr. Chips,' said Saint Toad.

Did you ever take the underground from Charing Cross
to one of the suburbs? You know, that long ride without
stops when you're totally in the dark and everything seems
to be rushing by outside in the opposite direction? Relativity, the laboratory-smock people call it. In fact, it was
even more like going up a chimney than going forward in
a tunnel, but it was like both at the same time, if you
follow me. Relativity. A bitter-looking old man went by,
dressed in turn-of-the-century Yankee clothing, muttering
something about 'Carcosa.' An antique Pontiac car followed him, with four Italians in it looking confused – it
was slow enough for me to spot the year, definitely 1936,
and even to read the license plates, Rhode Island AW-
1472. Then a black man, not a Negro or a wog, but a really
truly black man, without a face and I'd hate to tell you
what he had where the face should have been. All the
while, there was this bleating or squealing that seemed to
say 'Tekeli-li! Tekeli-li!' Another man, English-looking
but in early 19th-century clothing; he looked my way, surprised, and said, 'I only walked around the horses!' I
could sympathize: I only opened a bleeding door. A giant
beetle, who looked at me more intelligently than any bug
I ever saw before – he seemed to be going in a different
direction, if there was direction in this place. A white-

haired old man with startling blue eyes, who shouted
'Roderick Usher!' as he flew by. Then a whole parade of
pentagons and other mathematical shapes that seemed to
be talking to each other in some language of the past or
the future or wherever they called home. And by now it
wasn't so much like a tunnel or even a chimney but a kind
of roller coaster with dips and loops but not the sort you
find in a place like Brighton – I think I saw this kind of
curve once, on a blackboard, when a class in non-Euclidean
geometry had used the room before my own class in Eng
Lit Pope to Swinb. and Neo-Raph. Then I passed a shoggoth or it passed me, and let me say that their pictures
simply do not do them justice: I am ready to go anywhere
and confront any peril on H.M. Service but I pray to the
Lord Harry I never have to get that close to one of those
chaps again. Next came a jerk, or cusp is probably the
word: I recognized something: Ingolstadt, the middle of
the university. Then we were off again, but not for long,
another cusp: Stonehenge. A bunch of hooded people,
right out of a Yank movie about the KKK, were busy
with some gruesome mummery right in the center of the
stones, yelling ferociously about some ruddy goat with a
thousand young, and the stars were all wrong overhead.
Well, you pick up your education where you can – now I
know, even if I can't tell any bloody academic how I know,
that Stonehenge is much older than we think. Whizz, bang,
we're off again, and now ships are floating by – everything
from old Yankee clippers to modern luxury liners, all of
them signaling the old S.O.S. semaphore desperately – and
a bunch of airplanes following in their wake. I realized that
part must be the Bermuda Triangle, and about then it
dawned that the turn-of-the-century Yank with the bitter
face might be Ambrose Bierce. I still hadn't the foggiest
who all those other chaps were. Then along came a girl, a
dog, a lion, a tin man and a scarecrow. A real puzzler, that:
was I visiting real places or just places in people's minds?
Or was there a difference? When the mock turtle, the
walrus, the carpenter and another little girl came along,
my faith in the difference began to crumble. Or did some
of those writer blokes know how to tap into this alternate
world or fifth dimension or whatever it was? The shoggoth

came by again (or was it his twin brother?) and shouted,
or I should say, gibbered, 'Yog Sothoth Neblod Zin,' and
I could tell that was something perfectly filthy by the tone
of his voice. I mean, after all, I can take a queer propo-
sition without biffing the offender on the nose – one must
be cosmopolitan, you know – but I would vastly prefer to
have such offers coming out of human mouths, or at the
very least out of mouths rather than orifices that shouldn't
properly be talking at all. But you would have to see a
shoggoth yourself, God forbid, to appreciate what I mean.
The next stop was quite a refrigerator, miles and miles of
it, and that's where the creature who kept up that howling
of 'Tekeli-li! Tekeli-li!' hung his hat. Or its hat. I shan't
attempt to do him, or it, justice. That *Necronomicon* said
about Yog Sothoth that 'Kadath in the cold waste hath
known him,' and now I realized that 'known' was used
there in the Biblical sense. I just hope he, or it, stays in
the cold waste. You wouldn't want to meet him, or it, on
the Strand at midday, believe me. His habits were even
worse than his ancestry, and why he couldn't scrape off
some of the seaweed and barnacles is beyond me; he was
rather like Saint Toad in his notions of sartorial splendor
and table etiquette, if you take my meaning. But I was off
again, the curvature was getting sharper and the cusps
more frequent. There was no mistaking the Heads where I
arrived next: Easter Island. I had a moment to reflect on
how those Heads resembled Tlaloc and the lloigor of Fernando Poo and then this kink's version of a Cook's Tour
moved on, and there I was at the last stop.

'Damn, blast and thunder!' I said, looking at Manolete
turning his veronica and Concepcion lying there with her
poor throat cut. 'Now that absolutely does tear it.'

I decided not to toddle over to the Starry Wisdom
Church this time around. There *is* a limit, after all.

Instead, I went out into Tequila y Mota Street and approached the church but kept my distance, trying to figure
where BUGGER kept the Time Machine.

While I was reflecting on that, I heard the first pistol
shot.

Then a volley.

The next thing I knew the whole population of Fernando

Poo – Cubans descended from the prisoners shipped there when it was a penal colony in the 19th century, Spaniards from colonial days, blacks, wogs, and whatnot – were on Tequila y Mota Street using up all the munitions they owned. It was the countercoup, of course – the Captain Puta crowd who unseated Tequila y Mota and prevented the nuclear war – but I didn't know that at the time, so I dashed into the nearest doorway and tried to duck the flying bullets, which were coming, mind you, as thick as the darling buds in May. It was hairy. And one Spanish bloke – gay as a tree full of parrots from his trot and his carriage, goes by waving an old cutlass out of a book and shouting, 'Better to die on our feet than to live on our knees!' – headed straightway into a group of Regular Army who had finally turned out to try to stop this business. He waded right into them, cutting heads like a pirate, until they shot him as full of holes as Auntie's drawers. That's your Spaniards: even the queers have balls.

Well, this wasn't my show, so I backed up, opened the door and stepped into the building. I just had a moment to recognize *which* building I had picked, when Saint Toad gave me his bilious eye and said, 'You again!'

The trip was less interesting this time (I had seen it before, after all) and I had time to think a bit and realize that old frog-face wasn't using a Time Machine or any mechanical device at all. Then I was in front of a pyramid – they missed that stop last time – and I waited to arrive back in the Hotel Durrutti. To my surprise, when there was a final jerk in the dimensions or whatever they were, I found myself someplace else.

00005, in fact, was in an enormous marbled room deliberately designed to impress the bejesus out of any and all visitors. Pillars reached up to cyclopean heights, supporting a ceiling too high and murky to be visible, and every wall, of which there seemed to be five, was the same impenetrable ivory-grained marble. The eyes instinctively sought the gigantic throne, in the shape of an apple with a seat carved out of it, and made of a flawless gold which gleamed the more brightly in the dim lighting; and the old man who sat on the throne, his white beard reaching almost to the lap of his much whiter robe, commanded attention when he spoke: 'If I may be trite,' he said in a resonant voice, 'you are welcome, my son.'

This still wasn't High Church, but it was a definite improvement over the digs where Saint Toad and his loathsome objets d'art festered. Still, 00005's British common sense was disturbed. 'I say,' he ventured, 'you're not some sort of mystic, are you? I must tell you that I don't intend to convert to anything heathen.'

'Conversion, as you understand it,' the aged figure told him placidly, 'consists of pounding one's own words into a man's ears until they start coming out of his mouth. Nothing is of less interest to me. You need have no fear on that ground.'

'I see.' 00005 pondered. 'This wouldn't be Shangri-La or some such place, would it?'

'This is Dallas, Texas, my son.' The old man's eyes bore a slight twinkle although his demeanor otherwise remained grave. 'We are below the sewers of Dealy Plaza, and I am the Dealy Lama.'

00005 shook his head. 'I don't mind having my leg pulled,' he began.

'I am the Dealy Lama,' the old man repeated, 'and this is the headquarters of the Erisian Liberation Front.'

'A joke's a joke,' Chips said, 'but how did you manage that frog-faced creature back in the Starry Wisdom Church?'

'Tsathoggua? He is not managed by us. We saved you from him, in fact. Twice.'

'Tsathoggua?' Chips repeated. 'I thought the swine's name was Saint Toad.'

'To be sure, that is one of his names. When he first appeared, in Hyperborea, he was known as Tsathoggua, and that is how he is recorded in the Pnakotic Manuscripts, the *Necronomicon* and other classics. The Atlantean high priests, Klarkash Ton and Lhuv Kerapht, wrote the best descriptions of him, but their works have not survived, except in our own archives.'

'You *do* put on a good front,' 00005 said sincerely. 'I suppose, fairly soon, you'll get around to telling me that I have been brought here due to some karma or other?' He was actually wishing there were some place to sit down. No doubt, it added to the Lama's dignity to sit while Chips had to stand, but it had been a hard night already and his feet hurt.

'Yes, I have many revelations for you,' the old man said.

'I was afraid of that. Isn't there some place where I can bring my arse to anchor, as my uncle Sid would say, before I listen to your wisdom? I'm sure it's going to be a long time in the telling.'

The old man ignored this. 'This is the turning point in history,' he said. 'All the forces of Evil, dispersed and often in conflict before, have been brought together under one sign, the eye in the pyramid. All the forces of Good have been gathered, also, under the sign of the apple.'

'I see,' 00005 nodded. 'And you want to enlist me on the side of Good?'

'Not at all,' the old man cried, bouncing up and down in his seat with laughter. 'I want to invite you to stay here with us while the damned fools fight it out aboveground.'

00005 frowned. 'That isn't a sporting attitude,' he said disapprovingly; but then he grinned. 'Oh, I almost fell for it, didn't I? You *are* pulling my leg!'

'I am telling you the truth,' the old man said vehemently. 'How do you suppose I have lived to this advanced age? By running off to join in every idiotic barroom brawl, world war, or Armageddon that comes along? Let me remind you of the street where we picked you up; it is entirely typical of the proceedings during the Kali Yuga. Those imbeciles are using live ammunition, son. Do you want me to tell you the secret of longevity, lad – *my* secret? I have lived so outrageously long because,' he spoke with deliberate emphasis, 'I don't give a fuck for Good and Evil.'

'I should be ashamed to say so, if I were you,' Chips replied coolly. 'If the whole world felt like you, we'd all be a sorry kettle of fish.'

'Very well,' the old man started to raise an arm. 'I'll send you back to Saint Toad.'

'Wait!' Chips stirred uneasily. 'Couldn't you send me to confront Evil in one of its, ah, more human forms?'

'Aha,' the old man sneered. 'You want the lesser Evil, is it? Those false choices are passing away, even as we speak. If you want to confront Evil, you will have to confront it on its own terms, not in the form that suits your own mediocre concepts of a Last Judgment. Stay here with me, lad. Evil is much more nasty than you imagine.'

'Never,' Chips said firmly. ' "Ours not to reason why, Ours but to do or die!" ' Any Englishman would tell you the same.'

'No doubt,' the old man snickered. 'Your countrymen are as fat-headed as these Texans above us. Glorifying that idiotic Light Brigade the way these bumpkins brag about their defeat at the Alamo! As if stepping in front of a steamroller were the most admirable thing a man could do with his time. Let me tell you a story, son.'

'You may if you wish,' 00005 said stiffly. 'But no cynical parable will change my sense of Right and Duty.'

'Actually, you're glad of the interlude; you're not all that eager to face the powers of Tsathoggua again. Let that pass.' The old man shifted to a more comfortable position and, still oblivious of Chips' tired shifting from leg to leg, began:

This is the story of Our lady of Discord, Eris, daughter of Chaos, mother of Fortuna. You have read some of it in Bullfinch, no doubt, but his is the exoteric version. I am about to give you the Inside Story.

Is the thought of a unicorn a real thought? In a sense, that is the basic question of philosophy—

I thought you were going to tell me a story, not launch into some dreary German metaphysics. I had enough of that at the University.

Quite so. The thought of a unicorn is a real thought, then, to be brief. So is the thought of the Redeemer on the Cross, the Cow who Jumped Over the Moon, the lost continent of Mu, the Gross National Product, the Square Root of Minus One, and anything else capable of mobilizing emotional energy. And so, in a sense, Eris and the other Olympians were, and are, real. At the same time, in another sense, there is only one True God and your redeemer in His only begotten son; and the lloigor, like Tsathoggua, are real enough to reach out and draw you into their world,

which is on the other side of Nightmare. But I promised
to keep the philosophy to a minimum.

You recall the story of the Golden Apple, in the exoteric
and expurgated version at least? The true version is the
same, up to a point. Zeus, a terrible old bore by the way,
did throw a bash on Olympus, and he did slight Our Lady
by not inviting Her. She did make an apple, but it was
Acapulco Gold, not metallic gold. She wrote Korhhisti,
on it, *to the prettiest one*, and rolled it into the banquet
hall. Everybody – not just the goddesses; that's a male
chauvinist myth – started fighting over who had the right
to smoke it. Paris was never called in to pass judgment;
that's all some poet's fancy. The Trojan War was just another imperialistic rumble and had no connection with
these events at all.

What really happened was that everybody was squab-
bling over the apple and working up a sweat and pushing
one another around and pretty soon their vibrations –
Gods have very high vibration, exactly at the speed of light,
in fact – heated up the apple enough to unleash some heavy
fumes. In a word, the Olympians all got stoned.

And they saw a Vision, or a series of Visions.

In the first Vision, they saw Yahweh, a neighboring god
with a world of his own which overlapped theirs in some
places. He was clearing the set to change its valence and
start a new show. His method struck them as rather bar-
barous. He was, in fact, drowning everybody – except one
family that he allowed to escape in an Ark.

'This is Chaos,' said Hermes. 'That Yahweh is a *mean*
mother', even for a god.'

And they looked at the Vision more closely, and because they could see into the future and were all (like
every intelligent entity) rabid Laurel and Hardy fans and
because they were zonked on the weed, they saw that
Yahweh bore the face of Oliver Hardy. All around him,
below the mountain on which he lived (his world was flat),
the waters rose and rose. They saw drowning men, drowning women, innocent babes sinking beneath the waves.
They were ready to vomit. And then Another came and
stood beside Yahweh, looking at the panorama of horrors
below, and he was Yahweh's Adversary, and, stoned as

they were, he looked like Stanley Laurel to them. And then Yahweh spoke, in the eternal words of Oliver Hardy: 'Now look what *you* made me do,' he said.

And that was the first Vision.

They looked again, and they saw Lee Harvey Oswald perched in the window of the Texas School Book Depository; and he, again, wore the face of Stanley Laurel. And, because this world had been created by a great god named Earl Warren, Oswald fired the only shots that day, and John Fitzgerald Kennedy was, as the Salvation Army charmingly expressed it, 'promoted to glory.'

'This is Confusion,' said Athena with her owl-eyes flashing, for she was more familiar with the world created by the god Mark Lane.

Then they saw a hallway, and Oswald-Laurel was led out between two policemen. Suddenly Jack Ruby, with the face of Oliver Hardy, stepped forward and fired a pistol right into that frail little body. And then Ruby spoke the eternal words, to the corpse at his feet: 'Now look what *you* made me do,' he said.

And that was the second Vision.

Next, they saw a city of 550,000 men, women and children, and in an instant the city vanished; shadows remained where the men were gone, a firestorm raged, burning pimps and infants and an old statue of a happy Buddha and mice and dogs and old men and lovers; and a mushroom cloud arose above it all. This was in a world created by the cruelest of all gods, *Realpolitik*.

'This is Discord,' said Apollo, disturbed, laying down his lute.

Harry Truman, a servant of Realpolitik, wearing the face of Oliver Hardy, looked upon his work and saw that it was good. But beside him, Albert Einstein, a servant of that most elusive and gnomic of gods, Truth, burst into tears, the familiar tears of Stanley Laurel facing the consequences of his own karma. For a brief instant, Truman was troubled, but then he remembered the eternal words: 'Now look what *you* made me do,' he said.

And that was the third Vision.

Now they saw trains, many trains, all of them running on time, and the trains criss-crossed Europe and ran 24 hours a day, and they all came to a few destinations that were alike. There, the human cargo was stamped, catalogued, processed, executed with gas, tabulated, recorded, stamped again, cremated and disposed.

'This is Bureaucracy,' said Dionysus, and he smashed his wine jug in anger; beside him, his lynx glared balefully.

And then they saw the man who had ordered this, Adolf Hitler, wearing still the mask of Oliver Hardy, and he turned to a certain rich man, Baron Rothschild, wearing the mask of Stanley Laurel, and they knew this was the world created by the god Hegel and the angel Thesis was meeting the demon Antithesis. Then Hitler spoke the eternal words: 'Now look what *you* made me do,' he said.

And that was the fourth Vision.

They did then look further and, lo, high as they were they saw the founding of a great republic and proclamations hailing new gods named Due Process and Equal Rights for All. And they saw many in high places in the republic form a separate cult and worship Mammon and Power. And the Republic became an Empire, and soon Due Process and Equal Rights for All were not worshipped, and even Mammon and Power were given only lip-service, for the true god of all was now the impotent What Can I Do and his dull brother What We Did Yesterday and his ugly and vicious sister Get Them Before They Get Us.

'This is Aftermath,' said Hera, and her bosom shook with tears for the fate of the children of that nation.

And they saw many bombings, many riots, many rooftop snipers, many Molotov cocktails. And they saw the capital city in ruins, and the leader, wearing the face of Stanley Laurel, taken prisoner amid the rubble of his palace. And they saw the chief of the revolutionaries look about at the rubble and the streets full of corpses, and then they heard him sigh, and then he addressed the leader, and he spoke the eternal words: 'Now look what *you* made me do,' he said.

And that was the fifth Vision.

And now the Olympians were coming down and they looked at each other in uncertainty and dismay. Zeus himself spoke first.

'Man,' he said, 'that was Heavy Grass.'

'*Far* fuckin out,' Hermes agreed solemnly.

'Tree fuckin mendous,' added Dionysus, petting his lynx.

'We were really fuckin *into* it,' Hera summed up, for all.

And they turned their eyes again on the Golden Apple and read the word Our Lady Eris had written upon it, that most multiordinal of all words, Korhhisti. And they knew that each god and goddess, and each man and woman, was in the privacy of the heart, the prettiest one, the fairest; the most innocent, the Best. And they repented themselves of not having invited Our Lady Eris to their party, and they summoned her forth and asked her, 'Why did you never tell us before that all categories are false and all Good and Evil a delusion of limited perspective?'

And Eris said, 'As men and women are actors on a stage of our devising, so are we actors on the stage devised by the Five Fates. You had to believe in Good and Evil and pass judgments on your creatures, the men and women below. It was a curse the Fates put upon you! But now you have come to the Great Doubt and you are free.'

The Olympians thereupon lost interest in the god-game and soon were forgotten by humanity. For She had shown them a great Light, and a great Light destroys shadows; and we are all, gods and mortals, nothing else but gliding shadows. Do you believe that?

'No,' said Fission Chips.

'Very well,' the Dealy Lama said somberly. 'Begone, back to the world of maya!'

And Fission Chips whirled head over heels into a vortex of bleatings and squealings, as time and space were given another sharp tug and, nearly a month later, head *over heels, the Midget is up and tottering across Route 91 as the rented Ford Brontosaurus shrieks to a stop and Saul and Barney are out the doors (every cop instinct telling them that a man who runs from an accident is hiding something) but John* Dillinger, *driving toward Vegas from the north,* continues to hum 'Good-bye forever old sweethearts and gals, God . . . bless . . . *you* . . .' *and the same tug in space-time grips Adam Weishaupt two centuries earlier, causing him to abandon his planned soft sell and* blurt out to an astonished Johann Wolfgang von Goethe, *'Spielen Sie Strip Schnipp-Schnapp?'* and Chips, hearing Weishaupt's words, is back in the graveyard at Ingolstadt as four dark figures move away in dusk.

'Strip Schnipp-Schnapp?' Goethe asks, putting hand on chin in a pose that was later to become famous, *'Das ist dein hoch Zauberwerk?'*

'Ja, ja,' Weishaupt says nervously, *'Der Zweck heiligte die Mittel.'*

Ingolstadt always reminds me of the set of a bleeding Frankenstein movie, and, after Saint Toad and that shoggoth chap and the old Lama with his wog metaphysics, it was no help at all to have an invisible voice ask me to join him in a bawdy card game. I've faced some weird scenes in H.M. Service but this Fernando Poo caper was turning out to be outright unwholesome, in fact *unheimlich* as these krauts would say. And, in the distance, I began to hear wog music, but with a Yank beat to it, and suddenly I knew the worst: that blasted Lama or Saint Toad or somebody had lifted nearly a month out of my life. I had walked into Saint Toad's after midnight on March 31 (call it April 1, then) and this would be April 30 or May 1. *Walpurgisnacht.* When all the kraut ghosts are out. And I was probably considered dead back in London. And if I called in and tried to explain what had happened, old W. would be downright *psychiatric* about the matter, oh, he'd be sure I was well around the bend. It was a rum go either way.

Then I remembered that the old Lama in Dallas had said he was sending me to the final battle between Good and Evil. This was probably it, right here, right now, this night in Ingolstadt. A bit breathtaking to think of that. I wondered when the Angels of the Lord would appear: bloody soon, I hoped. It would be nice to have them around when Old Nick unleashed the shoggoth and Saint Toad and that lot.

So I toddled out into the streets of Ingolstadt and started sniffing around for the old sulphur and brimstone.

And half a mile below and twelve hours earlier, George Dorn and Stella Maris were smoking some Alamout Black hash with Harry Coin.

'You haven't got a bad punch for an intellectual,' Coin said with warm regard.

'You're pretty good at rape yourself,' George replied, 'for the world's most incompetent assassin.'

Coin started to draw back his lips in an angry snarl, but the hash was too strong. 'Hagbard told you, Ace?' he asked bashfully.

'He told me most of it,' George said. 'I know that everybody on this ship once worked for the Illuminati directly or for one of their governments. I know that Hagbard has been an outlaw for more than two decades—'

'Twenty-three years exactly,' Stella said archly.

'That figures,' George nodded. 'Twenty-three years, then, and never killed anybody until that incident with the spider ships four days ago.'

'Oh, he *killed* us.' Harry said dreamily, drawing on the pipe. 'What he does is worse than capital punishment, while it's going on. I can't say I'm the same man I was before. But it's pretty bad until you come through.'

'I know,' George grinned. 'I've had a few samples myself.'

'Hagbard's system,' Stella said, 'is very simple. He just gives you a good look at your own face in a mirror. He lets you see the puppet strings. It's still up to you to break them. He's never forced anyone to do anything that goes against their heart. Of course,' she frowned in concentration, 'he does sort of maneuver you into places where you have to find out in a hurry just what your heart *is* saying to you. Did he ever tell you about the Indians?'

'The Shoshone?' George asked. 'The cesspool gag?'

'Let's play a game,' Coin interrupted, sinking lower in his chair as the hash hit him harder. 'One of us in this room is a Martian, and we've got to guess from the conversation which one it is.'

'Okay,' Stella said easily. 'Not the Shoshone,' she told George, 'the Mohawk.'

'You're not the Martian,' Coin giggled. 'You stick to the subject, and that's a human trait.'

George, trying to decide if the octopus on the wall was somehow connected with the Martian riddle, said, 'I want to hear about Hagbard and the Mohawk. Maybe that will

help us identify the Martian. You think up good games,'
he added kindly, 'for a guy who was sent on seven assassination missions and fucked up every one of them.'

'I'm dumb but I'm lucky,' Coin said. 'There was always
somebody else there blasting away at the same time. Politicians are *awfully* unpopular these days, Ace.'

This was a myth, Hagbard had confided to George. Until
Harry Coin had completed his course in the Celine System,
it was better if he believed himself the world's most unsuccessful assassin rather than face the truth: that he had
goofed only on his first job (Dallas, November 22, 1963)
and really had killed five men since then. Of course, even
if Hagbard wasn't a holy man any longer, he was still
tricky; maybe Harry had, indeed, missed every time. Perhaps Hagbard was keeping the image of Harry as mass
murderer in George's mind to see if George could relate
to the man's present instead of being hung up on his 'past.'

At least I've learned this much, George thought. The
word 'past' is always in quotes for me, now.

'The Mohawk,' Stella said, leaning back lazily (George's
male organ or penis or dick or whatever the hell is the
natural word, if there is a natural word, well, my cock,
then, my delicious ever-hungry cock rose a centimeter as
her blouse tightened on her breasts, Lord God, we'd been
humping like wart hogs in rutting season for hours and
hours and hours and I was still horny and still in love with
her and I probably always would be, but then again maybe I'm the Martian). Well, in fact, the old pussy hunter
didn't rise more than a millimeter, not a centimeter, and
he was as slow as an old man getting out of bed in January.
I had just about fucked until my brains came out my ears,
even before Harry brought in the hash and wanted to talk.
Looking for the Martian. Looking for the governor of
Dorn. Looking for the Illuminati. Krishna chasing his tail
around the curved space of the Einsteinian universe until
he disappears up his own ass, leaving behind a behind:
the back of the void: the Dorn theory of circutheosodom-
ognosis. 'Owned some land,' she continued. That beautiful
black face, like ebon melody: yes, no painter could show
but Bach could hint the delight of those purple-tinted lips
in that black face, saying, 'And the government wanted to

steal the land. To build a dam.' The inside of her cunt had
that purple hue to it, also, and there was a tawny beige in
her palm, like a Caucasian's skin, there were so many
delights in her body, and in mine, too, treasures that
couldn't be spent in a million years of the most tender and
violent fucking. 'Hagbard was the engineer hired to build
the dam, but when he found out that the Indians would be
dispossessed and relocated on less fertile ground, he refused
the job.' Eris, Eros spelled sideways. 'He broke his con-
tract, so the government sued him,' she said. 'That's how
he got to be a close friend with the Mohawk.'

Which was all pure crapperoo. Obviously, Hagbard had
gone to court as a lawyer for the Indians, but that one
touch of shame in him had kept him from admitting to
Stella that he had once been a lawyer, so he made up that
bit about being the engineer on the dam to explain how
he got involved in the case.

'He helped them move when they were dispossessed.' I
could see bronze men and women moving in twilight, a
hill in the background. 'This was a long time ago, back in
the '50s, I think. (Hagbard was a hell of a lot older than
he looked.) One Indian was carrying a racoon he said was
his grandfather. He was a very old man himself. He said
Grandfather could remember General Washington and
how he changed after he became President. (He would be
there tonight, that being who had once been George
Washington and Adam Weishaupt: he of whom Hitler
had said, "He is already among us. He is intrepid and
terrible, I am afraid of him.") Hagbard says he kept thinking of Patrick Henry, the one man who saw what had happened at the Constitutional Convention. It was Henry who
had looked at the Constitution and said right away, "I
smell a rat. It squints toward monarchy." The Old Indian,
whose name was Uncle John Feather, said that Grandfather, when he was a man, could speak to all animals. He
said the Mohawk Nation was more than the living, it was
the soul and the soil joined together. When the land was
taken, some of the soul died. He said that was why he
couldn't speak to all animals but only to those who had
once been part of his family.' The soul is in the blood,
moving the blood. It is in the night especially. Nutley is a

typical Catholic-dominated New Jersey town, and the Dorns are Baptists, so I was hemmed in two ways, but even as a boy I used to walk along the Passaic looking for Indian arrowheads, and the soul would move when I found one. Who was the anthropologist who thought the Ojibway believed all rocks were alive? A chief had straightened him out: 'Open your eyes,' he said, 'and you'll see *which* rocks are alive.' We haven't had our Frobenius yet. American anthropology is like virgins writing about sex.

'*I* know *who* the *Martian* is,' Coin crooned in a singsong. 'But I'm not telling. Not yet.' That man who was either the most successful or the most unsuccessful assassin of the 20th century and who had raped me (which was supposed to destroy my manhood forever according to some idiots) was smashed out of his skull and he looked so happy that I was happy *for* him.

'Hagbard,' Stella went on, 'stood there like a tree. He was paralyzed. Finally, old Uncle John Feather asked what was the matter.'

Stella leaned forward, her face more richly black against the golden octopus on the wall. 'Hagbard had foreseen the ecological catastrophe. He had seen the rise of the Welfare State, Warrior Liberalism (as he calls it) and the spread of Marxism out of Russia across the world. He saw why it all had to happen, with or without the Illuminati helping it along. He understood the Snafu Principle.'

He had worked all that night, after explaining to Uncle John Feather that he was troubled in his heart at the tragedy of the Mohawk (not mentioning the more enormous tragedy coming at the planet, the tragedy which the old man understood already in his own terms); hard work, carrying pitiful cheap furniture from cabins onto trucks, tying whole households' possessions with tough ropes; he was sweating and winded when they finished shortly before dawn. The next day, he had burned his naturalization papers and put the ashes in an envelope addressed to the President of the United States, with a brief note: 'Everything relevant is ruled irrelevant. Everything material is ruled immaterial. An ex-citizen.' The ashes of his Army Reserve discharge went to the Secretary of Defense with a briefer note: '*Non serviam.* An ex-slave.' That year's income tax form went to the Secretary of the Treasury, after he wiped his ass on it; the note said: 'Try robbing a poor box. *Der Einziege*.' His fury still mounting, he grabbed his copy of *Das Kapital* off the book-shelf, smiling bitterly at the memory of his sarcastic marginal notes, scrawled 'Without private property there is no private life' on the flyleaf, and mailed it to Josef Stalin in the Kremlin. Then he buzzed his secretary, gave her three months pay in lieu of notice of dismissal and walked out of his law office forever. He had declared war on all governments of the world.

His afternoon was spent giving away his savings, which at that time amounted to seventy thousand dollars. Some he gave to drunks on the street, some to little boys or little girls in parks; when the Stock Exchange closed, he was on Wall Street, handing out fat bundles of bills to the wealthiest-looking men he could spot, telling them, 'Enjoy it. Before you die, it won't be worth shit.' That night he slept on a bench in Grand Central Terminal; in the morning, flat broke, he signed on as A.B.S. aboard a merchant ship to Norway.

That summer he tramped across Europe working as tourist guide, cook, tutor, any odd job that fell his way, but mostly talking and listening. About politics. He heard that the Marshall Plan was a sneaky way of robbing Europe under the pretense of helping it; that Stalin would have more trouble with Tito than he had had with Trotsky; that the Viet Minh would surrender soon and the French would retake Indo-China; that nobody in Germany was a Nazi anymore; that everybody in Germany was still a Nazi; that Dewey would unseat Truman easily.

During his last walking tour of Europe, in the 1930s, he had heard that Hitler only wanted Czechoslovakia and would do anything to avoid war with England; that Stalin's troubles with Trotsky would never end; that all Europe would go socialist after the next war; that America would certainly enter the war when it came; that America would certainly stay out of the war when it came.

One idea had remained fairly constant, however, and he heard it everywhere. That idea was that more government, tougher government, more honest government was the answer to all human problems.

Hagbard began making notes for the treatise that later became *Never Whistle While You're Pissing*. He began with a section that he later moved to the middle of the book:

It is now theoretically possible to link the human nervous system into a radio network so that, micro-miniaturized receivers being implanted in people's brains, the messages coming out of these radios would be indistinguishable to the subjects from the voice of their own thoughts. One central transmitter, located in the nation's capital, could broadcast all day long what the authorities wanted the people to believe. The average man on the receiving end of these broadcasts would not even know he was a robot; he would think it was his own voice he was listening to. The average woman could be treated similarly.

It is ironic that people will find such a concept both shocking and frightening. Like Orwell's *1984*, this is not a fantasy of the future but a parable of the present. Every citizen in every authoritarian society already has such a 'radio' built into his or her brain. This radio is the little voice that asks, each time a desire is formed, 'Is it safe? Will my wife (my husband/my boss/my church/my community) approve? Will people ridicule and mock me? Will the police come and arrest me?' This little voice the Freudians call 'The Superego,' with Freud himself vividly characterized as 'the ego's harsh master.' With a more functional approach, Perls, Hefferline and Goodman, in *Gestalt Therapy*, describe this process as 'a set of conditioned verbal habits.'

This set, which is fairly uniform throughout any authoritarian society, determines the actions which will, and will not, occur there. Let us consider humanity a biogram (the basic DNA blueprint of the human organism and its potentials) united with a logogram (this set of 'conditioned verbal habits'). The biogram has not changed in several hundred thousand years; the logogram is different in each society. When the logogram reinforces the biogram, we have a liber-

tarian society, such as still can be found among some
American Indian tribes. Like Confucianism before it
became authoritarian and rigidified, American Indian
ethics is based on speaking from the heart and acting
from the heart – that is, from the biogram.

No authoritarian society can tolerate this. All
authority is based on conditioning men and women to
act from the logogram, since the logogram is a set
created by those in authority.

Every authoritarian logogram divides society, as it
divides the individual, into alienated halves. Those at
the bottom suffer what I shall call the *burden of
nescience*. The natural sensory activity of the biogram
– what the person sees, hears, smells, tastes, feels, and,
above all, what the organism as a whole, or as a
potential whole, *wants* – is always *irrelevant and immaterial*. The authoritarian logogram, not the field of
sensed experience, determines what is relevant and
material. This is as true of a highly paid advertising
copywriter as it is of an engine lathe operator. The
person acts, not on personal experience and the evalu-
ations of the nervous system, but on the orders from
above. Thus, personal experience and personal judgment being nonoperational, these functions become
also less 'real.' They exist, if at all, only in that fantasy
land which Freud called the Unconscious. Since nobody has found a way to prove that the Freudian
Unconscious really exists, it can be doubted that personal experience and personal judgment exist; it is an
act of faith to assume they do. The organism has become, as Marx said, 'a tool, a machine, a robot.'

Those at the top of the authoritarian pyramid, however, suffer an equal and opposite *burden of omniscience*. All that is forbidden to the servile class – the
web of perception, evaluation and participation in the
sensed universe – is demanded of the members of the
master class. They must attempt to do the seeing,
hearing, smelling, tasting, feeling and decision-making
for the whole society.

But a man with a gun is told only that which people
assume will not provoke him to pull the trigger. Since

all authority and government are based on force, the master class, with its burden of omniscience, faces the servile class, with its burden of nescience, precisely as a highwayman faces his victim. *Communication is possible only between equals.* The master class never abstracts enough information from the servile class to know what is actually going on in the world where the actual productivity of society occurs. Furthermore the logogram of any authoritarian society remains fairly inflexible as time passes, but everything else in the universe constantly changes. The result can only be progressive disorientation among the rulers. The end is debacle.

The schizophrenia of authoritarianism exists both in the individual and in the whole society.

I call this the Snafu Principle.

That autumn, Hagbard settled in Rome. He worked as a tourist guide, amusing himself by combining authentic Roman history with Cecil B. DeMille (none of the tourists ever caught him out); he also spent long hours scrutinizing the published reports of Interpol. His *Wanderjahr* was ending; he was preparing for action. Never subject to guilt or masochism, he had one reason only for his dispersal of his savings: to prove to himself that what he intended could be done starting from zero. When winter arrived, his studies were complete: Interpol's crime statistics had very kindly provided him with a list of those commodities which, either because of tariffs intended to stifle competition or because of 'morals' laws, could become the foundation of a successful career in smuggling.

One year later, in the Hotel Claridge on Forty-fourth Street in New York, Hagbard was placed under arrest by two U.S. narcotics agents named Calley and Eichmann. 'Don't take it too hard,' Calley said. 'We're only following orders.'

'It's okay,' Hagbard said, 'don't feel guilty. But what are you going to do with my cats?'

Calley knelt on the floor and examined the kittens thoughtfully, scratching one under the chin, rubbing the ear of the other. 'What's their names?' he asked.

'The male is called Vagina,' Hagbard said. 'The female
I call Penis.'

'The male is called *what*?' Eichmann asked, blinking.

'The male is Vagina, and the female is Penis,' Hagbard
said innocently, 'but there's a metaphysic behind it. First,
you have to ask yourself, which appeared earlier on this
planet, life or death? Have you ever thought about that?'

'This guy is nuts,' Calley told Eichmann.

'You've got to realize,' Hagbard went on, 'that life is a
coming apart and death is a coming together. Does that
help?'

('I never know whether Hagbard is talking profundity
or asininity,' George said dreamily, toking away.)

'Reincarnation works *backward in time*,' Hagbard went
on, as the narcs opened drawers and peered under chairs.
'You always get reborn into an earlier historical period.
Mussolini is a witch in the 14th century now, and catching
hell from the Inquisitors for his bum karma in this age.
People who "remember" the past are all deluded. The
only ones who really remember past incarnations remember
the *future*, and they become science-fiction writers.'

(A little old lady from Chicago walked into George's
room with a collection can marked Mothers March Against
Phimosis. He gave her a dime and she thanked him and
left. After the door closed, George wondered if she had
been a hallucination or just a woman who had fallen
through a space-time warp and landed on the *Leif
Erikson*.)

'What the hell are these?' Eichmann asked. He had been
searching Hagbard's closet and found some red, white and
blue bumper stickers. The top half of each letter was blue
with white stars, and the bottom half was red-and-white
stripes; they looked patriotic as all get-out. The slogan
formed this way was

LEGALIZE ABORTION
PREGNANCY IS A JEWISH PLOT!

Hagbard had been circulating these in neighborhoods
like the Yorkville section of Manhattan, the western
suburbs of Chicago, and other places where old-fashioned

Father Coughlin-Joe McCarthy style Irish Catholic fascism was still strong. This was a trial run on the logogram-biogram double-bind tactic out of which the Dealy Lama later developed Operation Mindfuck.

'Patriotic stickers,' Hagbard explained.

'Well, they *look* patriotic . . .' Eichmann conceded dubiously.

('Did a little woman from Chicago just walk through this room?' George asked.

'No,' Harry Coin said, toking again. 'I didn't see any woman from Chicago. But *I* know *who* the Martian *is*.')

'What the hell are these?' Calley asked. He had found some business-size cards saying RED in green letters and GREEN in red letters.

('When you're out of it all the way, on the mountain,' George asked, 'that's neither the biogram nor the logo-gram, right? What the hell is it, then?')

'An antigram,' Hagbard explained, still helpful.

'The cards are an antigram?' Eichmann repeated, be-wildered.

'I may have to place you under arrest and take you downtown,' Hagbard warned. 'You've both been very naughty boys. Breaking and entering. Pointing a gun at me – that's technically assault with a deadly weapon. Seiz-ing my narcotics – that's theft. All sorts of invasion of privacy. Very, very naughty.'

'*You* can't arrest *us*,' Eichmann whined. '*We're* sup-posed to arrest *you*.'

'Which is red and which is green?' Hagbard asked. 'Look again,' They looked and RED was now really red and GREEN was really green. (Actually, the tints changed according to the angle at which Hagbard held the card, but he wasn't giving away his secrets to them.) 'I can also change up and down,' he added. 'Worse yet, I clog zippers. Neither one of you can open your fly right now, for instance. My real gimmick, though, is reversing revolvers. Try to shoot me and the bullets will come out the back and you'll never use your good right hand again. Try it and see if I'm bluffing.'

'Can't you go a little easy on us, officer?' Eichmann

took out his wallet. 'A cop's salary ain't the greatest in the world, eh?' He nudged Hagbard insinuatingly.

'Are you trying to bribe me?' Hagbard asked sternly.

'Why not?' Harry Coin whined. 'You got nothing to gain by killing me. Take the money and put me off the sub at the first island you pass.'

'Well,' Hagbard said thoughtfully, counting the money.

'I can get more,' Harry added. 'I can send it to you.'

'I'm sure.' Hagbard put the money in his clam-shell ash-tray and struck a match. There was a brief, merry blaze, and Hagbard asked calmly, 'Do you have any other induce-ments to offer?'

'I'll tell you anything you want to know about the Illuminati!' Harry shrieked, really frightened now, realiz-ing that he was in the hands of a madman to whom money meant nothing.

'I know more about the Illuminati than you do,' Hag-bard replied, looking bored. 'Give me a philosophic reason, Harry. Is there any purpose in allowing a specimen like you to go on preying on the weak and innocent?'

'Honest, I'll go straight. I'll join your side. I'll work for you, kill anybody you want.'

'That's a possibility,' Hagbard conceded. 'It's a slim one, though. The world is full of killers and potential killers. Thanks to the Illuminati and their governments, there's hardly an adult male alive who hasn't had some military training. What makes you think I couldn't go out on the streets of any large city and find ten better-qualified killers than you inside an afternoon?'

'Okay, okay,' Harry said, breathing hard. 'I don't have no college education, but I'm not a fool either. Your men dragged me from Mad Dog Jail to this submarine. You want *something*, Ace. Otherwise, I'd be dead already.'

'Yes, I want something.' Hagbard leaned back in his chair. 'Now you're getting warm, Harry. I want something but I won't tell you what it is. You've got to produce it and show it to me without any clues or hints. And if you can't do that, I really will have you killed. I shit you not, fellow. This is my version of a trial for your past crimes. I'm the judge and the jury and you've got to win an acquittal without knowing the rules. How do you like that game?'

'It ain't fair.'

'It's more of a chance than you gave any of the men you shot, isn't it?'

Harry Coin licked his lips. 'I think you're bluffing,' he ventured finally. 'You're some chicken-shit liberal who doesn't believe in capital punishment. You're looking for an excuse to *not* kill me.'

'Look into my eyes, Harry. Do you see any mercy in them?'

Coin began to perspire and finally looked down into his lap. 'Okay,' he said hollowly. 'How much time do I have?'

Hagbard opened his drawer and took out his revolver. He cracked it open, showing the bullets, and quickly snapped it closed again. He slipped the safety catch – a procedure he later found unnecessary with George Dorn, who knew nothing about guns – and aimed at Harry's belly. 'Three days and three minutes are both too long,' he said casually. 'If you're ever going to get it, you're going to get it now.'

'Mama,' Coin heard himself exclaim.

'You're going to shit your pants in a moment,' Hagbard said coldly. 'Better not. I find bad smells offensive, and I might shoot you just for that. And mama isn't here, so don't call her again.'

Coin saw himself lunging across the room, the gun roaring in mid-leap, but at least trying to get his hands on this bastard's throat before dying.

'Pointless,' Hagbard grinned icily. 'You'd never get out of the chair.' His finger tightened slightly, and Coin's gut churned; he knew enough about guns to know how easy it was to have an accident, and he thought of the gun going off even before the bastard Celine intended it to, maybe even as he was on the edge of guessing the goddam riddle, the pointlessness of it was the final horror, and he looked again into those eyes without guilt or pity or any weakness he could exploit; then, for the first time in his life, Harry Coin knew peace, as he relaxed into death.

'Good enough,' Hagbard said from far away, snapping the safety back in place. 'You've got more on the ball than either of us realized.'

Harry slowly came back and looked at that face and those eyes. 'God,' he said.

'I'm going to give you the gun in a minute,' Hagbard went on. 'Then it's *my* turn to sweat. Of course, if you kill me you'll never get off this sub alive, but maybe you'll think that's worthwhile, just for revenge. On the other hand, maybe you'll be curious about that instant of peace – and you'll wonder if there's an easier way to get back there' and if I can teach it to you. Maybe. One more thing, before I toss you the gun. Everybody who joins me does it by free choice. When you said you'd come over to my side just because you were afraid of dying, you had no value to me at all. Here's the gun, Harry. Now, I want you to check it. There are no gimmicks, no missing firing pin or anything like that. No other tricks, either – nobody watching you through a peephole and ready to gun you down the minute you aim at me, or anything like that. I'm totally at your mercy. What are you going to do?'

Harry examined the gun carefully, and looked back at Hagbard. He had never studied kinesics and orgonomy as Hagbard had, but he could read enough of the human face and body to know what was going on in the other man. Hagbard had that same peace he himself had experienced for a moment.

'You win, you bastard,' Harry said, tossing the gun back. 'I want to know how you do it.'

'Part of you already knows,' Hagbard smiled gently, putting the gun back in the drawer. 'You just did it, didn't you?'

'What would he have done if I did block?' Harry asked Stella in present time.

'Something. I don't know. A sudden act of some sort that scared you more than the gun. He plays it by ear. The Celine System is never twice the same.'

'Then I was right, he *wouldn't* have killed me. It was all bluff.'

'Yes and no.' Stella looked past Harry and George, into the distance. 'He wasn't acting with you, he was manifesting. The mercilessness was quite real. There was no sentimentality involved in saving you. He did it because it's part of his Demonstration.'

'His Demonstration?' George asked, thinking of geometry problems and the neat Q.E.D. at the bottom, back in Nutley years and years ago.

'I've known Hagbard longer than she has,' Eichmann said. 'In fact, Calley and I were among the first people he enlisted. I've watched him over the years, and I still don't understand him. But I understand the Demonstration.'

'You know,' George said absently, 'when you two first came in, I thought you were a hallucination.'

'You never saw us at dinner, because we work in the kitchen,' Calley explained. 'We eat after everybody else.'

'Only a small part of the crew are former criminals,' Stella told George, who was looking confused. 'Rehabilitating a Harry Coin – pardon me, Harry – doesn't really excite Hagbard much. Rehabilitating policemen and politicians, and teaching them useful trades, is work that really turns Hagbard on.'

'But not for sentimental reasons,' Eichmann emphasized. 'It's part of his Demonstration.'

'It's his Memorial to the Mohawk Nation, too,' Stella said. 'That trial set him off. He tried a direct frontal assault that time, attempting to cut through the logogram with a scalpel. It didn't work, of course; it never does. Then he decided: "Very well, I'll put them where words can't help, and see what they do then." That's his Demonstration.'

Hagbard, actually – well, not *actually*; this is just what he told me – had started with two handicaps, intending to prove that they weren't handicaps. The first was that he would have a bank balance of exactly $00.00 at the beginning, and the second was that he would never kill another human being throughout the Demonstration. That which was to be proved (namely, that government is a hallucination, or a self-fulfilling prophecy) could be shown only if all his equipment, including money and people, came to him through honest trade or voluntary association. Under these rules, he could not shoot even in self-defense, for the biogram of government servants was to be preserved, and only their logograms could be disconnected, deactivated and defused. The Celine System was a consistent, although flexible, assault on the specific conditioned reflex – that

which compelled people to look outside themselves, to a
god or a government, for direction or strength. The servants of government all carried weapons; Hagbard's insane
scheme depended on rendering the weapons harmless. He
called this the Tar-Baby Principle ('You Are Attached To
What You Attack').

Being a man of certain morbid self-insight, he realized
that he himself exemplified the Tar-Baby Principle and
that his attacks on government kept him perpetually
attached to it. It was his malign and insidious notion that
government was even more attached to *him*; that his existence *qua* anarchist *qua* smuggler *qua* outlaw aroused
greater energetic streaming in government people than their
existence aroused in him: that, in short, he was the Tar
Baby on which they could not resist hurling themselves in
anger and fear: an electro-chemical reaction in which he
could bond them to himself just as the Tar Baby captured
anyone who swung a fist at it.

More (there was always more, with Hagbard), he had
been impressed, on reading Weishaupt's *Uber Strip
Schnipp-Schnapp, Weltspielen and Funfwissenschaft*, by
the passage on the Order of Assassins, which read:

> Surrounded by Moslem maniacs on one side and
> Christian maniacs on the other, the wise Lord Hassan
> preserved his people and his cult by bringing the art
> of assassination to esthetic perfection. With just a few
> daggers strategically placed in exactly the right throats,
> he found Wisdom's alternative to war, and preserved
> the peoples by killing their leaders. Truly, his was a
> most exemplary life of grandmotherly kindness.

'*Grossmutterlich Gefälligkeit*,' muttered Hagbard, who
had been reading this in the original German, 'now where
have I heard that before?'

In a second, he remembered: the *Mu-Mon-Kan* or
'Gateless Gate' of Rinzai Zen contained a story about a
monk who kept asking a Zen Master, 'What is the Buddha?' Each time he asked, he got hit upside the head with
the Master's staff. Finally discouraged, he left and sought
enlightenment with another Master, who asked him why he

had left the previous teacher. When the poor gawk explained, the second Master gave him the ontological hotfoot: 'Go back to your previous Master at once,' he cried, 'and apologize for not showing enough appreciation of his grandmotherly kindness!'

Hagbard was not surprised that Weishaupt evidently knew, in 1776 when *Uber Strip Schnipp-Schnapp* was written, about a book which hadn't yet been translated into any European tongue; he was astonished, however, that even the evil Ingolstadt *Zauberer* had understood the rudiments of the Tar-Baby Principle. It never pays to underestimate the Illuminati, he thought then – for the first time. He was to think it many times in the next two and a half decades.

On April 24, when he told Stella to deliver some Kallisti Gold to George's stateroom, Hagbard had already asked FUCKUP the odds that Illuminati ships would arrive in Peos within the time he intended to be there. The answer was better than 100-to-1. He thought about what that meant, then buzzed to have Harry Coin sent in.

Harry swaggered to a chair, trying to look insolent, and said, 'So you're the leader of the Discordians, eh?'

'Yes,' Hagbard said evenly, 'and on this ship, my word is law. *Wipe that silly grin off your face and sit up straight.*' He observed the involuntary stiffening of Harry's body before the man caught himself and remembered to maintain his slouch. Typical: Coin could resist the key conditioning phrases, but only with effort. 'Listen,' he said softly *'I will tell you only one more time'* – another Bavarian Fire Drill, that— 'This is my ship. You will address me as Captain Celine. You will *come to attention* when I talk to you. Otherwise . . .' he let the phrase trail off.

Slowly, Coin shifted to a more respectful kinesic posture – immediately modifying it by grinning more insolently. Well, that was good; the streak of rebellion ran deep. The breathing was not bad for a professional criminal: the only block seemed to be at the bottom of the exhalation. The grin was a defense against tears, of course, as with most chronic American smilers. Hagbard attempted a probe: Harry's father was the kind who pretended to consider the case and to toy with forgiveness before he would administer the thrashing.

'Is that better?' Harry asked, accentuating his respectful posture and grinning more sarcastically.

'A little,' Hagbard said, sounding mollified. 'But I don't know what I'm going to do with you, Harry. That's a bad bunch you've been mixed up with, very *un-American*.' He paused to get a reaction to the word; it came at once.

'Their money is as good as anyone's,' Harry said defiantly. His shoes crept backwards, as he spoke, and his neck decreased an inch – the turtle reflex, Hagbard called it; and it was a sure sign of the repressed guilt denied by the man's voice.

'You were born pretty poor, weren't you?' Hagbard asked, in a neutral tone.

'Poor? We was white niggers.'

'Well, I guess there's some excuse for you . . .' Hagbard watched: the grin grew wider, the body imperceptibly moved back toward slouching. 'But, to turn on *your own country*, Harry. That's bad. That's the lowest thing a human being can do. It's like turning against *your own mother*.' The toes curled inward again, tentatively. What did Harry's father say before wielding the belt? Hagbard caught it: 'Harry,' he repeated it gravely, 'you haven't been acting like a *proper white man*. You've been acting like you got *nigger blood*.'

The grin stretched to the breaking point and became a grimace, the body stiffened to the most respectful possible posture. 'Now, look here, sir,' Harry began, 'you got no call to talk to me that way—'

'And you're not even *ashamed*,' Hagbard ran over him. 'You don't show any *remorse*.' He shook his head with profound discouragement. 'I can't let you wander around loose, committing more crimes and treasons. I'm going to have to feed you to the sharks.'

'Listen, Captain Celine, sir, I've got a money belt under this shirt and it's full of more hundred-dollar bills than you ever saw at one time . . .'

'Are you trying to bribe me?' Hagbard asked sternly; the rest of the scene would be easy, he reflected. Part of his mind drifted to the Illuminati ships he would meet at

Peos. There was no way to use the Celine System without communicating, and he knew the crew would be 'protected' against him by some Illuminati variation on the ear wax of Ulysses' men passing the Sirens. The money would go in the giant clam-shell ashtray, a real shocker for a man like Coin, but what would he do about the Illuminati ships?

When the time came to produce the gun, he slipped the safety off viciously. If I'm going to join the ancient brotherhood of killers, he thought morosely, maybe I should have the stomach to start with a visible target. 'Three days and three minutes are both too long,' he said, trying to sound casual, 'if you're ever going to get it, you're going to get it now.' They would be at Peos in less than an hour, he thought, as Coin involuntarily cried 'Mama.' Like Dutch Schultz, Hagbard reflected; like how many others? It would be interesting to interview doctors and nurses and find out how many people passed out with that primordial cry for the All-Protector on their lips . . . but Harry finally surrendered, abdicated, left the robot running itself according to the biogram. He was no longer sitting in an insolent slouch, a respectful attention, a guilty cramp . . . He was simply sitting. He was ready for death.

'Good enough,' Hagbard said. 'You've got more on the ball than either of us realized.' The man would now transfer his submissive reflexes to Hagbard; and the next stage would be longer and harder, before he learned to stop playing roles entirely and just manifest as he had in the face of extinction.

The gun gambit was variation #2 of the third basic tactic in the Celine System; it had five usual sequels. Hagbard picked the most dangerous one – he usually did, since he didn't much like the gun gambit at all, and could only stomach it if he gave most of the subjects a chance at the other role. This time, however, he knew he had another motive: somewhere, deep inside, a coward in him hoped Harry Coin was crazier than he had estimated and would, in fact, shoot; that way Hagbard could avoid the decision awaiting him in Peos.

'You win, you bastard,' Coin's voice said; Hagbard came back and quickly rushed through a small verbal

game involving Hell images picked up from Harry's childhood. When he had Coin sent back to his room, under
light security, he slouched in his chair and rubbed his eyes
tiredly. He probed for Dorn and found the Dealy Lama
was on that channel, broadcasting.

—Leave the kid alone, he beamed. It's my turn now. Go
contemplate your navel, you old fraud.

A shower of rose petals was the nonverbal answer. The
Lama faded out. George went on rapping to himself on
the themes planted by the ELF leader: Odd, the big red
one. Eye think it was his I. The eye of Apollo. His luminous I.

—Aye, trust me not, Hagbard beamed. Trust not a man
who's rich in flax – his morals may be sadly lax. (Some of
my own doubts getting in here, he thought.) Her name is
Stella Maris. Black star of the seas. (I won't tell him who
she and Mavis really are.) George, I want you in the captain's control room.

George should start with variation #1, the *Liebestod* or
orgasm-death trip, Hagbard decided. Make him aware of
the extent to which he treats women as objects – and, of
course, give him some mystical hogwash later to gloss it
over temporarily, so the doubt will be pushed into the unconscious for a while. Yes: George was already on a porno-
graphy trip, very similar to Atlanta Hope and Smiling Jim
Treponema, except that in his case it was ego-dystonic.

'That was a good trick,' George said a few moment's
later in the captain's control room, 'how you got me up on
the bridge with that telepathy thing.'

Hagbard, still thinking about the decision in Peos, tried
to look innocent when he replied, 'I called you on the
intercom.' He realized that he was whistling and pissing at
once, worrying about Peos as well as about George, and
brought himself back sharply. 'Absurd' was the word in
George's mind – absurd innocence. Well, Hagbard thought,
I fucked that one up.

'You think I can't tell a voice in my head from a voice
in my ears?' George demanded. Hagbard roared with
laughter, totally in the present again; but after George had
been sent to the chapel for his initiation, the problem returned. Either the Demonstration failed, or the Demonstra-

tion failed. Double bind. Damned both ways. It was infuriating, but all the books had warned him long ago: 'As ye give, so shall ye get.' He had used the Celine System on quite a few people over nearly three decades, and now he was in the middle of a classic Celine Trap himself. There was no correct answer, except to give up trying.

When the moment came, though, he found that part of him had not given up trying. 'Ready for destruction of enemy ships,' said Howard.

Hagbard shook his head. George was remembering some crazy incident in which he had tried to commit suicide while standing by the Passaic River, and Hagbard kept picking up parts of that bum trip while trying to clear his own head. 'I wish we could communicate with them,' he said aloud, realizing that he was possibly blowing the guru game by revealing his inner doubts to George. 'I wish I could give them a chance to surrender ...'

'You don't want them too close when they go,' said Howard.

'Are your people out of the way?' Hagbard asked in agony.

'Of course,' the dolphin replied irritably. 'Quit this hesitating. This is no time to be a humanitarian.'

'The sea is crueler than the land,' Hagbard protested, but then he added 'sometimes.'

'The sea is cleaner than the land,' Howard replied. Hagbard tried to focus – the dolphin was obviously aware of his distress, and soon George would be (no: a quick probe showed George had retreated from the scene into the past and was shouting, 'You silly sons of bitches,' at somebody named Carlo). 'These people have been your enemies for thirty thousand years.'

'I'm not that old,' Hagbard said wearily. The Demonstration had failed. He was committed, and others with him were now committed. Hagbard reached out a brown finger, let it rest on a white button on the railing in front of him, then pressed it decisively. 'That's all there is to it,' he said quietly.

('Be a wise-ass then! When you start flunking half your subjects, perhaps you'll come back to reality.' A voice long, long ago ... at Harvard ... And once, in the South,

he had been moved by a very simple, a ridiculously simple,
Fundamentalist hymn:

> Jesus walked this lonesome valley
> He had to walk it all alone
> Nobody else could walk there for Him
> He had to walk it by Himself.

I will walk this lonesome valley, Hagbard thought bitterly, all by myself, all the way to Ingolstadt and the final
confrontation. But it's meaningless now, the Demonstration
has failed; all I can do is pick up the pieces and salvage
what I can. Starting with Dorn right here and right now.)

Hate, like molten lead, drips from the wounded sky . . .
they call it air pollution . . . August Personage dials slowly,
with the cunt-starved eyes of a medieval saint . . . 'God
lies!' Weishaupt cried in the middle of his first trip, 'God
is Hate!' . . . Harry Coin is crumpled in his chair . . .
George's head hangs at an angle, like a doll with a broken
spring . . . Stella doesn't move . . . They are not dead but
stoned . . .

Abe Reles blew the whistle on the entire Murder Inc.
organization in 1940 . . . He named Charley Workman as
the chief gun in the Dutch Schultz massacre . . . He gave
the details proving the roles of Lepke (who was executed)
and Luciano (who was imprisoned and, later, exiled) . . .
He kept his mouth shut about certain other things, however . . . But Drake was worried. He gave orders to Maldonado, who conveyed them to a capo, who passed them
on to some soldiers . . . Reles was guarded by five policemen but nonetheless he went out his hotel window and
spread like jam on the ground below . . . There were mut-
terings in the press . . . The coroner's jury couldn't believe
that five cops were on the take from the Syndicate . . .
Reles's death was declared to be suicide . . . But in 1943,
as the Final Solution moved into high gear, Lepke announced he wanted to talk before his execution . . . Tom
Dewey, alive by grace of the Dutchman's death, was
governor, and he granted a stay of execution . . . Lepke
spent twenty-four hours with Justice Department officials
and it was announced later that he refused to reveal any-

thing of significance . . . One of the officials had been brought back from State to work with Justice because of his background on Schultz and the Big Six Syndicate . . . He said little, but Lepke read a lot in his eyes . . . His name, of course, was Winifred . . . Lepke understood: as Bela Lugosi once said, there are worse things than dying . . .

In 1932 the infant son of aviator Charles Lindbergh Jr. was kidnapped . . . Already at that time, a heist of that dimension could not be permitted in the Northeast without the consent of a full-fledged don of the Mafia . . . Even a capo could not authorize it alone . . . The aviator's father, Congressman Charles Lindberg Sr., had been an outspoken critic of the Federal Reserve monopoly . . . Among other things, he had charged on the floor of Congress, 'Under the Federal Reserve Act panics are scientifically created; the present one is the first scientifically created one worked out as we figure a mathematical problem . . .' The go-between in delivering the ransom money was Jafsie Condon, Dutch Schultz's old high school principal . . . 'It's got to be one of them coincidences,' as Marty Krompier said later . . .

John Dillinger arrived in Dallas on the morning of November 22, 1963, and rented an Avis at the airport. He drove out to Dealy Plaza and scouted the terrain. The Triple Underpass where Harry Coin was supposed to stand when doing the job was under observation from a railroadman's shack, he noted; it occurred to him that the man in that shack would not have a long life expectancy. There would be a lot of other eyewitnesses, he realized, and the JAMs couldn't protect them all, not even with the help of the LDD. It was going to be bad all around . . . In fact, the man in the railroad shack, S. M. Holland, told a story that didn't jibe with the Earl Warren version, and later died when his car went off the road under circumstances that aroused speculation among those given to speculating; the coroner's jury called it an accident . . . Dillinger found his spot in the thickly wooded part of the Grassy Knoll and waited until Harry Coin appeared on the Underpass. He made himself relax and looked around to be sure that he was invisible from everywhere but a helicopter (there were no helicopters: the Illuminati's top double agent

within the Secret Service had seen to that). A movement in
the School Book Depository caught his eye. Something not
kosher up there. He swung his binoculars . . . and caught
another head, ducking quickly, atop the Dal-Tex building.
An Italian, very young . . . That was bad. If one of Maldonado's soldiers was here, either the Illuminati were
aware they had a double agent in their midst and had
hired two assassins, or else the Syndicate was acting on its
own. John panned back to the School Book Depository:
whoever that clown was, he had a rifle, too, and he was
being cagey: definitely not Secret Service.

This was a piss-cutter.

John's original plan was to plug Harry Coin before Coin
could get a bead on the young Hegelian from Boston. Now,
he had three men to knock out at once. It couldn't be done.
There was no human way of hitting more than two of those
targets – all three of them in different areas and at different
elevations – before the fuzz were swarming all over him.
The third would have time to do the job while that was
happening. It was what Hagbard called an existential *koan*.

'Shit, piss and industrial waste,' John muttered, quoting
another Celinism.

Well, save what you can, as Harry Pierpont always said
when a bank job went sour in the middle. Save what you
can and haul ass out of that place.

If Kennedy had to die, and obviously it was in the cards
or in the *I Ching* at least (which probably explained why
Hagbard, after consulting that computer of his, refused to
get involved in this caper), then 'save what you can' could
only be applied, in this case, to mean: screw the Illuminati. He would give them a mystery they would never
solve.

The motorcade was already in front of the School Book
Depository, and the gazebo up there might start blasting
at any minute, if Harry Coin or the Mafiosos weren't
quicker. Dillinger hoisted his rifle, quickly sighted on John
F. Kennedy's skull, and thought briefly, *Even if it falls
through and doesn't remain an enigma to bug the Illuminati, think of those wild headlines when I'm caught:
PRESIDENT SHOT BY JOHN DILLINGER, people will*

think Orson Welles is publishing the papers now, and then he tightened his finger.

('Murder?' George asked. 'It's hard not to think of Good and Evil when a man's games get that hairy.'

'During the Kali Yuga,' Stella replied, 'almost all our games are played with live ammunition. Haven't you noticed?')

The three shots blew brains into Jackie Kennedy's lap and Dillinger, whirling in amazement, saw the man start to run out of the Grassy Knoll down into the street. John set off in pursuit and caught a glimpse of the face as the killer mingled in the crowd below.

'Christ!' John said. *'Him?'*

Stella toked again – she never seemed to think she was sufficiently stoned. 'Wait,' she said. 'There's a passage in *Never Whistle While You're Pissing* that goes into this a bit.' She got up, walking quite slowly like all potheads, and rummaged among the books on the wall shelf. 'You know the old saying, "different strokes for different folks"?' she asked over her shoulder. 'Hagbard and FUCKUP have classified sixty-four thousand personality types, depending on which strokes, or gambits, they use most often in relating to others.' She found the book and carefully walked back to her chair. 'For instance,' she said slowly. 'Right now, you can intersect my life line in a number of ways, from kissing my hand to slitting my throat. Between those extremes, you can, let's say, carry on an intellectual conversation with sexual flirtation underneath it, or an intellectual conversation with sexual flirtation and also with kinesic signals indicating that the flirtation is only a game and you don't really want me to respond, and on an even deeper level you can be sending other signals indicating that actually you do want me to respond after all but you're not ready to admit that to yourself. In authoritarian society, as we know it, people are usually sending either very simple dominance signals – "I'm going to master you, and you better accept it before I get really nasty" – or submissive signals – "You're going to master me, and I'm reconciled to it." '

'Lord in Heaven,' Harry Coin said softly. 'That was what my first session with him was all about. I tried

dominance signals to bluff him, and it didn't work. So I
tried submissive signals, which is the only other gimmick
I ever knew, and that didn't work either. So I just gave
up.'

'Your brain gave up,' Stella corrected. 'The strategy
center, for dealing with human relations in authoritarian
society, was exhausted. It had nothing left to try. Then the
Robot took over. The biogram. You acted from the heart.'

'But what has redundance got to do with this?' George
asked.

'Here's the passage,' Stella said. She began to read
aloud:

> People exist on a spectrum from the most redun-
> dant to the most flexible. The latter, unless they are
> thoroughly trained in psychodynamics, are always at
> a disadvantage to the former in social interactions.
> The redundant do not change their script; the flexible
> continually keep changing, trying to find a way of
> relating constructively. Eventually, the flexible ones
> find the 'proper' gambit, and communication, of a
> sort, is possible. They are now on the set created by
> the redundant person, and they act out his or her
> script.
> The steady exponential growth of bureaucracy is
> not due to Parkinson's Law alone. The State, by mak-
> ing itself even more redundant, incorporates more
> people into its set and forces them to follow its script.

'That's heavy,' George said, 'but I'll be damned if I can
see how it applies to Jesus *or* Emperor Norton.'

'Exactly!' Harry Coin chortled. 'And that ends the game.
You've just proven what I suspected all along. *You're* the
Martian!'

'Don't raise your voice,' Calley said drowsily from the
floor. 'I can see hundreds of blissful Buddhas floating
through the air . . .'

A single blissful Buddha, meanwhile – together with an
inverted Satanic cross, a peace symbol, a pentagon and the
Eye in the Triangle – were taking up Danny Pricefixer's
attention, back in New York. He had finally decided to

play his hunch about the *Confrontation* bombing and the five associated disappearances. The decision came after he and the acting head of Homicide received a thorough ass-chewing from the Police Commissioner himself. 'Malik is gone. The Walsh woman is gone. This Dorn kid was taken right out of a jail in Texas. Two of my best men, Goodman and Muldoon, are gone. The Feds are nasty and I can tell they know something that makes this case even more important than five possible murders alone would account for. I want you to report some kind of progress before the day is over, or I'll replace you with Post-Toasties Junior G-Men.'

When they escaped into the hall, Pricefixer asked the man from Homicide, Van Meter, 'What are you going to do?'

'Go back and give my men the same ass-chewing. They'll produce.' Van Meter didn't really sound convinced. 'What are *you* going to do?' he added lamely.

'I'm going to play a hunch,' Danny said, and he walked down to Bunco-Fraud, where he exchanged some words with a detective named Sergeant Joe Friday who always insisted on trying to act like his namesake in the famous television series.

'I want a mystic,' Danny said.

'Palmist, crystal-gazer, witch, astrologer . . . any preference?' Friday asked.

'The technique doesn't matter. I want one you've never been able to pin anything on. One you investigated and found a little scary . . . as if she or he really did have something on the ball.'

'I know the one you want,' Friday said emphatically, hitting the intercom button on his phone. 'R & I,' he said and waited. 'Carella? Send up the package on Mama Sutra.'

The package, when it shot out of the interoffice tube, proved to be all that Danny had hoped for. Mama Sutra had no arrests. She had been investigated several times – usually at the demand of rich husbands who thought she had too much influence over their wives, and once at the demand of the board of directors of a public utility who thought the president of the firm consulted too often with

her – but none of her activities involved any claims that
could be construed to be in violation of the fraud laws.
Furthermore, she had dealt with the extremely wealthy for
many years and had never played any games remotely like
an *okanna borra* or Gypsy Switch on any of them. Her
business card, included in the package, modestly offered
only 'spiritual insight,' but she evidently delivered it in
horse doctor's doses: one detective, after interviewing her,
quit the force and entered a Trappist monastery in Ken-
tucky, a second became questionable and finally useless in
the eyes of his superiors because of an incessant series of
memos he wrote urging that New York be the first American city to experiment with the English system of unarmed
policemen, and a third announced that he had been a
closet queen for two decades and began sporting a Gay
Liberation button, necessitating his immediate transfer to
the Vice Squad.

'This is my woman,' Pricefixer said; and an hour later,
he sat in her waiting room studying the blissful Buddha
and other occult accessories, feeling like a horse's ass.
This was really going way out on a limb, he knew, and his
only excuse was that Saul Goodman frequently cracked
hopeless cases by making equally bizarre jumps. Danny
was ready to jump: the disappearance of Professor Marsh,
in Arkham, was connected with the *Confrontation* mystery,
and both were connected with Fernando Poo and the gods
of Atlantis.

The receptionist, an attractive young Chinese woman
named Mao something-or-other, put down her phone and
said, 'You can go right in.'

Danny opened the door and walked into a completely
austere room, white as the North Pole. The white walls had
no paintings, the white rug was solid white without any
design in it, and Mama Sutra's desk and the Danish chair
facing it were also white. He realized that the total lack of
occult paraphernalia, together with the lack of color, was
certainly more impressive than heavy curtains, shadows,
smoldering candles and a crystal ball.

Mama Sutra looked like Maria Ouspenskaya, the old
actress who was always popping up on the late late show
to tell Lon Chaney Jr. that he would always walk the

'thorny path' of lycanthropy until 'all tears empty into the sea.'

'What can I do for you?' she asked in a brisk, business-like manner.

'I'm a detective on the New York Police,' Danny said, showing her his badge. 'I'm not here to hassle you or give you any trouble. I need knowledge and advice, and I'll pay for it out of my own pocket.'

She smiled gently. 'The other officers, who investigated me for fraud in the past, must have created quite a legend at police headquarters. I promise no miracles, and my knowledge is limited. Perhaps I can help you; perhaps not. There will be no fee, in either case. Being in a sensitive profession, I would like to keep on friendly terms with the police.'

Danny nodded. 'Thanks,' he said. 'Here's the story . . .'

'Wait.' Mama Sutra frowned. 'I think I am picking up something already. Yes. *District Attorney Wade. Clark. The ship is sinking. 2422. If I can't live as I please, let me die when I choose.* Does any of that mean anything to you?'

'Only the first part,' Danny said, perplexed. 'I suspect that the matter I'm investigating goes back at least as far as the assassination of John F. Kennedy. The man who handled the original investigation of that killing, in Dallas, was District Attorney Henry Wade. The rest of it doesn't help at all, though. Where did you get it from?'

'There are . . . vibrations . . . and I register them.' Mama Sutra smiled again. 'That's the best explanation I can offer. It just happens, and I've learned how to use it. Somewhat. I hope some day before I die a psychologist will go far enough out in his investigations to find something that will explain to *me* what I do. The sinking ship is meaningless? How about the date, *June 15, 1904?* That seems to be on the same wave.'

Pricefixer shook his head. 'No help, as they say in poker.'

'Wait,' Mama Sutra said. 'It means something to me. There was an Irish writer, James Joyce, who studied the theosophy of Blavatski and the mysticism of the Golden Dawn Society. He wrote a novel in which all the action takes place on June 16, 1904. The novel is called *Ulysses*, and is impregnated on every page with coded mystical revelations. And, yes, now I remember, there is a shipwreck mentioned in it. Joyce made all the background details historically accurate, so he included what was actually in the Dublin papers that day – the book takes place in Dublin, you see – and one of the stories concerned the sinking of the ship, *General Slocum*, in New York Harbor the day before, June 15.'

'Did you say Golden Dawn?' Pricefixer demanded excitedly.

'Yes. Does that help?'

'It just adds to the confusion, but at least it shows you're on the right track. The case I'm working on seems to be connected with the disappearance of a professor from a university in Massachusetts several years ago, and he left behind some notes that mentioned the Golden Dawn Society and . . . let's see . . . some of its members. Aleister Crowley is one name I remember.'

'*To Mega Theiron*,' Mama Sutra said slowly, beginning to pale slightly. 'Young man, what you are involved in is very serious. Much more than an ordinary police officer could understand. But you are not an ordinary police officer or you wouldn't have come to me in the first place. Let me tell you flatly, then, that what you have stumbled upon is something that could very easily involve both James Joyce's mysticism and the assassination of President John Kennedy. But to understand it you will have to stretch your mind to the breaking point. Let me suggest that you wait while I have my receptionist make you a rather stiff drink.'

'Can't drink on duty, ma'am,' Danny said sadly. Mama Sutra took a deep breath. 'Very well. You'll have to take it cold and struggle with it as best you can.'

'Does it involve the lloigor?' Danny asked hesitantly.

'Yes. You already have a large part of the puzzle if you know that much.'

'Ma'am,' Danny said, 'I think I'll have that drink. Bourbon, if you have it.'

2422, he thought while Mama Sutra spoke to the receptionist, that's even crazier than the rest of this. 2 plus

4 plus 2 plus 2. Adds up to 10. The base of the decimal system. What the hell does that mean? Or 24 plus 22 adds up to 46. That's two times 23, the number missing in between 24 and 22. Another enigma. And 2 times 4 times 2 times 2 is, let's see, 32. Law of falling bodies. High school physics class. 32 feet per second per second. And 32 is 23 backwards. Nuts.

Miss Mao entered with a tray. 'Your drink, sir,' she said softly. Danny took the glass and watched her gracefully walk back toward the door. *Mao* is Chinese for cat, he remembered from his years in Army Intelligence, and she certainly moved like a cat. *Mao:* onomatopoeia they call that. Like kids calling a dog 'woof-woof.' Come to think of it, that's how we got the word 'wolf.' Funny, I never thought of that before. Oh, the pentagram outside, and the pentagram in those old Lon Chaney Wolf Man movies. Malik's mystery mutts. Enough of that.

He took a stiff wallop of the bourbon and said, 'Go ahead. Start. I'll take some more of the medicine when my mind starts crumbling.'

'I'll give it to you raw,' Mama Sutra said quietly. 'The earth has already been invaded from outer space. It is not some threat in the future, for writers to play with. It happened, a long time ago. Fifty million years ago, to be exact.'

Danny took another belt of his drink. 'The lloigor,' he said.

'That was their generic name for themselves. There were several races of them. Shoggoths and Tcho-Tchos and Dholes and Tikis and Wendigos, for instance. They were not entirely composed of matter as we understand it, and they do not occupy space and time in the concrete way that furniture does. They are not sound waves or radio waves or anything like that either, but think of them that way for a while. It's better than not having any mental picture of them at all. Did you take any physics in high school?'

'Nothing like relativity,' Danny said, realizing that he was believing all this.

'Sound and light?' she asked.

'A little.'

'Then you probably know two elementary experiments.

Project a white light through a prism and a spectrum appears on the screen behind the prism. You've seen that?'

'Yes.'

'And the experiment with a glass tube that has a thin layer of colored powder on the bottom, when you send a sound wave through it?'

'Yeah. And the wave leaves little marks at each of its valleys and you can see them in the powder.' The track of the invisible wave in a visible medium.

'Very well. Now you can picture, perhaps, how the lloigor, although not made of matter as we understand it, can manifest themselves in matter, leaving traces that show, let us say, a cross section of what they really are.'

Danny nodded, totally absorbed.

'From our point of view,' Mama Sutra went on, 'they are intolerably hideous in these manifestations. There is a reason for that. They were the source of the worst terrors experienced by the first humans. Our DNA code still carries an aversion and terror toward them, and this activates a part of our minds which the psychologist Jung called the Collective Unconscious. That is where all myth and art come from. Everything frightening, loathsome and terrible – in the folklore, in the paintings and statues, in the legends and epics of every people on earth – contains a partial image of a manifestation of the lloigor. "As a foulness shall ye know Them," a great Arab poet wrote.'

'And they've been at war with us through all history?' Danny asked unhappily.

'Not at all. Are the stockyards at war with the cattle? It's nothing like war at all,' Mama Sutra said simply. 'It's just that they *own* us.'

'I see,' Danny said. 'Yes, of course. I see.' He looked into his empty glass dismally. 'Could I have another?' he murmured.

After Miss Mao had brought him another bourbon, he took a huge swallow and slouched forward in his chair. 'There's nothing we can do about it?' he asked.

'There is one group that has been trying to liberate humanity,' Mama Sutra said. 'But lloigor have great powers to warp and distort minds. This group is the most maligned, slandered and hated people on earth. All the evil they seek to prevent has been attributed to them. They operate in secret because otherwise they would be destroyed. Even now, the John Birch Society and various other fanatics – including an evil genius named Hagbard Celine – struggle ceaselessly to combat the group of whom I speak. They have many names, the Great White Brotherhood, the Brethren of the Rosy Cross, the Golden Dawn . . . usually, though they are known as the Illuminati.'

'Yes!' Danny cried excitedly. 'There was a whole bunch of memos about them at the scene of the crime that started this case.'

'And the memos, I would wager, portrayed them in an unfavorable light?'

'Sure did,' Danny agreed. 'Made them seem the worst bastards in history. Pardon me, ma'am.' I'm getting drunk, he thought.

'That is how they are usually portrayed,' Mama Sutra said sadly. 'Their enemies are many, and they are few . . .'

'Who are their enemies?' Danny leaned forward eagerly.

'The Cult of the Yellow Sign,' Mama Sutra replied. 'This is a group serving one particular lloigor called Hastur. They live in such terror of this being that they usually call him He Who Is Not To Be Named. Hastur resides in a mysterious place called Hali, which was formerly a lake but is now just desert. Hali was by a great city in the lost civilzation of Carcosa. You look as if those names mean something to you?'

'Yes. They were in the notes of the professor who disappeared. The other case that I was convinced was connected with this one.'

'They have been mentioned – unwisely, I think – by certain writers, such as Bierce and Chambers and Lovecraft and Bloch and Derleth. Carcosa was located where the Gobi Desert is at present. The major cities were Hali, Mnar and Sarnath. The Cult of the Yellow Sign has managed to conceal all this rather thoroughly, although a few archeologists have published some interesting speculations about the Gobi area. Most of the evidence of a great civilization before Sumer and Egypt has been either hidden or doctored so that it seems to point to Atlantis. Actually, Atlantis never existed, but the Cult of the Yellow Sign carefully keeps the myth alive so nobody will discover what went on, and still goes on, in the Gobian wastelands. You see, the Cult of the Yellow Sign still goes there, on certain occasions, to worship and make certain transactions with Hastur, and with Shub Niggurath, a lloigor who is known in mystical literature as the Black Goat with a Thousand Young, and with Nyarlathotep, who appears either as a solid black man, not a Negro but black as an abyss, or else as a gigantic faceless flute player. But I repeat: you cannot understand the lloigor by these manifestations or cross sections into our space-time continuum. Do you believe in God?'

'Yes,' Danny answered, startled by the sudden personal question.

'Take a little more of your drink. I must tell you now that your God is another manifestation of some lloigor. That is how religion began, and how the lloigor and their servants in the Cult of the Yellow Sign continue it. Have you ever had what is called a religious or mystical experience?'

'No,' Danny said, embarrassed.

'Good. Then your religion is just a matter of believing what you have been told and not of a personal emotional experience. All such experiences come from the lloigor, to enslave us. Revelations, visions, trances, miracles, all of it is a trap. Ordinary, normal people instinctively avoid such aberrations. Unfortunately, due to their gullibility and a concerted effort to brainwash them, they are willing to follow the witches and wizards and shamans who traffic in these matters. You see, and I urge you to take another drink right now, *every religious leader in human history has been a member of the Cult of the Yellow Sign and all their efforts are devoted to hoaxing, deluding and enslaving the rest of us.*'

Danny finished his glass and asked meekly, 'May I have more?'

Mama Sutra buzzed for Miss Mao and said, 'You're taking this part very well. People who *have* had religious visions take it very poorly; they don't want to know what foul source those experiences actually came from. The lloigor, of course, can be considered gods – or demons –

but it is more profitable, at this point in history, to just consider them another life form cast up by the universe, unfortunately superior to us and even more unfortunately inimical to us. You see, religion is always a matter of sacrifice, and whenever there is a sacrifice there is a victim – and also a person or entity profiting from the sacrifice. There is no religion in the world – not one – that is not a front for the Cult of the Yellow Sign. The Cult itself, like the lloigor, is of prehuman origin. It began among the snake people of Valusia, the peninsula that is now Europe, and then spread eastward to be adopted by the first humans in Carcosa. Always the purpose of the Cult has been to serve the lloigor, at the expense of other human beings. Since the rise of the Illuminati, the Cult has also acted to combat their work and discredit them.'

Danny was glad that Miss Mao arrived then with his third stiff bourbon. 'And who are the Illuminati and what is their goal?' he asked, belting away a strong swallow.

'Their founder,' Mama Sutra said, 'was the first man to think rationally about the lloigor. He realized that they were not supernatural, but just another aspect of nature; not all-powerful, but just more powerful than us; and that when they came "out of the heavens" they came from other worlds like this one. His name has come down to us in certain secret teachings and documents. It was Ma-lik.'

'Jesus,' Danny said, 'that's the name of the guy whose disappearance started all this.'

'The name meant "one who knows" in the Carcosan tongue. Among the Persians and some Arabs today it still exists but means "one who leads." His followers, the Illuminati, are those who have seen the light of reason – which is quite distinct from the stupefying and mind-destroying light in which the lloigor sometimes appear to overwhelm and mystify their servants in the Cult of the Yellow Sign. What Ma-lik sought, what the Illuminati still seek, is scientific knowledge that will surpass the powers of the lloigor, end mankind's enslavement and allow us to become self-owners instead of property.'

'How large is the Illuminati?'

'Very small. I don't know the exact number.' Mama Sutra sighed. 'I have never been accepted for membership.

Their standards are quite high. One must virtually be a walking encyclopedia to qualify for an initial interview. You must remember that this is the most dedicated, most persecuted, most secret group in the world. Everything they do, if not wiped off the records by the Cult of the Yellow Sign, is always misrepresented and pictured as malign, devious and totally evil. Indeed, any effort to be rational, to think scientifically, to discover or publish a new truth, even by those outside the Illuminati, is always pictured in those colors by the Cult and all the religions which serve as its fronts. All churches, Protestant, Catholic, Jewish, Moslem, Hindu, Buddhist or whatever, have always opposed and persecuted science. The Cult of the Yellow Sign even fills the mass media with this propaganda. Their favourite stories are the one about the scientist who isn't fully human until he has a religious insight and recognizes "the higher powers" – the lloigor, that is – and the other one about the scientist who seeks truth without fear and causes a disaster. "He meddled with things man should leave alone" is always the punch line on that one. The same hatred of knowledge and glorification of superstition and ignorance permeates all human societies. How much more of this can you stand?' Mama Sutra asked abruptly.

'I don't honestly know,' Danny said wearily. 'It seems if I do get to the bottom of this business, it'll bring every power in this country down on my head. The least that'll happen is that I'll get kicked out of my job. More likely, I'll disappear like the man I'm looking for and the first two detectives on this case. But for my own satisfaction, I'd like to know the rest of the truth, before I bid you good day and look for a hole to hide in. You might also tell me how you can survive, knowing as much as you do.'

'I have studied much. I have a Shield. I cannot explain the Shield anymore than I can explain my ESP. I only know that it works. As to answering your other questions, first tell me about your investigation. Then I will be able to relate it to the Illuminati and the Cult of the Yellow Sign.'

Danny took another drink, closed his eyes for a minute and launched into his story. He began with the Marsh

disappearance in Arkham four years earlier, his perusal of
the missing professor's notes, his reading in the books
mentioned in those notes and his conclusion that a drug
cult was involved. Then he told of the *Confrontation*
bombing, his skimming of the Illuminati memos, the disappearance of Malik, Miss Walsh, Goodman and Muldoon,
and the frantic curiosity of the FBI. 'That's it,' he concluded. 'That's about all I know.'

Mama Sutra nodded thoughtfully, 'It is as I feared,' she
said finally. 'I think I can shed light on the matter, but you
will be well advised to leave the police force and seek the
protection of the Illuminati after you have heard. You are
already, at this very moment, in great peril.' She lapsed into
silence again, and then said, 'You will not see the picture of
what is happening now, until I give you more of the background.'

For the next hour, Danny Pricefixer sat transfixed as
Mama Sutra told him of the longest war in history, the
battle for the freedom of the human mind waged by the
Illuminati against the forces of slavery, superstition and
sorcery.

It began, she repeated, in ancient Carcosa when the first
humans were contacted by the serpent people of Valusia. The
latter brought with them certain fruits with strange powers.
These fruits would be called hallucinogens or psychedelics
today, Mama Sutra said, but what they did to the brain of
the eater was not in any sense a hallucination. It opened
him to invasion by the lloigor. The chief fruit used in these
rites was a botanical cousin of the modern apple, yellowish
or golden in color, and the snake people promised, 'Eat
of this and you shall become all-powerful.' In fact, the
eaters became enslaved by the lloigor, and especially by
Hastur, who took up residence in the Lake of Hali; distorted versions of what happened have come down to us
in various African legends about people who had com-
merce with snakes and lost their souls, in the Homeric tale
of the lotus eaters, in Genesis, and in the Arabic lore
utilized in the fiction of Robert W. Chambers, Ambrose
Bierce and others. Soon, the Cult of the Yellow Sign was
formed among the eaters of the golden apples, and its first
high priest, Gruad, bargained with Hastur for certain

powers in return for which the lloigor were fed on human
sacrifices. The people were told that the sacrifices were
good for the crops – and this, in fact, was partially true,
for the lloigor ate only the energy of the victim, and the
body, buried in the fields, gave back its nitrogen to the soil.
This was the beginning of religion – and of government.
Gruad controlled the Temple, and the Temple soon controlled Hali, and, then, all of Carcosa.

So things went for many thousands of years, until the
priests were rich, fat and decadent, while the citizens lived
in terror and slavery. The number of sacrifices increased
ever, for Hastur grew with each victim whose energy he
absorbed and his appetite grew with him. Finally, among
the people, there arose one who had been refused admission
to the priesthood, Ma-lik, and he taught that humanity
could become all-powerful, not through eating the golden
apples and sacrificing to the lloigor, but through a process
he called rational thought. He was, of course, fed to Hastur
as soon as the priests heard of this teaching, but he had
followers, and they quickly learned to keep their thoughts
private and plan their activities in secret. This was the age
of midnight arrests, purge trials and accelerating sacrifices
in Carcosa, Mama Sutra said, and eventually the followers
of Ma-lik – the few who had escaped extermination – fled
to the Thuranian subcontinent, which is now Europe.

There they met little people who had come down from
the north after the snake folk had exterminated each other
in some form of slow, insidious and stealthy civil war.
(Apparently, the snakes never met in a single battle during
all this time: the poison in the wine cup, the knife in the
back and similar subtle activities had slowly escalated to
the deadly level of actual warfare. The serpent people had
an aversion to *facing* an enemy as they killed him.) The
little people had had their own experiences with the lloigor,
long ago, but all they remembered were confused legends
about Orcs (whom Mama Sutra identified with the Tcho-
Tchos) and a great hero named Phroto who battled a
monster called Zaurn (evidently a shoggoth, Mama Sutra
said.)

Many millenniums passed, and the little people and the

followers of Ma-lik intermarried, producing basically the human race of today. A great law-giver named Kull tried to establish a rational society on Ma-lik's principles, and fought a battle with some of the serpent people who had surprisingly survived in hidden places; most of this got lost in exaggeration and legend. After more thousands of years, a barbarian named Konan or Conan arose, somehow, to the throne of Aquilonia, mightiest kingdom on the Thuranian sub-continent; Konan brooded much about the continuing horrors in Carcosa, which he sensed as a threat to the rest of the world. Finally, he disappeared, abdicating in favor of his son, Conn, and reputedly sailing *to the west*.

Konan, Mama Sutra said, was the same person who appeared in the Yucatan peninsula at that time and became known as Kukulan. He was evidently seeking, among the Mayan scientists, some knowledge or technology to use against the lloigor. Whatever happened, he left them, and only the legend of Kukulan, 'the feathered serpent,' remained. When the Aztecs came down from the north, Kukulan became Quetzalcoatl, and human sacrifice was instituted in his name. The lloigor, in some fashion, had turned the work of Konan around and made it serve their own ends.

Carcosa meanwhile perished. What happened is unknown, but some students of ancient lore suspect that Konan actually circumnavigated the globe, collecting knowledge as he went, and descended upon Carcosa with weapons that destroyed both the Cult of the Yellow Sign and all traces of the civilization that served it.

Throughout the rest of history, Mama Sutra went on, the Cult of the Yellow Sign never regained its former powers, but it has come very close in certain times and certain places. The lloigor continued to exist, of course, but could no longer manifest in our kind of space-time continuum unless the Cult performed very complicated technical operations, which were sometimes disguised as religious rituals and sometimes as wars, famines or other calamities.

Over the intervening ages, the Cult waged steady warfare against the one power that threatened them: ration-

ality. When they couldn't manifest a lloigor to blast a
mind, they learned to fake it; if real magic wasn't available,
stage magic served in its place. 'By "real magic," of course,'
Mama Sutra explained, 'I mean the technology of the
lloigor. As science-fiction writer Arthur C. Clarke has commented, any sufficiently advanced technology is indistinguishable from magic. The lloigor have that kind of
technology. That's how they got to earth from their star.'

'You mean their planet, don't you?' Danny asked.

'No, they lived originally on a star. I told you they were
not made of matter as we understand it. Incidentally, their
origin on a star explains why the pentagram or star shape
always attracts their attention and is one of the best ways
of summoning them. They invented that design. A star
doesn't look five-pointed to a human being, but that's what
it looks like to *them*.'

Finally, in the 18th century, the Age of Reason appeared to be at hand. Tentatively, as an experiment, one
branch of the Illuminati surfaced in Bavaria. They were
led by an ex-Jesuit named Adam Weishaupt who had inside knowledge of how the Cult of the Yellow Sign operated
and performed its hoaxes and 'miracles.' The real brain
behind this movement, however, was Weishaupt's wife,
Eve; but they knew that, even in the Age of Reason, humanity was not ready yet for a liberation movement led
by a woman, so Adam fronted for her.

The experiment was unsuccessful. The Cult of the Yellow Sign planted fake documents in the home of an Illuminatus named Zwack, whispered some hints to Bavarian
government and then watched with glee as the movement
was disbanded and hounded out of Germany.

A simultaneous experiment began in America, started
by two Illuminati named Jefferson and Franklin. Both
preached reason, like Weishaupt, but carefully did not
make his mistake of stating explicitly how this contradicted
religion and superstition. (This latter matter they discussed
only in their private letters.) Since Jefferson and Franklin
were national heroes, and since the rationalistic government
they helped to create seemed well established, the Cult of
the Yellow Sign dared not denounce them openly. One
trial balloon was attempted: the Reverend Jebediah

Morse, a high Yellow Sign adept, openly accused Jefferson of being an Illuminatus and charged him and his party with most of the crimes that had discredited Weishaupt in Bavaria. The American public was not deceived – but all subsequent Yellow Sign propaganda in America has rested on the original anti-Illuminati claims of Reverend Morse.

Due to Jefferson, one Illuminati symbol was adopted by the new government: the Eye on the Pyramid, representing knowledge of geometry and, hence, of the order of nature. This was to be used in later generations, if necessary, to indicate the truth about the founding of the U.S. government, since it was well understood that the Cult of the Yellow Sign would try to distort the facts as soon as possible. Another Illuminati work, of more immediate importance, was the Bill of Rights (the part of the Constitution still under most vigorous attack by the Yellow Sign fanatics) and certain key expressions in early documents, such as the reference to 'Nature and Nature's God' in the Declaration of Independence – as far as Jefferson dared to go in leavening traditional superstition with a natural-science admixture. And, of course, the first half-dozen Presidents were all high ranking Masons and Rosicrucians who understood at least the fundamentals of Illuminati philosophy.

Mama Sutra sighed briefly, and went on. All this, she said, is only the tip of the iceberg. Government actually plays a minor role in controlling people; far more important are the words and images that make up the semantic environment. The Cult of the Yellow Sign not only suppresses words and images that threaten their power, but infiltrates every branch of communications with their own ideology. Science and reason are forever mocked or portrayed as menacing. Wishful thinking, fantasy, religion, mysticism, occultism and magic are forever preached as the real solutions to all problems. Best-selling books teach people to *pray*, not *work*, for success. Movies win awards by showing a child's ignorant faith justified over the skepticism of adults. There is an astrology column in virtually every newspaper. More and more, the ideology of the Cult of the Yellow Sign is set forth openly, as the ideas of the Illuminati and the Founding Fathers are forgotten or distorted. One only has to think of any antidemocratic, antirational or antihumane idea out of the Dark Ages, Mama Sutra said, and one can immediately think of some popular religious columnist or some movie star who is blatantly expounding it and calling it 'Americanism.'

The Cult of the Yellow Sign, the old woman continued, is determined to destroy the United States, because it came closer than any other nation to the Illuminati ideals of free minds and free people and because it still retains a few tattered relics of Illuminism in its laws and customs.

This is where Mr. Hagbard Celine enters the picture, Mama Sutra said grimly.

Celine, she went on, was a brilliant but twisted personality, the son of an Italian pimp and a Norwegian prostitute. Raised in the underworld, he early developed a contempt and hatred for ordinary, decent society. The Mafia, recognizing his talents and predilections, took him in and financed his way through Harvard Law School. After graduation, he became an important mouthpiece for Syndicate hoodlums in trouble with the law. On the side, however, he also took some cases for American Indians, since this was a way of frustrating the government. In one particularly bitter battle, he attempted to stop the construction of a much-needed dam in upstate New York; his unbalanced behavior in the courtroom (which helped lose the case) indicated his deep attraction for the occult, since he had obviously been taken in by the superstitions of the Indians he served. Mafia dons conferred with leaders of the Cult of the Yellow Sign, and soon, Hagbard, who had been wandering around Europe aimlessly, was recruited to start a new front for the Cult, to fight the United States both politically and religiously. This front, Mama Sutra said, was called the Legion of Dynamic Discord, and, while it pretended to be against all governments, it was actually devoted only to harming the U.S. He was given a submarine (which he later claimed to have designed himself) and became an important cog in the Mafia heroin-smuggling business. More important, his crew – renegades and misfits from all nations – were indoctrinated in a deliberately nonsensical variety of mysticism.

An important center of Celine's heroin network, Mama

Sutra added, was a fake church in Santa Isobel on the island of Fernando Poo.

Obviously, Mama Sutra concluded, Joseph Malik, the editor of *Confrontation*, was investigating the Illuminati, deceived by the lies spread against them by Celine and the Yellow Sign adepts. As for Professor Marsh, his explorations in Fernando Poo may have revealed something about Celine's heroin ring.

'Then you think they're both dead,' Danny said somberly. 'And, probably, Goodman and Muldoon and Pat Walsh, the researcher, also.'

'Not necessarily. Celine, as I have told you, is both brilliant and quite insane. He has perfected his own form of brainwashing and it amuses him to recruit rather than destroy any possible opponent. It is quite possible that all of these people are working for him right now, against the Illuminati and the United States, which they will believe to be the major enemies of humanity.' Mama Sutra paused thoughtfully. 'However, that is far from sure. Events in the last few days have changed Celine for the worse. He is more insane, and more dangerous, than ever. The assassinations of April 25 all across the nation appear to be his work, engineered through the Mafia. He is striking out blindly against anyone he imagines may be an Illuminatus. Needless to say, most of the victims were not actually in the Illuminati, which is, as I have mentioned, a very small organization. Since he is in this violent and paranoid frame of mind, I fear for the lives of anyone associated with him.'

Danny was slumped forward in his chair, drunk, dejected and depressed. 'Now that I know,' he asked rhetorically, 'what can I do about it? My God, what can I do about it?'

I finally got around to reading *Telemachus Sneezed* on the flight to Munich, a touch of appropriate synchronicity, since Atlanta Hope (like the Illuminati's pet paperhanger) had an umbilical connection backward toward Clark Kent's old enemy Lothar and his festive burgher's unsure God. In fact, Atlanta wrote as if she had her own Diet of Worms for breakfast every morning. What made it even more fan-fuckin'-tastic was that she was on the same flight with me, sitting, in fact, a few seats ahead of me and to port, or starboard, or whatever is the correct word for right when you're in the air.

Mary Lou was with me; she was a hard woman to get out of your system once you'd made it with her. John had advanced me only enough money for my own passage, so I'd hustled some Alamout Black on Wells Street to raise the extra fare for her, and then I had to explain that it wasn't just a pleasure trip.

'What's all the mystery?' she had asked. 'Are you CIA or a Commie or something for Christ's sake?'

'If I told you,' I said, 'you wouldn't believe it. Just enjoy the music and the acid and whatever else is coming down, and when it happens you'll see it. You'd never believe it before you see it.'

'Simon Motherfucking Moon,' she told me gravely, 'after the yoga and sex you've taught me these last three days, I'm ready to believe anything.'

'Ghosts? The *grand zombi*?'

'Oh, there you go again, putting me on,' she protested.

'See?'

So it was more or less left at that and we smoked two joints and hopped a cab out to O'Hare, passing all the signs where they were tearing down lower-middle-class neighborhoods to turn them into upper-middle-class high-rise neighborhoods and each sign said, THIS IS ANOTHER IMPROVEMENT FOR CHICAGO—RICHARD J. DALEY, MAYOR. Of course, in the lower-class neighborhoods, they weren't tearing anything down, just waiting for the people to go on another rampage and burn it down. The signs there were all done with spray cans and had more variety: OFF THE PIG, BLACK P. STONE RUNS IT, POWER TO THE PEOPLE, FRED LIVES, ALMIGHTY LATIN KINGS RUN IT, and one that would have pleased Hagbard, OFF THE LANDLORDS. Then we got into the traffic on the Eisenhower Expressway (Miss Doris Day standing before Ike's picture in my old schoolroom flashed through memory like the ghost of an old hard-on, the flesh of her mammary) and we put on our gas masks and sat while the cab crawled along fast enough to possibly catch a senile snail with arthritis.

Mary Lou bought Edison Yerby's seventieth or eightieth

novel in the airport, which suited me fine since I like to read on airplanes myself. Looking around, I spotted *Telemachus Sneezed* and decided, what the hell, let's see how the other half thinks. So there we were at fifty thousand feet a few yards from the author herself and I was plunged deeply into the *donner-und-blitzen* metaphysics of God's lightning. Unlike the lamentable Austrian monorchoid, Atlanta wrote like she had balls, and she expressed her philosophy in a frame of fiction rather than autobiography. Pretty soon, I was in her prose up to my ass and sinking rapidly. Fiction always does that to me: I buy it completely and my critical faculties come into action only after I'm finished.

Briefly, then, *Telemachus Sneezed* deals with a time in the near future when we dirty, filthy, freaky, lazy, dope-smoking, frantic-fucking anarchists have brought Law and Order to a nervous collapse in America. The heroine, Taffy Rhinestone, is, like Atlanta was once herself, a member of Women's Liberation and a believer in socialism, anarchism, free abortions and the charisma of Che. Then comes the rude awakening: food riots, industrial stagnation, a reign of lawless looting and plunder, everything George Wallace ever warned us against – but the Supreme Court, who are all anarchists with names ending in *-stein* or *-farb* or *-berger* (there is no *overt* anti-Semitism in the book), keeps repealing laws and taking away the rights of policemen. Finally, in the fifth chapter – the climax of Book One – the heroine, poor toughy Taffy, gets raped *fifteen* times by an oversexed black brute right out of *The Birth of a Nation*, while a group of cops stand by cursing, wringing their hands and frothing at the mouth because the Supreme Court rulings won't allow them to take any action.

In Book Two, which takes place a few years later, things have degenerated even further and factory pollution has been replaced by a thick layer of marijuana smoke hanging over the country. The Supreme Court is gone, butchered by LSD crazed Mau-Maus who mistook them for a meeting of the Washington chapter of the Policemen's Benevolent Association. The President and a shadowy government-in-exile are skulking about Montreal, living a gloomy emigre existence; the Blind Tigers, a rather thinly dis-

guised caricature of the Black Panthers, are terrorizing
white women everywhere from Bangor to Walla Walla;
the crazy anarchists are forcing abortions on women
whether they want them or not; and television shows nothing but Maoist propaganda and Danish stag films. Women,
of course, are the worst sufferers in this blightmare, and,
despite all her karate lessons, Taffy has been raped so many
times, not only by standard vage-pen but orally and anally
as well, that she's practically a walking sperm bank. Then
comes the big surprise, the monstro-rape to end all rapes,
committed by a pure Aryan with hollow cheeks, a long
lean body, and a face that never changes expression.
'Everything is fire,' he tells her, as he pulls his prick out
afterwards, 'and don't you ever forget it.' Then he disappears.

Well, it turns out that Taffy has gone all icky-sticky-
gooey over this character, and she determines to find him
again and make an honest man of him. Meanwhile, however, a subplot is brewing, involving Taffy's evil brother,
Diamond Jim Rhinestone, an unscrupulous dope pusher
who is mixing heroin in his grass to make everybody an
addict and enslave them to him. Diamond Jim is allied
with the sinister Blind Tigers and a secret society, the
Enlightened Ones, who cannot achieve world government
as long as a patriotic and paranoid streak of nationalism
remains in America.

But the forces of evil are being stymied. A secret underground group has been formed, using the cross as their
symbol, and their slogan is appearing scrawled on walls
everywhere:

SAVE YOUR FEDERAL RESERVE NOTES, BOYS,
THE STATE WILL RISE AGAIN!

Unless this group is found and destroyed, Diamond Jim
will not be able to addict everyone to horse, the Blind
Tigers won't be able to rape the few remaining white
women they haven't gotten to yet, and the Enlightened
Ones will not succeed in creating one world government
and one monotonous soybean diet for the whole planet.
But a clue is discovered: the leader of the Underground is

a pure Aryan with hollow cheeks, a long lean body, and a
face that never changes expression. Furthermore, he is in
the habit of discussing Heracleitus for like seven hours on
end (this is a neat trick, because only about a hundred
sentences of the Dark Philosopher survive – but our hero,
it turns out, gives lengthy comments on them).

At this point there is a major digression, while a herd
of minor characters get on a Braniff jet for Ingolstadt. It
soon develops that the pilot is tripping on acid, the copilot
is bombed on Tangier hash and the stewardesses are all
speed freaks and dykes, only interested in balling each
other. Atlanta then takes you through the lives of each of
the passengers and shows that the catastrophe that is about
to befall them is richly deserved: all, in one way or another, had helped to create the Dope Grope or Fucks Fix
culture by denying the 'self-evident truth' of some hermetic
saying by Heracleitus. When the plane does a Steve Brodie
into the North Atlantic, everybody on board, including the
acid-tripping Captain Clark, are getting just what they
merit for having denied that reality is really fire.

Meanwhile, Taffy has hired a private detective named
Mickey 'Cocktails' Molotov to search for her lost Aryan
rapist with hollow cheeks. Before I could get into that, however, I was wondering about the synchronistic implications
of the previous section, and called over one of the stewardesses.

'Could you tell me the pilot's name?' I asked.

'*Namen?*' she replied. '*Ja, Gretchen.*'

'No, not your name,' I said, 'the pilot's name. *Namen
unser*, um, *Winginmacher*?'

'*Winginmacher?*' she repeated, dubiously, '*Ein Augenblick.*' She went away, while I looked up *Augenblick* in a
pocket German-English dictionary, and another stewardess,
with the identical uniform, the identical smile and the
identical blue eyes, came over, asking, '*Was wollen sie
haben?*'

I gave up on *Winginmacher*, obviously a bad guess. '*Gibt
mir, bitte,*' I said, '*die Namen unser Fliegenmacher.*' I
spread my arms, imitating the plane. '*Luft Fliegenmacher,*'
I repeated, adding helpfully, 'How about *Luft Piloten*?'

'It's *Pilot*, not *Piloten*,' she said with lots of teeth. 'His name is Captain Clark. Heathcliffe Clark.'

'*Danke*— Thanks,' I said glumly, and returned to *Telemachus Sneezed*, imagining friend Heathcliffe up front there weathering heights of *saure*-soaring and plunging into the ocean because, as Mallory said, it's there. An Englishman piloting a kraut airline, no less, just to remind me that I'm surrounded by the paradoxical paranoidal paranormal parameters of synchronicity. Their wandering ministerial Eye. Lord, I buried myself again in Atlanta Hope's egregious epic.

Cocktails Molotov, the private dick, starts looking for the Great American Rapist, with only one clue: an architectural blueprint that fell out of his pocket while he was tupping Taffy. Cocktails's method of investigation is classically simple: he beats up everybody he meets until they confess or reveal something that gives him a lead. Along the way he meets an effete snob type who makes a kind of William O. Douglas speech putting down all this brutality. Molotov explains, for seventeen pages, one of the longest monologues I ever read in a novel, that life is a battle between Good and Evil and the whole modern world is corrupt because people see things in shades of red-orange-yellow-green-blue-indigo-violet instead of in clear black and white.

Meanwhile, of course, everybody is still mostly involved in fucking, smoking grass and neglecting to invest their capital in growth industries, so America is slipping backward toward what Atlanta calls 'crapulous precapitalist chaos.'

At this point, another character enters the book, Howard Cork, a one-legged madman who commands a submarine called the *Life Eternal* and is battling *everybody* – the anarchists, the Communists, the Diamond Jim Rhinestone heroin cabal, the Blind Tigers, the Enlightened Ones, the U.S. government-in-exile, the still-nameless patriotic Underground and the Chicago Cubs – since he is convinced they are *all* fronting for a white whale of superhuman intelligence who is trying to take over the world on behalf of the cetaceans. ('No normal whale could do this,' he says after every TV newcast reveals further decay and chaos in

America, 'but a whale of superhuman intelligence . . . !')
This megalomaniac tub of blubber – the whale, not Howard
Cork – is responsible for the release of the famous late-
1960s record *Songs of the Blue Whales*, which has hypnotic
power to lead people into wild frenzies, dope-taking, rape
and loss of faith in Christianity. In fact, the whale is behind most of the cultural developments of recent decades,
influencing minds through hypnotic telepathy. 'First, he
introduced W. C. Fields,' Howard Cork rages to the dubi-
ous first mate, 'Buck' Star, 'then, when America's moral
fiber was sufficiently weakened, Liz and Dick and Andy
Warhol and rock music. Now, the Songs of the Blue
Whales!' Star becomes convinced that Captain Cork went
uncorked and wigged when he lost his leg during a simple
ingrown toenail operation bungled by a hip young chiropo-
dist stoned on mescaline. This suspicion is increased by the
moody mariner's insistence on wearing an old cork leg
instead of a modern prosthetic model, proclaiming, 'I was
born all Cork and I'm not going to die only three-fourths
Cork!'

Then comes a turnabout scene, and it is revealed that
Cork is actually not bananas at all but really a smooth
apple. In a meeting with a pure Aryan with hollow cheeks,
a long lean body, and a face that never changes expression,
it develops that the Captain is an agent of the Underground
which is called God's Lightning because of Heracleitus's
idea that God first manifested himself as a lightning bolt
which created the world. Instead of hunting the big white
whale, as the crew thinks, the *Life Eternal* is actually running munitions for the government-in-exile and God's
Lightning. When the hollow-cheeked leader leaves, he says
to Cork, 'Remember: the *way up* is the *way down*.'

Meanwhile, the Gateless Gate swung creakingly open
and started picking up some of the 'real' world. That is, I
began to recognize myself, again, as the ringmaster. All of
this information gets fed into me, entropy and negentropy
all synergized up in a wodge of wonderland, and I com-
pute it as well as my memory banks give it unto me to
understand these doings.

But, as Harry Coin, I enter Miss Portinari's suite somewhat diffidently. I am conscious of the ghosts of dead

pirates, only partly induced by this room's surrealist variety
of Hagbard's nautical taste in murals. In fact, Harry, in his
own language, had an asshole tight enough to shit bricks.
It was easy, now, to accept that long-haired hippie, George,
and even his black girlfriend as equals, but it just didn't
seem right to be asked to accept a *teenage girl* as a superior.
A couple days ago I would have been thinking how to get
into her panties. Now I was thinking how to get her into
my head. That Hagbard and his dope sure have screwed
up my sense of values worse than anything since I left
Biloxi.

And, for some reason, I could hear the Reverend Hill
pounding the Bible and hollering up a storm back there in
Biloxi, long ago, 'No remission without blood! No remission without blood, brothers and sisters! Saint Paul
says it and don't you forget it! No remission without the
blood of our Lord and Saviour Jesus Christ! Amen.'

And Hagbard reads FUCKUP's final analysis of the strategy and tactics in the Battle of Atlantis. All the evidence
is consistent with Assumption A, and inconsistent with
Assumption B, the mathematical part of FUCKUP has decided. Hagbard grinds his teeth in a savage grimace:
Assumption A is that the Illuminati spider ships were
under remote control, and Assumption B is that there were
human beings aboard them.

—Trust not a man who's rich in flax – his morals may
be sadly lax.

'Ready for destruction of enemy ships,' Howard's voice
came back to him.

'Are your people out of the way?'

'Of course. Quit this hesitating. This is no time to be a
humanitarian.'

(Assumption A is that the Illuminati spider ships were
under remote control.)

The sea is crueler than the land. Sometimes.

(None of the evidence is consistent with Assumption B.)

Hagbard reached out a brown finger, let it rest on a
white button on the railing in front of him, then pressed it
decisively. *That's all there is to it,* he said.

But that wasn't all there was to it. He had decided, coolly
and in his wrong mind, that if he was a murderer already

the final gambit might as well be one that would salvage part of the Demonstration. He had sent George to Drake (Bob, you're dead now, but did you ever understand, even for a moment, what I tried to tell you? What Jung tried to tell you even earlier?) and then twenty-four real men and women were dead, and now the bloodshed was escalating, and he wasn't sure that any part of the Demonstration could be saved.

'No remission without blood! No remission without blood, brothers and sisters . . . No remission without the blood of our Saviour and Lord Jesus Christ!'

I got into the Illuminati in 1951, when Joe McCarthy was riding high and everybody was looking for conspiracies everywhere. In my own naive way (I was a sophomore at New York University at the time) I was seeking to find myself, and I answered one of those Rosicrucian ads in the back of a girlie magazine. Of course, the Rosicrucians aren't a front in the simple way that the Birchers and other paranoids think; only a couple of plants at AMORC headquarters are Illuminati agents. But they select possible candidates at random, and we get slightly different mailings than those sent to the average new member. If we show the proper spirit, our mailings get more interesting and a personal contact is made. Well, pretty soon I swore the whole oath, including that silly part about never visiting Naples, which is just an expression of an old grudge of Weishaupt's, and I was admitted as Illuminatus Minerval with the name Ringo Erigena. Since I was majoring in law, I was instructed to seek a career in the FBI.

I met Eisenhower only once, at a very large and sumptuous ball. He called another agent and myself aside. 'Keep your eye on Mamie,' he said. 'If she has five martinis, or starts quoting John Wayne, get her upstairs *quick*.'

Kennedy I never even talked to, but Winifred (whose name in the order is Scotus Pythagoras) used to bitch about him a lot. 'This New Frontier stuff is dangerous,' Winifred would say testily, 'The man thinks he's living in a western movie. One big showdown, and the bad guys bite the dust. We'd best not let him last too long.'

You can imagine how upset I was when the Dallas caper

began to throw light on the whole overall pattern. Of
course, I didn't know what to do: Winifred was my only
superior in the government who was also a superior in the
Illuminati, but I had a lot of hunches and guesses about
some others, and I wouldn't want to bet that John Edgar
wasn't one of them, for instance. When the feeler came
from the CIA I went on what these kids today call a paranoid trip. It could have been coincidence or synchronicity,
but it could have been the Order, scanning me, and ensur-
ing that my involvement would get deeper.

('Most people in espionage don't know who they're
working for,' Winifred told me once, in that voice of silk
and satin and stilettos, 'especially the ones who only do
"small jobs." Suppose we find a French Canadian separa-
tist in Montreal who's in a position to provide certain information at certain times. We certainly don't ask him to
work for American Intelligence. That's no concern of his,
and even inimical to his real interests. So he's approached
by another very convincing French Canadian who has
"evidence" to prove he's an agent of the most secret of all
Quebec Libre underground movements. Or, if the Russians
find a woman in Nairobi who has access to certain offices
and happens to be anti-Communist and pro-English: no
sense in trying to recruit her for the MVD, right? The contact she meets has a full set of credentials and just the right
Oxford tone to convince her he's with M.5 in London.
And so it goes,' he ended dreamily, 'so it goes . . .')

My CIA contact really was CIA; I'm almost absolutely
willing to give odds around 60-40 on that. At least, he
knew the proper passwords to show that he was acting
under presidential orders, whatever that proves.

It was Hoover himself who ordered me to infiltrate God's
Lightning. Well, he didn't pick me alone; I was part of a
group, and a rousing pep talk he gave us. I can still remember him saying, 'Don't let their American flags fool
you. Look at those lightning bolts, right out of Nazi Germany, and, remember, the next thing to a godless Commie
is a godless Nazi. They're both against Free Enterprise.'
Of course, as soon as I was admitted to the Arlington
chapter of God's Lightning, I found out that Free Enterprise stood second only to Heracleitus in their pantheon.

J. Edgar did get some queer hornets in his headgear at times – like his fear that John Dillinger was really still alive some place, laughing at him. That was the dread that turned him against Melvin Purvis, the agent who gunned Dillinger down in Chicago, and he rode Purvis right out of the Bureau. Those of you with long memories will recall that poor Purvis ended up working for a breakfast cereal company, acting as titular head of the Post-Toasties Junior G-Men.

It was in God's Lightning that I read *Telemachus Sneezed*, which I still think is a rip-roaring good yarn. That scene where Taffy Rhinestone sees the new King on television and it's her old rapist friend with the gaunt cheeks and he says, 'My name is John Guilt' – man, that's *writing*. His hundred-and-three-page-long speech afterwards, explaining the importance of guilt and showing why all the anti-Heracleiteans and Freudians and relativists are destroying civilization by destroying guilt, certainly is persuasive – especially to somebody like me with three-going-on-four personalities each of which was betraying the others. I still quote his last line, 'Without guilt there can be no civilization.' Her nonfiction book, *Militarism: The Unknown Ideal for the New Heracleitean* is, I think, a distinct letdown, but the God's Lightning bumper stickers asking 'What Is John Guilt?' sure give people the creeps until they learn the answer.

I met Atlanta Hope herself at the time of the New York Draft Riots. That was, you will remember, when God's Lightning, disgusted with reports that the FBI was swamped in two years' backlog in draft resistance and draft evasion cases, decided to organize vigilante groups to hunt down the hippie-yippie-commie-pacifist scum themselves. As soon as they entered the East Village – which harbored, as they suspected, hundreds of thousands of bearded, long-haired and otherwise semivisible fugitives from the Vietnam, Cambodia, Thailand, Laos, Taiwan, Costa Rica, Chile and Tierra del Fuego conflicts – they began to encounter both suspects and resistance. After the third hour, the Mayor ordered the police to cordon the area. The police, of course, were on the side of God's Lightning and did all they could to aid their mayhem against the Great

Unwashed while preventing reciprocal mayhem. After the third day, the Governor called out the National Guard. The Guard, who were mostly draft-dodgers at heart themselves, tried to even the score, and even help the Dregs and Drugs a bit. After the third week, the President declared that part of Manhattan a disaster area and sent in the Red Cross to help the survivors.

I was in the thick and din of it (you have no idea how bizarre civil war gets when one side uses trash cans as a large part of their arsenal) and even met Joe Malik, prematurely, under a Silver Wraith Rolls Royce where he had crawled to take notes near the front line and I had crept to nurse wounds received while being pushed through the window of the Peace Eye Bookstore – I have scars I could show you still – and a voice over my shoulder says that I should put in the fact that August Personage was trapped in a phone booth only a few feet away, suffering hideous paranoid delusions that in spite of all this chaos the police would trace his last obscene call and find him still in the booth afraid to come out and face the trash can covers and bullets and other miscellaneous metals in the air – and I even remember that the Rolls had license plate RPD-1, which suggests that a certain person of importance was also in that odd vicinity on some doubtless even odder errand. I met Atlanta herself a day later and a block north, on the scene where Taylor Mead was making his famous Last Stand. Atlanta grabbed my right arm (the wounded one: it made me wince) and howled something like, 'Welcome, brother in the True Faith! War is the Health of the State! Conflict is the creator of all things!' Seeing she was on a heavy Heracleitus wavelength, I quoted, with great passion, 'Men should fight for the Laws as they would for the walls of the city!' That won her and I was Atlanta's Personal Lieutenant for the rest of the battle.

Atlanta remembered me from the Riots and I was summoned to organize the first tactical strikes against Nader's Raiders. If I do say so myself, I did a commendable job; it earned me a raise from the Bureau, a tight but genuinely pleased smile from my CIA drop, a promotion to Illuminatus Prelator from Winifred – and another audience with Atlanta Hope which led to my initiation into the A∴A∴,

the supersecret conspiracy for which she was really working. (The A∴A∴ is so arcane that even now I can't reveal
the full name hinted in those initials.) My secret name was
Prince of Wands E; I got the Prince of Wands by picking
a Tarot card at random, and she gave me the E herself –
from which I deduced that there were four other Princes
of Wands, together with five Kings of Swords, and so forth,
meaning that the A∴A∴ was something special in even
esoteric realms, since it was a worldwide conspiracy with
no more than three hundred ninety members (five times the
number of cards in the Tarot deck). The name fairly suited
me – I wouldn't want to be Hanged Man D or Fool A –
and I was happy that the Prince is known for his multiple
personalities.

If I had been three and a half agents before (my role in
God's Lightning a fairly straightforward one, at least from
GL's point of view, since I was only asked to smash, not
to spy) there was no doubt that I was four agents now, be-
longing to the FBI, the CIA, the Illuminati and the A∴A∴
and betraying each of them to at least one and sometimes
two or three of the others. (Yes, I had been converted to
the A∴A∴ during their initiation; if I could describe that
most amazing ritual you would not wonder why.) Then
came the Vice President's brainstorm about economizing
on agents, and I began to get transferred on loan to the
CIA frequently, whereupon the Bureau discretely asked me
to report anything interesting that I observed. This, however, I perceive as a further complexification of my four-
way psychic stretch and not as the inevitable, irrefragable
and synergetic fifth step.

And I was right. For it was only in the last year that I
entered the terminal stage, or *Grumment* as the Order calls
it, due to those curious events which led me from Robert
Putney Drake to Hagbard Celine.

I was sent to the Council on Foreign Relations banquet
carrying the credentials of a Pinkerton detective; my supposed role as private dick was to keep an eye on the jewels
of the ladies and other valuables. My real job was to place
a small bug on the table where Robert Putney Drake would
be sitting; I was on loan to IRS that week, and they didn't
know that Justice had standing orders never to prosecute

him for anything, so they were trying·to prove he had concealed income. Naturally, I also had an ear peeled for anything that might be of import for the Illuminati, the
A∴ A∴ and the CIA, if my Lincoln Memorial contact
really was CIA and not Military or Naval Intelligence or
somebody else entirely. (You can be sure I often meditated
on the possibility that he might be Moscow, Peking or
Havana, and Winifred told me once that the Illuminati had
reason to believe him part of an advance-guard fifth column
sent by invaders from Alpha Centauri – but Grand Masters
of the Illuminati are notorious put-on artists, and I didn't
buy that yarn any more than I bought the tale that had
originally brought me into the Illuminati, the one about
them being a conspiracy to establish a world government
run by British Israelites.) Conspiracy was its own reward
to me, now; I didn't care what I was conspiring *for*. Art
for art's sake. Not whether you betray or preserve but how
you play the game. I sometimes even identified it with the
A∴ A∴ notion of the Great Work, for in the twisting
labyrinths of my selves I was beginning to find the rough
sketch for a soul.

There was a hawk-faced wop at Drake's table, very elegant in a spanking new tuxedo, but the cop in me made
him as illegit. Sometimes you can make a subject precisely,
as bunco-con, safe-blower, armed or whatnot, but I could
only place him vaguely somewhere on that side of the game;
in fact, I associated him with images of piracy on the high
seas or the kind of gambits the Borgias played. Somehow
the conversation got around to a new book by somebody
named Mortimer Adler who had already written a hundred or so great books if I understood the drift. One banker
type at the table was terribly keen on this Adler and
especially on his latest great book. 'He says that we and
the Communists share the same Great Tradition' (I could
hear the caps by the way he pronounced the term) 'and we
must join together against the one force that really does
threaten civilization – anarchism!'

There were several objections, in which Drake didn't
take part (he just sat back, puffing his cigar and looking
agreeable to everyone, but I could see boredom under the
surface) and the banker tried to explain the Great Tradi-

tion, which was a bit over my head, and, judging by the expressions around the table, a bit over everybody else's head, too, when the hawk-faced dago spoke up suddenly.

'I can put the Great Tradition in one word,' he said calmly. 'Privilege.'

Old Drake suddenly stopped looking agreeable-but-bored – he seemed both interested and amused. 'One seldom encounters such a refreshing freedom from euphemism,' he said, leaning forward. 'But perhaps I am reading too much into your remark, sir?'

Hawk-face sipped at his champagne and patted his mouth with a napkin before answering. 'I think not,' he said at last. 'Privilege is defined in most dictionaries as a right or immunity giving special favors or benefits to those who hold it. Another meaning in Webster is "not subject to the usual rules or penalties." The invaluable thesaurus gives such synonyms as power, authority, birthright, franchise, patent, grant, favor and, I'm sad to say, pretension. Surely, we all know what privilege is in *this* club, don't we, gentlemen? Do I have to remind you of the Latin roots, *privi*, private, and *lege*, law, and point out in detail how we have created our Private Law over here, just as the Politburo have created their own private law in their own sphere of influence?'

'But that's not the Great Tradition,' the banker type said (later, I learned that he was actually a college professor; Drake was the only banker at that table). 'What Mr. Adler means by the Great Tradition—'

'What Mortimer means by the Great Tardition,' hawk-face interrupted rudely, 'is a set of myths and fables invented to legitimize or sugar-coat the institution of privilege. Correct me if I'm wrong,' he added more politely but with a sardonic grin.

'He means,' the true believer said, 'the undeniable axioms, the time-tested truths, the shared wisdom of the ages, the . . .'

'The myths and fables,' hawk-face contributed gently.

'The sacred, time-tested wisdom of the ages,' the other went on, becoming redundant. 'The basic bedrock of civil society, of civilization. And we do share that with the Communists. And it is just that common humanistic tradi-

tion that the young anarchists, on both sides of the Iron
Curtain, are blaspheming, denying and trying to destroy. It
has nothing to do with privilege at all.'

'Pardon me,' the dark man said. 'Are you a college professor?'

'Certainly. I'm head of the Political Science Department
at Harvard!'

'Oh,' the dark man shrugged. 'I'm sorry for talking so
bluntly before you. I thought I was entirely surrounded by
men of business and finance.'

The professor was just starting to look as if he spotted
the implied insult in that formal apology when Drake interrupted.

'Quite so. No need to shock our paid idealists and turn
them into vulgar realists overnight. At the same time, is it
absolutely necessary to state what we all know in such a
manner as to imply a rather hostile and outside viewpoint?
Who are you and what is your trade, sir?'

'Hagbard Celine. Import-export. Gold and Appel Trans-
fers here in New York. A few other small establishments
in other ports.' As he spoke my image of piracy and Borgia
stealth came back strongly. 'And we're not children here,'
he added, 'so why should we avoid frank language?'

The professor, taken aback a foot or so by this turn in
the conversation, sat perplexed as Drake replied:

'So. Civilization is privilege – or Private Law, as you
say so literally. And we all know where Private Law comes
from, except the poor professor here – out of the barrel of
a gun, in the words of a gentleman whose bluntness you
would appreciate. Is it your conclusion, then, that Adler is,
for all his naivete, correct, and we have more in common
with the Communist rulers than we have setting us at
odds?'

'Let me *illuminate* you further,' Celine said – and the
way he pronounced the verb made me jump. Drake's blue
eyes flashed a bit, too, but that didn't surprise me: anybody as rich as IRS thought he was, would *have* to be On
the Inside.

'Privilege implies exclusion from privilege, just as advantage implies disadvantage.' Celine went on. 'In the same
mathematically reciprocal way, profit implies loss. If you

and I exchange equal goods, that is trade: neither of us profits and neither of us loses. But if we exchange unequal goods, one of us profits and the other loses. Mathematically. Certainly. Now, such mathematically unequal exchanges will always occur because some traders will be shrewder than others. But in total freedom – in anarchy – such unequal exchanges will be sporadic and irregular. A phenomenon of unpredictable periodicity, mathematically speaking. Now look about you, professor – raise your nose from your great books and survey the actual world as it is – and you will not observe such unpredictable functions. You will observe, instead, a mathematically smooth function, a steady profit accruing to one group and an equally steady loss accumulating for all others. Why is this, professor? Because the system is not free or random, any mathematician would tell you *a priori*. Well, then, where is the determining function, the factor that controls the other variables? You have named it yourself, or Mr. Adler has: the Great Tradition. Privilege, I prefer to call it. When A meets B in the marketplace, they do not bargain as equals. A bargains from a position of privilege; hence, he always profits and B always loses. There is no more Free Market here than there is on the other side of the Iron Curtain. The privileges, or Private Laws – the rules of the game, as promulgated by the Politburo and the General Congress of the Communist Party on that side and by the U.S. government and the Federal Reserve Board on this side – are slightly different; that's all. And it is this that is threatened by anarchists, and by the repressed anarchist in each of us,' he concluded, strongly emphasizing the last clause, staring at Drake, not at the professor.

The professor had a lot more to say in a hurry then, about the laws of society being the laws of nature and the laws of nature being the laws of God, but I decided it was time to circulate a bit more so I didn't hear the rest of the conversation. The IRS has a complete tape of it, I'm sure, since I had placed the bug long before the meal.

The next time I saw Robert Putney Drake was a turning point. I was being sent to New York again, on a mission for Naval Intelligence this time, and Winifred gave me a message that had to be delivered to Drake personally;

the Order wouldn't trust any mechanical communication device. Strangely, my CIA drop also gave me a message for Drake, and it was the same message. That didn't jar me any, since it merely confirmed some of what I had begun to suspect by then.

I went to this office on Wall Street, near the corner of Broad (just about where I'd be toiling at Corporate Law, if my family had had its way) and I told his secretary, 'Knigge of Pyramid Productions to see Mr. Drake.' That was the password that week; Knigge had been a Bavarian baron and second-in-command to Weishaupt in the original AISB. I sat and cooled my heels awhile, studying the decor, which was heavily Elizabethan and made me wonder if Drake had some private notion about being a reincarnation of his famous ancestor.

Finally, Drake's door opened and who stood there but Atlanta Hope, looking kind of wild-eyed and distraught. Drake had his arm on her shoulder and he said piously, 'May your work hasten the day when America returns to purity.' She stumbled past me in a kind of daze and I was ushered into his office. He motioned me to an overstuffed chair and stared at my face until something clicked. 'Another Knigge in the woodpile,' he laughed suddenly. 'The last time I saw you, you were a Pinkerton detective.' You had to admire a memory like that; it had been a year since the CFR banquet and I hadn't done anything to attract his attention that night.

'I'm FBI as well as being in the Order,' I said, leaving out a few things.

'You're more than that,' he said flatly, sitting behind a desk as big as some kids' playgrounds. 'But I have enough on my mind this week without prying into how many sides you're playing. What's the message?'

'It comes from the Order and the CIA both,' I said, to be clear and relatively above-board. 'This it is: *The Taiwan heroin shipments will not arrive on time. The Laotian opium fields are temporarily in the hands of the Pathet Lao. Don't believe the Pentagon releases about our troops having the Laotian situation under control.* No answer required.' I started to rise.

'Wait, damn it,' Drake said, frowning. 'This is more important than you realize.' His face went blank and I could tell his mind was racing like an engine with governor off; it was impressive. 'What's your rank in the Order?' he asked finally.

'Illuminatus Prelator,' I confessed, humbly.

'Not nearly high enough. But you have more practical espionage experience than a great many higher members. You'll have to do.' The old barracuda relaxed, having come to a decision. 'How much do you know about the Cult of the Black Mother?' he asked.

'The most militant and most secret Black Power group in the country,' I said carefully. 'They avoid publicity instead of seeking it, because their strategy is based on an eventual coup d'etat, not on revolution. Until a minute ago, I thought no white man in the country even knew of their existence, except those of us in the FBI. The Bureau has never reported on them to other government agencies, because we're ashamed to admit we've never been able to keep an informer inside for long. They all die of natural causes, that's what bugs us.'

'Nobody in the Order has ever told you the truth?' Drake demanded.

'No,' I said, curious. 'I thought what I just told you was the truth.'

'Winifred is more closed-mouth than he needs to be,' Drake said. 'The Cult of the Black Mother is entirely controlled by the Order. They monitor ghetto affairs for us. Right now, they predict a revival of 1960s-style uprisings for late summer in Harlem, on the West Side of Chicago, and in Detroit. They need to up the addiction rate at least eighteen percent, hopefully twenty or twenty-five percent, in all those areas, or the property damage will be even more enormous than we are prepared to absorb.

'They can't do it, if they have to cut their present stock even more than it's already cut. There just has to be more junk in the ghettoes or all hell will break loose by August.'

I began to realize that he had used the word 'monitor' in its strict cybernetic meaning.

'There's only one alternative,' Drake went on. 'The black market. There's a very cunning and well-organized group that's been trying to crack the CIA-Syndicate heroin mon-

opoly for quite a while now. The Cult of the Black Mother
will have to deal with them directly. I don't want the Order
involved at all – that would make it messy, and besides
we'll have to crush this group later, when we're able to
pierce their cover.'

The upshot of it was that I found myself on One Hundred Tenth Street in Harlem, feeling very white and un-
bulletproof, entering a restaurant called The Signifying
Monkey. Walking through a lot of hostile stares, I went
direct to the coffee-colored woman at the cash register and
said, 'I've got a tombstone disposition.'

She gave me a piercing look and muttered, 'Upstairs,
after the men's room, the door marked Private. Knock
five times.' She grinned maliciously, 'And if you're not
kosher, kiss your white ass good-bye, brother.'

I went up the stairs, found the door, knocked five times,
and one eye in an ebony face looked out at me stonily.
'White,' he said.

'Man,' I replied.

'Native,' he came back.

'Born,' I finished. A bolt slipped on a chain and the door
opened the rest of the way. I never did find out whose idea
of a joke that password was – they had lifted it from the
Ku Klux Klan, of course. The room I was in was heavy
with marijuana smoke, but I could see that it was decently
furnished and dominated by an enormous statue of Kali,
the Black Mother; I had visions of weird *Gunga Din* rites
and shouts of 'Kill for the love of Kali!' There were four
other men in the room, in addition to the one who let me
in, and two reefers were circulating, one deosil and one
widdershins.

'Who you from?' a voice asked in the murk.

'AISB,' I answered carefully, 'And I'm to speak to
Hassan i Sabbah X.'

'You're speaking to him,' said the tallest and blackest
character in the bunch, passing me a reefer. I took a quick,
deep draw and, Christ, it was good. I'd been half addicted
ever since the March on the Pentagon in 1967, where I
walked right behind Norman Mailer part of the way, and
later fell in with some hippies who were sitting on the
steps smoking it. I say I was half addicted since then, be-

cause two of me believe, as a loyal government employee, that the old government publications claiming marijuana is addicting must be true or the government wouldn't have printed them. Fortunately, the other two of me know that it isn't addicting, so I don't go through very bad withdrawal when it's scarce.

I started to outline the situation to Hassan i Sabbah X but the other joint came around, widdershins, and I took a drag on that. 'A man could get stoned doing this,' I said facetiously.

'*Yeah*,' a satisfied black voice agreed in the gloom.

Well, by the time I explained the problem to Hassan, I was so bombed that I immediately let him recruit me for the next step, on his rationalization that a white man could handle it easier than a black man. Actually, I was curious to contact this group of heroin pirates.

Hassan wrote the address carefully. 'Now, here's the passwords,' he said. 'You say, "Do what thou wilt shall be the whole of the Law." Don't say "Do what you will" – they can't stand anybody fucking around with the words, it has something to do with magic. She replies, "Love is the law, love under will." Then you finish it with "Every man and woman is a star." Got it?'

You can bet your ass I got it. I was almost goggle-eyed. It was the passwords of the A∴ A∴.

'One more thing,' Hassan added, 'be sure to ask for Miss Mao, *not* Mama Sutra. Mama isn't cleared for this.'

(As the Braniff jet took off from Kennedy International, Simon was already deep into *Telemachus Sneezed* again. He didn't notice the preoccupied-looking red-headed young man who took the seat across the aisle; if he had, he would have immediately made the identification, *cop*. He was reading, 'Factory smog is a symbol of progress, of the divine fire of industry, of the flaming deity of Heracleitus.')

HARRY KRISHNA HARRY KRISHNA HARRY HARRY

Harry Coin didn't know what the drug was; Miss Portinari had merely said, 'It takes you further than pot,' and handed him the tablet. It might be that LSD the hippies use, he reflected, or it might be something else entirely that Hagbard and FUCKUP had concocted in the ship's laboratory. Miss Portinari went on chanting:

HARRY RAMA HARRY RAMA HARRY HARRY

Obediently, he continued to stare into the aquamarine pool between them; she wore a yellow robe and sat placidly in the lotus position.

('I've gotta know,' he had told her. 'I can't go around with two sets of memories and never be sure which are real and which Hagbard just put in my head like a man puts a baby into a woman. Did I kill all those people or didn't I?'

'You must be in the proper frame of mind before you can accept the answer,' she had replied remotely.)

HARRY COINSHA HARRY COINSHA HARRY HARRY

Was she changing the chant or was it the drug? He tried to keep calm and continue staring into the pool, as she had ordered, but the porcelain design around it was changing. Instead of two dolphins chasing each other's tails like the astrological sign of Pisces (the age that was ending, according to Hagbard), it was now one long serpentlike creature trying to swallow *its own* tail.

That's me, he thought. A lot of people have told me I'm as thin and long as a snake.

And it's everybody else, too (he realized suddenly). I'm seeing what George told me: the Self pursuing the Self and trying to govern it, the Self trying to swallow the Self.

But as he stared, fascinated, the pool turned red, blood red, the color of guilt, and he felt it reach out and try to pull him down into it, into red oblivion. a void made flush.

'It's alive,' he screamed. 'Jesus Motherfucking Christ!'

Miss Portinari casually stirred the pool, remote and calm, and its spiral inward slowly turned back to aquamarine. Harry felt himself blushing, *it was only a hallucination*, and muttered, 'Pardon my language, ma'am.'

'Don't apologize,' she said sharply. 'The most important truths always appear first as blasphemies or obscenities. That's why every great innovator is persecuted. And the sacraments look obscene, too, to an outsider. The eucharist is just sublimated cannibalism, to the unawakened. When the Pope kisses the feet of the laity, he looks like an old toe-queen to some people. The rites of Pan look like a suburban orgy. Think about what you said. Since it has five words and fits the Law of Fives, it is especially significant.'

This is a weird bunch, but they know important things, Harry reminded himself. He looked deep into the blue spiral and silently repeated to himself, 'It's alive, Jesus Motherfucking Christ, it's alive . . .'

Jesus, looking strangely hawk-faced and Hagbardian, rose from the pool. 'This is my *bodhi*,' he said, pointing. Harry looked and saw Buddha sitting beneath the bodhi-tree. 'Tat TVam Asi,' he said, and the falling leaves of the tree turned into millions of TV sets all broadcasting the same Laurel and Hardy movie. 'Now look what you made me do,' Hardy was saying . . . In a previous incarnation, Harry saw himself as a centurion, Semper Cuni Linctus, driving the nails into the cross. 'Look,' he said to Jesus, 'nothing personal. I'm only following orders.' 'So am I,' Jesus said, 'My Father's orders. Aren't we all?'

'Look into the pool,' Miss Portinari repeated. 'Just look into the pool.'

It was like each Chinese box had another Chinese box inside it; but the best of all belonged to Miss Mao Tsu-hsi. We were reclining in her trim but elegant pad on West Eighty-seventh Street, passing a joint back and forth and comparing multiple identities. We were naked on a bear-skin rug, a dream come true, for she was my ideal woman. 'I got into the A∴ A∴ first, Tobias,' she was saying. 'They recruited me at a Ba'Hai meeting – they have cruisers out, looking for likely prospects, in every mystical group from Subud to Scientology, you know. Then Naval Intelligence contacted me and I reported to them on what the A∴ A∴ was up to. I'm not flexible as you, though, and my loyalties tend to stay fairly constant – chiefly I was reporting to A∴ A∴ what I gleaned from Naval Intelligence. I did believe in the A∴ A∴ basically. Until I met *Him*.'

'That reminds me,' I said, jealous of the worshipful way

she said *Him* as if talking about a god. 'If he's coming soon, shouldn't we get up and put some clothes on?'

'If you want to be bourgeois,' she said.

While we were dressing, I remembered something. 'By the way,' I asked casually, 'who are you spying on Mama Sutra for – the A∴A∴, Naval Intelligence, or *Him?*'

'All three of them.' She was starting to pull her panties on, and I said suddenly, 'Wait.' I knelt and kissed her pussy one last time, 'For the nicest Chinese box I've ever opened in this whole case,' I said gallantly. That was my Illuminati training; as an FBI man, I was ashamed of such a perverted act.

We finished dressing and she was pouring some wine (a light German vintage from, of all places, Bavaria) when the knock came.

Miss Mao sidled over to the door in her slinky Chinese dress and said softly, 'Hail Eris.'

'All hail Discordia,' came a voice from outside. She slipped the lock and a little fat man walked in. My first reaction was astonishment; he didn't look anything like the superintellectual superhero she had described.

'Hagbard couldn't come,' he said briefly. 'I'll handle the sale, and initiate *you*,' with a glance at me, 'into the Legion of Dynamic Discord, if you're really ready, as Miss Mao says, to battle every government on earth and the Illuminati to boot.'

'I'm ready,' I said passionately. 'I'm tired being a puppet on four sets of strings.' (Actually, I know I just wanted a fifth set.)

'Good,' he said. 'Put her there,' and he held out his hand. As we shook, he said, '*Episkopos* Jim Cartwright of the Mad Dog Cabal.'

'Tobias Knight,' I said, 'of the FBI, the CIA, the A∴ A∴ and Illuminati.'

He blinked briefly. 'I've met double agents and triple agents, but you're the first quadruple agent in my experience. I guess this was inevitable, by the Law of Fives. Welcome to the fifth ring of the world's oldest continuous Five Ring Circus. Prepare for Death and Rebirth.'

JESUS MOTHERFUCKING CHRIST IT'S ALIVE . . .

The dreadful carnage continues . . .

Witches

7: THE FEUD

The chilling horror series by
JAMES DARKE

John Ferris, the hero of James Darke's spine-tingling
horror books, has suffered grievously from the
ministrations of those evil men and women who worship
the Black Arts. But they are still on his trail.

Not many leagues distant, in cellars that reeked of
monkshood, henbane and thorn-apple, dark-garbed
figures with arcane names were pursuing their gruesome
rites by the sinister light of black candles. And before
long even the watchful Ferris would be lured into their
midst, and find himself as helpless as a new-born babe in
the face of their fiendish magic . . .

HORROR   0 7221 5201 9   £1.95

Don't miss:
THE PRISONER   THE MEETING
THE TRIAL   THE KILLING
THE TORTURE   THE PLAGUE
THE ESCAPE

From the Hugo and Nebula award-winning author

TIME
PATROLMAN
by POUL ANDERSON

DEFENDER OF THE PAST . . .

The creaking Phoenician ship slowly approached its destination. Everard gazed out over the sparkling water at the ancient port of Tyre. "A grand sight indeed," he murmured to the captain, glad of the easy electrocram method of learning the language. His gaze went forward again; the city reminded him not a little of New York.

Time patrolmen like Everard guard the past. No matter how good or evil an event, it must be held inviolate. The slightest slip, and Time would become Chaos, and all that has ever been or will ever be will tumble into darkness. When the Birth of Civilization is endangered by the malign counter-emperor Varagan, the patrol must be on its mettle . . .

SCIENCE FICTION   0 7221 1290 4   £2.50

Also by Poul Anderson in Sphere Books:

THREE WORLDS TO CONQUER   A KNIGHT OF GHOSTS AND SHADOWS
THE PEOPLE OF THE WIND   DANCER FROM ATLANTIS
THE AVATAR   ORION SHALL RISE
MIRKHEIM   TWILIGHT WORLD
A CIRCUS OF HELLS   THE MERMAN'S CHILDREN
THERE WILL BE TIME   THE BROKEN SWORD
                                 THE LONG NIGHT

The classic Amber series continues

ROGER ZELAZNY
TRUMPS OF DOOM

RETURN TO AMBER – The irresistible powers of the kingdom beyond imagination draw Merlin, son of Corwin, back to the magical realm . . .

Merlin is content to bide the time when he will activate his superhuman strength and genius and claim his birthright.

But that time arrives all too soon when the terrible forces of evil drive him mercilessly from Earth, and upon reaching Amber, he finds the domain in awesome, bloody contention.

And in every strange darkness of his fantastic crusade, there stalks a figure determined to destroy Merlin and wipe out the wondrous world of Amber . . .

SCIENCE FICTION   0 7221 9410 2   £2.50

Also by Roger Zelazny in Sphere Science Fiction:

DAMNATION ALLEY
MY NAME IS LEGION
EYE OF CAT

In the Amber series
NINE PRINCES IN AMBER
THE COURTS OF CHAOS
SIGN OF THE UNICORN
THE GUNS OF AVALON
THE HAND OF OBERON

A selection of bestsellers from SPHERE

FICTION

STREET SONG	Emma Blair	£3.50 ☐
GOLDEN TRIPLE TIME	Zoe Garrison	£2.95 ☐
BEACHES	Iris Rainer Dart	£2.95 ☐
RAINBOW SOLDIERS	Walter Winward	£3.50 ☐
FAMILY ALBUM	Danielle Steel	£2.95 ☐

FILM AND TV TIE-IN

MONA LISA	John Luther Novak	£2.50 ☐
BLOCKBUSTERS GOLD RUN		£1.95 ☐
9½ WEEKS	Elizabeth McNeil	£1.95 ☐
BOON	Anthony Masters	£2.50 ☐
AUF WIEDERSEHEN PET 2	Fred Taylor	£2.75 ☐

NON-FICTION

BURTON: THE MAN BEHIND THE MYTH	Penny Junor	£2.95 ☐
THE DISAPPEARED	John Simpson & Jana Bennett	£4.95 ☐
THE LAST NAZI: THE LIFE AND TIMES OF JOSEPH MENGELE	Gerald Astor	£3.50 ☐
THE FALL OF SAIGON	David Butler	£3.95 ☐
LET'S FACE IT	Christine Piff	£2.50 ☐

All Sphere books are available at your local bookshop or newsagent, or can be ordered direct from the publisher. Just tick the titles you want and fill in the form below.

Name _____

Address _____

_____

Write to Sphere Books, Cash Sales Department, P.O. Box 11, Falmouth, Cornwall TR10 9EN.

Please enclose a cheque or postal order to the value of the cover price plus:

UK: 55p for the first book, 22p for the second book and 14p for each additional book ordered to a maximum charge of £1.75.

OVERSEAS: £1.00 for the first book plus 25p per copy for each additional book.

BFPO & EIRE: 55p for the first book, 22p for the second book plus 14p per copy for the next 7 books, thereafter 8p per book.

Sphere Books reserve the right to show new retail prices on covers which may differ from those previously advertised in the text or elsewhere, and to increase postal rates in accordance with the PO.